WARRIOR OF
THE HEART

A whisper of legend has brought the hand-some barbarian to this treacherous country. It is here that Kolby of Apelstadt seeks the magic golden apples that will heal his dying father and restore his barren lands. Yet passion diverts Kolby from his steady course—an aching in his soul for the be-witching, endangered lady called Raven.

LADY OF WINTER

He appeared out of the mist to save her from the deadly fury of evil men. And now brave Kolby is Lady Raven's protector, igniting a raging fire within that consumes the breath-less beauty gloriously and utterly. But their love is in gravest peril. For it is Raven who guards the precious knowledge Kolby most fervently desires—a sacred secret she must never reveal . . . even at the cost of her heart.

Other Avon Romantic Treasures by
Emma Merritt

LADY OF SUMMER
LORD OF THUNDER

*If You've Enjoyed This Book,
Be Sure to Read These Other*
AVON ROMANTIC TREASURES

THE MACKINNON'S BRIDE *by Tanya Anne Crosby*
PHANTOM IN TIME *by Eugenia Riley*
RUNAWAY MAGIC *by Deborah Gordon*
WILD ROSES *by Miriam Minger*
YOU AND NO OTHER *by Cathy Maxwell*

Coming Soon

SILVER MOON SONG *by Genell Dellin*

EMMA MERRITT

LADY OF WINTER

An Avon Romantic Treasure

AVON BOOKS ◆ NEW YORK

LADY OF WINTER is an original publication of Avon Books. This work has never before appeared in book form. This work is a novel. Any similarity to actual persons or events is purely coincidental.

AVON BOOKS
A division of
The Hearst Corporation
1350 Avenue of the Americas
New York, New York 10019

Copyright © 1996 by The Estate of Emma Merritt
Inside cover author photo by F.E. Alexander
Published by arrangement with the author
Library of Congress Catalog Card Number: 95-96048
ISBN: 0-380-77985-4

First Avon Books Printing: November 1996

AVON TRADEMARK REG. U.S. PAT. OFF. AND IN OTHER COUNTRIES, MARCA REGISTRADA, HECHO EN U.S.A.

Printed in the U.S.A.

RA   10 9 8 7 6 5 4 3 2 1

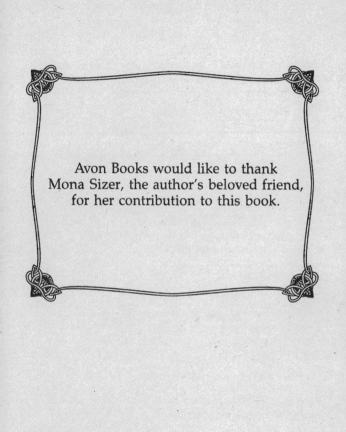

Avon Books would like to thank
Mona Sizer, the author's beloved friend,
for her contribution to this book.

Chapter 1

Scottish Highlands
Province of Inverness
Nameless Eve
December 22, A.D. *631*

No man stirred on the Nameless Day or its eve. Each year on that day, the sun shone its pale light for the shortest time before it was consumed by the longest hours of darkness. At that time the power of Hel, the midnight hag, was strongest, and the unwary traveler risked the danger of being pulled down into her gaping pit.

No one stirred except the Viking barbarian known as Kolby of Apelstadt. For he feared nothing, not human, not beast, not god.

He cared nothing for the darkness of Nameless Eve even as it enshrouded him. The fearsome-looking warrior strode along the edge of a thick woodland of looming birch, rowan, and oak. His long fur-lined cloak swung heavy around him. His giant shadow stretched ahead of him across the crystalline white snow.

The wind blew. The heavy cloak lifted away from the calves of his fur-lined leather boots. Snowflakes swirled gently. He felt their nip against his cheeks

1

and lips and on the ends of his lashes. They gathered on his hood and shoulders, twinkling momentarily before they melted.

His feet made soft crunching sounds as he led his golden-brown stallion across the clearing and wound through the stand of snow-covered trees. Deeper into the forest Kolby moved, certain he would soon reach the cave where he would take shelter for the night.

The stallion snorted softly and threw up its head. Instantly alert, Kolby stopped and looked around. Just ahead, the trees ended and the land sloped gently upward, its snow cover pristine and glistening. Kolby took another step and then another. His eyes burned across the dazzling expanse. At the top of the hill he saw a woman.

A woman! It couldn't be, not in this weather, not on Nameless Eve. Thinking he was snow-blinded, he brushed his gloves over his eyes and looked again. She was still there. He couldn't be mistaken.

She stood beside a massive table comprised of a smooth granite slab laid atop two short standing stones. *An altar*, he thought with a spurt of contempt for all superstitious and useless practices. He knew a moment of regret that she should be a part of such. Still he did not turn away and leave her to her rituals.

A fire blazed before the altar, yet she seemed surrounded by barren bushes and trees, their twigs encased in ice, their black boughs crowned with snow. Ice dripped from the underside of the altar. Wind swirled Hel's own cold around her. Yet, she seemed oblivious to it, to everything. To him.

After looping his horse's reins across a low-hanging limb, he crept forward, skirting the whiteness, keeping in the shadow of the trees, moving silently now that it suited his purpose.

Black hair, straight and long, hung below her buttocks. The wind teased the ends. As he watched, she slipped out of her luxuriant white fur robe. He couldn't believe his eyes. She must be mad. Beneath it she wore a filmy green kirtle with long, billowy sleeves. He couldn't forestall a shiver as he glimpsed her pale skin through the thin material.

And then he gasped. She unfastened a heavy golden girdle from her waist and dropped it atop the cloak. The wind blew fiercely. It picked up her kirtle and hair and wrapped them around her. As the fire leaped higher and sparks rose to join the swirling snow, she stepped closer until its glow bathed her. She tipped her face toward the sky until it was awash with moonlight.

Her lips moved.

Too far away to catch her words, he crept closer, infinitely curious, drawn by her beauty and the strangeness of the moment. The lowest, deepest notes of her voice reached his ears. The words were unintelligible, but the tones mesmerized him. Still concealed by the trees, he drew near enough to see what lay on the stone.

Her words ceased. She bowed her head, then turned to the altar. In the center she had placed a large golden bowl filled with apples. Fat candles burned at either end, flames whipping, wax streaming down their sides.

In front of them lay an object made of silver. More than a foot long, it had been wrought in the shape of a branch with leaves and blossoms cast of the same precious metal. More wonderful even than the silver were the three apples that hung from it—apples made of purest gold. Even as he marveled at the workmanship of the thing, the woman held it aloft in both hands. The wind carried her incantation aloft.

She laid the branch on the altar and picked up a gold and silver chalice, the bowl of which was shaped like an apple. Another incantantion, then she lifted the rim to her lips. Still chanting, she poured the libation over the sacrifice of apples, then lifted the empty cup to the sky. Another gust of wind whipped her hair and her kirtle about her. The snow swirled, the sparks leaped. Ice and fire enveloped her in their radiance.

Drawn to her, incapable of thought, Kolby moved from behind the tree. The snow crunched beneath his boots as he stepped into the clearing.

She whirled and looked directly at him. Her hair swirled around her. Then the wind caught it and set it across her high breasts with their pointed nipples, across the hollow of her flat belly. So much glorious, glistening hair covered her body like a black veil.

Her face was soft, pearlescent, radiant in the blending of the moon and the firelight. Long black lashes framed her glowing brown eyes.

Neither of them moved. Then she smiled, and Kolby thought he would die of pleasure. He lifted his arms. One step. Two.

In the depths of her eyes, he saw her growing wariness. He froze, studying her. She had about her an ageless air of innocence, yet she wasn't a young maid. He recognized the stirrings of desire within his body. Perhaps it flickered in his gaze still locked with hers. Another step. His own smile invited her.

Quick as thought, she bent. The links of golden girdle clinked as she swept it and the white fur robe to her breasts. For an instant her smile still trembled on her lips. Then she turned and ran into the darkness of the forest.

"Nay, lady!" Kolby shouted. "Wait! Please. I mean you no harm." He leaped to catch her. His foot crashed into a rock upthrust, its tip just below the surface of the snow. He stumbled. He caught himself before he fell, but the misstep had given her the start she needed to disappear.

Still he clambered after her tracks, slipping, staggering, cursing. How had she run so smoothly and lightly when he floundered in her wake like a wounded boar? Calling himself a clumsy fool, he stubbornly followed her footprints.

His foot slipped for the hundredth time. It toppled him against the trunk of a tall tree. The jolt created a cascade. Heavy, wet, white snow fell from its branches. It all but buried him. When he was able to plow his way through it, her tracks had disappeared.

He looked around him wildly. She had vanished. He shook his head in disbelief. It was as if she had never been.

A trickle of ice slid down his spine. It had nothing to do with the snow that had dropped on him and stopped him in his tracks. With a muttered exclamation, he threw off the superstitious nonsense. In the darkness anyone could lose his way, even a master tracker.

He determined to return to the altar and wait. She would come back for the treasure, for such was the value of the bowl, the chalice, and the branch that they could be deemed nothing less than a treasure.

The way seemed easier now, but, of course, he was following his own tracks this time. To his disappointment, when he returned to the hilltop where she had stood, all he found were a few apples lying in the center of the slab. All the beautiful objects were gone. She must have circled back, packed her belongings, and fled.

His eyes swept the circle around the heap of dying embers that had been the blazing fire. No sign of her footprints here either. The snow must have filled them instantly. She had vanished once again without a trace.

Kolby's relief upon reaching the shelter of the cave was tempered with disappointment. As he built a fire, unsaddled and fed his horse, he thought about the green kirtle, the glorious hair, and above all the tender smile.

After he had cared for his horse, Kolby spread his own pallet. His cloaks were thick, fur on one side, water-proofed leather on the other. He sat down on them and opened his evening meal of bread, cheese, and smoked meat. He washed it down with ale so cold it made his teeth ache. All the while he gazed out of the cave into the silver splendor of the night and thought about the woman. He should have known better than to approach someone engaged in a ritual. When he had started toward her, he had probably frightened her badly.

But he had wanted to get a little closer to her, to talk to her. He had heard the mellifluous voice as she murmured her prayers and songs. He had seen the glorious shape of her body through the soft kirtle. No, he would never forget the lady of the night, this lady of winter. He had never seen her before, yet she seemed strangely familiar.

In the distance Kolby heard a bird call—raucous, hoarse. He climbed to his feet and walked to the cave entrance. Above him, silhouetted against the silver moon, a huge raven circled and dipped. Moonlight burnished its wings to a high gloss. It glided effortlessly through the air as if one with the wind. It cawed again before it swooped down and landed on Kolby's shoulder.

The first time the raven had flown to him in the dark, he had been amazed. Bird masters had told him that ravens didn't fly at night. Yet his did. This raven was his friend, like no other, his chosen talisman and—though he wouldn't admit it to anyone—his link to the Otherworld. He told himself he wasn't gullible enough to believe that Odin ruled in Asgard with ravens on his shoulders to bring him news of all the doings of men. Still, he was pleased to have a friend of their kind, just in case.

He was especially fond of the bird. He had found it

as a nestling two summers ago, blown from the nest, too young to fly. When it had spread its tiny wings and ruffled its feathers defiantly, its courage had won his heart. He had rescued and cared for it. After it was grown, Kolby had released it, but it kept returning to him.

"Good evening, my friend." He ran his hand gently over the shiny feathers as he carried the bird back to the fire. "Indeed you are the Midnight Wind. I'm glad you returned for the night."

The bird's amber eyes glittered as it surveyed their quarters. It hopped from Kolby's shoulder to the stallion's back. The great horse tossed its head, its golden mane flying. It whinnied softly. As if it were an invitation to dine, the raven hopped to the ground and began to share the horse's meal.

"No question why you came." Kolby laughed softly. "I carry the grain sack."

Weary from the long march and the oppressive cold, he moved closer to the fire and began to undress. Staring dreamily into its flames, he seemed to see within their depths the lady of winter's luminous eyes and haunting lips curved in a smile.

If no man stirred on Nameless Eve, surely no woman stirred either.

No one but Raven, the lady born of the winter on the Nameless Day. Dedicated by her mother to the Great Mother Goddess in sacred ritual, Raven was a keeper of the land and a messenger to the heavens. As well, she was protected by the fierce triumvirate of lesser goddesses: Buanann, mother of heroes; Andraste, patroness of the British queen Boaddicea; and Cathubodua, raven of battle, from whom her name had come.

With their favor no harm would come to her on her special day. For this reason she had walked the night unattended. Now clad in a white fur robe, she slipped close to the entrance of the warrior's cave and watched him prepare for sleep. Who was he? she wondered. What man dared to walk on the night when the sun died?

He had taken her by surprise at the high grove altar. She doubted that any but herself knew of its existence. It belonged to the time of the Old Ones. She had taken it as her special place and each year traveled the long distance from her cloister to the lonely hills above Inverness to make her sacrifice and to offer her prayers to her birth goddess. Yet he had appeared there. Why he had done so troubled her deeply.

Inside the cave the warrior stood behind the fire, its glow illuminating his face and body. He removed his cloak, shaking melted snow into the fire, causing it to sizzle and snap. He spread his mantle close to the blaze to dry during the night and be ready for travel on the morrow.

All his clothing, of reddish-brown leather, was lined with fur. She noted with a shudder that the leather guards on his wrists and forearms were utilitarian. Devoid of shiny metals and jewels, they were deeply scuffed and worn. They had protected his skin from the snap of many powerful bowstrings. No doubt he had sent many an arrow on its way to the heart of an enemy.

He removed the belts from his waist and laid his sword and dagger next to his bow. He flexed his shoulders, drawing his tunic tight across his chest, emphasizing his thick muscularity and drawing attention to his sinewy arms.

In the darkness Raven felt her own muscles flex involuntarily. Mentally she scolded herself. She had seen many men more handsome than the Northlander, many who were more muscular. Still, she admitted, none were so intriguing. He stood alone, but his presence was such that had he been surrounded by people, he would have stood apart. He radiated strength and power that would always single him out.

He was a golden warrior, his eyes and hair the color of polished amber. Yet instinctively she knew the golden cast of his features was deceptive. He was dark, not light. Hard, not soft. His body was a study in hard lines and angles, in muscled perfection. His expression was black and grim, his eyes shadowed. Mysteries lurked in their depths. Mysteries Raven wanted to discover. Like a lodestone, he drew her to him.

As she studied those eyes, she saw beyond their color to the man inside. She saw in him a total absence of fear. That in itself did not bother her. But something did. He had no reverence. He didn't honor the holy day or its patron goddess by hanging the snippet of mistletoe over the entrance to his cave. This irreverence troubled Raven deeply. He was either a man without deep heartfelt emotions and convictions, or they were so deeply sequestered that no one, including himself, would ever find them.

Suddenly his muscles tensed. In one smooth motion, he bent and pulled his sword from its sheath. The metal hissed against the leather. When he straightened, his stance and expression were those of a warrior ready for battle. Holding his weapon, he slipped to the cave entrance and stared out. In the blink of an eye, he had become the predator, stalking his prey.

And she was the prey.

Raven ducked behind a small clump of trees and pressed her back against a trunk. She didn't make a sound, hardly dared to breathe. She had the feeling that he could see in the dark. The silence seemed to stretch on forever as he sought her with all his senses.

After a time he returned to the interior of the cave and built up the fire. She could hear him talking in soft tones to the raven and the horse.

She should leave now, vanish into the night and forget him as he would forget her. His presence would not let her leave. The heat of emotions she did not understand forced her back to her watching place.

Laying his sword down, he pulled one of the dry cloaks from his pack. At the same time that a brooch fell from among the folds, the fire popped and hissed. Sparks skittered through the air and across the floor of the cave.

Raven stared in fascination as the gold pin rolled toward the entrance. Jewel-studded, it glittered in the firelight. She expected him to pick it up, but he didn't. Apparently he was unaware that it had fallen. Wrapping the cloak about himself, he stretched out on the pallet.

Standing outside the cave entrance, Raven received the full blast of winter's chill. Enviously she watched the warrior, steed, and bird settle comfortably for the night. She wondered what would happen if she walked boldly into the firelight and joined him beside it. The thought made her shiver, but not with cold.

Chilled to the bone, the wind whipping through her damp winter clothing, she remained hidden behind the trees. Her gaze fastened on the brooch. The longer she stared at it, the more she wanted it—as a memento of this night, of this fascinating golden warrior.

Finally the fire burned low, and she heard the warrior's soft snore. She eased nearer to the entrance to the cave where the gold pin lay. The horse turned its head toward her. The raven hopped about and cocked a glittering eye. Neither sounded an alert. Raven hadn't feared they would. She was a keeper of the land, one with the plants and animals of the Highlands, at home in the dense forests that lay in the narrow glens between mountains and hills. She had spent the majority of her life around animals. They trusted her.

In his sleep, the warrior turned, presenting his back to her. Raven crept closer. Her fingers closed around the brooch. Clutching it tightly in her fist, she backed away. Out of hearing, she ran into the forest. She had no worry that the stranger would find her. By morning, snow would completely cover her footprints. She would be a long way from her high grove altar, bound for the cloister in Ross on the northeastern coast of Scotland.

Aye, by the time the golden-haired warrior awoke, she would be far away and safe within her own territory. In a patch of moonlight, she stopped only once and looked at the brooch lying flat on her palm. The jewels twinkled in the silvered light.

In the deepest part of her heart, she acknowledged that she had stolen a part of something that she could never have. A celibate cloistered priestess could never share the fireside with a Viking warrior. She slipped his brooch into the secret pocket of her cloak—into the secret part of her heart.

Chapter 2

Scottish Highlands
Province of Inverness
A.D. 632

Autumn settled crisply over the Highlands. A sharp wind blew and the morning sun shone brightly. Hilltop copses and valley woodlands painted Inverness in glorious shades of red, gold, and russet as the terrain rose and dipped. The sun layered the sky with luminescent shades of pink and lavender and orange.

Six mounted riders moved up the narrow mountain trail. Bradach, their Highlander guide, led the way. Kolby of Apelstadt followed behind him. Next came Kolby's four hand-picked Viking warriors—Durin, Aren, Thorfinn, and Sven. Although they were not wearing armor, they had brought it with them. Helmet and mail and extra weapons were stowed in leather packs that each man strapped to the back of his saddle. When they had answered Kolby's call to go a-viking, they had accepted war and death as possibilities.

Now Kolby led them from the northeastern coastal town of Glenmuir in Ross toward the interior. On a mission for his benefactor and liege, Kolby and his

12

men pushed steadily south down the coast. As they rode toward Inverness, the rocky mountainous terrain of the Highlands softened a little, giving way to glens and dales.

Trees no longer formed copses far apart but ran together to create belts of woodlands. In turn the woodlands gave way to thick deciduous forests of birch and rowan and oak. Conifers spiraled majestically into the skies. Where boulders and small bushes had bordered the earlier trails, now trees created arching canopies over the road.

"How much farther, Scotsman?" Kolby called.

Bradach hunched his shoulders. "We'll change direction soon."

He was a small man, older than the Northland warriors. Garbed in an unbelted shirt and sandals, he had left his knotty legs bare. A dirk hung from a leather lanyard over his neck and shoulder. The Northlanders had followed him now for several days. Once they had ended in the middle of a thick forest. Once they had come to the edge of a loch. He had shrugged and whined and insisted that the landmarks had been moved. He wasn't a warrior, as he was forever saying. He would lead them, but he would also stay out of harm's way.

Kolby had a proud warrior's contempt for mercenaries. Bradach's mistakes had more than irritated him. He didn't trust the man, but he and his men had come this far. They couldn't turn back without losing their chance of finding what they sought.

"Where the river forks," Bradach said, "the trail does also. One leads to the Shrine of the Great Mother Goddess, the other toward the trading port at Moray Firth. We won't take either of them. We'll take a pathway less traveled that will take us due south. No sense in taking a chance. We'll be moving deeper into the interior toward the borderlands."

Kolby nodded shortly. Bradach was doing exactly as he'd been told even though he grew more worried and more reluctant with every mile. They were not headed for the border of the Braelands, the foothills of the Highlands which were also known as the Lowlands. They were riding into territory that most people avoided. They were riding into the badlands themselves. First they would cross the headland of the loch called Ness. This despite the warnings.

Seamen swore that the loch was haunted, inhabited by a sea monster so huge that it swallowed ships whole. Others claimed to have seen strange creatures along its shores—fairy folk who tempted people to dance forever in the stone rings scattered about the Scottish countryside and shape changers who lured people to their deaths beneath the black waters.

The badlands themselves were the home of fearsome outlaws, men and women who'd been cast out of their homes and villages. They had banded together in misery in this wild, isolated land. From it they preyed on travelers and crofters both south and north.

According to Bradach, most who ventured across this border were not heard from again. Those who did return home often came back dim-witted and crazed.

Kolby had listened to the stories and dismissed them as superstitious bunk. Silly tales would not dissuade him from making this journey. Nothing would stop him from keeping his word, from fulfilling his quest.

Ura of Apelstadt had sent Kolby to find the sacred apple tree of the Great Mother Goddess and to return to Apelstadt with twenty of its magical apples. Betrayed and deserted by kith and kin, frightened that his last remaining vassal would also abandon him, Ura had made Kolby swear a blood oath to Odin that he would not return to Northland without the fruit.

To reassure his benefactor, Kolby had sworn, but the oath had not been necessary. Kolby would have searched for the tree in any case. He owed his liege a debt of gratitude that far outweighed a blood oath. When Kolby had been enslaved as a child, Ura had purchased him and given him a home. More important, the lord had later allowed the young man to buy his freedom. Moreover, Ura had used his friendship with a powerful thane to foster Kolby to Lord Lang of Ulfsbaer. Traditionally a nameless child would never be fostered by a noble. Kolby and Lord Lang's son Michael had become fast friends and fostered brothers.

Aye, Kolby's loyalty to Ura was based on far more than a sworn oath.

He had been searching for the apples for over a year, and he would continue to search. Resolute, his back straight, his shoulders squared, he rode toward the monster-ridden loch, toward the dark forest of the badlands. Here he would find the outlaw called Vaghn, who was willing to sell information about the location of this tree and its fruit, which was said to have the power to heal.

The warrior Durin urged his mount alongside Kolby's. He spoke softly, his words intended only for Kolby's ears. "Let this be the last, Kolby. If this venture proves futile, 'twill be time to return home. I have my doubts that a magical tree exists. And so I believe do you."

Kolby cast a sideways glance at his man. Durin had hit upon the ironic aspect of Ura's command. Kolby believed in no gods nor any magic. He believed in the strength of his arm, the stamina of his horse, and the loyalty of his men. Privately Kolby felt the healing apples were superstitious bunk, but he would not deny Ura his service. As long as there was a chance of finding *something*, as long as people insisted that *something* did exist, he couldn't give up the search.

"Aye, Durin, I'm sure you do," Kolby replied. "You think with me on every turn. You've always been skeptical. That's one of the reasons that I was so pleased when you agreed to sail with me."

Durin harrumphed. "Are you jesting with me?"

"Nay, my friend, I'm sincere," Kolby replied. "I like you because you say what you believe rather than what I want you to say. You make me think."

The wind rose, blowing through Kolby's short sun-bleached hair. It stirred the thick pale mane of his golden horse. So easily did he ride, so relaxed in the saddle, that man and beast seemed a part of each other. Both were fearsome creatures, emanating virile strength. Ironically they also embodied grace and beauty.

Kolby's cloak lay across the back of the saddle. He used it only in the morning and evening when it was chilly. Now he was clad in a blue tunic belted at the waist, his long sleeves tucked into his wrist guards. His fawn-colored trousers were cross-gartered from knee to ankle and stuffed into dark brown leather boots.

As for all Viking warriors, his primary weapons were the dagger and the long sword. Rather than carrying a battle-axe or spear as many of his comrades-in-arms did, he chose as his third weapon a fearsome longbow. During Kolby's travels in the far eastern kingdoms, he had acquired his in trade. His long arms and heavily muscled shoulders gave him a natural affinity for it, so now he carried it with him always.

"Bradach," Durin called to the guide, "all you Scotsmen believe the sacred tree exists, don't you?"

Bradach turned in the saddle and nodded. "We do."

"But not a one of you even knows anyone who has seen a living tree with silver branches and golden apples."

"Some of us have seen it," the guide protested. "Some few know its location. 'Tis a special tree. It bears the fruit of the gods themselves. 'Tis a symbol of their wisdom and knowledge."

"Or as elusive as their wisdom and knowledge," Durin scoffed.

The talk of apples made Kolby think of the woman he had seen on Nameless Eve, the lady of the winter night. She had held aloft an apple branch crafted out of silver. From it had hung three golden apples. He had thought perhaps this clue would have led him to discover her identity.

He had learned that any person born on the Nameless Day offered libation on its eve to the Great Mother Goddess. Such people used the symbol of the *craebh ciuil*, the silver branch with a cluster of three golden apples. As Kolby had continued his quest for the sacred tree, he had also searched for the woman. He looked for her in each woman he saw, questioned each person he met.

Unfortunately no one had given him answers. The apple was one of the most highly revered talismans of these Highlanders. No one so far would help him find the tree, and no one knew anything about his elusive woman of the night.

"You're a fool," Durin sneered to Bradach. "The whole lot of you with your heathen superstitions. And you, Kolby of Apelstadt, are the biggest fool of all. Golden apples. Silver branches. Hah!"

"Mayhap." Kolby took no umbrage from his friend's outburst. Instead he turned to Bradach. "How much farther to the badlands?"

"We shall be in them by nightfall."

"We are to meet àt the Sign of the Boar. 'Tis said that the outlaws gather there and drink their mead. How long until we reach it?"

Bradach studied the length of the shadows on the ground. "On the morrow for the morning meal.

Vaghn said he would wait for us until the noon hour."

"A loch that is haunted! Badlands filled with outlaws!" Frustrated, Durin waved his hand. "And we're going to pay a guide who's gotten us lost twice to guide us through a thick, dark forest filled with still more outlaws until we find this magical tree. Or until we have no booty left with which to buy his services."

Bradach spoke to no one in particular. "If you're frightened, mayhap you should remain here."

Durin glared at the Scotsman. "Nay, little man. I'm not frightened. But neither am I fool enough to believe in you."

Kolby laughed. "Either way, my friend, we shall have a great adventure."

"Aye," Durin agreed a little sourly, "for a verity we shall."

"No man knows the badlands better than Vaghn," Bradach insisted. "Basically he's a good man, who stays there because he has no other place to live. He was cast out many years ago because he went against a judgment of his overlord. The outlaws know he didn't really break the law, but they let him stay anyway even though he doesn't belong among them."

"To be sure. An honest man whom the outlaws respect," Durin drawled sarcastically.

"Or an innocent man."

"Bradach," Kolby warned, "I hope what you say and believe about this man is true."

"It is," Bradach replied. "You can trust me."

Durin hooted with laughter.

"We're following," Kolby said. "But be sure of this. If you lead us into a trap sprung by your outlaw friends, you will be the first to die."

They traveled for another hour, their progress

slower as they climbed a steep mountain trail so narrow that they were forced to ride single file. They had no reason to hurry. They would arrive at their destination long before the designated time to meet Vaghn.

Their horses' hooves rang on the rocky terrain. Their saddle leather creaked. The Northlanders talked quietly among themselves. All the while they maintained a sharp lookout for anything unusual. Seasoned veterans all, they remained constantly alert.

Suddenly Kolby flung up his hand. His ears, keener than the others', had heard a sound. Immediately his men halted their horses. Behind him every man's hand reached for his weapon; every man waited for his command. One second, two. Kolby motioned them forward.

Where the trail widened momentarily, Bradach reined his horse aside for Kolby and his men to ride by. Kolby heeled his horse into a trot. His men did likewise.

Up ahead they heard screams. Kolby slapped the reins across his stallion's withers. The big horse lengthened its stride and broke into a gallop. Down the path the men raced. As they neared the curve of the pathway, they heard raucous laughter. Metal clanged against metal.

Drawing his sword, Kolby reined the horse around the curve and into a small clearing. Then he sawed back on the reins and pulled the animal up on its hind legs. Blocking the way was an overturned cart, its central axle broken.

Three men clad in green tunics and trousers fought to defend it against at least a dozen outlaws wearing rags and skins. Three more of the defenders lay dead upon the ground. Two women wearing green robes with deep cowls huddled beneath the cart behind their tumbled goods. Bundles, sacks, portable furniture, supplies—all the many things necessary for a long journey lay tumbled on the ground.

This much Kolby took in at first glance. With a shout he flung himself from his horse and plunged into the fray. Right and left his sword hacked down on the shoulders of two of the attackers.

Behind him he heard shouts from his men and cries of alarm from the outlaws. He heard Durin's war cry as he launched himself from the saddle and brought down two of the outlaws with the weight of his mighty body. Young Aren leaped to the ground and cut the legs from under a burly ruffian before he could bash the brains of a wounded defender.

As a couple of the more cowardly outlaws turned and fled for their lives, Sven and Thorfinn galloped after them, shouting threats.

A hairy outlaw swung around at the noise and brandished his own axe. When Kolby ran to engage him, the man leaped over the overturned chests and swung his weapon within an inch of the heads of the huddled women.

"One step closer, ye hellhound, and they're dead!" he shouted.

"And you'll die with your next breath," Kolby roared. He pulled the longbow from his shoulder and nocked an arrow into his bowstring. Drawing it to his full extension, he aimed it at the outlaw's heart. "Leave them and you can have your life! Touch them and you die!"

The axe hung suspended above their heads. The bow drawn the full length of the arrow quivered as Kolby's muscles strained to hold its sixty-pound pull. "Make up your mind!" he shouted. "Another second and I'll shoot!"

With a growl the outlaw ducked behind the wagon and fled into the forest.

Kolby whirled to find that the rest of the outlaws

had fled as well. Slowly he brought the weapon down. With the arrow pointed to the ground, he eased the bow back to rest. Aren and Durin began to search the bodies of the dead outlaws for booty.

The men in green looked to their fellows who had fallen. One lifted a green and white standard and fitted it into the overturned wagon so it fluttered in the breeze.

Bradach urged his horse to Kolby's side. " 'Tis the colors of the Cloister of the Grove," he said, amazement tinging his voice. "A holy order of priestesses. The outlaws have attacked holy women."

Kolby shrugged. He wasn't surprised in the least. Only good people believed in the goodness of the gods and revered their representatives. He walked over to where the two women were crouched and dropped to one knee beside them.

"Are you all right, my ladies?"

Their cowls concealed their faces as their robes concealed their forms. Kolby couldn't see their features. Old or young, comely or ugly made no difference. They were women and deserving of his protection, whether or not he believed in their gods.

One of the women held out her hand in supplication. "Please. Please find the cloister satchels. Bring them to me. We mustn't let them fall into the hands of these outlaws."

"Madam, we'll look. Unless they carried off things before we arrived, your goods are probably all here." Kolby thrust his arrow back into his quiver and slung his bow over his shoulder. He motioned to Aren and Bradach, who had ridden up when the field was clear. Many pieces of luggage of both cloth and leather were scattered about.

"How will we recognize it?" the warrior asked.

The woman rose to her knees. "It's a double satchel, like a saddlebag but smaller, with connective shoulder straps."

He nodded and began turning over the goods in search of bags of the woman's description.

"The talisman of the grove is also burned into the leather flaps on both satchels," the priestess said. " 'Tis the *craebh ciuil*."

"By the goddess," Bradach breathed and fell to his knees to search anxiously through the goods.

Kolby curled his lip at the man's awe and reverence. He moved around the outer edge of the area, picking through the spilled contents. By luck he turned over and recognized the bags. He hoisted them aloft by one of the connective straps. "Is this what you're looking for?"

"Oh, aye," one of the women cried. "Thank you, young man. And the Mother Goddess's blessing be upon you."

For the first time, Kolby saw her face as she caught hold of the cart wheel and rose to her feet. She was middle-aged. The green cowl framed a beautiful face, lined and pale with a bright red bruise on her cheek. Her companion rose as well but held back as the first priestess advanced with trembling hands outstretched.

"I am Melanthe," she said. "Ancient One of the Cloister of the Grove. We must take these to the cloister immediately. They contain most sacred objects of great value. They must not be allowed to fall into the hands of unbelievers." She looked at him hopelessly. "But you are—"

"My lady." Kolby inclined his head as he set the surprisingly heavy satchels on the ground before her. "I am a Northlander. My faith is not yours, but I am an honorable man. I will not take your treasures. As soon as my men return, we will put your cart to rights and you can be on your way."

Her gentle eyes thanked him. She nodded as she bent to pick up the heavy satchels and hold them against harm. He turned to see Sven and Thorfinn returning through the trees. The three men in green had their heads together. They cast worried looks over their shoulders at the fierce Northlanders. He frowned and walked toward his men. Sometimes friends turned into foes once the danger was over.

Raven had pulled her mother beneath the wheels and held her there when the outlaws had attacked and overturned the cart. When her mother had risen, she had remained where she was, not speaking, not as concerned about the cloister satchels or their sacred contents as she should have been. Her entire attention was focused on *him*.

She stared at the golden warrior who had ridden to her rescue. Never had she thought to see him again, but it was *he*. She would have recognized him anywhere, day or night. He had haunted her dreams and slipped unbidden into her waking moments of quiet prayer and contemplation. He was the man who had surprised her at the high grove altar on Nameless Eve. Instinctively she pulled the cowl forward on her head. Easing her hand inside her robe, she ran it over her brooch, which hung from a chain next to her heart.

He didn't know her, but she had never forgotten him.

She couldn't let him know that she was the woman he had seen and pursued that long-ago night. Yet a part of her—that part close to her heart—urged her to. When he spoke to her mother, his deep rich voice called to her. Heat warmed her cheeks as she realized she wanted to hear it again and again. She wanted him to speak to her.

But such a thing wasn't possible. Never. She was a priestess, a high priestess, sequestered and celibate, in the most sacred of Druid orders. She was a Dryad. She had prayed and contemplated her path for many months before finally accepting the veils of the

Grove. Now no one must look upon her face, just as she must look no man in the face.

Still the fantasies troubled her. She imagined that the two of them—golden warrior and green maid—walked through the apple orchard at the Cloister of the Grove. They laughed and talked. He touched her cheek. She pushed back her cowl, and they looked at each other as man and woman, not as worshipper and priestess.

If she were not a priestess. And he were not a Northlander.

He was not of her faith. She had heard him say so. And even if he were, she could not come to him. For another person this introduction might have been simple, but not for Raven. Her past rushed in upon her, bringing with it a sick feeling of vulnerability. She felt safe only when she was in the cloister.

A fearsome yell turned all heads. The outlaw who had threatened to kill them slapped the flank of his horse and charged full tilt from the trees. Straight at Melanthe he galloped. With the same sword, he hooked the cloister satchels and flipped them from her arms.

The Ancient One screamed and hung on to the precious objects. The horse curvetted and came down, swinging her body with it.

"No. Let go. Mother!" Raven screamed as the outlaw shifted his sword to his other hand. "Mother!" She scrambled from underneath the cart. Her robes tripped her as she tried to rise. "Let her go!"

Across the clearing, Kolby drew his bow, but the outlaw reined the horse around again, putting the old woman between them.

"Melanthe!" Raven reached into the secret pocket of her tunic and pulled out her small dirk. This time she was able to get her feet under her and lunge toward the horse. Weapon in hand, she shouted at

Melanthe again, but her mother had both arms wrapped around the outlaw's leg.

The sword sang in the air as he whirled it above his head.

Raven shouted again. Hoisting her skirts, she clambered over the luggage.

If Melanthe heard her daughter, she ignored her. She would not turn loose, would not lose the sacred objects. Crazed, oblivious to everything but getting the cloister possessions, she reached again, caught his tunic, tried to pull herself up.

"Turn me loose, old one!" he snarled.

"Nay."

His sword blade flashed down. The flat of it smacked across Melanthe's forehead with terrific force. She stiffened and then her muscles went limp. Screaming, Raven dashed forward in time to catch her mother before she hit the ground.

The outlaw wheeled away with his loot.

At that moment more outlaws appeared among the trees. A hail of rocks and sharpened sticks flashed through the air as they renewed their attack. Northlander and Highlander fought side by side to defend themselves. Kolby sent arrow after arrow into the trees.

Raven knelt with her mother in her arms, shielding her from the battle with her own body. "How badly are you hurt?"

Melanthe's eyes blinked open. She pushed at her daughter with feeble hands. "Don't worry about me. Get the cloister satchels. We must have them."

"Your head—"

"I'm fine," Melanthe insisted. "Get the satchels."

Raven didn't move.

"Please, Raven," Melanthe begged, tears starting from her eyes. "You know I wouldn't ask if it weren't important."

Not understanding her mother's insistence, Raven nevertheless could not deny her. "I'll get them. Wait here."

She rose, striving for calm to assess the battle and make the correct move. Most of her men were dead or they were fighting for their lives. The strangers, led by the golden warrior and protected by their shields, had begun to move toward the trees. The outlaw with the cloister satchels wheeled his horse in a circle, exhorting his band to attack.

If she were to get the precious objects back, Raven reasoned, she was going to need more than her dirk. Frantically she began to search through the scattered goods, kicking luggage right and left and shoving the heavier boxes aside. She was searching for her blow-pipe and darts. Where were they? With the shouts and curses of battle resounding in her ears, she prayed to the Great Mother Goddess to help her.

Finally she found the long leather sheath and pulled out the slender reed. She extracted the quiver next, opened it, and pulled out a dart. Out of habit, she rolled the tiny, delicate cylinder in her hand. How she wished it were drugged, but she had used all her treated ones to protect herself against wolves as she gathered herbs at the Shrine of the Great Mother Goddess.

Never dreaming she would be attacked on her way home, Raven had not mixed more potion. Even untreated, the prick of the dart might provide her a slim chance to distract the outlaw so she could grab the satchels and run to safety.

Resolute, she moved along the periphery of the fighting. The outlaw was easy to see. Galloping his horse back and forth behind his men, he was intent on the battle. He halted his horse and stood in the saddle, sword aloft. Seizing her chance, oblivious to personal danger, she dashed forward. When she was close enough to get him in her sight, she raised the pipe to her mouth.

Even as she sucked in her breath, a horse galloped up behind her.

"What in the name of Odin are you doing?" a deep voice thundered.

An arm like iron banded her waist. A leather wrist guard dug through the double fabric of her tunic and robe and into the delicate skin of her midriff. She hung in the air like a sack of meal, her back to him, her buttocks in the air, rounded over his arm, her head and legs dangling.

"Put me down, you lack-witted fool!" Denied composure, she was pleased that the cowl covered her head. Out of its deep folds, she peered over her back at the golden warrior. He was enraged.

"Why didn't you two women stay in the cart out of the way?" he bellowed. "I had him in my sights."

"I did too! You just ruined my shot."

"Gods!" he yelled. "No woman can shoot straight. Not even with her mouth."

Rather than waste her breath in arguing, she tried to twist free. He tightened his grip, and she dropped the blowpipe. "Put me down."

For answer, he looked around him. "Where's the other woman?"

"By the cart."

"Odin's toes!" he cursed. "Why can't you two stay together?" In his anger he tightened his grip still more.

Raven gasped.

"Durin!" he shouted. "Rescue the other woman."

Raven raised her head. What she saw made her heart skip a beat. Melanthe had returned to the fray. Staggering, stumbling, she had nevertheless made her way across the road toward the forest. With single-minded determination, she pressed toward the outlaw who had draped the cloister satchels across his horse's withers.

"Melanthe!" Raven screamed. "Mother!"

The man must have heard her. He twisted in the saddle. His eyes met Raven's before they slid away to her mother. Green robes flapping, face set in a mask of pain, the Ancient One stumbled toward him, arms outstretched.

The outlaw's lips curled into a sneer. He dug his heels into his horse's flanks. As the animal leaped forward, the man leaned from the saddle and ran his sword into Melanthe's shoulder.

"Nooooo!"

The outlaw's horse swerved as he jerked the weapon free.

"Run for it!" he shouted to his cohort. He spurred his horse into the trees. The others broke off the fight and melted into the dimness behind him.

"Aren! Thorfinn! Sven!" the golden warrior shouted. "After them!"

Sobbing, clawing, Raven struggled in his arms, but he would not release her. His friend thrust the handle of his battle-axe into his belt as he ran to catch the stricken Ancient One before she sank to the ground. Gently he lifted her in his arms.

Melanthe's blood spread like a red river over the sleeve of her robe. It left a trail behind them as he carried her toward the cart.

"Let me down! Let me down!" Raven cried.

Gently, with seeming reluctance, the golden warrior lowered her to her feet. She did not wait for him to dismount but ran after the man who carried her mother. Behind her she heard the horse's hooves. Her captor of a moment ago now trotted his steed alongside her. "How is the old one, Durin?"

"She's wounded badly, Kolby," the man replied. Their eyes met and Durin shook his head.

"Bring her over here," Bradach called as he and two of the cloister warriors pushed the cart upright.

Durin placed his burden carefully on the tail of the cart, and Raven crawled in beside her. With trembling hands she brushed aside her mother's cloak. The tunic and sleeve were soaked with blood.

Raven slipped off her gloves and tucked them into her girdle. She caught the gold chain that hung from it and pulled up a leather sewing purse. From it she took her small gold scissors and cut away the drenched fabric. The wound was clean, but deep and low below the collarbone. At least one of Melanthe's ribs might have been scraped. Raven's heart sank. The lungs. The heart. So many vital organs! So much blood!

"'Tis a bad one," Melanthe whispered.

"Aye."

Raven pressed her hand over the wound to stop the bleeding. Hot and viscous, blood oozed between her fingers. For the first time she realized that Melanthe might die. The wound was critical and they had no herbs with which to doctor it. The outlaws had taken them when they stole the cloister satchels.

The golden warrior came to stand on the other side of the cart tail. "Can I do anything to help, my lady?"

"Bandages," she whispered, never taking her eyes from her mother. "I need bandages."

"Get them," he said to Bradach, who nodded and darted away.

As Raven waited for the guide to return, she was oblivious to the activity around them. The four Northlanders moved away and examined their horses and their gear. The cloister guards saw to their own wounds and laid the bodies of their comrades out for burial. One of them jogged into the woods in the direction the frightened oxen had taken.

The golden warrior moved away from the wagon to

squat at the edge of the clearing and study the
ground. He bent lower and lightly traced a circle in
the dust with his hand. Raven's distracted eyes
caught the gesture. Despite her concern for her mother, she stared at him. Kolby. His name was Kolby.

He scooted forward, still studying the ground.
Farther and farther up the trail, he repeated the ritual.

Melanthe began to murmur a prayer. Her voice
brought Raven's attention back abruptly. She lowered her head and placed her ear close to her mother's mouth. Melanthe prayed and called on the Great
Mother Goddess for wisdom and guidance. Her face
was as white as death.

Raven wished she could lay her hands over her
mother's, but she didn't dare. If she did, her mother's
blood and life would flow out onto the ground. When
she joined her voice to her mother's, her prayer was
for strength.

Bradach soon returned with a large piece of white
cloth.

"Take my scissors and cut it into bandages," Raven
ordered.

"I'll do that." The deep, resonant voice of the
golden warrior Kolby played along Raven's nerve
endings. The last time she had seen him he was
studying the ground. Now he had resumed his place
beside the cart and was gazing down at her. Sunshine
gleamed golden in his hair; it silhouetted him, emphasizing his great size and strength. Was his the
strength she had prayed for? Had the Great Mother
Goddess answered her prayer?

"Now that you've finished your examination of the
road." She couldn't keep the bitterness from her
voice.

"Aye," he replied without apology. " 'Tis a habit of
mine to study hoofprints. Sometimes they identify a
horse beyond doubt. Then when I find that horse

again, I can look up into the face of his rider." He repeated his question. "May I be of help?"

She shook her head. Taking the pieces of cloth Bradach handed her, she bandaged her mother's shoulder. "These will stem the flow a little but I also need—"

"Aye," the guide interrupted. "I know. Nature's remedy. Moss."

Raven nodded. "You know?"

"Aye, I'll hunt for some." He rose and strode away.

"Be sure to wash it for me," she called after him.

"You use moss in your dressings?" Kolby asked.

"Yes, if he can find some," she replied. "We press it against a bleeding wound. It seems to stem the flow of blood."

Both watched helplessly as the bright red stain began to appear through the freshly applied bandage. Raven choked back a sob.

Melanthe laid a trembling hand on Raven's arm. "I must make confession."

Terrified that her mother believed she was dying, Raven laid her hand over her mother's. "Plenty of time for that."

"No," came the whispered reply. "Now. Must."

Raven nodded. Without raising her head, she spoke to the warrior. "I beg you leave us, sir. The good mother and I would be alone."

"Now," Melanthe repeated.

He nodded curtly. His voice was stiff, as if he were disappointed that he could not remain near them. "There is much to do. Call if you need me."

Melanthe stared into her daughter's face. "The satchels?"

Raven hated to give the answer. "The bandits escaped with them."

"Nay." Melanthe's cry was an anguished whisper. Her fingers dug into Raven's arm. She tried to sit up, but the effort cost her too much. Gasping for breath, she sank back as fresh blood stained her bandages. "Get them back. We must get them back."

"The stolen goods were valuable," Raven protested gently, "but not irreplaceable. You needn't be so concerned about them."

"The shawl." This time when Melanthe sat up, she managed to stay. Her eyes were glazed, but she seemed oblivious to her pain.

With a gesture of impatience, Raven laid her hands on her mother's shoulders. She knew the shawls were important, but they were not priceless. Made of soft blue material, they were long, dipping down the back in a deep point. Each one was decorated with a silver fringe with tiny gold apple bells sewn intermittently around the hem. In each cloister the Ancient One wore a shawl on the Day of Apples when they celebrated the harvest of fruit.

"If we don't find it, I'll have Mother Barbara make us a new one, and we shall dedicate it to the Great Mother Goddess. The Sacred One will understand. Mother, please lie down."

But the loss of the sacred object possessed Melanthe entirely. "You must get the shawl."

"'Twill be all right," Raven assured her as she wondered at the strength necessary to finally make an old and wounded woman lie down again. "I'm sure we can borrow a shawl from another cloister before long."

"'Tis you who don't understand." Melanthe would have shouted the words had she had the strength. "'Tis not the shawl itself."

Puzzled, Raven ran a hand over her mother's brow. Was a fever setting in so soon? Was she delirious with pain?

"As the Ancient One, I have been entrusted with many secrets of the Druids."

"Aye."

Melanthe took a deep breath. "This year I was selected to be one of the Chosen Ones."

Raven stared at her mother. "This means you must know where the sacred tree is. I had no idea."

"You weren't supposed to. Only the Chosen Ones know each other. I have been given one of the sacred shawls for safekeeping. Now we must get it back." Her alarming pallor increased.

Raven knew that if her mother didn't stop exciting herself, she would be beyond help. "For a verity we can make another."

Again Melanthe caught her daughter's arm with surprising strength. "We need this one. Each little bell on the sacred shawl has an inscription, *ogham fedha*, on the inside. Together they give directions to the sacred apple grove of the Druids, hidden deep in the forestlands."

Wearily Raven rubbed her forehead. The implications for her people were staggering. "Nay, Mother. Tell me this isn't true."

"I swear by the Goddess." Though her face was as pale as a corpse, Melanthe's eyes burned with a zealot's light. "We must get the shawl back. With all its bells. If it is not returned and I die—"

"You will suffer dishonor in the Otherworld," Raven finished. Cold horror seeped into her soul. She shuddered.

"Aye, and so will the cloister and our land. Our orchards will die. You must promise me, Raven."

There could be no other answer. "I'll get the shawl back for you. I promise. I vow before the Great Mother Goddess."

Melanthe stared into her daughter's face, then relaxed back upon the rough wood. "You needn't be afraid. The Great Mother has protected you all your life. She will do so now."

For the first time the Ancient Once seemed able to rest. Raven held her mother's hand and looked away at the men who were bringing some semblance of order to the scene. Her heart was heavy not only with concern for Melanthe's health but also with worry about the shawl. If its secret was discovered, the riches it protected could be exploited by uncaring people. She thanked the Great Mother Goddess that the Northlander had sent his men after the thieves. She was sure they would overtake the outlaws, retrieve the cloister satchels, and return the holy shawl.

When Bradach came back from his successful search for moss, Raven removed the cloth bandages and pressed the moss gently over the wound. Then she covered it again with a fresh dressing.

"The shawl," Melanthe mumbled. "You must find it." Her mother's face had changed again. Now fever began to redden her cheekbones. Her eyes were glazing. "The shawl."

"I will." Raven clasped her hands tightly, shaken by the knowledge of what she was about to say. "I swear before you and before the Great Mother Goddess that I will recover the shawl."

Chapter 3

Sitting on the edge of the cart with the sun directly overhead, Raven watched Kolby stride toward her. As he came, he lifted his arm and wiped his sleeve over his forehead. He reminded her of how hot she was. Perspiration trickled down her back and between her breasts. While she needed her robe for the morning and evening chill, it was entirely too warm in the middle of the day.

The heavy clothing was one of the most disagreeable aspects of her life at the cloister, but now she welcomed it. The deep cowl hid her face from the golden warrior. Her body trembled at the thought of what he might do if he were to recognize her and remember how he had last seen her.

Kolby halted beside the cart. "How is your friend?"

"Her wound is very serious," Raven replied. Despite the bandages and the moss, blood continued to seep through the material. "We have no herbs with which to treat her."

"We have some few crude stuffs. You're welcome to use them," Kolby said. "Durin," he shouted, "bring my saddlebag."

He was a good man, truly helpful, Raven thought. Many men would not have been so patient with a wounded woman, or with any woman for that matter.

Raven almost raised her head to smile at him. Instead she tugged the cowl a little farther down. "Thank you, my lord, both for rescuing us and for sharing your medicines so freely."

Behind them, Northlanders and cloister guards began to wrestle with the central axle. The cart rocked to and fro as they sought to bind the splintered ends together with strips of ox hide. Melanthe moaned softly. Raven placed her hand on her mother's forehead. To Kolby she said, "Mother Melanthe and I owe you a debt of gratitude that we shall surely repay. May I know your full name, sir? I have heard only Kolby."

"Aye," he replied. "Kolby of Apelstadt from the kingdom of Northland."

She nodded gravely, taking care to keep her face completely concealed. "I am Raven nea Pryse of Ailean, High Priestess of the Cloister of the Grove. Our house is on the northeastern coast of Scotland near Ross."

"Raven," he murmured. "That's an unusual name."

"Not among Dryads. For us, the raven is a fearsome bird. We believe it is sacred because of its powerful link with the Otherworld. Sometimes it carries messages to those wise enough to hear. Many of us in the Highlands have this name."

Kolby covered what might have been a laugh with a cough. Unable to help herself, Raven peeked out from under her cowl. He was indeed grinning. As she watched, a black shadow passed over his face. He held up his arm. To her amazement a raven—the one she had seen beside him in the cave—dropped down onto his wrist guard with a flutter of feathers.

"Not so fearsome a bird," he told her, barely able to control his laughter. "No, nor sacred either. Midnight Wind is a thief and a beggar. If he could talk, I doubt you'd want to hear what he has to say."

Suddenly she remembered this man's lack of reverence, which had bothered her on that night long ago. "You don't believe in the Otherworld?" she accused softly.

"I've never been there." He shot a glance back at her, but she quickly ducked her head. His voice was definitely tinged with sarcasm. "But many do believe. It pleases them, I suppose. Away, you black outlaw." He stretched his arm aloft and the bird took wing with an indignant cawing.

"It is our link with all of life," Raven insisted. Again she was troubled by his lack of reverence. She wanted only the best for this man who had undoubtedly saved their lives. "This woman is Melanthe, the Ancient One of the Cloister of the Grove. Ordinarily she would be covered with a cowl and robe like me. We are a sequestered order of celibates, whose duty is to preserve that link for all our people."

When she would have said more, Durin strode up with a small leather bag. "Here is our store of medicines, my lady. The little we have."

"At least there will be something to help her," Raven said gratefully.

Kolby accepted it for her and set it on the bed of the cart. He untied the leather thongs that bound it. "Perhaps you will find herbs among our small supply that will help."

Again she wanted to raise her hood and smile at him. Feeling more constrained by her order than she had ever felt before, she bent her head over the bag and began to pull out some of the herbs.

Kolby bent his head close to hers to identify the few small bundles and packets and explain their uses.

She had to stop herself from drawing back in alarm. Never had she been more powerfullly aware of a man. She could feel his heat. The scents of him— leather and horses and hard-worked man—filled her nostrils, doubly stirring because she knew he had done the difficult tasks of a warrior for her, to save her life.

He appeared not to notice. Instead he said, "I think these two should help."

"I—I'll mix them together and brew a tea when we stop for the night." She held out her hand awkwardly. His fingers brushed her palm as he handed the herbs to her.

To cover her confusion, she looked around desperately. The shadows had begun to lengthen as the short northern afternoon rapidly wore on. Still they sat in the middle of the clearing far from home. Thank the Great Mother Goddess the guard had returned with the oxen. Now if the cart could only be fixed . . .

Folding his arms over his chest, Kolby loomed above her. "This is isolated and dangerous country, my lady. Particularly for holy women. What are you two doing out here alone?"

Raven had only just learned how dangerous it was for them, now that Melanthe had told her about the shawl. Still, she couldn't tell this man about the secret groves. He had no reverence for sacred things.

"We weren't alone," she denied, hoping she wouldn't have to lie. "Six cloister guards were with us. Besides, we've traveled this road before. Every year we've made an annual pilgrimage to the Shrine of the Great Mother Goddess. This is the first time misfortune has befallen us."

"According to our guide, that shrine is much farther south, near Argyll," Kolby pointed out. "You were on a road that leads through the badlands. Did you get lost?" He cast a skeptical eye in Bradach's direction. "Or did he?"

"We . . . er . . . were on our return trip to our cloister." Raven hated herself. This man had been so good to them and she was lying to him. And she wasn't a good liar. "That is—we—our cloister always turns off the main road. We travel to the port where we . . . er . . . trade." She was making a mess of this.

Kolby looked around at the strewn luggage and supplies that the thieves had not succeeded in taking. "You must not have traded very much," he said dryly. "Or maybe you didn't find what you wanted."

"Oh, we traded for . . . er . . . these things. Traders are eager to buy items from the Cloister of the Grove. We have quite a reputation. We especially enjoy trading with the . . . er . . Iberians."

"Iberians—hmm."

"That's right. Iberians. Merchants." She closed her eyes and set her lips tightly together.

"Madam," Kolby said. "I doubt you've ever met an Iberian merchant."

"You're right of course. That is why we travel with an armed escort," Raven argued. "I am a sequestered priestess. I don't actually meet with the merchants. My guard does."

He said nothing for a few moments. Carefully she drew the veil across the lower half of her face, at the same time managing to peep out from under it. He was looking directly at her, his face a study in disbelief. Hastily she ducked her head. He laughed. "Careful, my lady. You'll betray your vow."

She said nothing. What was there to say? She wished he would go away and leave her in peace. And still a part of her wanted him to stay. She and Melanthe were going to be desperately alone with a broken cart, one ox, and three guards, one of whom was wounded.

Their predicament had not escaped Kolby either, for he suddenly asked, "How far are you from your cloister?"

"By cart, four or five days. By this cart—" She shrugged her shoulders beneath the green robes. "Who knows? I told you our cloister is on the northeastern coast of Scotland near Ross."

"And how far is it to the shrine?"

Again she shrugged. "Another six or seven days."

"My lady, you're in trouble."

"Aye. I hope your men return shortly." The cart jolted as one of her guards began the task of loading their remaining goods in it. She took a deep breath and assumed the mantle of her wounded mother. She was in charge now. "It's most important that we get back to the cloister as quickly as possible. We will pay you for your valuable time and reward you generously as well for saving us."

He didn't answer. Unable to bear the suspense any longer, she caught up the edge of her veil and pulled it across the lower half of her face. He was frowning, his golden brows drawn together over his hawk's eyes.

"Your pardon, madam. We shall be leaving as soon as possible, but we won't be going directly to the cloister."

She almost dropped the veil. "What! Not going to the cloister!"

"Nay, madam, you said it would take four to five days to reach it. I can't afford to waste four or five days."

She couldn't believe her ears. "But we'll reward—"

"It's not a matter of reward."

She glared at him. He wasn't taking her seriously. So let him go. And good riddance to the irreverent, stubborn—"Then we'll go our way alone. We have guards."

"They were certainly effective when you were attacked before."

To her list of his faults, she added sarcasm. Oooh, how she hated him. "They will be more careful next time. They were . . . attacked from ambush."

"You have only three guards now and one is wounded." He looked at her pityingly. "Be glad I am

willing to take you with me. Pride and stupidity have
cost many a warrior his life."

She had never been so angry in her life. He had
actually called her proud and stupid. She! A high
priestess of the Cloister of the Grove. How dare he?
This barbarian. She knew what was best for them all.

She strove for calm. Nothing was achieved by
anger. "The Ancient One is badly hurt. She can get
the best care at the cloister. If we push the ox, and
travel long hours, we can possibly—"

"Nay, madam. If you are attacked again, she will
be killed."

"If you would escort us just until we get out of the
badlands, we'll give you all we have and promise—"

"You cannot travel quickly with her. As she is, she
may not survive the trip the rest of this day."

Raven's blood was boiling. He had backed her into
a corner with reason, but her anger refused to let her
see it. She actually stamped her foot. "Nothing is
more important than getting us to the Cloister of the
Grove."

"For you, madam. Not for me."

"For all of Scotland, Kolby of Apelstadt. I'm high
priestess of the largest and most revered cloister of all
the kingdoms, a keeper of the land. The Ancient
One—" She pointed to her mother's prone body. As
if somewhere in her consciousness, Melanthe heard;
she stirred and rolled her head from side to side. Her
lips moved soundlessly. "—the Ancient One is the
most sacred one among us all, the chosen of the Great
Mother Goddess. You must—"

Kolby folded his arms across his chest. Religious
people always had priorities that had nothing to do
with the things of this earth. These so-called directions from their gods always required that ordinary
people drop their most urgent business and run off
on some fool's errand.

He would not jeopardize his meeting with the

outlaw Vaghn. He had been searching for nearly two years, and this was the closest he had ever come to finding definitive information about Ura's sacred tree. Perhaps tomorrow he would discover once and forever where it existed. Or, more likely, that it didn't exist at all. At any rate by tomorrow night, he might have completed his quest and be able to return to his own homeland. Then he would have no trouble escorting the priestesses on the way back.

He sympathized with the woman, who was obviously distraught and incapable of rational thinking, but he was settled on his course. He would meet Vaghn for the morning meal at the Sign of the Boar in the badlands. Perhaps he could even arrange an escort for them there.

If that were not possible, then he would pay for their lodging until he could return and escort the foolish females himself.

"Some of you Northlanders live among us," Raven was saying. "They will thank you greatly and add rewards to mine if—"

Kolby shook his head.

"My brother-in-law Brian mac Logan has a friend who is from the Northland," she went on.

Kolby froze, staring at her face as he tried to imagine what she looked like behind the veil. A hot flush rose in her cheeks.

"I am a friend of mac Logan," he said reluctantly. Kolby knew the high priestess was intentionally reminding him of the universal law of friendship. A Northlander owed it to a friend to protect the friend's family. Raven had declared herself a part of mac Logan's family.

"You fought with him at the battle of Glenmuir," Raven said anxiously.

"Aye. I do not need to be reminded of that, madam."

"Then you are honor-bound to escort us." She could not keep the triumph from her voice.

He nodded, his lip curling with contempt at her attempt to shame him into doing his duty. "Aye, madam, and I will." He watched her eyes. "But not tomorrow."

He saw her hand clench in the green material. He held his breath, wondering if she would forget her vow and let him see her face.

"Riders coming!" Durin shouted.

Instantly Kolby reacted. Swinging away from the cart, he pulled the longbow from his shoulder. He motioned to the cloister guards, who obeyed him without question, arranging themselves in front of the cart to protect Raven and Melanthe. Bradach eased up to the back of the cart where he could guard the rear and give the alarm if needed.

After a swift gesture to Raven to keep her head down, Kolby raced across the clearing to join Durin. All waited, their bodies tense, their hands on their weapons. The thud of horses' hooves grew louder, closer. At last the riders rounded the curve.

Raven, peeking over the rim of the cart, felt her hopes plummet. The three Northlanders had returned alone.

The youngest of them, the one called Aren, leaped from his horse. "We lost them."

"How, lad?" Kolby put his arm around his minion's shoulder. "Their horses looked scrawny compared with ours."

"They disappeared in the trees. We were behind them. We could see them. Then, suddenly, they were gone." Aren looked to his fellows for confirmation. They nodded soberly.

"'Twas just as he said, Kolby," Thorfinn added.

"Shall we go again, my lord?" Aren asked. "Mayhap—"

Kolby shook his head. Patting the young man's shoulder, he stepped back. "Nay, lads. They're not worth our trouble."

For Raven his words were a catastrophe. The events of the past hour rushed in upon her. Her load was too heavy to bear. The cloister possessions had been looted. Her guards had been killed and wounded. Her beloved mother lay near death. And most terrible for all of Scotland, the sacred shawl had been stolen.

The Northlanders must not be allowed to abandon the search. They had to go out again and find the shawl. They had to. She flung herself from the cart. "No. No. No!"

Every man in the clearing turned to stare as she dashed toward Kolby, her green robes flaring out behind her. In her distress she quite forgot to hold the veil in place. The cowl blew back, leaving her face framed in fine white linen.

Unaware that Kolby stiffened in recognition, she flung herself at Aren. "Clumsy. You were clumsy. You made too much noise. They knew you were chasing them, so they turned aside one by one and disappeared. You were fooled. They'll meet back at an appointed place. I know they will. You can find it. You must look longer. You must!"

"Madam." A hand descended on her shoulder. Its hard grasp shocked her as Kolby spun her around. "Cease your raving."

"Raving!" She had never been accused of raving, had never been ordered to calm herself. Still his words made her aware too late of what she was doing. He was terribly close to being correct. Most especially because in her anger and frustration, she had betrayed her order, her vows, and herself. Only an uncharacteristic perversity made her want to deny his accusation.

"Aye!" His other hand fell on her. Both hard hands gripped her and pulled her away from his men.

"Raving." He bent over her, his fierce brows drawn together, a muscle in his jaw flickering as he sought to silence her. "I alone have the right to discipline my men. I alone have the right to order them to stay or to go. I would not tolerate such words spoken by a man, and I will not tolerate—"

"I do not rave." She made a special effort to lower her voice and put on a stern, cool expression.

His eyes widened. His anger gave way to puzzlement. "I know you," he said softly. "We have met before. Where?"

"No. We have never met. Never."

Too late, she struggled with one hand to catch up the veil and with the other to pull the cowl forward over her face. Too late, she remembered the vows she had taken to let no man look upon her, to remain forever with head bowed and features hidden. She was dedicated to the true contemplative life in which all her thoughts were directed toward the Great Mother Goddess.

"I have seen your face," he insisted.

"No," she whispered. "No. I am a sequestered priestess. We could never—"

"We have," he insisted. "I'll remember it. It will come to me." She saw a small smile play around his mouth, lifting the corners of his well-shaped lips. "I never forget a face. And soon I'll remember where I've seen you before."

"No. No." She jerked away from him and fumbled to put her shielding garments into place. Hiding her hands inside the sleeves of her garment, shrinking in its folds, she sought to compose herself.

One lapse in nine years was surely permissible, was her fleeting thought. Surely the goddess would forgive one lapse when she had felt so desperate, so alone, so devoid of control. Her greatest strength had been her composure and thoughtfulness, her ability to view a situation calmly from various perspectives and to make sound judgments. Surely in the grip of strong passion—

She took a deep, steadying breath. "I apologize, sir. You are quite right to chastise my behavior." Even as she spoke, she wished she had not put the cowl back in place. She couldn't even see how he was taking her words. Her frustration was acute. No help for it but to push on. "I apologize," she repeated. "I don't ordinarily behave like this. Please believe that I was overcome by desperation. Those evil men have gravely wounded the Ancient One of the cloister and have escaped with holy objects."

She was almost sure he wouldn't change his mind, but she couldn't turn from her purpose. She waved her hand toward Kolby's men. "I must confess, sir, I'm at a loss to understand your leniency with men who have performed inadequately."

"Inadequately!" Durin of the battle-axe scoffed loudly. "Inadequately. I'll have you know—"

His leader must have waved him to silence because the speech broke off. Then Kolby's hand, tanned and battle-scarred, appeared beneath the cowl. Though she shivered and tried to avoid his questing fingers, they found her chin and tipped it back. For his eyes only, she turned her face into the light of day. "I sent my men after the attackers not to retrieve your property, but to make sure they did not return and harm us," he informed her coldly. "My warriors and I have no personal quarrel with them, no score to settle. They stole nothing of ours."

"Cloister shame is shame for us all," Raven countered.

"That might be true for you Highlanders," Kolby said, "but not for me and my warriors. We do not worship your gods. Indeed, I worship no god at all. My word and my lord are enough for me, just as this life is enough for me."

Her eyes glittered with shock. His words were like

knives. How could any man doubt the power of the gods? Of the Great Mother Goddess who appeared in all things of earth and all of heaven? He was truly a barbarian.

She tried one more desperate appeal based on the universal law of friendship. "Sir, I beg you to send your men out again. One more time. Please. If Mother Melanthe could know that the satchels were safe, the knowledge could very well save her life. She is dear to your Brian mac Logan and his wife Gwynneth."

He shook his head. To his men he said, "Finish loading the cart. Help those guards hitch the one oxen to it. Durin, unsaddle Bradach's horse. We'll hitch him in the other yoke. Aren, you give Bradach your horse and drive the cart."

That command pleased no one.

Young Aren scowled because he had to plod along behind an ox and a plug of a horse.

"I would rather Bradach drove," Raven protested immediately. "He is one of my countrymen. I will feel safer with him."

"I will drive the lady," Bradach agreed promptly.

Kolby's fists clenched. "Enough!" he thundered. "You will do as I command. Do not question me, Aren. As for you, Bradach, you'll ride ahead of us, as you did before. 'Tis my silver that hired you."

He locked gazes with Raven. "Do you have anything to say about my commands?"

She recognized an angry man when she saw one. "No, sir."

"Then let's be off." He raised his voice. "Mount up, all!"

"We can't leave without—" she began, but he caught her by the arm.

"Come with me. Don't speak to the men again." He dragged her across the clearing to the cart and boosted her up beside her mother.

When she would have jumped back down again, he held up his hand, his finger pointed only inches from her nose. "Later! I'll want a full explanation later."

She seized his hand with both her own. "Barbarian. There are things of inestimable value in those satchels. You must get them back."

His piercing stare caught and held hers. Unaccustomed as she was to meeting anyone's eyes, least of all a fierce warrior's, she almost quailed before him. Then she rallied and returned his stare.

"What things of inestimable value?" he sneered.

Instantly she released his hand and lifted her chin. "I command great respect throughout Scotland," she informed him. "If I should send word that you are not to be trusted, you would soon find your sojourn here most distressing and quite unprofitable."

"What things?" he repeated, clearly unimpressed with her recital of her power.

She hated to tell him because she knew he would scoff. She hated to be in the presence of such irreverence. Otherwise, he was a noble man who aroused unfamiliar feelings within her. She dropped her eyes. "A sacred shawl."

He was silent for so long she could not bear the suspense. When she looked at him, she found him grinning. "Stop it!"

"Stop what?"

"Stop grinning, you fool. It is an object sacred to the Great Mother Goddess. It is beyond price."

He laughed. "I'm sure it's worth very little. Those satchels couldn't have been very heavy. 'Tis not as if they contained gold or silver. Besides, if your Great Mother Goddess is so great, why can't she protect her own things?"

"Don't—don't blaspheme." Raven could feel tears starting in her eyes. Why wouldn't he understand? Why, with hundreds of brave and able men in

Scotland, had she been rescued by one who believed in nothing?

" 'Tis holy, sacred, magic. The Dryads at the Shrine of the Great Mother Goddess presented the shawl to Melanthe, the Ancient One of the Cloister of the Grove. It belongs to the Great Mother Goddess, and Melanthe cannot bear the shame of having it stolen from her. As priestesses we have a duty to protect the Great Goddess's possessions."

"As I said, if she's so great, why can't she protect her own things?"

Their conversation was interrupted when the cart swayed as Aren climbed aboard, still scowling. Durin led Kolby's horse forward. Kolby tossed his leg over the golden stallion's back and swung into the saddle. "Scout ahead," he told his man. "We didn't do enough damage to those outlaws. We don't want another attack."

"Aye, sir."

Kolby looked around one last time. Bradach reluctantly waited at the head of the clearing. Thorfinn and Sven sat their horses next. On foot the cloister guards stood on either side of the team to help Aren control them until they settled into their stride. The wounded guard, Melanthe, and Raven waited in the cart.

Kolby glanced at the sun already speeding down the horizon. They had so much time to make up. Still, he could do no less. "Forward! We're off to the Sign of the Boar."

The cart jolted forward and Melanthe groaned. Raven had her hands full making her mother comfortable. She could only grind her teeth as the procession moved slowly into the badlands.

From the thick limb of a tall tree far up the side of the mountain road, two men watched the cart and its escort.

The outlaw who had stolen the satchels and stabbed the Ancient One cursed softly.

The man beside him didn't even look at him. "You're an idiot, Magdu. You had them all. You could have killed them all and taken everything. Loot for all of your men."

"The Northlanders attacked out of nowhere, Donnal. We didn't have any idea they were near," Magdu whined. "And who would have thought they would have interfered? We were lucky to get away with what we got." He looked longingly at the satchels slung over his chief's shoulder. "When are we going to divide the loot?"

"When we get it all." The leader watched the procession until it wound out of sight. "When we get it all. And the woman. You're being paid for the woman too. Let's follow the Northlander for a while. They'll have to stop for the night soon. I'm sure he's too high-principled to get rid of his wounded."

The man called Donnal shifted his body until he was belly-down on the limb and let himself down to the full extension of his arms. From that position he dropped lightly to the ground. He pulled his mount's reins from around a low bush, then vaulted into the saddle and kicked the animal into a lope. His henchman cursed again, more loudly this time. He too let himself to the ground. Though he spat in the tracks of his leader, he still climbed his horse and followed his master into the forest.

The sun was already behind the trees when the procession plodded out of the forest and onto the shores of a long lake. In the evening shadows its surface might have been a sheet of glass, so still was it, with hardly a ripple. Its color was not blue, or gray, or green, but shiny black from the layers of peat that floated in its depths. Along the shoreline, pale gray mist rose as the black lake still reflected the sun's heat to mix with the coolness of the forests. An oppressive stillness lay over everything. The loch looked as if it belonged to another world and had no part in the dealings of men.

Raising his arm to signal a halt, Kolby guided his stallion alongside Bradach. "What is this place?"

" 'Tis Loch Ness, sir," the Highlander replied. "On the other side of its shores are none but the bad. A good man who goes there is liable never to return."

Kolby's mouth twisted. "Then it's a good thing I'm not a good man. Otherwise I might be in danger."

"We should camp here for the night," Bradach said nervously. He made as if to dismount.

"Hold on." Kolby crossed his arms over his chest as he ran his eye along the distant shoreline. An hour of daylight yet remained and the road lay clear before them. "You're changing your tale, Highlander. When we were preparing for this journey, you assured me that we would spend the night in an abandoned village on the south side of the loch. You said it was safer than staying on this side where we would be in the open, easy prey for outlaws."

Bradach threw a quick glance toward the cart. "Aye, my lord, but having the ladies with us, especially the old one, changes matters."

Kolby looked at him in disgust. "Aye, it does change matters. They must be dispatched to the safest place. Let us—"

Raven spoke over the edge of the cart. "Let us turn this wretched thing around and head for the north of Scotland. We'll all be killed if we ride farther into the badlands."

Kolby twisted in the saddle to glare at her. All the men had heard her words, including her dire prediction of death for them all. "Hold your tongue, woman!"

"I don't want to go into the badlands," she insisted.

"I don't want to go into the badlands either,"

Kolby growled. She was the most argumentative female he had ever known. "But I have to. I don't want you traveling in my company, but here you are. I don't want to have to argue over every decision that I make and every order that I give. But here you are questioning me. Now hear me, lady. If you want my escort, you'll have to travel with me and do my bidding.

"Bradach, lead us to the abandoned village by the quickest and most direct way."

Raven dropped down on the cart bed with a dejected thud. She was helpless and she didn't like it one bit. The situation was becoming more grave by the minute. Her mother was very ill. They were moving deep into the badlands, where dangerous outlaws lived. They were traveling alongside a lake infamous throughout Scotland for evil spirits that dwelt on its shores and in its depths. Every mile they covered carried them farther away from the sacred objects.

The barbarian had reduced her to the verge of tears. He had destroyed her maturity and self-possession just as the oppressive heat was destroying her will to wear the habit of her order. She let the cowl fall back onto her shoulders. The linen wimple was soaked beneath it. If only she could take it off as well.

She leaned against the railing and squeezed her eyes tightly shut. If one tear fell, it would turn into a flood.

"Are you all right, my lady?" Kolby's deep voice rumbled above her.

Without opening her eyes she answered. "As well as can be expected under the circumstances."

An object brushed her shoulder. She opened her eyes to find him dangling two bags beside her. "Food and drink."

Surprised, she straightened. Suddenly she realized how hungry she was. She also remembered the night at the mountain cave when she had watched him eat. Soft memories returned to block out the harsh ones. They added to her growing confusion. One minute he repelled her with callousness; the next he drew her with kindness and consideration. She didn't know what to think. Warriors traveled light. This man was sharing what little they had with her. Her own guards were also partaking of a share.

"Thank you." She lowered the bags to the cart bed beside Melanthe. Despite her own thirst, she first held the ale to her mother's parched lips. At first the liquid ran down the sides of her mouth. Then the unconscious woman seemed to rouse. Although her eyes remained closed, her hand lifted, fumbled and caught at the bag, and she drank greedily.

Raven was terribly aware of the Viking as he rode beside the cart. Her fingers shook as she found a piece of cheese about the size of a man's thumb and tore off a piece of bread. The crust was so tough she had to soften it by pouring a little ale over it, but she managed to choke it all down.

Quickly she returned both bags to Kolby. "Thank you, sir. I feel much better now."

Though he accepted them, he did not ride off, but continued beside her, staring at her face. "I'm sure I've seen you," he remarked. "But where?"

"Perhaps you've seen my sister," Raven suggested hastily. "She's Gwynneth nea Pryse of Ailean. She's the wife of the seafarer Brian mac Logan. She is a seafarer also and has sailed to foreign lands."

He shook his head. "I know Gwynneth. She competed in the Great Hall after the battle of Glenmuir." His mouth curled in self-deprecation. "She outshot me. On that day she was the better archer."

Raven nodded. "She is wonderful."

"She is an exceptional woman. But you are not she.

And when I see your face, I don't think of her. Instead—" He closed his eyes, as if trying to conjure up a picture.

She held her breath.

At length he shook his head. "I will remember eventually."

She could only hope and pray that he would not. Melanthe stirred and whimpered. Raven poured water onto a cloth and washed her mother's face.

"How did your mother come to be a priestess?" he asked.

"She entered the Cloister of the Grove after she and my father were divorced."

"And you went with her into the cloister?"

He was getting terribly close to her personal business. She wondered whether she should answer him or not. Reluctantly she said, "Not for many years. Since I am the heir to the high seat, I lived with my father and his second wife and Gwynneth. I didn't enter the cloister until I was much older."

If he asked the next question, she would not answer it. She would not tell him about her disgrace. To forestall the question she quickly asked one of her own. "What of yourself, sir? Have you pledged fealty to one of the thieves who styles himself a lord? Is that why you travel this way and in such haste?"

His eyebrows flew up. For a space, she thought he wouldn't answer her. Her question was impolite, but perhaps it would drive him away.

"I have business with an outlaw," he replied at last. "That does not make me a thief."

"Are you seeking your fame and fortune?"

"You might say that."

He was as close-mouthed as she. Between the two of them, they had a great store of secrets. " 'Twould be better found outside the badlands," she gibed. "Great lords are always searching for champions.

They pay good bounty for services rendered. Petty lords—no more than thieves—pay little or nothing."

He caught her implication. His jaw clenched until a tendon showed in his neck. "I go where I must."

"Only outlaws who join together can survive in the badlands."

He looked at her from beneath his golden lashes. His tone was mockingly polite. "Do you worry about me, Holy Mother?"

Holy Mother! She would guess that she was five or more years younger than he. Certainly not old enough to be his mother. For the first time since she had taken her vows, she deeply resented being called Holy Mother. The Northlander made her feel as if she were the Ancient One of the cloister. She didn't feel holy or motherly. This man stirred her womanly instincts, not her religious ones. He reminded her that she was young. He sent her blood boiling through her veins.

And she could do nothing about such feelings except conceal them as best she could. "Aye," she replied, surprised that she sounded so calm. "I am. I'm grateful that you came along when you did and saved us."

"I did what any honorable warrior would," he replied, clearly uncomfortable with her compliments. "I was taught to repect you and your mother as holy women, whether or not I believe in your gods. According to the universal laws of friendship, you are my charges now. I shall protect you at all costs."

She smiled slightly. "The costs could be quite high."

"I expect they will be, my lady."

Chapter 4

Night shadows fell across them as they rounded the tip of the lake. The darkness was complete. A dense canopy of leaves from overhanging trees closed off the stars and the moon. They might have been in a cave except for the night sounds of the creatures all around them.

An owl hooted mournfully somewhere to the left. In a distant glen a wolf howled. His fellow answered. Crickets chirped. Night beetles clicked. The very leaves of the trees seemed to be talking to each other as they rustled softly.

Kolby rode alongside Bradach. "Where is this abandoned village?" he asked. "This is like the dominion of Hel herself."

In the cart Raven heard his comment and thought much the same thing. "I wonder you do not fear to be beside the haunted waters of Loch Ness."

He halted his horse. "What mean you? Haunted waters?"

Had she detected a note of concern in his voice? She sincerely hoped so. "Oh, there may be a kelpie abroad somewhere this night."

One of the cloister guards muttered a quick prayer. Both of them were hanging on to the sides of the cart

for dear life. Kolby reined the stallion alongside them.
She could see his face, a pale oval in the dimness.

"What's a kelpie?" Kolby demanded.

"Ah, you don't know." She lowered her voice to a
whisper. Good Highlanders knew to fear the badlands of Scotland. It would do the Northlanders good
to fear them also. "A kelpie is a water horse. A pony
so beautiful that no one can resist the sight of him.
All want to mount him. But beware. For he's a shape
changer. Once the person has mounted him, he will
gallop straightaway into the loch. There he will
change into a fearsome monster and devour his
rider."

Kolby laughed softly. "If a man were foolish
enough to ride a wild horse into a loch, he deserves
his fate. A wise man would slip from his back."

"Ah, but he can't." Raven was enjoying herself
thoroughly now. "His skin is adhesive. Once a human touches it, there is no escaping his fate."

The guards muttered in agreement, but Kolby
hooted at their fears. He leaned over the cart rail,
almost in a conspiratorial manner. "You don't believe
that yourself, my lady. You're trying to throw a scare
into me, so I'll turn back and take you to your
damned cloister."

"Would I do that to you, sir?" she asked demurely.

"You would indeed. Listen, while I make my own
fate." He lifted his hands to his mouth and bird calls
whistled through the air. They waited. He called
again. Tension mounted. Then they heard the answering trill. Still they waited until out of the dense
undergrowth a rider emerged.

"What news of this abandoned village?" Kolby
asked.

"Straight ahead," Durin replied, "less than half a
league."

"Good. Lead the way." Kolby guided his horse up

alongside Bradach. "Despite your efforts, Highlander, it looks as though we'll find a village after all."

"My lord," Bradach protested, but Kolby cuffed him on the shoulder and ordered Durin to his best speed.

Hand on his sword, Kolby rode his stallion through the village. The miserable cluster of buildings was barely worthy of the name. What protection it might offer was moot. The state of the walls and roofs would have to be investigated to discover what shelter it might provide.

The "village" consisted of the remains of four huts, two on either side of a lane that led up a gentle slope to a somewhat larger building that had probably served as a mead hall. Motioning his men on toward it, Kolby rode his horse up to one of the huts. He discovered that its low roof was fallen in. Gray flecks of whitewash remained here and there in the wattle, but it too was fast weathering away. All the huts were the same, he guessed. Weeds overgrew the lane. The remains of cart sheds, kennels, and pens among them suggested what the buildings had originally been used for.

In front of the mead hall, his men were already dismounting. Soon several torches were blazing. Kolby noted with satisfaction that his Northlanders disappeared in different directions without command. They would scout the surrounding area and establish guard posts.

They were good men. He had trained them well. He swung down from the stallion at the cart tail in time to help Raven stand on solid ground. Her face in the torchlight looked drained of color. He was sorry that he had pushed her so hard, but to spend the night in the open would have been asking for another raid. Here at least they could have some protection for their backs.

"Just a few more minutes," he said, trying to encourage the exhausted woman. "Your guards are searching the mead hall. When they tell us it's safe, I can carry her inside and let her rest in peace for the night."

"I thank you." Raven looked up into his face. The leaping torchlight cast shadows into her eyes and cheeks. "What can I do to help?"

"Select a place for your lady mother."

Raven strode up the broad steps to the door of the mead hall, only to turn away with a moan of disappointment. The reason for the abandonment of the village became clear. The inside of the large building had been gutted by fire. Only the four walls and the door hanging askew by a single leather hinge remained.

"A place to stable our horses," Kolby said, coming up behind her. "Nothing more." He ran his hand over the door and the leather strap. "This can be easily repaired so that it shuts. Our mounts will be protected from the outlaws."

Sudden exhaustion made Raven reel where she stood. Her shifting vision took in the ominous shadows that hovered over them. Trees took on frightful shapes. They were bent and grotesque; their limbs looked like clawing hands. She could easily imagine the outlaws lurking behind them ready to attack.

Even as she shivered, she felt Kolby's arm slip around her waist. "Steady, my lady."

She nodded. "You're right. I must be strong."

"Let's find shelter for you and your lady mother." He was surprisingly gentle, not like a barbarian at all. Bearing a torch in one hand and keeping his arm around her, he guided her across the street to one of the smaller buildings.

She should have pulled away from him and walked alone. That she allowed him to touch her was a sin in light of her vows. It might be regarded as a sign of weakness that she could ill-afford. He might think she would fall in easily with his plans—whatever those might be.

Yet his arm was so welcome. Warm feelings all unbidden welled up inside her. Before she had entered the cloister, she had loved her father's touch. She, her mother, and her sister had always been affectionate. Now she had been so many years without it that this warrior's gentle assumption of some of her burden left her weak and shaky.

Enough, she told herself. She straightened a little awkwardly and pulled away from him.

He let her go without comment and gave the door a hard push with his hand. It creaked inward, its bottom dragging across a wooden floor. Kolby thrust the torch ahead of him and stepped into the house. "Someone of importance lived here," he said. "The room is large. Planks cover the floor."

Raven followed him into the room, and was also surprised by its size. First, she looked up. "The thatch still keeps out the sky," she announced hopefully.

Kolby walked to the door in the opposite wall. He opened it and swept the torch around. "It has a second chamber," he announced. "And by the look of it a room or maybe two beyond that."

He stood back to allow Raven to enter. The chamber was obviously for sleeping, for it had an elevated wooden platform at one side. On it was the frame of a bed, covered with dust. The remains of a canopy hung in shreds from the posts.

She moved toward it as if mesmerized. A flash. A trick of the shadows. Almost too swift to register on the mind's eyes, she imagined she saw a man and his wife sleeping in that bed—a golden warrior wrapped in his wife's long black hair. They were nude, his hard, sun-browned body contrasting with her soft pale skin.

She blinked. The bed was again a dusty frame, the shreds of its canopy stirred by the heat of Kolby's torch.

"The master's bed," Kolby said. His voice was so near, so soft that Raven felt its timbre all along her nerves. She clenched her hands against the sensations it evoked.

"Aye," she murmured, tapping down her absurd fantasies.

He mounted the platform by its three broad steps. "It still has the bed slats. We can make a mattress of brush, and your mother can rest here." He glanced upward. "Unfortunately the thatch hasn't survived in here. She'd have to sleep in the open air."

"I think her own pallet beside the fire pit in the first chamber will suit her well. If you bring in the brush from the cart, it will be enough," Raven said. He had been generous to help her find a place. She would be generous not to send his men out in the middle of the night to cut brush.

"As you will, my lady." Together they left the house.

"Durin!" he shouted.

"Aye, sir." The warrior with the battle-axe materialized out of the darkness.

"We'll put the women in this house with the luggage. All of it," he said significantly. "We'll take the hut across the street. Horses and ox in the mead hall. Post guards to patrol. Relief every four hours."

"Right you are." Durin loped away to carry out Kolby's orders.

Raven waited until Kolby turned back to her. "Where is the stream?" she asked.

He pointed back in the direction they had come. Then he cleared his throat. "My lady, I know you and your mother are holy women, dedicated to the gods, but I don't think it would be wise for you to go to the

stream for your ablutions. We're surrounded by outlaws, and . . ." He paused, as if trying to decide
whether to say more. She could see his face darken in
the ruddy light of torches. Was he blushing? "My
warriors are men, and you are a woman."

Raven laughed. She couldn't help a small spurt of
pleasure at the thought that she had troubled him. "I
have told you that I'm quite mature. I shouldn't think
I'd be a temptation to them."

"Any female would, lady," he replied coarsely,
"regardless of her age."

"Oh." The words stung her pride. *But I don't interest
you*, she thought. *Not one iota.* She knew a moment of
madness wherein she was tempted to pull the wimple
from her head and shake out her hair. She wondered
what he would do. Would he recognize her?

She clasped her hands tightly together. "I wasn't
going to bathe at the stream." *Curb your own imagina-
tion, sir.* "Among our luggage are several large basins.
I thought I might carry water in it, to bathe my
mother's wounds and to wash the worst of the dirt
from my own hands and face."

His face cleared instantly. The ruddy color faded
away. "Good."

He cupped his chin with his hand and rubbed his
index finger over his upper lip. "You must keep close,
my lady. You'll probably never see the outlaws until
they attack. Bradach will be taking us to the Sign of
the Boar in the early morning. I'll leave Durin here to
guard you. He's the strongest and bravest of men. You
can trust him to do what he thinks is best. Your hut
will be the building we'll fall back to in case of attack.
For that reason we'll put all our luggage with yours.
While we're gone, do nothing to reveal yourself. If
you must go outside, use your robe and cowl to cover
yourself completely."

"I will," she promised, determined to keep her word.

Much later, Raven knelt beside Melanthe's pallet. It had been laid a safe distance from the fire pit where the Northlander called Aren had built a small fire. On a clean cloth at her mother's side, Raven had laid out the herbs, spoons, pestle and mortar, and mixing bowls. Other utensils—two more cauldrons, a basin, and a water pail—were set handily between her and the fire pit. The rest of their luggage had been piled in the corner. A cauldron of water bubbled amid the glowing coals.

Raven knelt beside her mother. Tenderly she brushed her hand over the knot on Melanthe's forehead. She breathed a soft prayer to the Great Mother Goddess who had turned the outlaw's blade to the flat before he could strike.

Melanthe's skin was hot to the touch. Raven breathed a second prayer before she bent to loosen the bandages.

A shadow fell across her. She did not need to look up to know that Kolby had entered. His leather garments creaked as he hunkered down beside her. "Any change?"

Raven pushed aside the torn robe and tunic. She unbound the dressing and tossed the moss into the fire. It had served its purpose well, for the bleeding had stopped. The wound was frightening to behold. It was a deep gash between three and four inches long, surrounded by bruised and torn flesh. One glance told her the situation was very grave. Still she tried to be optimistic. "She's breathing easier. There are no red streaks radiating from the wound."

Kolby held the torch closer. "I have seen much worse from which men recovered."

Raven nodded, at the same time thinking that his

words offered no real consolation. A young, powerful man was quite a different person from an older woman who was receiving only the crudest of medical care. Her lips moving in silent prayers, Raven bathed the wound and placed fresh dressings on it.

Wind blew crisply through the room. It fluttered the torch. "Do you wish me to close the shutters?"

Raven sighed. Ordinarily she would have been chilled, but not tonight. The unusual heat of the day had combined with her own emotional state and unaccustomed exertion. She couldn't remember when she had been so hot. She wanted the shutters open, so she could enjoy the coolness. More, she wanted to remove the robe and cowl because they had begun to oppress her.

Yet she did not dare. "Yes. Thank you."

He closed the window and bolted it before bidding her good night. At the door he paused. "Rest well, my lady. My men and I will guard you. If you need anything, you have only to call out."

Kolby stepped into the brisk night air.

Memory niggled at the back of his mind. The sight of Raven's face in firelight had raised another image. He knew he had seen her face before, reddened by firelight, exalted with inner fire.

But where?

He stood in the middle of the street, staring at the door he had just closed. A raucous cry reached his ears. From the inky trees came the flap of powerful wings. Kolby lifted his arm. Midnight Wind flew directly to him. His wings stirred the air as he hovered in flight, then dropped down, his talons closing over the leather wrist guard.

Kolby stroked the silky feathers. "Tell me the secret, and I'll believe you really are one of Odin's messengers." His words were soft, for the bird's ears only. "Tell me the secret that I cannot recall. Who is she? Where did she come from?"

Feeling as if she carried the weight of the world on her shoulders, Raven bent to check on her mother once more. Melanthe slept quietly, her breathing regular and slow. Raven adjusted a blanket over her shoulder and left her for the night.

Then, covering her hands with her gloves, she hoisted the cauldron of hot water out of the fire pit. Staggering slightly with her load, she carried it into the second room. The thatch might be gone, but unless thieves or Northlanders came, it would be private.

She closed the connecting door. Hood, cowl, and wimple came off in one sharp movement. The night air, so refreshing she could drink it, touched her heated face. It blew against the dampened tendrils on her cheeks and forehead. Off came her robe, to lie in a pool around her feet. She stretched her arms toward the midnight sky, then stooped and lifted her tunic. It followed the rest of her garments, and she sighed with relief.

For one long glorious minute, she stood there, letting the breeze revive and invigorate her. Only the brooch that she had taken on the night before the Nameless Day remained on her body. It lay between her breasts, held there by a gold chain. She put her hands to her neck and lifted her heavy hair. Eyes closed, she waited for her burdens to lift as well.

She didn't rouse until she felt the gentle teasing of material against her calves. She looked down. Dark stains covered her green garments. Melanthe's blood. There would be no rest for her this night.

Stooping, she unlaced her boots and stepped out of them. After stripping off the rest of her clothes, she went to the basin and poured water over the top of her head. It sluiced down her naked body. She had always loved a bath. Tonight her pleasure was almost pagan. She didn't mind that she was chilled and her teeth were chattering. It was a blessed relief from the heat.

When she was finished, she wrung as much water as she could out of her hair and slipped into her second tunic. Leaving the rest of her clothing behind, she returned to the main room. There she spread her own pallet beside her mother's. Sitting cross-legged on it, she began to brush her hair dry with long smooth strokes.

Tomorrow she would think about how to get the sacred shawl back. It couldn't have disappeared forever. She wanted to cry at the thought of the gold and silver objects that adorned it. Surely the Great Mother Goddess would not allow them to be cut from it and melted down as part of a heathen outlaw's booty. When she returned to the Cloister of the Grove, she would appeal to the thanes of Ross. They would place their finest warriors at her disposal. The shawl must come back into Melanthe's possession for the good of all Scotland.

At last, exhausted, Raven lay down and pulled the blankets up. She would not think about the Northlander. He would be in her life for just a moment. A matter of days. A couple of chance encounters. No more.

She would return to her sequestered life of peace and serenity.

She closed her eyes, only to see the golden warrior. She went to sleep, only to dream of him.

Raven opened her eyes and gazed around her. Sunlight dappled her face and brightened the room. For a moment she was disoriented. Then she remembered. She was in an abandoned village in the badlands south of Loch Ness with a Northlander named Kolby of Apelstadt.

She glanced up. The thatch that had appeared so thick the night before was actually thin in places. The sun felt wonderful, but she dared not lie there and enjoy it.

Aching in every bone, she pushed herself up and knelt beside her mother. "Melanthe," she whispered. "Are you awake?"

Her mother didn't answer.

Raven shook her gently, but Melanthe didn't respond. Raven examined her mother's head wound in the bright light of day. It was violently discolored, but the swelling might have abated just a bit. Still Raven worried. She had heard of people receiving blows to the head that caused them to go into deep sleeps from which they never awakened. Their limbs drew up, their spines curved until their bodies curled into tight balls. They slowly wasted away.

Throwing off such terrible thoughts, she rose and put on her robe, shuddering at the rusty stains that were fearfully evident in the sunlight. She didn't pull the wimple or cowl over her head. Instead she crossed the room and opened the shutters to stand for a moment in the sunlight.

When the voices of the Northlanders carried to her, she hastily stepped back into the room and reluctantly covered her head. Returning to the pallet, she laid out herbs from which to prepare Melanthe's medicine. Only a small amount of water remained in the cauldron, but she set it in the heart of the fire pit where the coals still burned.

Then she unfastened Melanthe's bandage.

With a sinking heart she observed the tiny red lines radiating from the gash. They were a sure sign that inflammation was spreading through her mother's body. Conscious that there was so little she could do, she crushed and mixed the last of the Northlander's herbs and prepared a poultice with a few drops of hot water. She smeared this mixture on the wound and covered it with a clean cloth.

Leaving Melanthe unmoving, Raven carried the cauldron to the door. On its threshold she stopped, spellbound.

Wearing only leather trousers and knee-high boots, Kolby strode out of the forest into the street. Freshly shaved and bathed, he looked rested and vibrant. His wet hair was brushed back from his face in deep waves.

A leather pack, a full-sleeved linen shirt, and a leather vest were slung over one broad shoulder. Over the other hung his sword strap. In the morning sunlight, his chest was finely dusted with golden-brown hair that swirled down his abdomen over his firm stomach to narrow hips encased in tight trousers.

Caught unawares, her mind open and unprotected by the cloister rituals, Raven felt heat curl in her belly. Her heart stepped up its rhythm. She was suddenly aware of the weight of Kolby's brooch hanging between her breasts. It could not hang heavier if he had placed it there himself as a sign of his ownership.

He was perfectly formed, every line, every angle of his body a study of excellence. He reminded her of an exquisite piece of art, except he was flesh and blood, warm and moving. Her fingers flexed unconsciously, reaching for him. The contour of his male body drew her like a magnet. He was a barbarian who scoffed at the very idea of the Great Mother Goddess. At the very least she should pity him. At the very most she should despise him. But she didn't. She only wanted to touch him, to adore the perfection of his body.

And that was terribly wrong. One should adore only the goddess. He was just a man. Preyed on by conflicting emotions, she stepped back into the shadow of the doorway.

Kolby strode up the street and halted in front of a small fire his man had built. "Durin, why are you preparing a morning meal? We're to break our fast with Vaghn at the Sign of the Boar."

"Not me," the warrior snarled. He continued turning a chunk of bread on a stick above his tiny flame. "I've lived a long time because I don't trust guides like the one we've got and I don't fight on an empty stomach."

"You think we're going into a fight?"

Durin raised one shaggy eyebrow. "You don't trust that guide any more than I do. And you don't trust the outlaws. Otherwise why all the guards?" He lifted his bread and blew on an edge that had blackened. "Me, I'm getting ready. I want to live a little longer."

Raven stepped out of the house. She had set her cowl in place and now she walked with a sedate gait toward the fire. "Good morrow, sirs."

Kolby looked up. "Good morrow, lady. I trust you slept well."

"Aye," she replied. "To my surprise, I did."

The golden warrior strode toward her and for the first time she did not try to hide her face beneath the cowl. To what purpose? He had seen her already and she found she couldn't take her eyes off him. She wondered what he looked like without his clothes. Although she had never confessed her licentious thoughts to anyone, she had wondered that ever since she'd seen him on Nameless Eve.

"We shall leave soon," Kolby told her. "Do whatever you have to do outside in the next few minutes. After we're gone, return to your hut and bar the door. I'll post your cloister guards at opposite ends of the street. Don't come out again until we come back."

He set his pack down and shrugged the sword

strap from his shoulder. Acting as unconcerned as if she were one of his men, he pulled his tunic over his head and down over his muscled torso. He strapped on his wrist guards and donned his vest.

The thought flickered through Raven's mind that he reminded her of her father. Pryse mac Russ had exuded just such an aura of male arrogance and power. Even the leather clothing worn by the Northlander resembled her father's garb. Excitement surrounded him, communicated itself to her, made her breath catch in her throat. He was as wild and untamed as the beasts whose skins he wore.

Lifting his arms, Kolby shoved his hands through his hair, finger-combing the long strands. They flowed through his fingers like fine, golden floss. Raven's own fingers itched to follow his.

His sweet smile transformed his face. "How's your mother this morning?"

The question forced Raven back to an unpleasant reality. Her excitement vanished. She threw a glance at the door and the dim room beyond where Melanthe lay. "No better, and the inflammation is spreading. I hope you can finish your business here shortly, so we can be on our way to the cloister."

"As quickly as I can, I assure you," he replied. "Shall I ask the outlaws if they have any medicines they can spare or trade?"

Raven wrinkled her nose. "I wish we had more medicine, but I doubt that anything they have would be trustworthy."

"As you will, my lady." He nodded shortly before turning away.

He would be gone soon. She would be alone with her gravely ill mother and the three cloister guards who prided themselves on their stoicism. The forest was very close and dense. She took a step toward Kolby. Unable to stop herself, she held out her hand. "How long will you be gone?"

He looked around, his eyes drawn to the pale fingers with their short-trimmed nails. Instantly she doubled her fist and thrust it into the sleeve of her other arm.

He moved closer to her. She tried to hide her face, but he tipped her chin up. His gaze locked with hers. "Perhaps only a few hours. Perhaps all day. Perhaps longer. The man we will meet seldom receives visitors from the other side of the border. He will take advantage of our company. We will hunt, feast, and play games. I will take great care to lose several times, so that he will parley with me in a good mood. Will you miss me?"

How dare he insult her with such a provocative question! She snapped her head aside. "I merely asked for information," she replied coldly. "I will spend the day caring for my mother and praying for her safety and for all in your company."

He gave a short bark of laughter. "Don't bother to pray for mine. My sword is my safety."

"If you prefer to think—"

The hoarse cawing of a bird overhead drew their attention upward. Kolby looked up to see Midnight Wind circling high above them.

He scooped up his sword belt and buckled it around his lean middle. "Riders," he said succinctly. "Coming fast."

"How do you know?" Raven asked.

He pointed upward. "The raven told me. Return to your house. Close the door and bar it."

She resented the way he ordered her around. Scotland was her country, not his, even though this area was without law. Whoever approached would have more in common with her than with him. She held her ground.

He wheeled away and ran toward the mead hall. "Riders!"

Durin kicked dust over his fire. Along with the

other Northlanders, he hurried to don mail and helmet and take up a defensive position. The tension in the air was almost palpable. Travelers were always wary of visitors.

"Bradach, what say you?" Kolby shouted to the Highlander.

The man emerged from the mead hall where he had bedded down with the horses. His eyes were bleary and he looked confused.

Kolby shook him hard. "What say you? Friend or foe?"

The Scot listened to the fast approaching hoof-beats. He looked apologetic. "The chance that these newcomers are our foe is greater than their being our friend."

Kolby pushed him away in disgust.

"Ready, men." He looked back to find Raven still standing in the middle of the street. "Damn you! Take cover, my lady." He raced toward her.

"You have no right to order me about," she objected. "These are my people. The chances are good that they will respect holy women."

Kolby looked like a man who'd been driven too far. He caught her arm in a punishing grip and dragged her back to the hut. "Most likely they care nothing for anything except looting. They will kill us if they can. What they will do to you and your lady mother before they kill you does not bear thinking about."

Raven's cowl slipped off her head and left her face exposed. She must have revealed the fear his words instilled in her.

His grip softened. His eyes gleamed as his gaze fastened on her face with renewed interest. "My lady, you say you are a matron, but believe me, you are wondrous fair."

She hadn't been paid a compliment in years. She had almost forgotten what it was to be admired by a man. It shook her, clove her tongue to the roof of her mouth. She felt the heat of his big hand through the cloth of her robe. His eyes had turned from hard to soft, as warm as polished amber. Pleasure glided through her body as he shifted his grasp to take her hand. She knew he meant the gesture as comfort, but for her it was more. While he thought her a pitiful object to be protected, he stirred her womanly instincts.

Heat rose in her cheeks. He mustn't see her blush. She inclined her head. Her gaze dropped to his hand. It was scarred and callused, yet it was holding her so gently. As easily as it could wield a sword or dagger, now it consoled. It took life; it promised life. These were contradictions that made up Kolby the Northlander.

Young Aren galloped down the street. "Kolby! Kolby! Riders coming! Fast!"

Raven withdrew her hands from Kolby's clasp and stepped back.

The young scout swung off the horse in front of his leader.

"How many, lad?" Kolby asked.

"About twenty."

"Four to one," Raven gasped.

"We have fought greater odds and won," Kolby assured her.

"Aye," the others gathered around them agreed.

"What did they look like?"

"Bright," the lad answered. "Banners of all colors are flying. The leader is an older man. He wears shiny black trousers. They are puffy and bagged out, cross-gartered from below his knees to his boots. His banner is vermillion, the same color as his shirt."

" 'Tis Vaghn," Bradach called. At the Highlander's words, the others stepped back to allow him to approach Kolby.

"You can't be sure." The warrior eyed Bradach steadily. "What else, Aren?"

"These people are riding scrawny horses like the outlaws who attacked the priestesses. They could be part of the same band."

"Nay, 'tis Vaghn," Bradach insisted. "The outlaws who attacked the women weren't wearing colorful clothing like Vaghn's outlaws. They didn't fly bright-colored banners."

"A man can change his clothes," Durin pointed out sourly.

Kolby nodded in agreement. He pressed forward, intimidating the smaller Scotsman. "Why would he come here?"

Bradach retreated, putting up a hand to turn the Northlander's wrath away. "He wants to p-protect his forest," he stammered. "He wants to find out who is moving about in his territory." He managed an apologetic smile. "This village is an advantage. Really. Just as I told you. It's your camp. You can . . . er . . ."

"Set an ambush!" Kolby thundered. "We are honorable warriors. We don't fight that way."

"I never meant—"

"If there's going to be a fight, let me take my mother and leave," Raven said.

"Nay!" Kolby swung around, his brows drawn together in an angry scowl. "You'll be safer here than out in the forest somewhere."

"That's what you claimed when you led us across the border into this forsaken land."

The other men looked at her as if she had lost her mind. She realized she was arguing with the man whom they all obeyed without question. His hand was clenched around the hilt of his sword.

"If the outlaws have found us in this village, lady, they would certainly have seen us if we camped in the open on the other side of the loch."

"But—"

"That's my last word!" he shouted. "Go inside that

building and stay there. Don't disobey my orders again."

She gasped. But she had no choice. She could hear the horses drawing nearer. Her own escape was cut off. She turned on her heel and strode into the dark interior.

"And keep that cowl and robe on!" was his parting shot.

She slammed the door shut.

Chapter 5

Raven lowered the oaken bar across the door. Swinging around, she leaned against it, her heart pounding. Outlaws were approaching. Perhaps they were some of the same ones who had attacked her and her mother. The thought that the black-hearted, sacrilegious thief who had ruthlessly stabbed the Ancient One might actually ride into this village and be welcomed by Kolby and his men infuriated her.

Bradach had insisted that they were the men Kolby was supposed to meet at the Sign of the Boar, but he hadn't actually seen them. Raven had come to agree with Kolby. The guide was untrustworthy. For all any of them knew, he might be in league with the outlaws.

She had never felt so helpless or so trapped. She hurried across the room and sank to her knees beside her mother. Tears started in her eyes as she saw the faint flush of fever on Melanthe's white cheek. She lifted her wrist. Her pulsebeat was fast and irregular.

They were many leagues away from the cloister, from warmth, from comfort, from help. Friends there awaited their return and news from the shrine. They awaited the goods Raven and Melanthe were bringing them.

How distressed the priestesses would be if they knew their high priestess and their Ancient One were locked in a ruined house in an abandoned village. If these fast-approaching horsemen attacked and killed them all, the women of the cloister would never know what became of them. Neither would Pryse and Gwynneth, her father and sister.

Outside, Kolby shouted more orders. The sound of running footsteps reached Raven as the Vikings hid among the trees and rocks to disguise their strength in preparation for any eventuality. She pulled the covers up to her mother's chin and rose. She must be prepared also. Better to violate her cloister vows than allow her mother to be raped and murdered. She would be her own champion, and in case of an attack, would defend her mother and herself for as long as she could.

She had only her knife and her blowpipe, useless against violent men armed with swords and bows and arrows. If the outlaws came through the door, they would hack her to pieces before her drugs could take effect. Her only chance was to aid Kolby and his defenders by shooting from the window.

She arranged the darts on the floor beside the window and cracked the shutters the width of the pipe. As she leaned the weapon at the ready, she smiled at herself. Perhaps she was more like Gwynneth than she knew. How quickly she was abandoning peaceful philosophies for the militant ones of a warrior!

The luggage! Both hers and the Northlanders'. She stared at Kolby's brown leather packs. They did not contain clothing. He had gotten fresh garments this morning from another place. She strode over to the bags and opened the first one.

Of course, gold and silver. It was not very heavy. A small amount. A bribe? A reward? She felt a little safer, but only a little. If thieves were riding to attack

them, Kolby would defend the treasure with his life.
Since she and her mother shared the room with such
treasure, perhaps they would be saved incidentally.

For double assurance, she would hide it. If they
were overrun, she might bargain information for
freedom. She began to kick at the edges of the floor
planks. Moving slowly across the floor, she finally
found what she sought. A loose plank yielded to her
boot toes and to her straining fingers. At last she
pried it up and stuffed the treasure bags beneath it.
Then she stamped the board back into place and
scuffed dust and dried thatch across it.

From her luggage, she produced a dirk. She
pressed her other hand against her tunic and felt the
bulge of its mate. The larger one she belted around
her waist. If the Great Mother Goddess allowed her to
fight, she would use the larger dirk against her
enemies. The smaller one, she would save to dispatch
her mother and spare her the pain and indignity of
rape.

She bent and pressed a kiss on her mother's
forehead before slipping to the window and fitting
the blowpipe into the crack.

The street outside was empty. The Northlanders as
well as her guards had all disappeared from view.
The horses' hooves were very near now, moving
slowly.

Then the golden warrior stepped into her line of
vision.

In the gleaming morning light, he was as beautiful
as one of his own warrior gods. His helmet gleamed.
His long hair lay on his massive shoulders. One hand
clasped the hilt of his sword. In the other he carried
his mighty longbow.

She could not keep silent. Opening the window
wider, she called, "May the Great Mother Goddess
protect you, Kolby of Apelstadt."

He looked in her direction. "If you want to call on the gods, Odin and Thor the Thunderer would be better choices, my lady. With a bit of Loki's craft thrown in."

She waved her arm. "Odin and Thor and Loki."

"May your Great Mother Goddess protect you," he replied. "Now close the shutter and bolt it tight."

Raven pulled the shutter almost closed. She slipped a dart into the blowpipe and fitted the slender rod into the opening. No one would notice it. Only an inch or two protruded.

Kolby began to walk down the street. Durin and Aren fell into step behind him. Raven could not help herself. Like a magnet, she edged sideways, keeping him always in view.

The visitors, some twenty strong, halted their horses at one end of the street. As Aren had reported, they were a colorful lot. Their bright shirts, trousers, caps, and cloaks looked to have been gathered from the booty of many thieving raids. Saddle blankets, woven in a variety of brilliant hues, covered their horses' rumps.

Raven scanned their faces. Her spirits lifted a bit when she recognized none of them. These were a different band of thieves from the ones who had attacked her. Her second observation was that Vaghn and his men had fallen upon hard times. Or more likely, there had never been good times. Thievery must be a very chancy business.

Closer inspection revealed the true state of the motley dress. The materials were faded and soiled, their edges tattered. Obviously no care was taken to dress them all in one color to give a uniform appearance. They looked like what they were, a ragged band of outlaws. Even their mounts looked scrawny and underfed in comparison to the sleek, powerful Northland horses.

The leader raised his hand and the whole group moved toward the Vikings. Raven noticed with some contempt that Bradach, the Highlander guide, took great care to stand directly behind Durin. The big Viking caressed his battle-axe as if his fingers itched to pull it from his belt.

The horses' bridles clinked, the saddle leather creaked, the hooves kicked up little puffs of dust from the street. Then Raven started in surprise. A few women, weapons strapped about their waists, spears in their hands, rode among the men. Side by side in the same tattered garb, they could be distinguished only because they had no beards.

The leader was an older man, but his hair was jet-black, his brow encircled by a tooled leather headband. His shirt was yellow, dyed with precious saffron that had no doubt been stolen from some eastern trader. His trousers were black. As if flaunting the civilized world, he wore a huge gold torque around his neck and a gold earring in his ear. For him at least thievery had paid well.

His sleeveless vest was embroidered in green, blue, vermillion, and black floss. Like all Highlanders, he wore a sword and dirk.

Bradach inched forward and whispered at Kolby's back. "It's Vaghn."

At that minute the outlaw spoke. "You're trespassing, stranger!"

Kolby took a step in front of his cohort. "This village was abandoned."

"It belongs to me." The outlaw grinned slyly. "I was planning to rebuild the mead hall next spring."

"You can start tonight if you like," Kolby countered. "We stabled our horses in it."

The man threw back his head and laughed. The rich sound echoed off the mead hall's doors. "It belongs to me. But I'm reasonable. I provide anything for a price. To stable your horses, one silver piece per horse. A gold piece for each of you. Two for you, big man."

Bradach stepped out from behind Durin and shuffled down the street. "Good morrow, Vaghn."

"That's Lord Vaghn to you, Bradach, you idiot. What'd you bring 'em here for?" He scowled darkly at the guide.

Bradach fell back a step. "I—I—"

Kolby brushed the guide aside. "You know why I've come. Give me the information I seek and we'll leave."

Vaghn ran his eyes over Kolby's muscular body, as if he was calculating his strength. His eyes narrowed as he ended by staring into Kolby's eyes, as if he judged the power of the Viking's will.

At last he laughed a little uneasily and dismounted from his horse, then handed the reins to a servant. "Your Viking is a brave warrior, Bradach. He'd have to be to set up camp on this side of the border."

"Aye, he is that." Bradach edged back in between the two men. "He doesn't trust me," he muttered. "Nor you."

"He has the right of that. There's none of us can be trusted. We'll steal the horses from under the saddles." He laughed again.

Bradach joined him, but with much less humor. "He's promised me money. He has brought gold for you."

Vaghn nodded, his eyes glowing with interest. "I'll take it. It makes being an outcast bearable." He touched the heavy gold torque. "Good things sometimes fall into our hands. Honest men on the other side don't get such things." He brushed past Bradach and came to stand in front of Kolby. He slapped his own chest. "In the badlands I am the king."

Kolby said nothing. His cold stare went past the strange-looking figure to the guide. "Bradach. Introduce me to your friend."

The Highlander hurried forward. "Lord Vaghn, I have brought Lord Kolby of Apelstadt in the far Northland."

"Ah. At last." The outlaw king grinned. "You are a brave man to have crossed the haunted loch."

"A wary one," Kolby replied. "We circled around it."

Vaghn frowned as though the answer was not quite to his liking. Then Kolby saw respect in the depth of his obsidian eyes. The outlaw leaned forward so the others could not hear. "You have the gold we agreed upon?"

Kolby nodded. "In my saddle packs. Two pounds."

"Ah, good." His black eyes scanned the street, looking for a trap. "Only two men with you?"

"You can count them," Kolby said.

"But you have more." Vaghn made the statement as fact.

"As do you." Kolby came abreast of the man. Shoulder to shoulder they stood, a contrast of light and dark.

Vaghn raised his eyebrows. Appearing casual, he strolled up the street toward the mead hall. Raven drew back as he stopped in front of the window where she watched. He put his hand on their cart standing to one side. His black eyes scanned the house. They narrowed. She was sure they had found the blowpipe between the shutters. She dared not move. He might guess a weapon was being aimed at him, but he could not be sure. Or if he did, it might make him cautious.

The outlaw king patted the battered cart. To Kolby he said, "I did not expect you to travel by oxcart."

Kolby glanced quickly at Bradach. The man dropped his eyes. The Northlander shrugged. "It's slow but sure."

"More like something a woman would require." Vaghn moved around the cart, as if he were studying it. His hand trailed along the railing. He stooped to look beneath it. When he saw where the axle had been repaired, he nodded. "Something such as two priestesses would require."

Kolby tensed, his bow at the ready.

Vaghn leaned back and crossed his arms. "Priestesses of the Cloister of the Grove."

Raven bit her lip. Bradach must have slipped out in the night and told this outlaw everything. He was no better than an outlaw himself.

Kolby must have concluded the same thing, for he threw Bradach a look that promised retribution.

Bradach hurried to his side. "Lord Kolby, I know what you're thinking and I swear—"

Kolby's fist shot out and connected with Bradach's chin. The guide catapulted backward and slammed down hard. The dust rose around him. "Swear nothing, Scot. Your damned tongue will rot out at the root with so much lying."

Bradach had sense enough to stay down, Raven noted. Distracted by the scuffle, she realized too late that she could no longer see Vaghn. Before she could pull the blowpipe back, the outlaw's hand shot up and grasped the end of it. Before she could draw in the breath to use it, he had wrenched it from her grasp and tossed it into the street. With a cry of triumph, he jerked the shutters back.

On a craggy rock above the village, the thieves who had botched the robbery of the cloister priestesses watched the scuffle. In particular Donnal, their leader, stared hard, his eyes straining to count the numbers of Northlanders and outlaws in Vaghn's band. When he saw them all enter the mead hall, he motioned to his henchman Magdu.

"Now's the time. Get your stupid self and that band of idiots you ride with down there and finish the job."

"In broad daylight?" the thief whined.

"You attacked the cloister priestesses in broad daylight."

"Aye, but we could run in any direction if they fought back too hard. It'd be a man's life if one of 'em was to see us and trap us inside one of them huts. Brained like a sheep we'd be as we tried to run out through the door. The Northlanders are too handy with battle-axes."

His leader shook his head in contempt. "We'll set up a distraction if we need one. If someone comes out of the mead hall, we'll raise a cry that's bound to bring them all into the forest. You can escape when they go running."

Magdu considered. They had been interrupted yesterday. A few minutes more and the whole party would have been dead or gone and the rest of the rich pickings could have been carted off. He hated to leave a job unfinished.

"A distraction, you say."

"Aye."

Magdu shrugged. Motioning to two of his men, he threw a leg over his horse's back and led the way down the narrow trail.

By the light of day, the cause of the mead hall's destruction was clearly revealed. It had met the fate that came sooner or later to most of the halls where men met to boast of their deeds, tell stories of their heroes, and drink the fermented honey that loosened their tongues. When sparks from the fire pit rose along with the smoke, sometimes they ignited the thatch. Flames roared toward the sky and turned the roof into a raging inferno, but left the carved walls almost intact.

The outlaws arranged themselves around the interior of those walls. Vaghn lounged on the platform that had once been the dais where the chieftain had sat above his men to dispense justice.

Raven stood before him, her cowl pulled low over her face, her hands tucked into the sleeves of her robe. Too late! Too, too late! She had violated the rules of sequestration, and now she was paying the price. Vaghn had seen her face, and now he wanted her. She shuddered to think of the horrible injustice about to be done here.

Kolby stood behind her. His four Northlanders and the two cloister guards flanked him. His fierce scowl should have quelled them all.

"What do you want for her?" The outlaw rubbed his earring between his thumb and index finger. His lecherous grin proclaimed why he asked the question.

Raven's belly clenched. Fear and anger warred within her. They were tamped down by the cold realization that the best she could do for her mother and for herself was hold her peace.

She had disobeyed Kolby. He had told her not to show herself in any way. He had brought gold to pay these outlaws. For what, she didn't know, but somehow she had become part of his problem. If she angered him again, he might very well leave her. Her fate was in his hands.

Humiliation burned in her. She was a high priestess of the Cloister of the Grove, one of the guardians of the Shrine of the Great Mother Goddess. Her mother was a Chosen One. Yet they were at the mercy of an unbeliever and an outlaw, items of barter between them.

Vaghn continued to smile, unimpressed. "If she's not for sale, then surely you'll barter for her."

Vaghn's band were all armed to the teeth. Although the women cast hostile looks at Raven, the men leered openly. Kolby's own men were tense, worried. Kolby hesitated. "I hadn't thought about an exchange. There's the old one to be considered. Were you wanting to trade them for the information you have for me?"

Vaghn's smile slipped. He sat up straighter. "Nay, I want the gold. I've already made plans for its use. But I want that woman too. And the old one if she doesn't die."

"Ah, but you don't have anything to trade for them," Kolby pointed out.

"Your lives," came the silky reply.

"Too rich a price if you should lose your own." Kolby's retort was filled with significance.

"You might lose yours too. What do you care? She's a priestess. You only chanced upon her a day ago."

"Bradach must have gotten no sleep at all last night, shuttling back and forth between our camp and yours," Kolby remarked to no one in particular.

While the guide cringed, Vaghn's fingers slid suggestively over his heavy gold torque. "I have other valuable possessions with which to barter. In fact, I have many commodities you might find interesting. Come. Let's look through them." He started to rise.

Kolby held up his hand. "Not so fast. First let's discuss the matter that brings me here. It is of more import than the women."

Vaghn laughed shortly. "We have so few women here beyond the loch that nothing else is of more import."

"Do you want her for yourself?" Kolby asked.

Vaghn glanced at a large-bosomed woman with a tangled mass of red hair. She wore a gold chain around her neck and several gold bracelets on her arms. The outlaw shook his head.

"Nay. I have my own. I want her for my men. I have to keep them satisfied else they'll desert me. A lord on the other side of the border can afford to lose a man occasionally. An outlaw in the badlands can't.

Presently my warriors have plenty of gold and silver, but only a few women. They want more."

Kolby looked squarely at Raven. While this exchange was going on, she had been peeping out from under the cowl. Their eyes met. Hastily she looked away.

Kolby shrugged. "What are you offering in exchange for her?"

A low gasp escaped Raven. She swayed where she stood. She had thought Kolby an honorable man.

Vaghn shrugged. "What do you wish?"

"The way to the sacred apple tree."

Raven whirled around to stare at him. What had the barbarian to do with the sacred apple tree? Why was he seeking it?

"You wish for the stars," Vaghn said, sneering.

"It is what I came for. Nothing else in this desolate place is of value to me." Kolby looked contemptuously at the ruined building open to the sky. It was a poor place even for an outlaw to hold court.

"It's true I could bring you a step closer to getting your wish."

Kolby's muscles tensed, though he maintained a stoic demeanor. Raven knew, as surely as the Northlander did, that someone like Vaghn would probably break his promise once he got what he wanted.

"The gold was to pay for that information," Kolby replied. "If you don't possess it, then we've nothing to talk about and I've wasted my trip."

Vaghn looked alarmed. If Kolby and his men chose to ride out of the badlands, they would take their gold and silver with them. The outlaws would lose many men attempting to stop them.

Raven clasped her hands together and prayed hard. With Melanthe so gravely wounded, they could not travel fast enough. Kolby would surely leave them. She wanted to throw herself at him and scream that he had betrayed them both. She had begged him not to take them into the badlands, but he had refused to listen.

"I'm curious, Vaghn," Kolby said suddenly. "Why barter for these women when you can abduct any you want? 'Tis customary to raid for them when they are in scarce supply."

" 'Tis customary on the other side, but not over here. It would incite the Highlanders. They might take a notion to invade us."

"Surely you're not afraid of a good fight," Kolby jeered.

"Nay, I'm not afraid." The outlaw looked truly insulted. "Just prudent. There are other outlaws in the badlands. They raid and rampage among themselves. We have to be constantly on the alert against them. There's one vicious bastard right now—" He shrugged. "I ask you, man to man, what sort of leader would I be if I started a fight with trained warriors from the other side when I had dogs nipping at my heels in my own backyard?"

"I see your point." Kolby allowed himself a small smile.

Vaghn jumped down from the dais and caught Raven's arm. She tried to pull away, but he held her easily. "Do you claim this woman?"

Kolby didn't hesitate. One long stride brought him to her. He grasped her other arm. "Aye."

The hard grip of both men lifted Raven up on her toes. Fear and anger spurted through her, but she was powerless. Like two bad children they were fighting over her as if she were a toy.

"As your woman?" Vaghn insisted, his black beard bristling.

"Aye."

His grip loosened. "Then you're going to have to show your mark of ownership."

Raven managed to pull herself from his grasp. How she wished she could pull herself away from Kolby too, but he held her tight. Vaghn's demand could mean several things, none of them pleasant for her.

"My word isn't enough?" Kolby demanded.

"Damona." Vaghn waved the red-haired woman forward. "Show your mark."

Glaring angrily, Damona pulled down the neck of her shirt. A V had been branded into the white skin of her shoulder. A reddened, puffy scar testified to how painful and deep the wound must have been.

Raven felt faint. Without a doubt her knees would have buckled and she would have collapsed if Kolby hadn't kept his grip on her arm.

"We sometimes brand our slaves," Kolby said. "Never our women."

"Then perhaps you'd care to authenticate your claim in a different way," Vaghn suggested. Again his voice turned silky. Raven hated him more by the minute. He was enjoying this game of cat and mouse that caused her such humiliation and kept Kolby from his quest. What purpose could he have for tormenting them?

Kolby looked bored. "And I suppose you also have laws that stipulate how this is to be done."

"Aye. That we do." Vaghn's teeth looked very white in his tangle of black beard. "There's a new Christian custom that makes sense to us outlaws. A man either mates with his new woman in the presence of those he trusts to give an honest report, or he gives us proof of the rupture of her maidenhead."

Anger, followed closely by humiliation, surged through Raven. To be treated as if she were a piece of property! Even Alba O'Illand, the brute who had driven her into the cloister, had never denied that she was a human being. Her hands beneath the sleeves of her robe balled into tight fists. She had learned more about the cruelty and callousness of men in the last two days than in the whole of her previous life.

She took a moment to wonder why the outlaw

demanded proof of her virginity. Highlanders never demanded it from the women they claimed.

"What if she has no maidenhead to rupture?" Kolby asked.

Breath hissed out from between Raven's lips. At that moment she swore that she would exact vengeance upon him for this scene. He had led her to it and now participated in it.

"'Twould serve you well to have a witness when you mate with her. If you can't prove that you mated with or deflowered her, my men and every other able-bodied man who happens upon you will be challenging you for her."

"This is all beside the point," Kolby protested angrily. "I don't have time to waste with this."

Vaghn smiled. "Then you don't have time to waste with her. Give her to me and then we'll get down to business."

Raven looked at the outlaws. They were a tough lot with cold, merciless eyes set in hard, battle-scarred faces. Their women had the same cold look stamped over weariness of spirit. They looked dead to emotion and feeling. Raven could only pity them their hard lives.

As if he read her thoughts, Vaghn directed his next statement to her. "My warriors are civilized in comparison to others who live here."

Kolby heaved a sigh, as if he were approaching a tedious task. "I will authenticate my claim."

"No!" Raven cried.

"Silence."

"You have no right."

Kolby caught her arm again and jerked her aside. He put his face close to hers in the shadow of the cowl. "Do you want me to trade for you? Fool. I'm trying to save all our lives." His long arm wrapped around her waist and clamped her to his side. He raised his head. "Henceforth, you and she and everyone else in this camp and under the sound of my voice will know that she belongs to Kolby of Apelstadt of Northland."

"No!" Raven struggled. "No!"

He stooped to wrap his other arm around the back of her knees. Even as she realized his purpose, it was too late. He had lifted her off the ground and slung her over his shoulder.

The outlaws cheered.

Raven clawed at Kolby's back. She couldn't believe this nightmare was happening. She had trusted him to obey the universal custom of friendship. He had promised to protect her, to see that she returned safely to the Cloister of the Grove. Earlier he had told her that he respected her position as high priestess. He knew she was celibate. Surely he was making this gesture to save her from the outlaws.

He swung around. Grinning, Durin jumped to open the mead hall door. Like hungry wolves the outlaws rose to follow them, their lips pulled back from their teeth in bestial grins.

Raven tossed her head. "You dare not!" she screamed at Vaghn, who followed hard on Kolby's heels. "You dare not! I am a sequestered Dryad. He will damn my soul to the Underworld for all eternity. And yours too." She pointed an accusing hand at Vaghn. "If I am dishonored, the land will be also. Because I am a keeper of the land, any harm done to me will bring pestilence and plague upon the land and its people. Upon you! Upon you all!"

For an instant the outlaws stared. Then they burst out laughing. "What do you think we care about the land, priestess?" Vaghn sneered. "The land doesn't care about us."

"Be quiet, woman!" Kolby slapped her bottom as he strode down the steps of the mead hall.

She tried again. "Vaghn!" she shouted. "You gave him the chance to barter. What about me?"

The outlaw stopped laughing. "Wait a minute."

Kolby halted at the door to the hut where he and his men had slept the previous night.

Raven tried to squirm off his shoulder, but he wouldn't let her go. She was forced to make her offer from the most undignified of positions. Still, Vaghn was listening. The rest of his outlaws trooped out through the mead hall door, determined not to miss any of the fun.

"I am the high priestess of the Cloister of the Grove," she began in what she hoped was a calm and authoritative voice. "You would do well not to offend the Great Mother Goddess. She will curse you and your land."

The men looked at one another and at Vaghn. They shook their heads. One red-bearded brute went so far as to give a short laugh.

Vaghn looked bored. "But my men aren't frightened of her curses, my lady. Ever since each of us crossed the haunted loch, we've lived under the curse of not one but all gods. The kelpie of the loch, the long-necked water horse called Each Uisge, keeps away all the other gods. They don't dare cross his path. So we play around in his shadow. We don't have names or clans. What more can we fear?"

Raven should have remembered with whom she was dealing. These people had no souls and no consciences. Her voice broke in her desperation when she said, "Then if you will guarantee my mother and me safe passage out of the badlands to the Cloister of the Grove, I shall give you treasures the like of which you have never seen."

There was a moment of silence while they calculated piles of gold and silver.

"She promises treasure, Vaghn," Damona offered timidly.

"Let me see the booty," the outlaw demanded.

How large the attack of the other outlaw band

loomed now. Their thievery would keep her from controlling her fate! To her chagrin she had to admit, "I have none with me."

Vaghn scowled. Snarling beneath their breaths, the outlaws pulled back.

"I have personal wealth," Raven rushed on to say. "Some of it is at the cloister, some in the king's village in Ailean. Gold and jewels I crafted and designed myself. No one in all the lands will have possessions as beautiful and rich as yours."

"The high king's seat at Ailean!" Vaghn hooted. "I'm sure Pryse mac Russ would welcome us with open arms. Just before he hanged us from the nearest tree, and good riddance. Your offer isn't enough to tempt us out of the safety of our kingdom, my lady."

"Please, my lord outlaw—"

"Enough," Kolby snarled. He gripped her so hard that his fingers were bruising her skin beneath her robes. With a booted foot he kicked open the door to the hut. "Durin, guard the door. I'll bring proof of her maidenhead when the deed is done."

She caught hold of the door frame and stopped him before he could enter. "I am the daughter of the Nameless Day!" she screamed. "The Goddess will curse you."

The grip on her thighs lessened. Kolby lowered her with such swiftness that she staggered. "You!" he exclaimed. "Now I know where I saw you." He pushed the cowl back. His rough fingers slid in between her chin and the linen wimple. With one tug he ripped it from her head. Her long black hair tumbled down her back.

" 'Tis you."

He had recognized her. He had seen her all but naked on the Nameless Eve. With a cry of horror, she bolted. Across the road she ran, pushing warriors and outlaws aside.

Inside the hut where her mother lay, she caught up

a thick stick from the pile beside the fire pit. When Kolby came through the door, she swung it at his face with all her might.

Kolby barely managed to throw up his arms in time to ward off the blow.

"You have betrayed me," she cried. "Me and my mother. You brought me here and now you'll destroy me." She swung at him again. The stick struck him on the shoulder. He caught it and wrenched it from her hand.

She drew the dirk from her belt and flung herself at him. Before he could catch her wrist, she had drawn a long red scratch down his forearm.

"Ow!"

The window was crowded with outlaw and warrior faces. At least six grinning men, among them Vaghn and Durin, watched with lascivious pleasure. The rest crowded in at the door. From their catcalls and malicious suggestions, Raven knew that not one single person cared about her.

"The woman disputes your claim," Vaghn called when he could control his laughter. "She obviously doesn't want your attentions, Northlander."

"She has no voice in the matter," Kolby growled. He leaped from side to side as Raven stabbed and slashed to drive him away. He feinted right, then dived in left under her guard.

One big arm encircled her, slamming her against his chest. One hand slid down her arm and captured her wrist before her dirk could do any more damage. Their bodies were plastered together from breast to thighs.

He stared into her eyes. Then his mouth swooped down to fasten on hers. The kiss was all about plunder, domination, punishment. She was stunned. For a heartbeat, her resistance collapsed. The kiss deepened. The barbarian unbeliever seemed to drink her soul.

Abruptly she came to life and kicked his shin. When he cried out in pain, she wrenched her wrist. His grip tightened.

His open mouth slid along the side of her cheek. His lips against her ear, he snarled softly, "If you wish to keep your maidenhead and your integrity, trust me."

"You mean that if I wish to allow you in my bed, rather than the outlaw, I had better trust you." She tried to kick him again, but his arm tightened around her waist, forcing the breath from her lungs. At the same time, he gave her wrist a powerful twist. Pain shot up her arm as her fingers opened and the dirk fell to the floor.

"You've lived behind that cloister wall too long," he muttered. "You lack good judgment. I doubt your intelligence."

She fought more fiercely, wiggling against him. But he was no longer aware of her pounding fists and flailing legs. She knew the minute he felt her woman's body. His manhood hardened against her belly. His chest heaved, crushing her breasts. Hardness against softness. His anger and frustration disappeared. Passion assumed command—elemental and instinctive.

Kolby sucked in air. He was lusting for her. She was the lady of winter. The mystery woman of the Nameless Eve. The celibate. Now he knew that beneath these robes—all this enveloping green material—was a young and tender body. Supple and graceful. He remembered how she had looked as she lifted the branch of silver, remembered how her breasts had pressed against the fabric of her pale green gown. Remembered—

Everyone around them seemed to melt away. Only Kolby and Raven existed.

Was he dreaming?

He had found the lady of winter. This priestess who had fought against him and fought with him. He could not believe he had found her. If he believed in fate, he would think they had been destined to meet again. Otherwise how could they have been brought together in such a fashion?

He spun away. The red-haired woman Damona stood in the doorway. He pointed to her. "Stay here with the lady's mother."

Damona looked to Vaghn for confirmation. The outlaw nodded.

"No," Raven gasped. "Melanthe needs care."

"I'll take care of her." Damona came hesitantly into the room. "I have some skill."

Raven hurried to her mother's side. Melanthe lay on the pallet, eyes closed. Her mouth continued to move from time to time, but she had not regained consciousness. Raven bit her lip. "She needs water or wine. Please tell me you'll make her drink some."

"I will," Damona promised. Then she bent closer to whisper to Raven. "Go with him. You don't have a choice. Either go with dignity or you will lose it."

"Come, my lady." Kolby took her arm and raised her to her feet. He read the fear in her eyes as he took her hand in his. "You must do as I say."

As he led her out, the ranks parted for them. Straight across the street, they walked. His men followed several paces behind them. As he led her across the threshold, Durin closed the door behind them.

Once inside, Kolby turned to look at her. Her face was flushed, her dark eyes wild. They roved the crude room's confines.

"You cannot escape, my lady," he said gently.

She raised her head. Her color was high in her pale cheeks. Her long black hair hung like a shiny dark curtain down her back to below her buttocks. Soon he would see beneath the robe she wore.

He wouldn't take her against her will. The rules of friendship required that he protect Brian mac Logan's sister-in-law, especially since he had vowed to do so. But at the same time he vowed to see the whole of her. She owed him that much for the trouble she had put him to.

"Come here."

She didn't move. Her mouth tightened as she waited for his hands.

He reached out and ran his fingertips over her smooth cheekbones. Her lips trembled. The tiniest of whimpers escaped between them before she pressed them tight together. Then he stooped and lifted the green gown over her head.

He dropped it at her feet. She blinked at the sound of the heavy wool falling. It was a solid sound, as if a piece of armor had been removed. In a sense it had. The outer shell was gone and the priestess was no more.

Beneath the gown she wore a white kirtle with long, billowy sleeves and a girdle cinched around her waist. With a twist to the corner of his mouth, he noted the second dirk slipped into a small scabbard beneath it.

"That's your third blade," he noted. " 'Tis a strange cloister that supplies their priestesses with so many weapons." He flipped it out and dropped it into the folds of the green robe. His eyes continued to take in her form. No matron here, he observed with pleasure. The girdle pulled the material softly over her full breasts.

The sheer white linen was in marked contrast to her long black hair. His fingers trembled as he touched it—something he had dreamed of doing since he had first seen her in the high grove altar. Like silk, her hair glided through his fingers.

"Do you remember me?" he asked.

She nodded.

"Why didn't you tell me who you were when I questioned you?"

"I couldn't. I wasn't even supposed to be there. I'm a sequestered Dryad."

"No more sequestered then than now. And again a long way from your cloister, just as you were on Nameless Eve." He smiled at the memory and also at the thought that she wasn't quite the sequestered holy woman that she would like everyone to believe. He wondered what her story was.

She stirred a bit uncomfortably. "'Twas the eve of my birthday. I was at my special high altar, making an offering to the goddess of my day."

"You ran away. I looked for you, but I couldn't find you."

"I didn't want to be found." She looked away from his handsome face, his strong, brown hands so close to her flesh. "I—There would be no point."

"I'm a master tracker," he argued. "I should have found you." His hands slid down her arms and settled on her waist. His fingers worked at the girdle. It too fell away. The linen settled into looser folds. "What's this?"

Immediately her hand flew to her breast.

He caught it. With his other hand he pulled the gold object from beneath the low neck of the kirtle. He stared at it incredulously. "This is mine. How came you by it? I lost it the night—"

She would have twisted away, but he held her fast. "It isn't. It's—"

"You were there," he accused. "Somehow you came into my cave that night and stole it from me."

"No."

"Why?"

"I didn't do it." Suddenly she stopped, mortally ashamed of the words falling from her lips. She was lying. But what difference did a few lies make? She had broken so many of her vows. Everything had gone wrong, beginning with the night of the Nameless Eve. One could almost believe the Great Mother Goddess had deserted her.

"You did," he insisted inexorably.

"You're right. I took it," she admitted in a low voice. "I don't know why. I just wanted—"

"—to remember me." He was smiling now. "And you've never forgotten me. Nor I you."

She unfastened the chain from around her neck and handed the brooch to him. "Take it. I return it to you."

"Too late." He laughed softly, placing the chain once again around her neck. "It's yours. Ah, if I had known, all of this wouldn't have been necessary. I'd have had you pull that out. Vaghn's woman might have had a brand, but my woman wears my symbol next to her heart." He laughed again and dragged her against him.

"No."

His mouth came down on hers. His kiss was long and passionate.

She submitted, her own body heating and her heart stepping up its rhythm. She kept telling herself that she had no choice. She was helpless. She couldn't very well run from him in her underdress.

But she very much doubted she could run anyway.

Her mind sought frantically for some way to avert this disaster. She wrenched herself away from him when he paused to draw a breath.

"You must stop!" she commanded. "I am forbidden to you. And to all men. I am the high priestess of the Cloister of the Grove, a holy woman to be respected and protected. I have taken a vow of celibacy. More than that, I am the sister-in-law to your friend Brian mac Logan. I am of noble birth, daughter of Pryse mac Russ, High King of Ailean."

Nothing else mattered to Kolby but the last sentence. Her words drove a knife deep into a wound that had remained open and painful since he was old enough to understand about such things—his ignoble beginnings. He was a nameless Northlander without family and clan. He was not worthy of her.

But he wanted this woman. In some dark dawning of his mind, he suspected that this imperious priestess was the woman for him.

Suddenly it became doubly important for him to find the sacred tree. Then Ura would adopt him and he would have a steading, a title, and a name. He stepped back.

Outside, the outlaws waited restlessly. Coarse jokes and foul suggestions reached Kolby's ears. That Raven heard and understood was conveyed by the scarlet blush that rose in her cheeks.

She had been in his mind from the moment he had first seen her. She had run away from him, stolen from him, defied him, and disobeyed him. Most important, she had refused to trust him to protect her and the cloister valuables. He should have left her long ago.

But he hadn't. Instead he had brought her into the badlands and stripped away her cowl and robe. Now, to protect her, he must brand her as his own.

Raven's dark eyes dilated with fright. She must truly believe that her Great Mother Goddess had forsaken her as she stood nearly naked, exposed to his burning eyes, a horde of filthy outlaws shouting obscenities outside.

She bit her lip, blinking rapidly, then tears began trickling down her cheeks. Try as she would, she couldn't control them. She swiped at them with her hands in a childish gesture.

Kolby bent and picked up her robe. Gently he wrapped it around her shoulders. "Don't cry, little priestess," he murmured in her ear. "All will be well."

She caught her breath to try to stifle a sob. "How can it?"

"Trust me."

She raised her head. Her dark eyes found his, caught between hope and fear.

"You're not—you don't intend to—"

He didn't want to mislead her as to his intentions. "Aye, lady, I am and I do. I must."

"So I'm to be traded for the information you seek." Despite her tears, the words were laced with contempt.

"Aye, and to protect you and your mother. And to save my men from having to fight a battle they might well lose."

"Surely there is something else that we can do."

At least she had changed the word to "we."

"Nothing."

Outside the hut, tension between outlaws and Northlanders remained high. Aren and Durin guarded the door. Thorfinn took up a post at the door to the mead hall, where he could survey the street. Sven took his post at the other end.

Alongside the huts on the opposite side of the street, the outlaws arranged themselves in watchful attitudes. The other women joined Damona in the hut where Melanthe lay. Only Vaghn appeared to be at ease. He sprawled in the bed of the oxcart, his arms beneath his head, basking in the sun.

Bradach regarded him covertly, then shuffled to his side. Under Durin's scowl, the guide spoke to the outlaw in low tones. "Do you have the information the Northlander seeks?"

Vaghn opened one basilisk eye. He had an open man's contempt for men who lived by subterfuge. "Mayhap."

"He has the gold," Bradach confirmed. "I've seen it."

"Then I have news to give him. When *I* see it. Not before. Maybe he'll like my news, maybe not. Once he hears it, he'll have to decide what to do with it."

Bradach wet his lips uneasily. "If you're playing games—"

"If I am, what difference does it make to you?"

The guide glanced at Durin. "He might take it into his head to kill me."

"Small loss."

"Great loss for you," Bradach reminded him. "You need me, Vaghn. Without me you'll never get back to the other side."

For an instant Vaghn looked murderous. Bradach fell back a step. Then Vaghn's dark expression was gone, replaced by one of supreme indifference. "I'm not likely to make it to the other side in this life, Bradach. Don't overvalue yourself."

"But can you give him information that will lead him to the sacred tree?"

Vaghn closed his eyes against the sun's glare. "I would say so. If he's deserving of the fruit, he'll have no problem. If he's not, he's a dead man."

Chapter 6

Kolby left Raven's side to stare at the old bar that held the door shut. A good kick by Vaghn's foot and the thing would fly out of the rotten wood. The Northlanders' personal luggage had already been ransacked by outlaws during the meeting in the mead hall. Even the water bags had been emptied in their search for coins and trinkets. He cursed flatly at the waste, wondering if even now the outlaws were discovering the sacks of gold and silver he'd left with the women in the other hut.

He gathered the packs in this hut and slung them onto a dry place on the floor. Then he collected the clothing and dropped it on top. Several planks remained on a frame along one wall. He wrenched one of these up and strode back to the door.

Raven watched him, curious in spite of herself. "What are you doing?"

"I don't trust this bar. With this plank against the door, we'll make it a bit harder for them." With the heel of his boot, he kicked out a short trench and set the plank in it. Then he let the plank fall so that the other end was braced against the door beside the bolt. "There." He dusted his hands with a smile of satisfaction.

His simple safeguard did nothing to reassure Raven. She felt helpless. She had no weapons. Desperately she scanned the floor. Finally she saw a glint of metal half-buried in the mud. Edging closer, she rubbed it with her shoe, succeeding in uncovering more. Her eyes strained to make it out. It was a broken dagger blade. Quick as thought, she swept it up. It was of good quality. Possibly one of the outlaws had broken it in his careless search.

It was not the weapon she would have wanted, its point broken, its hilt end jagged, but it was better than none at all. She lowered her arm to her side and turned her hand under the folds of her kirtle.

Kolby closed the shutter and dropped the bar into place. Shadows enveloped the room, their darkness broken by the thin lines of sunshine edging in through cracks and holes in the thatched roof. Studying the room, he slowly turned; he walked from one corner to the next. Finally he stopped.

The shadows cloaked him. She knew he was there, but she couldn't see his face. He was a massive silhouette looming large. As the shadows of the forest had loomed over them last night, Raven felt him towering over her now. Although the situation was tense, fraught with an unsettling element of the unknown, Raven found that she was less frightened than excited.

"Come over here," he ordered.

"Nay." Her stomach churned. Her heart pounded against her ribs like a smithy's hammer.

He sighed wearily and stepped into one of the small pools of golden light.

Despite her resolve, she took a step backward. "I won't let you take me without a fight," she promised. Her voice sounded hollow to her own ears.

He planted his hands on his hips and stared at her, until time seemed to lengthen into eternity. Finally he walked over and hooked his foot beneath the plank.

"Shall I open this door and disclaim you? Would you rather take your chances with them?" He stared significantly at her breasts pushing against the fine linen of her kirtle. "Barter with them, lady, and learn what jewel they are intent on having."

When it was put like that, she had no choice. "You must know I would not!"

"Then the matter is settled. We will do what we have to do to survive. I will come one step closer to achieving my quest. You will come one step closer to returning safe and sound to your cloister. You will cease your silliness."

Yesterday he had accused her of being hysterical; now he was calling her silly. No one had ever made such accusations before.

He waved his hand to one corner. " 'Tis darkest over there, where the wall has no cracks and the roof no holes. We'll be most concealed from prying eyes." He let a sardonic smile twist his mouth. "Unless, of course, you would prefer a witness. In that case, Vaghn would be glad to oblige."

"No." She shuddered at the memory of the outlaw's gaze crawling over her. "No."

Kolby nodded. He returned to the luggage and rummaged through it until he found a riding pack, two large bags connected with a leather strap that could be slung over an animal's rump or a man's shoulder. Tooled in the leather was a beautiful runic inscription. He held the bag up, a narrow stream of sunlight framing the letters. He ran his index finger over them. "This is my mark."

"Your name."

He could not keep a note of bitterness out of his voice. "Such as it is. Not like some people, who can claim a high king for a father."

He unfastened one of the bags and drew out a garment. It whispered in the dark like silk, and when it flashed through a thin line of sunshine, she saw that the material was glistening yellow. It was a dress cloak for festive occasions. A golden cloak for a golden warrior.

He was going to use it as the sheet that would testify to what had been her maiden status—after he had destroyed it forever.

With a sinking heart, Raven watched him spread the cloak on the floor. The pallet where they would mate! The enormity of what was about to be done to her struck her forcibly. This man was going to enter her body, hurt her, tear her, whether she was willing or not.

The outlaws would demand proof that she had been deflowered, and her maiden blood would be easily visible on that cloak. In the minds of the outlaws she would be marked as Kolby's possession, more surely than if he encircled her neck with that leather strap inscribed with his name. She would thereafter be his property. And the story would spread throughout Scotland that a priestess of the Cloister of the Grove had lost her virginity to a Viking by Christian custom.

She should kill Kolby and then herself. But she didn't want to die. "Please. Please don't do this," Raven begged. "If I alone were to suffer from the shame, I wouldn't put up a fight, but I'm a representative of the earth, a keeper of the land. If I behave shamefully, I bring that shame to the earth."

She stared at the golden cloak laid at her feet. When Kolby didn't answer, she looked up.

"You must deal with your vows and your shame in your own way," he replied. "At least you'll be alive to deal with them. I have to deal with Vaghn and his outlaws, and this is the only way I know to do so."

Her hand tight on the broken silver blade, she

lifted it between them. The jagged edge of the hilt would tear her hand as she drove it into his body. Their blood would mingle as it spilled into the dirt. "I won't make mating easy."

With a wry smile, he walked closer to her. "I haven't found dealing with you in any way easy, lady. Why should it be any different now?"

Her hand was shaking. Still she held the weapon between them.

He spread his arms wide, as if inviting her to use it. "If there were another way of protecting us, lady, I would take it. This is the only way I know to make you mine and ensure everyone knows it. There must be no doubt that I am your champion."

She lifted her chin. "You could pledge your fealty to me."

He laughed shortly. "Madam, you have seen these outlaws for yourself. You heard what Vaghn said. These are men who fear nothing because they have nothing to lose but their lives. They enjoy exercising even the smallest bit of power because they have none. Declaring my fealty to you wouldn't pacify them. They don't honor our laws or customs except when they can turn them to their own use, as they have today. Otherwise they have created their own. We're in their territory and must obey them."

"Have I no choice in the matter?" Her trembling hand clenched around the knife so tightly that he could not doubt that it was cutting her tender skin.

Still he gave her the truth. She had the choice to kill him and then herself. He wouldn't take it from her until the very last minute. He hoped she would see sense. "None," he answered. "Without Vaghn we're alone in the badlands. And my purpose is thwarted, perhaps forever."

The morning sun, filtering through a hole in the roof, blazed down on Kolby, burnishing his hair to amber-gold, reminding her once again of his power.

Nameless he might be, but someone of great importance had fathered him, she had no doubt. She looked into his face. It was hard, rugged like the Northland from where he had come. She gazed into his eyes. She saw steely resolve in their depths.

Her grip on the blade loosened. It tilted downward. A drop of blood slid down the edge and clung on the tip.

"Your only choice at the moment is whether you would rather belong to me or to Vaghn." Even as he finished speaking, he realized he had chosen the wrong words. Defiance glittered in her eyes.

"I won't *belong* to either of you." Her hand grew steady. She lifted the knife. "I shall kill you, Northlander, and him too if he tries to take me."

"I doubt you could do that," he pointed out reasonably. "I would wager that my battle skills are more sharply honed than yours, lady, and I'm a much bigger man than you are a woman." He paused. "Even if you did kill me, you can be certain Vaghn wouldn't meet you one to one as I am. He would have his men swarm all over you and pin you down. You would be helpless to move while he enjoyed every minute of your degradation."

She shuddered. Her grip on the knife tightened.

Kolby held out his hands. "Again I say, madam, which is it to be? Me or the outlaw?"

Fearfully she stared at him as he stepped closer. He totally disregarded the blade she held.

Within slashing distance of the knife, he unbuckled his wrist guards, first the left, then the right, to reveal his powerfully muscled forearms and wrists. As if he were shedding his skin, he let the guards fall to the floor. Out of habit he reached for his weapons belt. Then he remembered he had given it to Durin.

Again he held out his hand. She refused to take it. He took a step toward her. She took a step backward.

When she was flush with the wall, he halted. She still held the blade, the last barrier, between them.

"That's as far as you can go." He took another step.

Two tears followed the paths of others down her cheeks. Angrily she wiped them away. She didn't want him to see her crying. In that moment of distraction, he caught the blade and pulled it from her unresisting fingers. Dropping it at their feet, he leaned in close, his chest pressing against her breasts. He slipped his arms around her and drew her near. As the soft warmth of her lower body melded against him, his manhood surged to life.

She snapped her head aside, pressing her cheek against the rough wall behind her. He buried his face in the curve of her neck and shoulder thus exposed. He inhaled deeply of her sweet herbal fragrance. His whole body shuddered with need. Did she tremble with fear or with the same need?

Since he had accepted Ura's quest, he had taken no woman. He was as close to understanding celibacy as he was ever likely to be. Yet he honored her choice. Never would he take an unwilling woman.

He caught the tie at the neckline of her kirtle and pulled it free. The bodice sagged, the material falling away from her shoulders and sliding down her arms. Slowly it revealed the most beautiful body Kolby had ever seen. Smooth skin the color of rich cream. Full, rounded breasts with darkened aureolas, the peaks hard. He had to press his lips into a thin line to keep from sampling their sweetness.

He wanted to see her naked and let her see him before they did more than touch. He pushed the kirtle lower around the supple line of her abdomen and flat stomach. Her hips flared gently below that. He closed his eyes against the thunderous beat of his heart.

He let the kirtle fall to the floor, let his gaze rest on

the blue-black triangle of hair at the juncture of her thighs. Dazed by her beauty, he couldn't find words.

From a long way off, her voice rasped in his ears. "Whether I fight or not, you will be taking me against my will."

Slowly, reverently, he let his gaze move up her body until it rested on the pendant between her breasts. "I don't think so," he whispered. "I think you have been waiting for me for almost a year now."

"You lie," she cried. "Where did you get such an idea?"

"From my pendant." He closed his hand round it. The backs of his fingers brushed her breast. "It's warm from the heat of your body. You stole it from me to remind you."

"No."

"I say yes." He pulled her toward him by the chain. "I say that this pendant became your talisman until I joined you. You were so certain we would meet again that you stole it."

She dropped her eyes as his lips touched her forehead.

"Tell the truth."

"Aye." If they had not been heart to heart, he wouldn't have heard the soft escape of her breath.

"Ah." He pulled back. Golden eyes, soft and warm, measured hers. "Now we learn the truth."

"I want to," she confessed, "but I mustn't. I am a keeper of the land and all its elements."

He placed his lips on her temple. Down the side of her cheek to the lobe of her ear, he traced little nibbling kisses. "I am one of the elements of the land," he murmured. "Would you be my keeper, lady?"

The tension in the room heightened, changing subtly. Anger and fear gave way to curiosity and tingling excitement. Shadows lost their ominous cast

to become soft and intimate. Sunlight streamed
through the cracks in the shutters to touch the man
and woman with golden warmth. It whetted their
desires.

Priestess was transforming into woman, warrior
into man, both into lovers.

Just as her knees buckled, Kolby swept her up into
his arms and laid her on his cloak. Her hair fanned
out around her, making a black cloak against the
gold. Her eyes were luminous as she watched him
strip off his vest and tunic. Keeping on his trousers
and boots, he stretched out and leaned over her. He
brushed her hair from her face and traced her lips
with his fingertip.

Involuntarily she shifted her hips. Only a fraction,
but he smiled. Raven caught the smile with her own
fingers. "I have fought many battles in my life, but
none like this, Northlander."

"You fight the same battle that every woman does.
And every woman loses if she is a woman at all." He
buried his face against her throat again, inhaling her
womanly scent, enjoying her softness, the satin texture of her flesh. So often he had dreamed of doing
this.

"I'm not fighting you or the outlaws. I'm fighting
myself." Her voice, hoarse with desire, broke into his
thoughts. "And I'm fighting the gods, the immortals
who cannot lose."

A thwacking noise and a burst of raucous laughter
from outside made her jump.

"It's all right," Kolby whispered. "I have you."

"I'm much afraid you do," she whispered back.
Still, the noise had intruded on the dream. "I don't
understand why they are demanding proof of my
virginity. Highlanders have never put great value on
such."

"They are testing me." He slid more closely against
her and slipped his arm under her head.

"Why?"

"In mating with the lady of the Nameless Day, in taking the virginal celibate dedicated to the Great Mother Goddess, I am proving my disregard of Highland law. If I take you, I become an outlaw like them. Every Highlander's hand will be turned against me. In taking you, I prove I'm a man of my word and an outsider no longer."

"And are you a man of your word?"

"Aye. By the letter."

He captured her mouth before she could question him further. For the first time his tongue slid between her lips, tasting her sweetness, sliding over the satiny surfaces, until her tense body relaxed. Then his mouth whispered across her cheek to her ear. "To convince the outlaws that we have mated, you're going to have to cooperate with me."

"But you've admitted you're an equivocator. How can I believe you?"

"I must authenticate my claim. That hasn't changed."

"I don't understand," she faltered. "What is going to happen? Either you take my virginity or you don't."

"Let's just see what happens." His chest rubbed against her nipple, and her breasts swelled. They throbbed pleasantly, sending wonderful sensations throughout her body. He lifted his head, and she brushed her hands over his chest, loving the crisp golden hair beneath her palms.

In an uncontrollable impulse to repay the pleasure, she caught his face in her hands, bringing his lips to hers, and she gently kissed him.

It was a light, tentative kiss, the mere whisper of lips. It was the sweetness that Kolby had dreamed of having ever since he had first seen Raven at the high grove altar, a sweetness he had despaired of ever knowing. At that moment he was content to hold and caress her. He enjoyed a satisfaction that carnal fulfillment rarely gave him.

"I know 'tis a great weakness in me," she confessed, "but I've wanted to taste you for so long."

She traced one finger over his thick brows, down the bridge of his nose. She smoothed her palms over his hair as she had dreamed of doing since she had first seen him. "The golden warrior," she murmured. "That's what I always called you."

"My lady of winter," he replied.

"That's what a woman is called when she is born on the Nameless Day. How did you know?"

"The first time I saw you," Kolby said, "I wondered if you were Freya of the snow-white bosom. The gown you wore . . . um . . . revealed more than it concealed."

"Who is Freya?"

"She is the Northlander's goddess of love and beauty. When you disappeared, I was afraid I had imagined it all and that I would never find you."

"Then you can understand why I stole your brooch. I believed you would never find me again. You shouldn't have. I should be hidden away in a cloister."

"And I should be paying an outlaw for information to end my quest." He fell to kissing her again. "But it didn't happen."

She returned his kisses. When they stopped for breath, she asked, "How could I be a Northlander's idea of a goddess? Aren't all your goddesses golden-haired and blue-eyed?"

He chuckled softly. "Since I've never seen one, I have no expectations."

"Are you disappointed that I'm not a goddess—golden-haired and blue-eyed?"

"I would have been disappointed if you *had* been a

goddess. A goddess would have gotten herself out of this fix with Thor's thunderbolts. She wouldn't have waited around for me to save her.''

Raven sighed with a mixture of sorrow and joy. ''Thank the goddess then. I'm quite mortal.''

''Enough conversation,'' Kolby commanded softly. ''Pretend you're kissing me. I think I saw someone peeking through one of the cracks.''

She smiled. ''You're equivocating again. But even if no one is looking, I'll kiss you.''

He pressed his lips against hers; she wrapped her arms around him. Sweet, sweet happiness flowed through him. Now he understood why in all these years of having women, his hunger had not been assuaged. Always he had been searching for the woman of his soul, for *this* woman.

She was his destined mate. The woman he had yearned for, the only one who would bring peace to his heart. He wondered how he would keep from taking her today, how he could stay away from her. Already desire pumped through him, so hot, so forceful, he could hardly think of anything but his own need.

He knew he shouldn't touch her any more than was necessary to convince Vaghn and the outlaws that he had taken her. Paradoxically he couldn't keep his hands off her. He wouldn't force her. That wasn't his way. But he had to touch her. She was so smooth. Silky. Soft. Seductive. And for the moment—at least for this moment—she was his.

''I suppose we have to do this.'' She squirmed beneath him, touching him with her body, branding him with her flesh.

''Aye, lady.''

He spread kisses over her face and neck, across her shoulders, in the hollows of satiny skin below her collarbone, down to her breasts. Breathing heavily, he was determined to stop at the top of the gentle swell, but the hardened tip drew him like a lodestone. He ached to take it into his mouth, to roll his tongue around it, to suck. Desire speared through him, reminding him ever more strongly how long he had been without a woman—reminding him how much he wanted her.

"They mustn't suspect." His voice was thick.

Raven shivered from the onslaught of emotions. She had never dreamed such feelings existed and that they could flow through her. Desire had been a warm emotion stirring faintly on rare occasions when the worship of the Great Mother Goddess became ecstatic. Now she applied those feelings to something of this earth. To her own feelings, which permeated her lower belly. From there they spread hotly through her entire body.

This mustn't happen. She tossed her head restlessly, seeking control.

He smoothed her hair from her temple, then lowered his head until his lips touched hers. She moaned softly. It was wonderful but not enough. She moved her legs, trying to insinuate them closer to him. She felt the bulge of his lower body. It was large, startling. Even through the leather trousers, he was hot. It was the glory of his manhood.

"What—" Beneath his lips, she opened her mouth.

He groaned, swallowed her word, and wrapped his arms tighter about her. His lips grew more moist, the kiss hotter as his tongue stroked her mouth. Raven caught his hand and moved it to the juncture of her thighs. Still holding him, she pressed his palm against the triangle of hair. She was so needy, she had become the instigator.

Kolby knew he should remove his hand. She was innocent, unseasoned in mating. He wasn't. But she felt so good to him. So warm. Her talisman was the apple, and it was an appropriate symbol, he thought. She was like the delicate blossom. Each spring a fragile netting of gossamer petals spread over the orchard. Each autumn, rich, succulent fruit weighed down the bows. Raven's breathtaking beauty and fragile fragrance were a promise of the full fruition of her love.

For Raven his touch had stirred doubts as never before. She had always been told that her magical powers were great because she was born on the day when the Great Mother Goddess walked the earth and celebrated her completeness, when she and the Great Father God came together in a mystical union. Raven had accepted that she was one with this great goddess.

But she would swear that Kolby was more magical than she. Golden and majestic, he was a manifestation of the Great Father God himself. He had only to touch her and her body sang. Joy flowed through her. He brought a completeness to her that she had not experienced before.

She felt the tips of his fingers where they burned her untrammeled flesh. They excited her beyond imagining. They whetted her desire. They made her aware of what she had been missing all these years. She knew the glory that Gwynneth knew. And she envied her.

He removed his hand from her secret spot, leaving her with a void of despair. Her lower body twisted with longing; hunger drove her. She arched against his hand. She wanted more, needed more. She would have more.

Still kissing her, he slid his hand lower, his fingers moving closer and closer to the center of her femininity.

He touched her there. Warm and moist, she pulsated against him; she trembled. The pressure of his fingers lightened.

"Nay." She covered his hand with hers.

He caught her lips in another kiss, a fuller one this

time, his tongue making gentle forays into her mouth. She opened wider to receive him. She loved the sweet roughness of his tongue as it brushed against her teeth, her cheeks, as it clashed with her tongue for dominance. She was breathing harder; she was fighting for more caresses, fighting to touch him as he touched her.

He continued to love her, his fingers stroking, sending her higher and higher. She truly felt as if she were one with the Great Mother Goddess, as if somehow they were one united self, beneath the body of the Great Father God. Joy like silver radiance spiraled through her.

It filled her until she overflowed.

Her body convulsed, and he held her closely and whispered in her ear. Catching the back of her head in his hand, he pressed their mouths together. In such fashion he received the cry of her first pleasure. It became the essence of their kiss. It was as if she had burst into tiny lights, strewn across the midnight sky.

She clung to him, burying her head against his chest and not speaking for a long time. When at last she found her voice, it was a mere thread of sound. "I have never felt like this before."

He kissed her forehead, her eyelids, the tip of her nose. "How do you feel?"

She thought for a long time, trying to sort through the deep and conflicting emotions. Had he really only touched her with his fingers? At last she decided upon the word. "Happy."

"Aye." He kissed her mouth again, and her lips trembled.

"Confused," she confessed.

"I would imagine so." He brushed his mouth across her cheek to her temple and gathered her more tightly against him. "I want to know something."

It was a measure of how completely at ease she was that she did not even flinch from his request.

"Why did you become a celibate priestess?"

Reality flooded in upon her. Still, his question was a fair one, given the total response of her body, heart, and mind to the simple touch of his fingers.

"Nine years ago I was dishonored." She shuddered at the memory.

He held her tighter. "How?"

"A man, my betrothed, publicly rejected me. What he did shamed me and my family beyond measure. My father was ready to swear a terrible vengeance. Then the man made everything right with Pryse. He married my younger sister."

Her voice broke. "I—I had no choice. I was an embarrassment to all. I retreated to my mother's cloister."

She gasped as Kolby's grasp tightened. She couldn't draw a breath. Instantly his hold eased.

His voice in her ear promised vengeance. "Name him and he will die."

She shrugged. "He is already dead. And Gwynneth is married to the man of her dreams, your friend Brian mac Logan. All has been made well."

"Except that you are locked up for the rest of your life."

He didn't understand. She hadn't told it well. "I love the Great Mother Goddess," she tried to explain. "I have everything and more."

He pushed his hand down against her mound. Though she gasped, he pushed harder, twisting his palm back and forth, stirring new sensations in her. "Everything?"

She arched her back, trying to escape his hand. "Stop it."

When he lifted his hand, she felt her hips rise involuntarily to follow it. A whimper escaped her.

He placed his lips against her ear. "Remember how you feel."

"Guilty and embarrassed," she replied.

He jerked his head back. "Nay."

She laid a finger over his mouth. Her cheeks were flushed, her eyes smoky. "I begged you not to mate with me, but I really wanted you to. I couldn't keep my hands off you. I am content with what we did, but I still want more. And I can't have it."

He pushed up on one arm and caught her chin in his hand. "Be happy, my lady. Acknowledge the pleasure that my touch created in you. And you can feel a little confusion. But you mustn't feel guilty or embarrassed. You've done nothing to be ashamed of."

"I was a virgin. I took a vow of celibacy."

He rolled onto his back to stare upward at the dust motes drifting in the shafts of sunlight. "No god or person should demand that," he muttered.

"The Goddess didn't," Raven said. "I freely offered it to her."

"In exchange for sanctuary," he pointed out. "She doesn't seem a very generous goddess to me. In fact she doesn't seem like a goddess at all. Just a name that some people mouth so they can shuffle others off rather than stand by them as they should."

She raised up and put her hand over his lips. "Don't blaspheme. There would have been a war had I not gone. My father and my friends might have died."

He sighed. "Then know that from my point of view, and from the point of view of your goddess, you're still celibate. And your maidenhead is intact."

Raven felt her cheeks grow warm. She tucked her head beneath his chin. Beneath her ear she could hear the steady thrum of his heart. She felt she could lie like this forever. "You're embarrassing me again."

"I didn't mean to," he said. He closed his arms around her and hugged her gently. "I was explaining that you're the same person you were when I brought you into the room."

"I'm not," she replied. "And I would be foolish if I thought so. I'll never be the same."

Kolby had touched her heart and soul. He had authenticated his claim. He had branded her his possession. He might as well cut the leather strap from the pack and fasten it around her neck, for all to see his name upon her. He had engraved his name on her heart and soul. Because of love she would be forever bound to him.

He reached behind them and bunched her kirtle in his fist, making sure he grabbed the blade that was lying beneath it. Her blood was still on it, but it had dried. He brought the garment around and stuffed it between them.

"It's time for us to dress." As he spoke, he eased the jagged metal from the folds of the cloth.

When she saw it, her mouth formed an O. "What are you going to do?"

"Keep your eyes open and your mouth closed."

He rose on his knees. With one hand he opened his leather trousers and pulled them down, exposing the honey-brown hair of his groin. Her eyes widened as she saw the dark male root of his masculinity. The jagged edge flashed down.

She winced.

A tiny cut streamed blood into the hair.

"Sweet Mother Goddess—" she began.

He lowered himself upon her. She felt him smear the hot blood into the hair at the bottom of her belly. Then he slid down and smeared himself over the silken cloak.

"That should do the trick," he muttered. In a movement so graceful, it made her want him all over again, he pressed himself straight up on his powerful arms, pulled his feet up under him and sprang erect.

In one fell swoop they were all marked. She, he, and the cloak all bore the stains that authenticated his claim.

"Now," he said, pulling up his trousers and refastening them. "I've protected us all. The outlaw has the information that I must have if I'm to complete my mission. And your virginity is still intact."

He had done this for her. He could have left her and her mother to the mercy of the first band of outlaws. He hadn't had to rescue them. No one would ever have known that he had seen them. He owed them no allegiance. For a long time he had thought of Raven as a disagreeable and matronly priestess. Yet he had fought for her and found a way for her to retain her virtue and integrity.

She rose and slipped on the white kirtle. As it slid down her body, some drops of blood were smeared onto the snowy material. She didn't care that her clothing might be ruined. She only cared that she was party to a deception. Suddenly she regretted that this was Kolby's blood, not the result of their having mated.

He swept up the golden cloak and folded it neatly over his arm, so that the bloodstains showed.

She touched the rich folds regretfully. "It's ruined. Your cloak. 'Tis a fine one."

"Which do you prefer that I save—the garment, or you and your mother?"

She caught up her girdle and buckled it around her middle. She held up the wimple, then discarded it. It was too torn to be of service. Her robe came next. The folds enveloped her like a prison. Her moment of freedom was gone. She wanted to cry.

Last, she took the knife blade from him. Kneeling, she drove it back into the muddy floor from whence it had come. With her boot she scuffed mud and dust over it.

Then she caught up his wrist guards, thinking she could at least do him the small service of helping him to dress, but he wouldn't allow it. "Leave those with the luggage," he told her. "I want them to see no wound on my body. I hope Vaghn won't check too closely to find where the blood came from."

She pulled the cowl over her head to hide her blushes, but he tipped it back and kissed her hard and thoroughly. There was nothing gentle about it. He branded her, crushing her lips. Then, instead of taking his mouth away, he slid it down over her jaw to her neck. Innocent of what he had in mind, she yelped in pain when he bit her hard enough to leave a bruise on her soft flesh.

"Now." He grinned in the old cynical way. "We'll return to Vaghn for inspection." He draped his tunic and vest over his shoulder and jerked open the door.

Sunshine burst into the room. They stood for a moment blinking as their eyes became accustomed to the glare. Then they stepped out into the street.

Vaghn gave a cheer and swung down from the oxcart. The Northlanders turned. Their eyes took in their thane's nude torso, his broad smile. They too smiled. The outlaws who were lounging near the mead hall left off their game of draughts and rose to gather round.

Squinting first at the cloak and then at the couple, Vaghn strode toward them. He stared so blatantly that Raven felt as if he knew what had actually happened in the room. She halted, frightened. How could he know that the blood wasn't hers? Her mind argued that all blood was red and left a bright stain. But still he studied her, adding to her embarrassment.

Vaghn halted in front of them and hooted with laughter. "Ah, Lord Kolby, you rode her well."

Raven could have died of shame. Then Vaghn's hand came up to touch her chin and turn her head aside. He was looking at the mark on her neck. Her eyes flashed fire. How dare he touch her, a priestess?

Except that in his eyes, she was no longer a priestess.

She looked around the circle of grinning faces.

Every man among them thought she was deflowered, that her virgin blood stained that golden silk.

Durin slapped Kolby's shoulder and held out a hand. They shook vigorously. The others gathered round him too. They were congratulating him for raping her. Were all men such monsters?

But it hadn't been rape. He hadn't hurt her. Perhaps he did deserve to be congratulated. Thanks to his skill and consideration, she had not fought him off. She had said she would. She had intended to do so. She had declared herself the champion of her vows, but she had capitulated without striking a blow. Her womanly desires had proved stronger than her commitment to the cloister.

"I have decided to have our parley here in the village," Vaghn announced loudly. "For now it is your village, Northlander."

"So that I can pay you extra booty for the use of it," Kolby rejoined.

"I'm a reasonable man," the outlaw replied. He turned to Raven. "So you really belong to him now."

The wind blew cold across her bare head. It picked up strands of hair and swept them across her face. It stirred her robes. Beneath the enveloping folds the tingling happiness had died. "Aye, outlaw." Her voice was as flat as a dry leaf rustling. "According to your laws, I belong to him. May the Great Mother Goddess forgive me. And have mercy on the land."

She saw a shadow darken Kolby's eyes as she turned from him and walked toward the shelter where her mother lay. Before Kolby had ridden to rescue her, Raven had experienced little guilt. Today she had made up for a lifetime without it. She had lied and deceived. She had violated one vow after another until nothing sacred remained.

Walking through the open door, she saw Damona sitting cross-legged on the floor beside her mother's pallet. The outlaw's wife rose in a graceful motion and came to Raven with outstretched hands. "There now. That wasn't so bad, was it?"

Raven longed to scream at her that it hadn't been bad. And yet it was the most terrible experience of her life. Only concern for her mother made her hold her peace. She dropped to her knees beside Melanthe and put her hand on her mother's forehead.

"I didn't have to change the dressing." Damona hovered over the pair, her hands clasping and unclasping. "But she became so restless that I worried she'd start bleeding again, so I gave her a sleeping potion. She's been sleeping peacefully ever since."

"Thank you." Though Raven despised this woman's tacit approval of rape, she appreciated the care the outlaw woman had given Melanthe.

Satisfied that there was nothing her mother needed for the moment, Raven sat back on her heels.

"You'd best wash your clothes before the blood sets," Damona suggested.

Raven looked down at Kolby's cloak, at his blood, at his sacrifice for her and her mother.

"Your dress is also stained," Damona said quietly, one woman to another. "You'd best wash it in cold water soon or the fabric will be ruined." She rubbed the hem between her fingers. "'Tis fine fabric, my lady, much too costly to waste. Let me take you to a safe spot where you can bathe. One of the other women will stay here with your mother until we return."

Raven sensed that Damona wanted to see for herself the stains on the under clothes. No doubt she would report them to Vaghn. Rather than protest, she rose. "Where is the best spot? Last night I bathed in here because I—"

"Aye, my lady, I know. Vaghn and I have camped here often. There's a secluded spot for us women where we bathe and wash our clothes. It's behind this building around the curve in the stream."

"Will the outlaws honor Kolby's claim on me?" Raven asked.

"Aye. You'll be left alone," Damona promised. "In order to survive in these wilds, Vaghn had to set up strict laws and customs. We belong only in the badlands. We're outcasts everywhere else. But when we violate one of our own laws, we're banished to the borderlands. Over there we are *dicenn*."

Raven shivered at the pronouncement of the damnable word. Aye, she thought, headless and faceless, without soul or honor, without name or clan. A fate no man or woman wanted.

"Like animals we would be hunted and killed. We would die but we would go nowhere." Damona's eyes filled with horror. "It would be the end." She laid her hand on Raven's shoulder. "Once a claim has been authenticated, it is honored because it is the only way to avoid *dicenn*."

While Damona called one of the other women inside, Raven found her personal satchel among the luggage. She pulled out the soiled robe she had worn yesterday. She had been much too worried about her mother to wash it last night. The blood would have set, and it might be ruined. Heavy-hearted, she gazed at the garments, one stained with her mother's blood, the other with Kolby's.

"This is the only other robe I have." She slung it over her arm. "I'll wash everything and put this back on. It will dry on me." At the door Raven stopped. "I just remembered. Since Kolby is in effect chief of this village now, and I am his woman, am I responsible for preparing the evening meal?"

"Nay. Vaghn wasn't sure how long the two of you would be closed up in the house, so we shall provide the food for tonight's meal. You can do it for your man tomorrow."

How right that sounded to Raven! She was to prepare a meal tomorrow. For her man. And how ironic! Damona had called Kolby her man. Raven had originally asked him to swear fealty to her, but he had refused. Now, under circumstances neither one of them could have foreseen, he was her champion, and she was his woman.

She was close to the spring when Damona called out. Raven turned. Another outlaw woman approached and handed her a soft dress in a pale rust color. The ribbons were bright russet, green, and yellow. The sleeves were short and the material was light and cool.

"An old gown of mine," Damona said. "You may wear it if you want to."

"'Tis very kind of you," Raven said, and realized that she truly meant it.

Chapter 7

Kolby caught Vaghn by the shoulder and spun him around. The outlaw growled and went for the knife in his belt, but he was no match for the younger man. Quick as a whiplash, the Viking plucked the weapon out of its scabbard and tossed it far out of reach. "I want my money and supplies returned immediately."

Vaghn's virulent curse turned to a whine. "What are you talking about?"

Kolby pushed him up against the door of the mead hall. "While you kept all of us here parleying this morning, some of your thieves went through our luggage. I didn't have time to figure out what was taken, but I want it back."

Vaghn straightened indignantly. "My men didn't take anything. They were all with me."

Kolby bared his teeth in a snarl.

"It's true! I swear!" Vaghn insisted.

Slowly Kolby released him. He was reasonably sure he could believe the man—in this at least. He had suspected all along that his men were being followed, probably by the thieves who had attacked the priestesses. But he had had to make sure. And he had to make Vaghn aware of what was happening without trying to enlist his aid. While there was seldom honor among thieves, Vaghn and his cut-throats wouldn't be anxious to help catch others, unless they saw a clear advantage to doing so, or unless they felt their territory was being invaded.

"Then you need to send some of your men out to see who's sneaking around. Your village could be next."

Vaghn appeared to consider. A sudden look of alarm registered in his hard face. "They didn't get my two pounds of gold, did they?"

Kolby grinned. "What if I said they did?"

Vaghn relaxed. "Then I'd say farewell."

"They didn't get it."

Under Damona's watchful stare, Raven stripped and bathed and cleaned her hair. Out of the corner of her eye, she saw the outlaw woman nod with satisfaction at the sight of the stains on the linen kirtle. She should have brought the torn wimple to use as a washcloth, she thought. It would have served as proof of rape.

She slipped her only other kirtle over her head. Wherever the white linen touched her wet skin, it clung and became transparent, but it was better than nothing. Kneeling on a stone, she began to wash her clothing in the free-running stream. The ice-cold water made short work of the new bloodstains. Unfortunately, Melanthe's blood had been too long neglected. The stains left circles that would show on the garment forever.

When all was as good as Raven could make it, she waded to the bank and slipped into the outlaw woman's dress. Then she walked beside Damona back to the village. For the first time in nine years, she walked with the sun on her head and the wind in her face. Her arms were bare, as was her throat with the marks of Kolby's mouth on her skin. She felt naked. When she turned into the street, outlaw and Northlander alike stared at her. She should be shrinking from their gaze, but what was the point? They had all seen her now. She felt strangely free.

With Damona's help she strung a drying line from one side of the room to the other. Across it she draped the wet clothing. Damona poured them each a drink of ale. Priestesses were forbidden alcoholic beverages, but she shared it willingly with the outlaw woman.

Aren came striding into the house and nodded respectfully. "The lords are parleying. They bid you both come."

Damona rose immediately. "I must go, my lady. Vaghn will want me with him." The way she scurried out made Raven pity her and thank Kolby again for his championing of her. Vaghn must not be an easy man to ride beside if Damona was as fearful as she seemed.

As soon as she was gone, Aren started toward the luggage. "Kolby also sent me to fetch his treasure sacks."

Raven crossed the room and pointed to the floor. "Dig here, sir. Not through our luggage."

In amazement Aren pulled up the plank and found the bags. The muscles in his arm barely flexed as he lifted them. Two pounds of gold was very little really. She wondered what Kolby wanted that it cost so little—or so much.

Raven followed Aren to the door where she leaned against the jamb and watched as he strode toward Kolby, who sat cross-legged in the square before the mead hall. Vaghn sat opposite him in much the same position. Their men lounged nearby. The tension heightened when Kolby's raven circled the gathering and dropped down to perch on top of one blackened timber.

Aren set the two bags in front of Kolby, who hefted each in turn as if demonstrating its weight for Vaghn.

The young man then spread a piece of black leather on the ground, opened the bags, and laid out the contents. First came two shawl clasps of braided gold. Kolby hefted each in his hand and proclaimed them to weigh a half-pound apiece.

Next came a curiously wrought piece such as Raven had never seen before. Always interested in new designs, she drew nearer to study it. It was a circular brooch made of silver with two dragon heads of gold, back to back at its top. A third dragon at the bottom had the brooch pin for his tongue. While it lacked the actual value of the solid gold pieces, the craftsmanship made it worth much more to the right buyer.

Finally Aren produced a double handful of coins, which he passed to Kolby. The lord of Apelstadt tossed them down with a dramatic flourish—a handful of elaborately chased gold pieces each nearly an inch in diameter and with a hook on its rim so the owner could attach them, according to custom, to a thin loop of gold wire or leather around his neck.

Vaghn licked his lips. His eyes shone with avarice. The other outlaws also snapped to attention. Damona leaned forward, her fingers flexed at the sight of the coins sliding across the gleaming leather. If one had landed in the dust, Raven was sure the outlaw woman would have snatched it up.

There was a tense silence. All hands hovered near their weapons. Then Vaghn sighed gustily. "You have brought me worthy treasure."

"I hope the information is as worthy," Kolby replied.

"It is." Vaghn leaned forward, looking more closely at the brooch. "May I?"

"Aye." Through narrowed eyes, Kolby watched the outlaw.

Vaghn picked up the heavy gold and silver piece.

Rolling it around in his hand, he spoke almost as if to himself. "The sacred apple tree is located in the heart of a forestland and is encircled by a huge bramble thicket."

Kolby's hand shot out like a stone. He plucked the brooch from Vaghn's hand. "I know that. All men know that."

Vaghn reached for a shawl clasp but then seemed to think better of it. "I have heard of a man who claims to have seen it."

"Every Scotsman I meet claims to know someone who has seen it," Kolby countered. Disgust curled the corners of his mouth. Off to his left Durin grunted, and he and Kolby exchanged glances.

Midnight Wind cawed again. The shiny bits of gold had attracted his eye. He spread his wings and dived, but Kolby was too quick for him. He waved the big bird away.

"Odin's ravens," he told Vaghn in a deep voice. "They fly everywhere and see the secrets of men. Then they return to perch on their master's shoulders and tell him what he needs to know."

Vaghn turned pale beneath his deeply weathered tan. "That one must not know much," he muttered. "He hasn't told you what you desire."

In the tense silence that followed, Kolby began methodically to stack the gold pieces.

A sigh went from the women. Their men began to growl.

"This man claims to know the very place where it is located," Vaghn insisted. "He saw it when he traveled through the dark forest."

"Why doesn't he himself take the sacred apples?" Durin called scornfully.

"He's a hermit. He has no need of them."

Another tale, Kolby thought wearily, but it was all he had to go on. A curse on this quest, on traveling this cold land rife with warring clans and outlaws. And the presence of the two cloister priestesses, one of them wounded, had more or less trapped him here. With his men he could easily fight his way out of this rabble, but to move helpless women would be impossible.

"Where is this dark forest?" he asked, barely suppressing his skepticism.

" 'Tis in the heart of the badlands." Vaghn reached forward again, this time for a gold coin. He turned it in his fingers, letting the sun glint off it. "Few of us venture into it. Those who do never return."

"A fine superstition," Kolby sneered. "I suppose the dark loch runs through it."

"Well, yes," Vaghn admitted. "But 'tis the truth, I tell you. I have known valiant men who've gone in. None has come out. 'Tis the tree of the Great Mother Goddess that you seek, and she protects it. She's hidden it deep within the cauldron of her body so that evildoers can't desecrate the tree's sacred fruit."

"How will I find this tree?"

Vaghn leaned forward, both hands poised to rake in the gold. His eyes dared Kolby. "I've already given you enough information for the gold you've brought."

Kolby leaned forward too. "You've told me nothing I didn't already know."

The outlaw leader gestured toward where Raven stood beside the oxcart. "Earlier you told me that your greatest desire was to find the sacred tree. Mine is to have the two women. In exchange for them, I'll bring you the man who claims to have seen the tree and is willing to lead you to it."

"No." Kolby never looked in Raven's direction. He didn't need to. He could see her in his mind's eye, growing more beautiful, more desirable with each passing hour. No longer dressed in the enveloping cloister robe, she wore instead the garb of an outlaw woman. A headband bound her forehead and allowed her glorious hair to hang free. An equally colorful band crisscrossed her bodice, drawing the rust-colored tunic tightly around her narrow waist. The soft garment emphasized the gentle flare of her hips. Beneath it her legs were long and shapely. He swallowed hard in an attempt to stem his excitement.

"She's a beautiful woman," Vaghn continued. "But if you think to keep her, you'll have to join our band, my Northland friend. Otherwise, she'll never be yours. All Highlanders know about Raven nea Pryse of Ailean. She's the woman of the Nameless Day—the lady of winter. Most of us belong to one god. She belongs to two—earth and sky—Great Mother Goddess."

Kolby acknowledged the truth of the outlaw's words. As things stood now . . . But if he found the tree and brought the apples to Ura, then he would be as good as any man, and fully worthy of her.

A gust of wind whirled a score of leaves across the street. A golden-red one slid under one of the shawl clasps.

"Autumn is upon us," Vaghn said.

Kolby waited. The man said nothing without a purpose.

"We outlaws have a forgathering each year at this time."

"I've heard of it."

"It's an autumn festival and trade fair that usually lasts about seven days. Most outlaws attend."

Kolby tried to picture such a thing with dozens and dozens of the motley crew about, drinking, gambling, picking fights. "Isn't it dangerous for all of you to gather in the same place at the same time?"

"Aye, but more dangerous if we don't. Each group of outlaws is like a clan." Vaghn warmed to his words as he explained. His eyes flashed, his gestures broadened. "For seven days we agree to put peace before war. It's vital to all of us. 'Tis good if we can settle boundary disputes without war and put our energy to most profitable business."

He leaned forward. "And here, my Northland friend, is where you come in. We exchange information. Not by what we say, because most of us lie anyway."

He looked around him for confirmation. The rest of his band laughed as if he had made a good joke.

"Oh, no," he went on. "But we can tell where the other has been by looking at his goods, at the clothes he wears. We can guess where he's going by the kinds of goods he trades for."

He put his big hand over the gold coins. "It's in the best interest of all of us to attend. The one who has seen the sacred tree will most likely be there." He looked intently at Kolby. "And I'll take you and your Northlanders with us, if you have the stomach for it. For a generous fee, of course."

Durin leaned forward. "It could be a trap."

Kolby shook his head. "The first one sprung in it would be Vaghn."

The outlaw nodded.

"I'm right, am I not?" Kolby said. "If they found you had brought me, they would kill us both?"

Vaghn nodded again. "They're not kind to interlopers."

When Kolby made no move toward the gold, Vaghn began to stack it, arranging the smaller coins on top of the larger ones.

At last Kolby spoke again. "Where do you meet for this forgathering?"

Another sigh went up among the outlaws. The tension eased considerably. One of the women actually laughed.

"The rendezvous point is a secret."

"As is the exact date, I suppose?"

"You suppose right. But if you wish to camp here in this village for a short while, I won't charge you too much." Vaghn looked around him. His band of outlaws laughed appreciatively. He grabbed up the ale bag and tossed it to Kolby. "Shall we drink to seal the bargain?"

"Nay," Kolby replied. "I want to meet the man who claims to have seen the tree, and I also want the two priestesses."

"You drive a hard bargain." Vaghn chewed a blade of grass. "The woman means so much to you."

"Aye."

Vaghn shrugged. "I hate to see our bartering end here."

Kolby looked at the gold disappearing into the outlaw's bag. "Would you consider anything else?"

"I'm a trader." Vaghn spread his arms wide. "I take anything that may turn a profit. That fine horse of yours for instance."

Kolby looked back at Raven's hut and thought of her stolen satchels heavy with cloister jewelry and the holy shawl. He had brought her and Melanthe into his trouble. The least he could do was get them out—with their integrity and possessions intact.

"The outlaws who attacked the priestesses took valuable goods."

"Mayhap cloister jewelry," Vaghn prompted, licking his lips at the thought. He was mightily tempted. Such precious pieces were renowned for their craftsmanship and exquisite design. Of all valuables, they were the most sought after. Vikings and godless outlaws had raided for them for years.

"Aye. Cloister jewelry. Inset with jewels and magical charms and blessed by the ladies of the Shrine of the Great Mother Goddess. Items of incalculable value." Kolby concealed his amusement at his own huckstering. It was one of the skills he had had to learn on this damnable quest. He supposed when he was too old to go a-viking, he could become a merchant. He seemed to have a talent for selling.

"But the thieves are many days from here," Vaghn protested.

Kolby rose and stretched his legs. Aren hurried forward to pick up the square of black leather. "Perhaps. And perhaps not. Remember I told you our luggage was ransacked."

Vaghn's eyes widened. "Do you think—?"

"I do. And I plan this night to slip out of the village and track the thieves."

"In the dark?" Vaghn asked incredulously.

"If the moon is bright, I can track them. I can find the trail. I'll move faster than they will. They may even move in a circle. They know we're all here now, but they're greedy. They know we're bartering." He looked up toward the hills. "They could be sitting up there on a rock right now watching us."

The outlaws looked around warily. A couple of them sprang up, bows at the ready, bent on hunting for those who dared spy upon them.

"Don't be so hasty," Kolby advised. "They killed three men and wounded a fourth, and stabbed a woman who was trying to protect her possessions. These are not simple thieves. I suggest that you all post guards and stay close together. Otherwise, they might decide to strike again."

Damona dropped to one knee beside Vaghn and whispered in his ear. He nodded sagely. "My wife says that there are all manner of wonderful things in the satchels. We should have our pick of anything of value."

"When I get what I seek, they're yours," Kolby promised, thinking that Raven would be furious if she knew he was trading her belongings. But the situation didn't give him much choice. He needed to have done with this and be gone.

Vaghn smiled fondly at Damona. "In that case my wife advises me to accept your offer. The thieves' loot is more valuable to us than the women. With it, we can buy many healthy women."

"Nay, Vaghn," snarled a red-bearded outlaw. "Don't listen to Damona. This is a bad trade. We don't know that any of this is true. What we do know is that the women are here with us now. We've been waiting a long time."

Vaghn grinned. "Patience, Rangwald. Patience. Damona reminded me that slaves will attend the forgathering."

"We've never been able to trade for one there," the outlaw grumbled. "The chiefs of the other bands always have the better items."

"Not at this forgathering," Vaghn declared. "Not if we have jewelry crafted at the Cloister of the Grove." He turned back to Kolby. "Get me the cloister goods, and I'll deliver the man to you."

"One more request," Kolby said. "When I leave, I should like two of my men, Durin and Aren, to leave also and return the women to the other side of the border."

"If we let the women go," Rangwald protested, "we can't ensure that you'll come back."

"You have the information I'm seeking," Kolby replied.

"You could meet with others who have the same, possibly more," Vaghn said. "You could have planned it among you. The three of you make for the border today. The others slip away under cover of darkness. Forget it."

"I have given my word to them," Kolby said.

"I have given mine."

The two men stared at each other, neither willing to trust the other.

"You have authenticated your ownership," Vaghn

said at last. "This is the most important law of the badlands. 'Tis one that every man enforces—or he soon loses all he possesses. No one in my band will violate it. I guarantee your woman's safety."

Kolby stared at him, then looked at the hardened faces of the outlaw band.

"I am an outlaw, Viking." Vaghn's black eyes glittered in his dark face. "But I am a man of my word."

Outlaws and Vikings seemed to shake themselves mentally. Almost to a man they began to move around and gather in small groups to talk among themselves.

Vaghn unplugged the stopper of the ale bag and handed it to Kolby. "Shall we drink to our trade?"

Kolby took the bag but did not lift it to his mouth. His face hard, he stared at Vaghn. "If any harm comes to my women, outlaw, I shall kill every one of you, and I swear you'll go first."

Bradach shuffled closer. "I'll go with you tonight, Lord Kolby. My skills—"

"You'll remain here," Kolby commanded. "You'll be needed as a guide later. I don't need you for this. I'll be following a trail." With that, he held the bag aloft. *"Skoal!"*

His men heard his word and as he drank, they shouted their answer. He passed the bag around to them and then returned it to Vaghn. After several drinks, passing the bag back and forth among themselves, the outlaw said, "You would be wise to trade for two of my horses."

Kolby shook his head. He had seen the outlaw's horses and knew them to be scrawny, windbroken nags. "I'll trust mine. He and I work well together. He's strong enough to carry me."

Vaghn wiped the back of his hand across his mouth. "Oh, he's prettier, I'll grant you that. But he's not bred to our clime." He waved his hand to his own black stallion with a white blaze down its face. "These are Highland horses. They thrive on rough pasture and need little extra feeding. They're first-rate riding ponies, as I'm sure yours is, but they're used to crossing boggy land and climbing mountains. They'll never slide over the cliff with you."

Kolby looked at the black as if he might consider it. In the process of looking it over, he did not miss the swollen hock. A bowed tendon, he suspected.

Thinking Kolby might make a trade for the Northlander's fine horse, Vaghn redoubled his efforts. "If the thieves you're chasing are riding horses like these, you'll be at a disadvantage, Lord Kolby. Theirs can outrun your horses with no trouble."

Not with a leg like that, Kolby thought. The black would pull up lame before he had gone a quarter-mile. "Another time," he said. "This time we have the advantage. They won't know they're being chased."

Vaghn shrugged. He waved his men to gather round. "Now we shall seal our agreement with games."

Games at the end of the parley guaranteed the bargain. While Kolby would rather have begun his pursuit of the cloister thieves, he nodded his willingness to participate. His departure would be an insult to Vaghn, a man whose goodwill he needed, and it might signal to the watchers in the hills—if such there be—that all was not as it should be. He must return quickly if he was to be able to send Raven and her mother safely on their way and continue his own hunt for the sacred tree.

"Games it is," he said, motioning to his men.

"Board games or battle games?" Vaghn asked. He glanced at his men knowingly, and they rumbled their approval. The thought that he might be able to best the Northlanders and demonstrate the superiority of his own men tickled Vaghn.

"You choose," Kolby said equably. "As long as we can wager, we'll enjoy the competition."

The one called Dughald hooted with laughter and waved his bow aloft. The others joined in his cheer. When they had quieted somewhat, Vaghn warned, "My men are good."

Kolby grinned at Durin, who nodded. "You'll need better to defeat mine."

His words proved prophetic, to the chagrin of the outlaws. One after another, they loosed their shafts into a target hung up against the wattle wall of the hut at the end of the street. Though the outlaws did well and managed to put their arrows within the two-inch-wide center of the target, they could not best Kolby's shot.

In one fluid movement, he drew an arrow, nocked it into the string, and let it fly almost without appearing to aim. It struck the target dead center.

A cheer went up from his men and a groan from the outlaws.

Next, Durin sent his battle-axe spinning into a log and split it in two.

None could best the tall Northlanders. The Scotsmen retreated in disgruntled defeat.

But Vaghn called them back together and handed out pieces of Kolby's gold to the winners. As the sun set, all lolled in front of the mead hall, exchanging wagers and boasting of their past feats of glory.

Preferring to sit with her mother, Raven had not joined the Northlanders during their games. But they were over now. The deal was struck. She waited anxiously for Kolby to come to her and tell her that she and Melanthe could leave now.

His shadow blocked the door of the hut. "My lady."

She sprang to her feet. He took her arm. "Walk

with me." He led her out into the sun. "You look worried."

She didn't want to go with him. She knew without a doubt that if he had brought good news, he would have told her. With a sinking heart she allowed him to lead her down the street and away from prying eyes.

When they were out of sight of the mead hall, she turned and gripped his arm. Her eyes were luminous with tears she could barely contain. "I fear Mother Melanthe's getting worse. Now that you and Vaghn have struck your deal, would you please ask two of your men to escort us to the cloister? I'm afraid that if she doesn't return there, she may die."

Kolby shook his head. "I can't. You'll have to wait a bit longer. Your mother can rest and gain strength here just as easily as she can—"

"She cannot!"

The patient and submissive cloister priestess had shed her nature with her clothes. The outlaw woman screamed at him. "She will die! And it will be your fault as much as it is the fault of the thieving murderer who struck the blow. You brought us here because it suited your aims. You care not what happens to us, so long as you find your cursed apples."

He caught her by the shoulders. "I care. You are my responsibility. I couldn't leave you after so many of your guards were killed and your cart damaged. Now you must wait one day more. At the most two. Then I swear—"

"Listen to him, lady." Vaghn had followed them and now he approached. "He has traded the cloister jewelry for your safety. He could have kept it for his own."

"It isn't his to trade," Raven said coldly.

"Nor is it yours at the moment," Vaghn pointed out reasonably. "Since the outlaws have it, it belongs to them."

"Then I'll go with you," Raven declared. "If what you say is true, then I'll find the cloister treasure and buy my way home for my mother and me."

Kolby caught hold of her arm. "You'll do nothing of the kind. You're my property now, as is everything that you own."

She twisted away from him. "I'll go with you. If I don't, you're liable to steal some of it for yourself."

"You'll stay and nurse your mother," Vaghn ordered coldly. "This is man's work."

She shot the outlaw a withering glance. "Don't you tell me what to do."

"Tell her!" Vaghn shouted at Kolby.

Kolby tried for reason. "I can travel much faster without you."

"Am I to be a hostage?" She turned away from them both and stared between the trees at the village street.

"Aye," Vaghn growled. "I want guarantee that the Northlander will return."

"He will," Raven said sarcastically. "Not for me, outlaw, but for the information you have to sell him. And he'll buy it with my gold."

"Too many people are willing to barter for information," Vaghn said. "I'm the only one who'll have the woman he wants."

Kolby waved the outlaw away. He put his hands on Raven's shoulders. "Vaghn will see that no harm comes to you or your mother. 'Tis best. Believe me. Trust me."

She spun around in his arms. "How can I? I've come to believe that you're as much of a thief as anyone in the badlands."

"Raven!"

"Let me go! Let me go!" She chopped the sides of her hands down on his forearms and wrestled free. She turned and ran back to the village.

Kolby stood with his hands on his hips, shaking his

head. He was disgusted with himself. Everything she said was true. And he couldn't guarantee that he would return with the cloister jewelry and the sacred shawl. His eyes blazing, he strode back to the mead hall.

"Saddle my horse," he commanded Durin. "And gather the men. I shall talk to them before I leave."

"When will that be?" Vaghn asked.

"Now," Kolby replied.

"Now!" the outlaw exclaimed. "Surely you can wait until we've feasted and celebrated."

"Nay. The sooner I ride, the sooner I'll find the stolen goods and return."

"It'll be dark before long," the outlaw pointed out.

Kolby was tired of arguing with him. He was a man of action. He wanted to get out of this morass that seemed to be sucking him down, and find the horse's hoofprint that he had seen earlier on the road. It was a print with an odd nick in the hoof; the animal's gait had thrown the hoof off to the side. He knew that horse. And when he looked up, he would see the rider's face—the face of a murderer.

Was it only three days ago that he had seen the print? He could scarcely believe so much had happened since then to set his life awry. He looked toward the hut where Raven undoubtedly paced, angry enough to run her dirk in under his ribs.

He was trying to decide whether to go to her when Durin emerged from the mead hall leading the horse. "The stallion's ready. Packs and victual bags are strapped to the saddle."

"Take them off," Kolby ordered. "I won't be gone that long."

He motioned his men to come close. Gravely he explained what he planned. "Join with the cloister guards and take care of the ladies. They are your first concern."

"Let me go with you," Aren begged.

He shook his head. "This is for me alone. I shall travel swiftly and silently, and be back before I need to eat."

He shook hands with Durin and pulled his friend toward him. For his ears only he said, "If I don't return, find the means to get them both back to the cloister. To stay here would mean the death of them both."

"Aye, sir." Durin gripped his young friend hard.

Kolby led the stallion to the door of the hut. "Lady, I beg you hear me."

Silence.

"I go to fetch your mother's shawl. If it is as important as you say, the gold that pays the freight is a small amount unworthy of consideration."

He heard a rush of footsteps and then Raven burst through the door to clasp his arms. "You didn't tell Vaghn about it."

"I didn't tell him."

She smiled a singularly sweet smile, a secret smile. "Then you'll be doubly and triply repaid. This I swear."

"I don't do it for payment." He took her hand. "I swear to you I have no wish to leave, but I have no choice. I was hoping to take you with me or to see that you were got safely away, but Vaghn wouldn't agree."

At the mention of the outlaw, she grew cold again. "In that case, we must all be patient."

"You are giving in without a fight, my lady," he teased her. For the first time since the bartering had begun, his smile was genuine.

She raised her hand in farewell. "Be sure you return safely."

A tumult of cawing broke them apart. Midnight Wind circled overhead.

"Is someone coming?" Raven asked, alarmed by the raven's noise.

"Probably not." The bird swooped down and lighted on Kolby's shoulder and pecked at his ear. "Nay." He ran his palm over the black back. The feathers glistened in the slanting light of late afternoon. "He's come to roost for the night. He'll be unhappy to be displaced."

She raised her hand to the bird's head. The creature ducked and wove, but finally allowed her to smooth his shiny feathers. "He can stay with me."

Kolby grinned. He couldn't believe she would be so kind to his pet. "Hear that, you beggar? You get to stay with the beautiful lady. I get to ride around in the cold all night long."

He passed the bird to her. Midnight Wind seemed happy to perch on her wrist, where he tucked his head to preen his feathers.

Anxious to be away, the golden stallion tossed its head up and down. The bit jingled.

"Be sure you return safely," she repeated.

"I shall bring your shawl," Kolby promised. "This I swear."

She stepped closer to him. "I want it—for my mother," she whispered, "but more, Viking, I want you to return—unharmed."

Unspoken words trembled between them. They wanted to say so much to each other, but neither spoke. They wanted to kiss each other, to hug each other tightly, but they didn't. She couldn't forget that she was a hostage because of him. He couldn't forget that by rescuing her, he had turned even farther from his quest.

Finally Kolby swung into the saddle. To Durin he said, "Keep all weapons by your side, ready for use."

Man and maiden watched in silence as he trotted the horse down the street into the fast-falling dusk.

Chapter 8

⌒◡⌒

Once within the trees, Kolby began to circle around the village, taking the turn that would lead him closest to the back of the hut where he and his men had spent the night. He had not traveled far when he found the tracks of at least two men, leading to it and then away. The tracks leading away were farther apart and deeper, as if they had been running carelessly now that their purpose was achieved.

Kolby tied the horse's reins to a tree and followed where the tracks led. As shadows lengthened and began to fade, he stooped lower and lower, his eyes searching. Within minutes he found what he sought, what every instinct, fine-honed by years of training and experience, told him to expect. A pair of horses had been tied at this spot. The tracks were many, crossing over and over each other, the ground churned. He followed the tracks that led away. After a couple of quick strides, the riders had sorted the animals out. One followed the other at a trot. Farther on, the trail widened. They galloped abreast.

In the dying light, Kolby saw what he had come to find. A hoofprint with a nick and the peculiar rolling of the hoof that accompanied it. The trail led almost straight up the side of the mountain.

Kolby thrust his fist into the air, aiming at the route

146

they had traveled. Then he spun and dashed back to his own mount.

For nearly an hour he guided the big horse through the thick forest that covered the side of the steep hill. Between the trees over his left shoulder, he would catch occasional glimpses of Loch Ness, lying like a black mirror at the bottom of the glen. The moon reflected like a single eye off its surface.

He did not doubt the thieves lay sleeping somewhere up ahead of him. Probably they'd made camp on top of the ridge where they could look down on the village and watch the goings-on. There they would wait for the chance to slip back down and plunder the women's hut as well. Only their fear that Melanthe might be conscious and give an alarm had kept them from raiding the priestesses' luggage earlier.

He was surprised by their persistence. That very single-mindedness troubled him. Why take the chance of crossing swords with more than a dozen armed men when there might be little left to steal? There were spoils for the taking elsewhere. Kolby wondered what prayers Raven had uttered to keep them nearby.

As he rode deeper, night's velvet cloak settled tightly around him. As he had many time before, he thanked Ura for fostering him with Lord Lang of Ulfsbaer. From him he had learned to blind-fight when he was a young boy. Under the earl's tutelage, his senses had become attuned to sounds and scents, and he had developed a sort of second sight. He didn't have to see to know a person was near.

Blindfolded, he and his fostered brother Michael had fought seasoned warriors with blunted weapons. Although they had not been slashed or stabbed, the lads had been badly bruised and had taken many a tumble before they were able to hear and to feel another person's presence.

A rush of feathers, a slow beating of wings, and Midnight Wind settled on his shoulder. Cawing softly, the bird hopped from Kolby's left shoulder to his right and back again. Kolby found a sparse handful of oat grains in the pocket of his cloak. He offered them to his friend. "What are you doing here, you crazy beggar? I left you safely tucked away for the night with a beautiful lady."

At that moment the stallion snorted and threw up its head. Bird and horse together alerted Kolby to the approach of another horse and rider. Someone was following on the track behind him. A small stand of trees, dense and dark, lay to his right. He reined the stallion off the road into them. Horse, Kolby, and raven were swallowed up in the shadows.

From his hiding place, Kolby focused all his senses on the approaching rider.

The night was so crisp and clear that the clop of the hooves rang clearly. Kolby slipped his bow from his shoulder, and Midnight Wind hopped down onto the stallion's neck.

After sliding off his mount, Kolby moved to the edge of the small thicket. Hidden behind the largest tree, he nocked his bow. As he waited, he studied the area around him. Then, staying in the darkest shadows, he moved around the circle until he stood where he could command both possible entrances to the area.

Suddenly the clop of the horse's hooves ceased. He listened but heard no sound. A chill ran up his spine. He had counted on the rider coming into the clearing unaware that he was being observed. Kolby waited.

Silence.

Then, like an apparition, a robed figure stepped into the small clearing. A dark silhouette. From the outline, it looked as if the rider had a bow slung over one shoulder.

His first thought was that one of his own men had

come after him. A thrill of fear went through him. Had something happened to Raven or her mother? For the priestess's sake, he hoped Melanthe would begin to improve, but perhaps she had taken a turn for the worst.

He hadn't liked the idea of leaving them in Vaghn's camp. Until he had given the outlaws something of great value—the cloister treasure—he would be unable to return them to the cloister without a fight. And they both might be injured, or even die, in an encounter with so many cutthroats.

Kolby watched the figure advance slowly into the clearing. Obviously it too was listening. Kolby didn't dare step out and identify himself. Suppose it was not one of his own men. Snagging his bow on his shoulder and returning the arrow to its quiver, he eased his dagger out of its sheath and slipped through the trees until he stood behind the stranger. He moved in closer. As he went to loop his arm around the intruder's neck, the figure jumped around and pressed the point of a dagger into Kolby's belly.

"I wouldn't if I were you." Raven's voice was harsh and threatening.

Kolby cursed at the realization that he could have been gutted.

"My lady!"

"My lord!" She stepped back.

He shook his head in disgust. He had mistaken the silhouette of her blowpipe for a longbow. "You followed me here when I ordered you to remain. Don't you realize you almost got your throat slit?"

"*Who* almost got slit?" came her mocking retort.

He acknowledged the truth with a grunt. Still angry, he tried a new tack. "I shouldn't be surprised that you followed me," he rumbled. "You've disobeyed or questioned every order I've ever given. But why did you act surprised? Weren't you looking for me?"

"Oh, aye," she replied cheekily, "but I thought you'd be harder to find."

She was teasing him, but her point was well-taken. He had not treated her with the respect she deserved. "How did you escape?"

"Damona helped me," Raven answered. "She agreed that you would need someone to help you—to guard your back trail. Obviously, we were right."

This time he actually growled.

"Oh, don't worry that I'll be missed. Damona promised not to report my disappearance until morning."

"Vaghn will be angry."

"So I told her. But she told me that parleying for peace with him is half the fun for her. She knows a man needs a woman even more than he thinks he does."

Kolby choked over these words. They revealed a side of Raven that was neither imperious priestess nor frightened girl. He had to lower his voice in an effort to make it stern. "Did you think how your escape will affect the safety of my men and your mother?"

"Damona said she'd explain to Vaghn. Because I left Melanthe with him, he would understand that I simply wanted to be with my man."

He laughed shortly. "Well, my lady, thanks to your efforts, you'll be *with your man*."

She laid a hand on his arm. A ray of moonlight illuminated her face. "Don't be angry."

"I'm not angry," he admitted. "What man would be angry to have a woman dare danger to be with him on a dark night in the depths of the forest? I'm frustrated."

"Because I'll slow you down."

"Nay, because you may be in danger."

"I won't," she assured him. "I can be a great help against the thieves."

As he took her arm to guide her back to his horse, his lips brushed against her ear. "Thieves may not be the greatest danger you have to face in the dark forest, lady."

She shivered.

He swung into the saddle and offered his arm to swing her up. When she was settled safely behind him, he started off at a slow pace. "How far back is your horse?"

"A little ways." It was the most natural thing in the world to put her arms around his waist. Her chin brushed his shoulder. "When I no longer heard you moving about, I decided to travel by foot. It's much quicker on foot among trees than it is by horse. Of course, I had to go quietly. There was always the danger you'd think I was one of the outlaws and shoot me."

"I never shoot someone I don't know," he told her dryly.

"I brought my blowpipe," she told him eagerly, like a child hoping for his approval. "Even though I couldn't make a poison potion."

"Your blowpipe isn't much of a weapon then, is it?"

"I wouldn't mind learning how to use a longbow," she admitted ruefully. "Perhaps you could teach me."

"Perhaps." What he wanted was to get her on her own horse, so her breasts wouldn't press against his back and her arms wouldn't hug him so warmly around the middle.

"Are you going to let me ride on with you?"

He sighed heavily. "Have I a choice, lady?"

"Nay." She knew she had won. She laughed and squeezed him a little harder. His manhood leaped to life.

He heard the smile in her voice and smiled himself despite his discomfort. Pleasing her gave him pleasure, even if she might present a problem later on. He was glad for her company, but he wondered how she had escaped Vaghn's camp. Despite what she believed to be Damona's cooperation, he wondered if this was some trap set by the outlaw.

They circled back to her horse. To his astonishment he found she had stolen Durin's Roman-nosed steed. The gelding was Durin's pride, as stubborn and hard to turn as his master. Kolby smiled at the thought of Durin's anger when he discovered the theft. The air would be blue with curses.

Kolby transferred Raven to her own saddle, and soon they were threading their way through the forest. Following the thieves' trail was slow going as the tall trees thinned out and the underbrush grew thicker. Since their voices carried far in the stillness, they spoke in low tones.

"How were you planning to get the satchels back?" she asked.

"By the simplest way." He rode bent over the cantle, his gaze on the ground. "I'll steal them. And then we'll run for Vaghn's village before they catch us."

"Slip into the camp and take them?" Amazement rang in her voice.

"Seems the easiest way to me. If they have other bags of loot, they might not even know they're gone until much later."

"If they have other bags of loot, you might not be able to find ours," she pointed out.

The moon was directly overhead now, the tracks of at least four horsemen clear in its light. After a moment's silence, she asked another question.

"Are you going to wait in the village for Vaghn and his outlaws to take you to the forgathering?"

"Aye, lady, I must. I must have the information he swears someone there can give me. I must fulfill my quest."

"Is this something you *must* do or something you *want* to do?"

"Both. I owe a debt of gratitude to Ura of Apelstadt, my benefactor and my liege. He was the man who gave me hope as a small boy. Therefore I've pledged to fulfill his desperate request."

Raven's tones were hushed, almost as if she spoke to herself. "We're both trapped by pledges to people we love and respect. But the pledges set our lives on paths other than those we would have chosen."

"Aye, you of all people know about such things." He remembered her impassioned tale of rejection by the man who should have been her husband, and of her family's subsequent shame. Like him, she had been thrust will-she, nill-she on such a path.

"Tell me how your pledge came about."

"I've carried my burden for what seems a long time now," he admitted slowly, "although it has not been nine years. When I was a small child, no more than four or five winters, Ura bought me from a slave trader."

"You were a slave!" Her royal blood and breeding instantly recoiled from him. Then her humanity mastered and buried those feelings.

"Aye," he whispered.

She hoped her incredulity had not embarrassed him. "You've risen far," she said lamely.

"Aye, but not far enough. Ura was a hard man, but he was just. He freed me and raised me as a member of his family."

"Ah. We perform such adoption ceremonies in Scotland. Your father must be very generous."

"He freed me," Kolby repeated, "but he didn't adopt me. When I came of age he fostered me to Lord Lang, the Earl of Ulfsbaer."

"Without a name, how could you be fostered?" Raven asked. "You—you must have a name. Else you would be—*dicenn*." She shook her head as the hopelessness of the situation struck her. "I know you have a name. I saw a mark—your mark—on your pack."

"Aye, lady, *my* mark, but not my family's mark. Ura and Lang fostered me out of their friendship for each other. During the years I spent with Lord Lang, he came to respect and like me. His son Michael and I became fast friends and foster brothers. Five years ago, I accepted the war dagger from Michael and sailed with him to the Highlands to avenge a wrong done to him and his father."

"I heard about that," she admitted. "You were right and just to do so. But you remained after Michael had avenged the shame and married the queen of Glen-muir?"

"Aye. I had come to think I might make my home here. Then Ura sent a message ordering me to return to Northland immediately. When I arrived, I found him dying."

"I'm sorry." She reined Durin's horse in close to the stallion and laid her hand over Kolby's. It was a gesture she had longed to make many times as a priestess, to console a penitent or a patient. But as a sequestered celibate, she had been forbidden to touch anyone in such a fashion. Now she did it with such naturalness that she wondered at herself. How easily such strictures had slipped away from her. Now she touched him with no guilt for having violated her vows. She wanted to touch him in other ways—this virile man who sent blood rushing through her body, who made her acutely aware of her femininity. Hastily she drew back.

"When I returned home, I didn't recognize my lord's steading," Kolby said bleakly. "It lay in ruins. Although it was spring, the plants and animals were wasting away. Many of the buildings lay in shambles. The Great House was in need of repair. The apple orchard—" He broke off and swallowed hard. "Ura and his wife, Nanna, had a large apple orchard that spread over many acres. It was Ura's pride and joy."

"Your liege sounds more like a keeper of the land than he does a warrior."

"He was both. It was he who taught me to love and honor the land. His sons, however, wanted nothing to do with his gardens and orchards. They wanted to loot and plunder. They were greedy men who argued continuously over which one would inherit the estate. One night when they were all drunk, they burned the fruit trees. They destroyed their own inheritance. In the end the three of them killed one another."

"Dear Heaven!" Raven murmured. "Brother murder is the most damnable of sins."

"Aye, Hel gathered them all up in one fell swoop and dragged them down."

They rode in silence, each thinking of the tragedy that had befallen the good old man.

Then Kolby shook himself out of his dream. "Ura's warriors saw this as an omen of the gods. They deserted him in a body and swore their allegiance to other lords."

"All except you," Raven guessed. "You were the only one to whom Ura could turn for help."

"Nay, he went first to his grandchildren," Kolby said. "He swore that the man who avenged his dishonor would inherit his estate. But his grandchildren wanted no part of revenge. With no love for him or the land, they sailed to other parts of Northland and went a-viking with men they considered greater warriors than Ura."

"A blighted clan," Raven muttered.

"Only then did my liege send for me."

They crossed a shallow pool of water where they could stop and let their horses drink.

"Ura wanted to adopt me," Kolby said, "and give me his name. The gods had smiled at me. My greatest desire was to have a name, no longer to be *dicenn*. I would belong to a clan. No. It would be *my* clan. The clan of the raven. I would be the chieftain and all my children would make up its sept."

As if he had heard his name, Midnight Wind dropped down out of nowhere and perched on Kolby's shoulder. His feathers brushed the Northlander's cheek. Then Kolby sent him on his way and returned his eyes to the ground. The tracks were clear in the soft sand.

"But first I had to perform a task," Kolby said. "It was one that would have the blessing and direction of the goddess Idunn, or so the priests tell us."

"Idunn. Who is she?"

"Ura knows her well, or so he says. She is the sister of Odin, the All-seeing. She tends the sacred apple tree of the gods. Its fruit supposedly keeps the gods young. She appeared to Ura in a vision and instructed him to send a golden warrior to find this tree. When he arrives, he is to pick no fewer than twenty apples and bring them back to Apelstadt. From them the warrior is to make a magical apple wine for Ura to drink. This wine will make him well. Then the warrior is to plant the seeds so they will heal the land."

"Ura believed you are the golden warrior?"

"Aye. He believed all I have told you."

"And do you believe it?"

He shrugged. "Enough to take its direction and try to make an old man happy."

"But this is truly marvelous." Raven laughed joyously. "For this, you will be adopted and given a name? You'll have an inheritance."

"Aye, but there's more," he added quietly. "Ura stipulated that, as the future heir to Apelstadt, I must marry."

Raven felt a cold chill settle in her belly. She didn't

want to think about Kolby's marrying. She didn't want to think about never seeing him again. "That comes to most of us sooner or later," she whispered. "My father heartily regrets his championing of Gwynneth and thrusting me into the cloister. More and more, he tries to persuade me to leave it and marry. He wants a grandchild who will inherit the high seat of Aliean."

"If you marry, you will marry a man of his choosing." Kolby's heart pounded as he awaited her reply. How quickly he had come to think of Raven as his woman!

"No. I may choose, but Father says my choices are limited. Many of the eligible men will turn me down, considering how old I am."

"How old *are* you?"

"A man should never ask a woman her age," she chided him. "However, I will tell you since you see me only as a priestess. "I'm twenty-and-nine."

"That's old for bearing your first child," he admitted. "But Nanna bore Ura's youngest son at thirty-and-nine."

"As a sequestered celibate, I won't be bearing any children."

The statement fell like an iron wall between them. Kolby knew a moment's pain. He could imagine Raven growing large with child, their child. He had often gazed at his friend's wives when they were pregnant. They had a glow about them that he thought beautiful. Had his mother looked like that when she carried him? Would a wife of his have this same glow if she were carrying his child? What would a child created by him and Raven look like? Would it be dark or fair? He knew such a babe would be high-spirited.

Kolby's fantasies carried Raven with him to Apelstadt, rebuilding the houses, planting the gardens and the orchards. She, who had been a keeper of the land, would love to see them grow. He saw her standing on the shore eagerly awaiting his return from his voyages.

But all this could never be.

He shoved those thoughts sternly from his mind. "Ura wanted me to choose a maiden so I could solemnize the betrothal before I left Northland. I refused. I told him I would wait until I returned with the sacred fruit. He could adopt me then and I would marry as befitted his true son."

Kolby remembered Ura's warning: *You must marry a woman of my choice, Kolby, one of the Northland, or you will not inherit. You will not have a name.*

"I hope you find the apples," Raven said. "I have heard many wondrous things about them. We priestesses of the Cloister of the Grove make our own replicas of our goddess's apples. In the olden times Cliodna, a fair goddess of the Otherworld, presented a silver branch of golden apples to a fallen hero. Around her shoulders flew three birds which then began to feed upon those apples. They sang so sweetly that they soothed the hero to sleep. When he awoke, his wounds were healed."

"A silver branch with three golden apples. Like the one you held above the altar on Nameless Eve," Kolby said.

"Aye. You saw my version of the *craebh ciuil*. I suppose all the goddesses possess them as well. When the Great Mother Goddess wields hers, it makes sweet music that inspires joy. The fruit from our orchard is sweet and healthy, and its juice can be made into a wine that links mortals directly with the goddess. It heals the sick and causes people to sleep. 'Tis said that in the hands of a deserving person, the magical branch with its cluster of apples can become a protective spear."

"I suppose the sacred apples of Idunn could give

youth to an old man if he was lucky enough to eat them. Of course, they're only food for the gods."

His bitter tone disturbed Raven. In the stillness of the night she couldn't conceal her concern any longer. "Why do you not believe?"

He reared up straight in the saddle. She could see the pale oval of his face in the darkness.

"Why do you not believe?" she repeated. "Every one of us—Highlander and Northlander—believes in gods and goddesses that seem to be very much the same. I daresay even the Christians have some sort of belief about magic apples. If so many people believe them, they must be real."

His voice had a hard edge. "Many people believe, but none can speak from experience. You tell me all about the sacred apple tree, but have you ever seen it?"

Regretfully she had to admit she hadn't. All the same, she wished she could tell him about the sacred shawl and what its bells told. But that was Melanthe's secret. She could not betray the Chosen One.

"And you are high priestess of the Cloister of the Grove. Surely you would be one whom the gods—"

"Don't." She reached out and caught hold of his arm. "Don't use my position as an excuse not to believe. I am not so virtuous."

"You are as virtuous a woman as any I've ever met. It must be legend. A tale."

"Nay." Her nails dug into the tender skin on the inside of his elbow. "'Tis real."

"Then, madam," he said in his most formal voice, "since the Great Mother Goddess is your personal goddess and she owns a real apple tree, can you not make supplication to her? I want only twenty of her apples to save my foster father's life. I'll not harm her tree in any way. And her gods don't need those apples to stay young as the Northland gods need Idunn's."

Kolby's plea, though uttered in a bitter, cynical tone, tugged at Raven's heart. She didn't know where the sacred tree actually was, but if they found the shawl, she would have access to the information. How ironic that he thought the cloister gold was more important! He was rescuing the shawl merely as an act of personal commitment. She thought she could see the plan of the Great Mother Goddess in this strange adventure.

Kolby had rescued her and Melanthe from the thieves. He had saved her from Vaghn's outlaws. Now he was helping her retrieve the sacred shawl that in all likelihood would lead the way to the sacred tree he sought.

Like all novitiates, she had taken a vow to protect the sacred apple tree. Yet only the Chosen Ones knew where it was located. Only they knew the way through the thorny brambles that protected and hid it from the eyes of greedy mankind. They gathered once a year to prune the brambles and to pick the yellow apples, a specific number of which were sent to each grove cloister. Many of the seeds were planted in their orchards. Others were pulverized for use in their medicinal potions.

"The Cloister of the Grove is surrounded by apple trees," Raven told him, her heart saddened because she couldn't help him. "The fruit has been blessed and is the choicest in the land. You are welcome to pick some. I shall give you our recipe for making our special wine, and you can replant your orchards in Apelstadt."

"In his vision Ura saw—"

"I know what he saw, but he won't know the difference. This orchard was started with seeds from the sacred tree, so in a way it too is sacred. They could save his life, Kolby, and if they do, they will be the miracle apples you are searching for."

"I would know the difference," he replied. "I must continue my search for the sacred apples. Only the apples of Idunn can save Ura and the land." Only they could give him a name. Only then would he feel entitled to the steading.

"For a man who doesn't believe in the gods, you certainly behave in godly ways."

He grunted and got down off the horse to search the ground. The terrain had grown steeper, the ground rocky. Their horses' hooves rang loudly in the night. "I'll go on alone," he told her. "You stay with the horses. I'll be back—"

She was already swinging down from the saddle. "We'll tie the reins to that bush," she contradicted. "I'll go with you. Two can search through thieves' loot twice as fast as one."

He opened his mouth to argue, then shrugged. "Be sure you keep up."

She grimaced at his back as he led the way of the trail. A fog began to rise among the rocks. "My lord, earlier today you asked me to put my trust in you. Tonight I'm asking you to do the same."

In the moonlight she saw his broad shoulders lift, but he didn't say anything.

"Have no more dealings with Vaghn and his outlaws. They don't know where the sacred tree is, nor do I believe they would meet anyone who did. Keepers of the land don't attend forgatherings of breakers of the laws of god and man. Vaghn will gladly accept the treasure in exchange for useless information—or offer a string of excuses as to why he has no information at all."

Kolby knew she was right, but it was the only hope he had. "Aye, lady. That is a risk I take. Unless you, who claim that the tree exists, can tell me where it is."

"I can't." She balked at telling him about

Melanthe. "But I have access to people who do. As soon as we return to the cloister, I'll go to the High Council of all the Druids. I'll tell him of your father's dream. I'll explain your quest. Since I am the high priestess of the cloister, they will do as I ask."

He snorted skeptically. "I'm sure they would be pleased to help a Viking."

"You have much more chance with them than with outlaws."

"Thank you for wanting to help me," Kolby said, "but I doubt they will reveal their secret."

"We can but try, my lord. If they refuse my request, I shall take it to the Ancient of Days and Nights, the High Druid priest, Sholto. I am determined on this." When Kolby didn't answer, she begged harder. "Please, my lord, consider it. You'll be much less likely to get a dirk between your ribs."

"I'll consider it." They rode a ways before he cleared his throat. "Lady, I know Lady Gwynneth well. She is a fair and honorable person. Why would your sister allow disgrace to fall upon you by wedding your betrothed?"

Raven had wondered the same thing herself. She could only believe that a combination of impetuous youth, the instinctive jealousy of a younger sister for an older one, and Alba's handsome face and persuasive powers had effected such a betrayal. Ordinarily she never talked of the broken betrothal without great pain, but now she found she didn't have the slightest apprehension. The golden warrior who sought a miracle had worked a miracle with her.

"When Alba O'Illand arrived from Eire, I was beside myself with joy, but he took an instant dislike to me. He crushed my happiness when he told me that he had fallen in love with my beautiful younger sister."

Kolby muttered a curse.

"I think she fell madly in love with him at first sight."

"The Lady Gwynneth I remember would have given him a knife in the ribs, or set her wildcat on him."

"Aye, now. But then she was very young. I was furious and ill with my own humiliation. I thought I could persuade him to love me. He didn't allow either of us the opportunity for love. To my disgrace, Gwynneth persuaded my father to break my betrothal to Alba. The two of them were wed."

"But you were the firstborn. The heir to the high seat," Kolby exclaimed incredulously. "Why would your father heap such shame upon you?"

"Gwynneth was the child of his heart. Her mother died when she was a wee babe. He and I raised her. We loved her, Lord Kolby. Later we brought Melanthe to be her tutor. She too fell deeply under Gwynneth's spell. All three of us spoiled her. We gave her whatever she wanted, and she grew up accustomed to taking without thinking of the consequences."

Raven's throat swelled painfully at the memory of Gwynneth's thoughtless cruelty. "She grew up quickly and painfully, so I heard. Her marriage to Alba ended in disaster on their wedding night. He proved to be a cruel man. He drank too much and beat her."

"At least you were spared that," Kolby commented.

"Aye. He would have maimed her for life, possibly even killed her, but her Highland wildcat sprang upon him and clawed him fiercely. Later my sister received a bill of divorcement, but judgment went against her. The assembly believed Alba when he accused her of claiming to be a virgin when she was not. They judged she was his property and he could punish her as he deemed fit. Rather than accept the judgment, she demanded to be outcast. My precious sister outcast."

"She did you and your whole family a great wrong," Kolby pronounced.

"Aye, but she did an even greater wrong to herself. Her shame was lifted only when Alba died. For a long while I was angry with her and refused to see either her or my father."

"And has that changed now?"

"Oh, aye. We've forgiven each other," Raven said. "When my father and I made amends, he thought I would leave the cloister. He was disappointed and angry when I refused." She sighed. "'Tis not easy to leave the cloister once you have joined it. He found that out to his sorrow."

After a moment's silence, Kolby said, "Like your sister, you became an outcast when Alba rejected you."

Surprised, Raven stopped dead in her tracks. "Nay. I'm not an outcast."

"I say you are. By law the assembly banished Gwynneth. By choice you banished yourself to a cloister."

"My father accuses me of hiding there," she admitted stiffly. "But I am not. As you have chosen to be a warrior, I have chosen to be a Dryad priestess."

"But you don't like the life."

"I do."

"My lady." His deep voice sent thrills down her spine. "I have kissed you and brought you to a woman's pleasure. You are ill-suited for the life of a celibate."

She halted in mid-stride. Thank the Goddess for the darkness. He could not see the flush rising to her cheeks. "A lord of good breeding would not remind me of that."

As if to forestall their argument, Midnight Wind

dropped down on Kolby's shoulder and plucked at the brooch that held his cloak together.

"He's looking for grain," Kolby said.

Raven's own stomach growled at the thought of food. "Should we stop for him to eat?"

Kolby laughed. "We don't have to stop for him, but we can stop for you and me."

She heaved a sigh of relief. "I couldn't climb another step. The way is steep and—"

"And cloister priestesses are not used to traveling for long distances on foot," Kolby finished for her.

They dropped down together in the middle of the trail, their backs against a huge boulder, their legs stretched out in front of them. From a pocket in his cloak, Kolby produced an oatcake, which he passed to Raven. "'Tis short rations," he apologized. "I didn't plan for you to accompany me."

Midnight Wind hopped from Kolby's shoulder onto Raven's lap. Surprised, Kolby stared at the bird. "He's never done that before."

"I have a way with animals." She brushed her hand over the bird's feathers. The raven turned his head and rubbed against her. "Melanthe claims it is because I was born on the Nameless Day."

"Did you name yourself when you entered the cloister?"

"My mother chose it for me," Raven replied. "She was so frightened to have given birth to a daughter of the night that she did everything she could to protect me. She invoked one of the holiest and most powerful birds to be my namesake. Then she performed a ritual that protects me and binds me to the Highlands, to its land, its water, its air, its sky. All gods and goddesses must safeguard me because I serve them as a keeper of the land. I cannot leave Scotland without risking death."

Midnight Wind pecked gently at her fingertips. Happy with this moment, Raven didn't want to cloud it with thoughts of her vows and oaths. She had loved talking to Kolby. He had proved to be so much more than a warrior. She found so much in him to love.

She directed her next statement to the bird. "I have a raven. Black Night. She's about your size."

Kolby looked interested. "How did you get her?"

"When I was gathering herbs, I found her wounded in the woods. Of course, I had to rescue her."

"Because she was a raven."

"Because she was hurt and needed help."

"Why don't you travel with her?" Kolby asked.

"She's safe at home. I crafted a large golden cage for her. She has her own great hall and high seat." She smiled tentatively. "I've even created her own jewelry, a delicate ring for her right claw and a delicate gold chain that attaches it to my cloak."

"How can you bind her with cage and chain? She's a creature of the wind," Kolby protested.

"I love her, so I protect her," Raven argued.

Kolby saw the similarity between Raven and her bird. Both were beautiful creatures of the wild. Both were in cages of different kinds. "Ravens belong to the gods and to the forest. They should be set free, not locked up."

"The cage is large," she explained defiantly. For the first time, she felt guilty about Black Night. "She has plenty of room to move about. The chain is quite delicate. She seems to be content with our arrangement." She paused and yawned widely. "I love her. I wouldn't harm her for the world. Nor could I bear to lose her."

Catching her yawn, Kolby opened his cloak and drew her under it. "We'll sleep for an hour." When she started to protest, he shook his head. "They can't be too much farther ahead. The rest will refresh our senses for what we must do."

He was a good man. So generous, so caring. She

snuggled against him, hearing the warm thrum of his heart close to her ear. Unthinkingly she placed her hand on his chest.

"My lady," his deep voice rumbled. "If you keep your hand there, I won't rest." He paused significantly. "And neither will you."

Abruptly the warm camaraderie they had been sharing ended. Raven stared into the darkness before her, frighteningly conscious of the physical man who held her. He was a mystery. She had never realized a man could be fierce and gentle, a warrior and a keeper of the land, a brother who would offer a cloak and a lover who would lay her down upon it. In her heart she knew that she and Kolby of Apelstadt could never share a simple friendship.

In the beginning she would have insisted that what she felt toward him was priestly charity. But to make that claim now would be a lie. What she felt for her golden warrior was desire, all-encompassing, all-consuming. She wanted to mate with him, to be with him always.

Feeling the heavy weight of her calling, as she had frequently during the past two days, she crossed her arms over her chest and leaned back against his arm. But she didn't sleep. Tired as she was, as much as her body ached, her heart ached more. Her orderly life had collapsed around her and her contentment with the cloister was lost forever.

To lie down with him, she realized, would mark a new beginning. She hugged herself tightly as another chill made her shiver.

"You're going to need your rest." Kolby's voice came softly out of the darkness.

"I thought you were asleep."

"How could I be with you quivering like a leaf?"

"I'm tired." She tried to excuse herself. "I'm not accustomed to climbing mountains in the middle of the night."

"Aye. Or being haggled over during the day."

She took a deep breath before she whispered the next sentence. "That's not all that's keeping me awake."

He said nothing.

She looked up at him, but his face was in darkness, the moon over his left shoulder.

"I'm thinking how much my life has changed since I met you."

"Aye, lady, so has mine."

"We've only known each other a few days. Hours really. You lust for my body, but you don't like me very much, do you?"

He considered his feelings. Better not to reveal them. Their vows had set them forever on different paths. "I desire you," he confessed. "I have ever since I saw you at the high grove altar. Most of the time I like you well enough. You can be presumptuous and arrogant—beyond everything that's right for a female. As well as obstinate and high-handed."

"I understand," Raven replied. "I feel the same way about you."

"Soon I shall return you and your mother to the cloister, and life as you knew it will resume."

"I shall return to the cloister, but not to life as I knew it. Now that I've met you, I'm no longer innocent. I know what my body wants." She shivered again.

His arm tightened around her as he sought to soothe her. "After I'm gone, I'll become a memory that will grow dimmer with each day that passes."

She turned in his arms, placing her hand on his chest again. This time she didn't take it away even when she felt him suck in a quick breath. "Before I met you, my life was centered on the cloister. I had no doubts about who I was or what path I had chosen. Now I'm desperately confused."

"You've experienced desire," he agreed. "I should

be sorry for that, but I'm not. No man who is a man could be sorry."

"You've experienced it before, haven't you?" she asked.

"Aye, lady. I haven't lived a sequestered or celibate life."

She slumped back against his arm. Her hand fell into her lap. "Even if I should leave the cloister, we have no future together. Our life threads are woven so that each of us is bound to his own land, my lord."

"I fear that's true." His chest heaved again.

Staring into each other's faces, they moved at the same time, closing the distance between them.

"My lord." She raised her hand and touched his cheek.

"My lady." He took her face between his palms and brushed his fingertips over her cheeks, her temples. "My lord, my lady," he mocked. "Viking. Priestess. Say rather nameless bastard and elder daughter of the high king."

She sucked in her breath on a sob.

He curled a strand of her hair around one of his fingers. "Do you realize that since we've met, we've not called each other by name?"

"Aye, my lord. Kolby," she whispered. "Kolby. Kolby." She wrapped her arms around him and snuggled her cheek against his chest.

Folding her in his arms, he laid his cheek on top of her head. "Raven."

Needing and wanting comfort more than passion, wishing they could undo what the fates had done to them, they held each other. They rubbed each other's backs. They twined their fingers in each other's hair.

"Kolby." She pulled back to stare into his night-shadowed face. "Kolby of Apelstadt. From the moment I saw you at my high grove altar, I thought you were the most handsome man in all the world."

"Raven. Raven nea Pryse of Ailean. My little raven.

From the moment I saw you I thought you were the most beautiful, desirable woman in the world." Her hair slid like silk through his fingers.

She had never felt such joy as she did to hear him call her name. At the same time she realized that he had no *son of* to add to his name. It was a great grief among both their peoples to be nameless. It grieved her to think how much he desired a family and a clan. Had Ura not had the foresight to foster Kolby to a Northland earl, people would have believed he was *dicenn.* Since he had friends and a fostered brother in lofty positions, no one questioned him.

"If I am adopted," Kolby said, as if he read her mind, "I shall be called Kolby Urassonn."

"You will find the apples," she promised, tempted more than she had ever been to reveal the secret of the bells on the shawl. "I know you will."

"Aye." Kolby smiled at her.

"Once you are adopted and have your name, you will visit our cloister. I shall call you Kolby Urassonn of Apelstadt in Northland." She chuckled. "My tongue will grow tired from saying it."

"More than anything else in the world, my sweet Raven, I want to hear you say it."

"I shall," she promised.

"Now, no more talk." He tucked her head against him. "Go to sleep. An hour and we must be up. We must find their camp before light."

Obediently she closed her eyes, but she didn't sleep. She thought of Kolby, of the man she cared about—the man she loved. She could never have him. Even if she abjured her vows, abdicated her position as high priestess, and left the cloister, they were each keepers of far distant lands. She was bound to Scotland and the Great Mother Goddess. He, to the Northland and Ura, his benefactor and his liege.

Chapter 9

"**M**y lady."

Raven felt the warmth of Kolby's hand on her shoulder. He shook it gently. Groggily she opened her eyes and looked into his face. Gazing into those wonderful amber eyes, she smiled. "My lord."

"We've overslept."

She realized that the bright light of day warmed them. "Oh. I'm so sorry. This was all my fault."

He glared down at her, mock-accusing. "Indeed it was. You promised not to slow me down and here you've made me lose half a night."

She looked so truly stricken that he couldn't bear to tease her any longer. "Though we may be very hungry before we return to Vaghn's village, I'm glad. I've wondered what you would be like when you first awakened." He brushed his hand through her hair, lifting the weight of it, holding it in his palm, letting it flow through his spread fingers.

She remembered that was one of the last things he had done the night before. She guessed that he was fascinated by black hair since he came from a land where nearly all the people were blond.

"What do you think I look like?" she murmured.

"You're beautiful, lady."

"You're blinded by the morning sun," she teased him. "The last thing I am in the morning is beautiful."

He had finger-combed his hair, but it was still tousled. It softened the angular hardness of his face. His eyes were warm, less wary than Raven had ever seen them. The beard that stubbled his face added strength to his features. He wasn't so beautiful, but he was much more dear.

"I had despaired of seeing you when you first awakened," she said. "You are the object of my delight. Yesterday when I saw you, you had been to the stream to bathe. You were half-naked. You disturbed me terribly with your masculinity."

He ducked his head as if her frank admission had embarrassed him. A hint of red stained his sharp cheekbones.

"'Tis a practice I began long ago when I started a-viking. When we travel, whether by land or sea or both, we must take advantage of the daylight. We're up early in the morning and travel as late as we can."

"You must love the sea," she murmured, a hint of regret in her voice. She hadn't set foot on a deck in nine years.

"Aye, lady, there is no greater pleasure in the world than standing on the deck of a ship. The snap of the wind in the sails, the taste of brine on your lips. A horizon that stretches on forever. The sunrise and sunset." He paused. "Have you never sailed with your sister?"

"Never. My duties were at the cloister. I never had cause to travel with her." It was her turn to duck her head. "I don't think she would have wanted me along anyway. When I say we have forgiven each other, I don't mean we are close friends."

He ignored the last comment. "One doesn't have to

have cause to travel," he said softly. "'Tis something you could do because you wanted to."

"Not a cloistered priestess." She saw his face darken. "But now I want to, Kolby. I want to desperately."

"Then, my lady, I promise that one day I'll take you sailing on my ship."

"Tell me about it."

Raven listened as he talked about his longship, the *Morning Star*. She imagined the brilliant display of shields as he sailed victoriously into port, the banners that unfurled from the mast, the sail tightly billowed with wind. She could imagine him at the rudder, steering his ship, shouting orders to his men, leading them to great victories and wondrous prizes. She tantalized herself until she wanted to cry.

She gulped back pain. "It sounds so adventurous, my lord."

"Always. There's always something new to see. A new land. A new invention. New faces."

"Where is your ship now?"

"Three of my warriors have it moored in a small harbor in Glenmuir."

"Soon you'll be marching to it," Raven said, "bearing the twenty sacred apples and looking forward to your new life."

He smiled and caught a leaf as it wafted down from the tree above them. "If you and I don't get on the move, I won't."

Raven loved to see him smile; it changed his entire countenance, made him seem more accessible and understanding, more the man of the house and of the field rather than the warrior. Suddenly she had a vision of a child. A small boy with white-blond hair holding up his arms to Kolby. The Northlander lifted him high on his chest. The child laughed and looked over his shoulder—at her. His eyes were brown. Dark, dark brown. Like hers.

Kolby pulled her to her feet and pointed her toward a narrow stream of water that bounded from stone to stone in a white cascade. "Make haste. We need to be on the move as quickly as we can."

As she followed him to the bank, despair settled over Raven. Kolby moved off in the opposite direction. She supposed he was going to bathe, but the water looked too cold and swift and shallow for her. She stared into its rushing depths, trying to read the future. The child. The child. How she wanted that child to be hers.

Ceasing to be a keeper of the land would be virtually impossible. Three holy women had accepted her vows: Mother Barbara, a priestess of the Cloister of the Grove; Mother Feich, a priestess who was also a seer and healer as well as Brian mac Logan's foster mother; and her own mother, Melanthe, Ancient One of the Cloister of the Grove and now a Chosen One among Dryads. All had been present to accept her vows; all had helped her support the insupportable in her retreat from the world.

She would have to ask each one in turn to release her. It wasn't possible. She couldn't face them and ask to leave the place that had given her sanctuary and lifted her up when she was in disgrace.

A sadness settled over Raven as she thought about her mother. How grievous was the wound? Had it become infected? Was Melanthe even now tossing with fever, calling for her daughter? She shouldn't be here with Kolby. She *wouldn't* be here, except that the sacred shawl with the inscribed bells loomed larger in importance than it ever had before. Not only her mother's, but now her beloved's fate depended on its return to the cloister.

Farther downstream, she heard splashing. Kolby must be completing his ablutions. He was infinitely

braver than she. When she dipped her hands in the
water to wash her face, her fingers went numb. The
water must be well below freezing. She dried herself
and strolled downstream in the direction her warrior
had taken.

The water leaped over a boulder. She went around
it and found a pool. And there she saw him. Seem-
ingly oblivious to the cold, he rolled and splashed in
the water like a dolphin. Morning light gleamed on
his wet hair, which was slicked back from his face. It
glimmered on his face and shoulders. Steam rose off
his skin. Then he rolled over. One long smooth stroke
brought him to the rocks. He hiked his legs under
him and rose. Water sluiced down his head, his chest
and abdomen, his flanks and thighs. He stepped out
onto a rock.

Raven caught her breath. He was naked. Sunlight
filtering through the canopy of trees caught his
magnificence and hewed him into one of the immortal champions. Massive shoulders tapered into a slim
waist, lean tight buttocks, and sinewy legs. She had
seen naked men before when tending to the ill and
wounded at the cloister, but none of them compared
to Kolby. His masculinity both fascinated and excited
her.

He turned and she saw his manhood.

Stooping, he picked up a piece of linen. Vigorously
he rubbed it over his face and hair, under his arms
and down his chest. His hands and the cloth dipped
lower. Mesmerized, she watched as they slid down
his abdomen, down the tight-muscled stomach to the
dark patch of pubic hair. He cupped his manhood,
gently drying it, then tossed the cloth onto a nearby
boulder.

Raven gazed unashamedly at his jutting arousal.
She sucked in her breath. She wanted to touch him.
Weak with feelings that she was only just beginning

to recognize, she leaned back against a tree, wondering what was happening to her. She had never allowed herself to be driven by carnality.

Trembling with emotion and the strain of being absolutely quiet, she crept away to her own bathing area. When she returned to camp, Kolby was offering her another oatcake and telling her that they had to eat it as they walked.

"Make haste," he said. "We don't want to lose them, not when we're so close."

Instead of suiting his own actions to his words, he leaned over her.

At the question in her eyes, he whispered, "Crumbs."

Using the pad of his thumb, he wiped the corners of her mouth.

"Strange," she told him. "I haven't taken a bite."

"I lied," he admitted. "I just wanted to touch you."

She studied his mouth and the texture of his sunbrowned skin. She wanted to taste him, to feel his warmth, the hardness of his body that could turn soft, the softness that could become hard. Even when he no longer brushed her mouth, he continued to hold her chin, to stare into her eyes.

"When I first saw your eyes, they reminded me of Baltic amber," she confessed. "I've never seen eyes so beautiful."

Kolby shook his head. Embarrassed, yet obviously pleased by her compliment, he traced the arch of her eyebrow with his fingertip. His thumb brushed the corner of her mouth. As if she were a trail that he wanted to travel over and over, or one that he wished to commit to memory because he would never travel it again, he studied her, putting down all the landmarks, making an indelible picture of it in his mind.

"My eyes are quite plain." Raven forestalled what she considered to be flattery. "Just brown. Not blue.

Blue eyes would be wonderful. My sister has blue eyes."

"Nay, I love your brown eyes. And they aren't plain. They are beautiful. I look into them and I see the forest. An enticement for living."

"All that in my eyes?" She smiled at his absurdities.

"And more," he insisted. "I'll have to spend hours reading them for you—when we have hours."

"I'd like that."

As she said the words, both of them knew they wouldn't have the opportunity for him to read her eyes any more than she would someday sail with him. Sadness clouded their faces even as Raven turned her face into his palm and kissed it. With her lips she chose the imaginary world. It offered her a joy that the real one seemed to be denying her.

The silence was broken by the chattering of a squirrel. In a tree above them, it scolded them for their presence, then flirted its tail angrily before dashing along the limb and disappearing into the foliage.

Raven cleared her throat and pulled away from Kolby's hand. "Do you think we'll find them today?"

"Undoubtedly." Kolby shielded his eyes against the sun and surveyed the gray crags of the ridge rising above the dark green trees. The answer made him sad. He hadn't looked to find such pleasure on this expedition. In fact, if he had been by himself, it would have been over by now. He wouldn't have stopped for the night to give her a chance to rest. He wouldn't have spent this time bathing.

But he wouldn't have had her companionship, or these precious moments of sharing the secrets of their hearts.

Raven looked around her also. "Where is Midnight Wind?"

"Exploring," Kolby replied. "He takes care of himself. I probably won't see him until later in the day."

"You never know if he's going to return, do you?"

"Nay. I never know."

She kicked at a pebble on the trail. "I wouldn't like that. I like my life well ordered. I don't want to live with uncertainty, worrying about the ones I love. Don't you worry about him?"

"I missed him at first," Kolby admitted. "But I've learned to live with the uncertainty. He has a right to his freedom. Perhaps one of these days he'll find another raven he prefers to me. A gorgeous female with blue-black feathers and an inviting eye." They both laughed. "Then I won't see him again."

Raven joined him and they moved up the trail.

Within the hour they were climbing hand over hand over sharp gray rocks. The track had disappeared, but Kolby was confident he would pick it up on the other side of the mountain.

Over her shoulder Raven could see Loch Ness, a silvery black expanse stretching out to the northern horizon. They were just a few yards from the top of the ridge when she caught Kolby's sleeve and pointed. "The village."

"Aye. The thieves sat up here somewhere close by and watched us. They wanted more." He looked at her soberly. "If we'd arrived half an hour later during their first attack, we'd have found nothing but the wreck of an oxcart and eight bodies."

She shuddered. "But we were a procession of religious pilgrims."

"Naught to them but prey."

"How can they not fear the vengeance of the Great Mother Goddess?"

He paused. His amber eyes flashed down at hers. He made a violent chopping motion with his hand. "Your Great Mother Goddess has been noticeably silent ever since all this began. She didn't protect

your guards or your mother, her own Ancient One, or
you for that matter. Her treasure, and an object that
you tell me is most sacred, now lie in the hands of
thieves. And you have no one to depend on but an
unbeliever."

Raven swallowed hard. She tried to stutter an
explanation, but he set his foot on a large boulder and
hiked himself up. His big hands closed over the sharp
rocks at the top of the ridge and he swung himself
over. He had disappeared from her view before she
could marshal her arguments.

On the other side of the ridge, Raven found Kolby
following a trail of sorts. A small patch of damp earth
revealed hoofprints deeply embedded. Kolby knelt
and traced them with his fingers.

Raven bent above him, staring at what appeared to
her a hopeless jumble in the bright light of day. "Can
you tell which are the freshest?"

"Most of the time." He pointed to one. "This is a
new one. See how it imprints over these. This one
underneath it is older. And it belongs to one of the
men who robbed you and your mother."

"You're sure?" Raven bent closer.

"Aye. I would know this footprint anywhere. See
the nick in the hoof? I saw one like this the day you
were attacked."

"When you were studying the trail?"

"Aye."

He rose and followed the tracks for a short distance. He left the trail and moved down into the
stunted trees at its edge. Lifting his head, he sniffed
and looked around.

"What's wrong?" Raven asked.

"Smoke. Someone didn't put out his fire."

He walked further through a stand of trees. Raven
followed him. In a small clearing, wisps of smoke
climbed weakly into the air. A few dull red embers
glowed near dry foliage.

"There." He strode to the fire and kicked dirt over the still glowing coals.

"How could anyone do that?" Raven exclaimed in horror. "They must know the laws of the forest."

He motioned her to be silent, then knelt beside the fire and slowly moved out, fanning around the campsite. Finally he stopped and traced the ground again. "The thieves who stole your goods aren't far away," he whispered. "My guess is that they are moving from place to place rather than setting up a permanent campsite. Less chance of a surprise that way. They may also be moving back toward the village to attempt another raid."

She looked alarmed, thinking of her mother once again at the mercy of murderous men.

After making sure that the fire was out, they moved on. Throughout the afternoon, Kolby followed the tracks. Raven shook her head in amazement as he pointed to a white mark on the side of a gray boulder where a piece of metal had scraped against it. Another time he showed her a rock overturned by a passing hoof, exposing fresh soil and dampness to the sunlight.

They were very close. Trained hunters that they were, both walked as quietly as a church procession. Neither one spoke for fear that their voices would carry and alert their quarry.

Then Kolby heard the rush of a stream. He tapped Raven on the arm and whispered, "They might be somewhere around here. This is a good place for a camp."

She nodded and followed him silently through the thin underbrush. As they reached a copse of trees, they saw a clearing at the edge of the stream. Gray boulders of medium size had formed a fortification of sorts. From behind one of them, a pale stream of smoke spiraled into the sky.

Kolby motioned her down. Together they crawled

closer. Raven could feel her heart pound with excitement. The hunt was coming to an end. How would she feel when she saw her human quarry for the first time? She knew she couldn't forgive the men who had stolen from her, murdered her guards, and grievously wounded her mother. Would she want to kill them?

Slithering on his stomach, Kolby moved off to the right. Cautiously he raised his head, then ducked back down again. He held up his hand to her, four long fingers splayed wide, then pointed.

She too raised her head. Four men sat around the small fire. Shaggy-haired with thick beards, they were indistinguishable one from the other. Shoulders hunched, cloaks pulled up around their ears, they roasted oatcakes and strips of meat on sticks. But beyond a boulder, closer to the stream and out of Kolby's line of vision, another man sat, his back to his companions, a gray hood pulled over his head. As she watched, he lifted a small bag of ale to his mouth and drank.

She pulled back from her vantage point and cautiously turned around. Kolby wasn't looking at her. Indeed he had disappeared. She suspected he had moved farther to the right, probably scouting the camp. Curiosity and a deep anxiety drove her to look again. Moving with great care, she slid around the side of the boulder and rose up, pressing her back against it to give herself greater stability.

She couldn't see the cloister satchels.

Suppose they had already disposed of that loot. Suppose these were not even the men who had robbed them. Kolby could be mistaken about the hoofprint. She looked again, stretching upward, moving cautiously from side to side and up and down to try to survey the camp through the foliage.

A hand touched her shoulder. Lips brushed her ear. "Careful."

She knew his touch. It was the only thing that kept her from crying out. She sank down against him. "I don't see the cloister satchels," she mouthed.

He lowered his mouth to her ear again. "Over on the left. Several large packs and satchels, some cloth, some leather. Yours is probably among them."

Raven couldn't be satisfied until she crawled over to where he pointed and looked her fill. A half-dozen horses were tethered there as well. One—a prick-eared dun—raised its head and stared hard at her. It snorted, then dropped its head and returned to grazing.

When she was sure the thieves had paid no attention to the horse, she eased up again to stare at the mound of baggage—much of it undoubtedly stolen. Her hands began to shake. It was so near yet still so far away. The cloister treasure, but more important, the shawl. It had preoccupied her mind since the thieves had attacked her and Melanthe.

In particular, she worried about the consequences that Melanthe would bear if it was not found. Raven had come to believe that her mother was so shocked by the garment's loss that she had given up the will to live. If it was returned to her, she was sure her mother would recover.

One of the thieves strode over to the mound of saddlebags. Almost angrily he tugged the satchels and packs aside. He opened one. Then another. The dun snorted again. The thief froze. He looked at the horse, then took a quick look around. Raven prayed that she was completely concealed.

Finally he found the one he sought. Leaving it without making any effort to restore the mound to order, he rejoined his companions. A surge of anger left Raven hot and light-headed. To toss sacred objects around as if they were of no account was a sacrilege. Even as she tamped down her anger, she told herself it was righteous wrath.

She slid down behind the rock and hugged herself. The cloister satchels were within reach. In a few hours—after nightfall—she and Kolby would retrieve them. She didn't doubt that her golden warrior would do as he said he would. They would take the shawl back to Melanthe and all would be well.

Except all wouldn't be well. At the same time that finding the shawl solved one of Raven's problems, it created another. When she held the shawl, she would also hold the answer to Kolby's quest. She would know the location of the sacred tree.

Nevertheless, if she renounced her vows to the goddess and left the cloister (admittedly, almost beyond the realm of comprehension), she would still be bound by her oath of silence in regard to the Grove secrets. She could never divulge the secret of the shawl.

Kolby motioned to her from a copse of trees and thick underbrush. She crawled to him and he led the way into its center. "We'll wait here," he whispered. "It won't be long before nightfall."

"Did you see the fifth man?"

"Yes. He doesn't seem to be part of them. Perhaps he's some traveler who's fallen in with them." Kolby stretched his long limbs out in front of him and prepared to rest. "Hope he doesn't have anything worth stealing."

"How will you find the satchels in the dark?" Raven asked.

"I might have to steal it all, make several trips. I'm counting on you to know your objects by feel. I'll return what we don't want and we'll be on our way."

"That sounds very dangerous."

His amber eyes hardened. "It might be. For them." He pulled the last oatcake from the pocket of his cloak and tore it in two. As he handed her the larger piece, he whispered, "Perhaps I should steal their food as well."

Her stomach grumbled as she began to chew. "A good idea."

The glow from behind the boulders grew brighter as the night darkened and the thieves built up the fire. The low drone of talking, occasional laughter, and the snorting of horses reached Raven and Kolby. Every so often Raven would ease up on her knees and look at them. The four were passing an ale bag back and forth among them. She looked at Kolby, impatience showing in her face, but he merely smiled and shrugged.

As she continued to watch, the talk grew louder and louder. The man who had sat apart suddenly strode up to the campfire. His features were still concealed by the shadows thrown by the leaping flames. He snatched the ale bag from one of the loungers and lifted it to his mouth. After drinking deeply, he wiped his mouth with the back of his hand. "Hush your complaining. You're being well-paid. There's more to be had out of that village down there. I won't return to Eire without it."

"Eire." Raven's lips formed the word. "Eire!" She dropped back down beside Kolby. "They're from Eire."

Kolby raised up with her. His sharp eyes marked the one who had spoken. Obviously the leader, he was tall and well-formed. He could not be the man who had stolen the cloister satchels and stabbed the priestess. Kolby looked at the other thieves with new eyes. This was no ordinary band of wandering outlaws. They had been hired, probably by the man who now berated them.

He put his mouth to Raven's ear. "Do you know him?"

She shook her head. "I can't see his face." She had not thought of Eire in many years. Certainly not since Alba O'Illand had betrayed her and married her half-sister. "Never saw him before. Why would an Irishman be here in Scotland?"

The next words were unintelligible as the thieves sitting around the campfire growled and shouted at their leader. He waited, his lip curled in disgust until they had fallen to grumbling. "Tomorrow we go again. It's decided."

One of the thieves blundered to his feet. "Nay, Donnal. We'll not go again. We've got more treasure than we can spend in a year. It'll cost our lives if we're caught."

Raven clutched her dirk. "He's the one," she whispered. "He stabbed Melanthe."

Kolby covered her hand. It was stone-cold and shaking. "Calm yourself," he murmured. "You can't charge out there and kill him. You're outnumbered."

He pulled her back down and held her tightly while she shook with the violence of emotions she had not known she possessed. The talk around the campfire rose higher.

"—prize—woman—Triath—" were the words that reached his ears.

"Triath," Raven whispered. "He's the high king of Clan O'Illand."

"Ah," Kolby said. "There's more to this than we thought. Much more."

The arguing had turned to shouting. Raven pulled herself from Kolby's arms and rose to her knees. What she saw made her blood run cold. The thief who had stabbed Melanthe had drawn his sword and slashed at the one called Donnal.

The man from Eire drew his own blade and dropped into a crouch. "Come and get it," he challenged. "You've been spoiling for it for days now, haven't you, laddie?"

His anger fueled by drink, the thief charged. The Irishman stepped aside. The knife blade driven by the force of the thief's weight slashed past his body. He had overextended himself. With no way to get his guard back up, he fell forward. His cry of fear became an anguished gurgle as Donnal's blade drove down into his back.

As his victim fell away, the Irishman pulled the knife free and whirled. His dripping blade pointed at the three remaining thieves, one after another. He dared them to come, but they had no stomach for it.

At last he pointed to the body. "Be hauling the guts out of camp and burying it under a rock down wind."

The order was a test of his authority. They hesitated only a minute before grasping the body by the feet and shoulders and lugging it out of the firelight.

Raven slid down the rock, her face pressed against the cold granite. It had happened so fast. So incredibly fast. She had just witnessed a murder. Never mind that the thief had stabbed her mother. He was a human being, yet he had been slaughtered like an animal.

Kolby held her hard while she wet his tunic with her tears. Neither one of them looked toward the thieves' camp again. The noise of the campfire ceased immediately. A low drone of voices quickly trailed off into silence, and the fire began to die.

Taking solace in Kolby's strength and warmth, Raven relished the closeness. She had been a strong woman for the past nine years. She had chosen her life and had lived it; she had made her own decisions and had suffered the consequences. But the events of the past few days overwhelmed her. Too much blood, too little peace. She was glad to lean on Kolby, to know that he was a man strong and wise enough to protect her from both men and demons.

For perhaps half an hour she allowed him to hold and caress her. Then she roused. She hadn't reckoned with the ghosts of her past haunting her after all these years. The O'Illands were after her, as they had been after Gwynneth. Now that her sister was out of their reach and safely married to Brian mac Logan, Triath must have settled on the older sister for revenge.

She could well imagine him sitting across the sea and brooding on the loss of his son. The Donnals were cousins to the O'Illands. Triath had probably brooded until he had gone mad. Now she feared she would never know a minute's peace.

She wanted to stay in Kolby's arms and let him comfort her. She wanted to have him fight her battles for her. But that wouldn't be fair to him. She pushed away and sat up. "Thank you. I'm all right now."

He put his hand on her arm. "I won't let these men hurt you. I promise, Raven. If you have need of a champion, know that I am yours."

He leaned closer until his face was only inches from hers. In the moonlight it was barely enough to see that the shadow of death still lurked in her staring eyes. "Listen to me. What we did wasn't altogether mating, but it was part of mating, and it was not pretense. You are mine. No one and nothing shall hurt you or any of your family."

She knew he was making a pledge to her. Still she pushed him away. "Thank you. Thank you for offering to be my champion. It is more than I would ever have dreamed. But this is a battle I must fight alone and in my own way. Once I have the shawl, I can return to Melanthe. Only the shawl. If it were not for the shawl, we could leave now."

He shook his head, about to speak, but she laid her fingers over his lips.

"My mother and I will return to the cloister. When she's fully recovered, we'll take shelter in another cloister, one Triath and the O'Illands know nothing about."

"That isn't fighting, lady. That's running. Do you plan to run for the rest of your life?"

"In a sense it's running," she acknowledged, "but

not for myself. This is the only way to protect Melanthe. I don't intend to have the O'Illands' curse anyone else I love."

"By denying yourself the joy of love," he said quietly.

"By denying myself a champion," she declared.

"I'll challenge them one by one," he promised. "How many can there be?"

She took his big hands in both of hers. His were so warm; hers, so cold. "Nay, I don't want you to die because of me. Let's just get the satchels and escape. No one need be the wiser. With any luck they won't notice until we've given the treasure to Vaghn and left with Melanthe."

He didn't say anything. He couldn't argue with her at this time, but he vowed to himself that she would never leave his side as long as she was in the slightest danger. The skill with which the man called Donnal had killed showed him to be a formidable enemy. Left unguarded, Raven would surely be taken.

In tense silence, they waited for the thieves to settle down for the night. Finally, when three of the men were wrapped in their cloaks and stretched out for sleep, Raven pulled out her blowpipe. Again Donnal had moved away from the others to take up his spot with his back to the boulder, completely hidden from the campsite. From where Kolby and Raven watched, they might not have known he was there.

"With all the boulders around them," Kolby said, "you're going to have a difficult time stunning the watchman."

"I'll have to get closer."

"We can't afford to awaken them."

"I won't," she promised. "Remember, I slipped into your cave without your knowing."

His white teeth flashed in a smile. "Aye, lady, so you did."

Crouching, she and Kolby laboriously wound their

way among the boulders, until they were closer to the camp, until she had the watchman in sight. She angled this way and that; she inched foward, backward, to the side. Finally she settled down into position, drew a few deep breaths, and raised the pipe.

For a second she wondered how she would feel if she were sending a poison dart into a member of Clan O'Illand. Could she do it? Could she kill a man? Coldly she put the mouthpiece between her lips, aimed, and shot the dart. The watchman jumped and slapped at his back before he settled down again. Minutes passed. Slowly his head lolled forward onto his chest.

"Well done," Kolby complimented her. "How long must we wait?"

"He's asleep," she said. "Hurry. It lasts for only a short time."

Kolby slipped into the camp and searched among the luggage, finding it a more difficult task than he had anticipated. Running his fingertips over the satchels, he encountered heavy sailcloth first, worn and tattered. He lifted those aside. A long bale, comparatively light for its size and shape, rolled and hit the ground with a thump.

The horses lifted their heads and stirred. One snorted and stamped. Kolby dropped to the ground and waited, holding his breath. He heard no sound from the fireside where the three men lay wrapped in their cloaks. The amount they had drunk was probably acting as a sleeping potion. Still—

One after another he searched through the bags. At last he found a leather satchel that weighed heavy in his hands—as heavy as lead, or gold. Beneath it was another pressed almost flat. Flat and light. He rubbed his hands over its surface. His fingers traced the *craebh ciuil* tooled into its flap. He had them. He rose with the light satchel and slung it over his shoulder.

The bells on the shawl tinkled. He froze on the spot. He had forgotten about the bells.

One of the thieves stirred and raised himself on one elbow. His back was to Kolby, but the warrior dared not move. One step and the bells might ring again.

In a graceful, effortless movement, Raven rose from behind a boulder and blew another dart. It caught the sleepy man in the shoulder. He grunted, slapped his hand over his chest, and lifted his head as if he were listening. Gradually his body slipped back into its bedroll. Quickly she reloaded the pipe, ready if another man should awaken.

Kolby slipped across the intervening space. He put his arm around her shoulder and together they hurried back to a log. Sliding behind it, she reached for the satchel.

"The shawl is here," Kolby whispered, "or at least the bells are."

She smiled. "I heard them."

She opened it and closed her hand over the fine wool. The bells tinkled. She felt a thrill of gladness and relief. Melanthe would recover!

"Did I get the right satchel?" Kolby asked.

"Aye." He heard the relief in her voice and he was thrilled to know that he had put it there. "These are the ones."

She slipped her hand inside the other satchel to feel the shape and weight of a couple of objects. Then she reached out her hand and caught his. In an impulsive gesture she brought his palm against her cheek. "You have brought everything, my champion."

His heart stepped up its beat. Then with a smile he shouldered the satchel with the gold objects in it. "Now," he said, "stay close to me. Don't let me get more than a step or two in front of you. If I do, call to me. We must travel fast and we have a long way to go."

Going back over the ridge was not as hard as coming up it the first time. Kolby took them by the most direct route and they made good time. On the other side, however, the weather had changed. A storm was blowing down the Moray Firth from the North Sea.

The air was heavy. Wind whipped their hair and clothing. Clouds scudded in to cover the moon. The loch boiled with whitecaps.

Kolby cursed softly. "A storm is blowing up. We don't dare get caught in the open on top of this crag. We'll be struck by lightning. Take my hand." She did so. "Now we run!"

Down the trail they pounded. It had taken them half a day to climb up from where they had left the horses. Now they seemed to fly down the mountain. Raven had never covered ground so quickly before. The golden warrior pulled her so fast that she took giant strides. If she stumbled, he didn't allow her to fall but dragged her onward.

All at once the air above the loch seemed to explode. Lightning crackled through a huge bank of clouds, stabbed down into the water in at least half a dozen places, and spread out in all directions. In almost the exact place where they had come over the ridge, it struck like a ball of fire, crumbling the rock and sending a plume of smoke upward.

As if the lightning had opened up the clouds, rain began to fall.

Kolby ducked his head and plunged onward. The water pelted them until Raven couldn't see. It plastered her hair against her cheeks. It filled her eyes, her nose, her mouth.

Suddenly Kolby tugged her off the trail, and she fell against the side of her mare. They had reached the horses.

Chapter 10

Kolby lifted Raven onto the stallion and slung the satchel of gold over the mare's withers. He tied the reins of both horses around his waist before continuing down the trail. But the way grew increasingly treacherous. Water sheeted down it, so fast it was like wading in a rushing stream. He held his breath for fear one of the horses would lose its footing and send them all sliding down the mountain.

The howling wind lashed the trees. Leaves, boughs, whole branches scraped their skin as the fury of the storm threatened to blow everything off the side of the mountain. Lightning streaked across the sky. Thunder boomed.

"We should stop!" Raven screamed above the din.

"I thought we could outride it, but we can't," he shouted over his shoulder. "We're going to have to take shelter until it blows over."

"Shelter!" she screamed back. "Where can we find shelter?"

"Yesterday I saw a small cave back from the trail. If I can find it, it will accommodate us and the animals." Whether he could find it was the question. His eyes were useless in the darkness. He did well to keep his feet under him and lead the horses downward at a snail's pace. Only when the lightning flashed could he see where he was going.

In the end a lightning flash showed him a dark hole in the side of the mountain. Praying that his eyes didn't deceive him, he led the mounts between the trees. Undergrowth tore at his trousers. He stumbled and staggered as rocks turned under his feet.

Another flash directly overhead made the landscape as bright as day. The thunder boomed in the same instant with deafening intensity. A bolt of jagged fire lanced down and split a tree off to the right.

Raven screamed. The mare neighed in panic and tried to bolt. Only the stallion's great strength and Kolby's courage kept the party together. By the light of the fire that blazed for a minute before the rain extinguished it, he could see to lead them into the cave.

The first thing he did was help Raven from the saddle. She was sobbing with relief. Kolby drew in deep draughts of breath. The horses too stood shivering, heads hanging, sides heaving as if they had run a mile. Just to be out of the pelting rain felt like a blessing. Icy water fell like a curtain in front of them. Likewise, a veritable waterfall poured off the overhang as the water raced down the mountainside.

Another flash of lightning revealed the back of the cave. Kolby caught a glimpse of a small pile of wood and the remains of a fire. He hurried to it and knelt to take an inventory. He had been lucky. Someone had been here before him. Within minutes he had pulled flint and striker from his saddlebag and struck a fire.

He took Raven's hand and guided her to it. She was numb with shock and cold. Without waiting for permission, he stripped her cloak off her and spread it on some rocks to dry.

He strung his own cloak over the cave entrance to keep out the rain. It deepened the shadows. Then he dropped in his tracks and bowed his head. He had done what he set out to do. They could rest here for the night.

The storm would pass and leave no trace for the thieves to follow if they noticed the missing satchels. He could imagine the storm striking the thieves' camp, putting out their fire. They would be too occupied with keeping dry to check their loot.

In the morning he could take Raven back to her mother and send them on their way. Why didn't that thought please him? Why did he feel as if an important part of his life was about to be torn away from him?

Raven was the first to raise her head and look around her. The orange glow of the flames created warmth and intimacy in the cavern's small confines. She saw Kolby sitting with his knees drawn up, his arms resting on them, his head bowed on his locked wrists.

He was her dear champion. He had brought her through safely. The adventure was almost over and they were going to succeed.

As if he felt her gaze on him, Kolby raised his head. His eyes glowed warm amber in the orange firelight. He held out his hand and she went into his embrace as if she belonged there.

"You should sleep," he told her. "We have a long way to travel yet. I took off your cloak. It's drying over there. You need to get as dry as you can."

She rested her head on his shoulder. Lightning flashed behind the Viking's cloak. Thunder boomed from farther away. She put her arms around his waist and hugged him close. "Do you think we should take our chances and ride on?"

He bent his head and placed his lips to her forehead. "Aye, lady, we should."

"But not because of the storm," she said, and lifted

her head so that his lips could trail down her temple onto her cheek.

"No," he agreed. "Not because of the storm."

She tilted her head back. When she looked into his face, she saw the same hunger reflected in his eyes that she felt in herself. Not bread, cheese, smoked meat, or the finest banquet, could assuage it for her. Emotions, white-hot and passionate, inundated her. She couldn't stop staring at him.

"Don't look at me like that, my lady," he warned. "I'm a man who's been hard put upon these many days since you came into my life."

"I know."

The cave was too small. The longer they remained here, side by side, the more it pushed them together. Abruptly Kolby reared up and stalked past his cloak to stare out into the driving rain. "It's not letting up," he called. "We're going to be here for a while."

He pulled the saddles from the horses' backs and used sheepskins to rub the animals down. Then he came back to join her at the fire. "At least the rain will wash away our tracks in case we left any for them to follow."

She had finger-combed her hair while he'd been gone. Now it waved around her face. She looked almost like a child except, of course, for the glorious body that the rain had revealed by wetting her garments, so that they clung to her everywhere. Sweet torment.

From the first moment he had seen her, he had been entranced by her physical beauty. But the longer he was around her, the more he learned about her, the more intrigued he became with the person she was inside. The more he came to recognize her worth. She was witty, with a dry sense of humor that he enjoyed. For a woman of peace, she was spirited. On the Nameless Eve he had thought she shone with the radiance of the moon. Tonight she was the embodiment of the lightning, wild and untamed, one with nature around her.

No man could have had a better partner on a mission. Kolby had known many men who neither thought nor acted as fast as she did. They had come over the mountain almost at a dead run, yet she had followed faithfully. She hadn't complained when he'd handled her roughly, or when the trees had whipped her face and body. He didn't doubt that she was bruised.

He licked his lips. He would like to lay his mouth over every bruise and kiss the soreness away.

Under his gaze she shifted and blushed. "You were very brave, Kolby of Apelstadt. You are a determined man. I have no doubt that you will find the sacred tree. I hope it's truly what you want."

He moved closer. "You sound as if you have doubts."

"Oh, not for you, but for myself." She looked away into the heart of the fire. "Before you came into my life, I knew what I wanted. Now I'm just as sure that I don't want it at all. If you find the tree, you'll leave. I don't think I'll ever see you again." She looked back at him. "But that is my loss, not yours."

He didn't say anything. Had he heard right? She was going to miss him.

Outside, the rain continued unabated. Inside, their desire for each other was also unceasing.

Kolby held out his hand. "Come, lady. Sit down and rest. There's no food to eat tonight, but at least we'll be warm. Tomorrow at first light we'll return to the village."

They sat together. A stick broke in the fire, sending up a little shower of sparks. "Do you think that Donnal person will be chasing us?" Raven asked. "By now they might have discovered the theft."

"I doubt they've discovered anything." He chuckled. "They were mostly drunk when they rolled up in their cloaks. Since the rain struck, they've no doubt been searching for someplace to keep warm and dry. They won't be thinking about anything else until morning."

"But then?"

"I doubt they'll associate the theft of the satchel with us. They'll think one or the other of them took it. After they've accused one another for a while, they'll think that maybe some other outlaws happened by. Since you're the one they're hunting and you're a priestess of the Cloister of the Grove, they'll think you've returned to the cloister."

"I *am* returning to the cloister," she reminded him.

He looked at her but said nothing. His expression so disturbed her that she sought to distract him. She reached for the cloister satchel, wanting to examine the contents more carefully, to reassure herself that all was as it should be.

First to come out was the shawl. She pressed its folds against her face. Cloister spun and cloister woven from the finest combed wool, it was soft against her face, yet strong. The tinkle of the bells filled the cave. The delicate chime drew Raven into its magic.

"It will heal Melanthe," she told him dreamily. "This will be as good a medicine as all the herbs in Scotland."

The bells tinkled again with a new sound. She dropped the shawl and stared at it in horror.

"What's wrong?" Kolby asked.

"It—it sounded like singing. Didn't you hear it?" She wrung her hands, trying to wipe the feel of the shawl from them.

He shrugged. "It made sweet music, my lady, but I didn't hear a voice. What matter if it is singing?"

"It heals the sick, but it also sings for the dead. It

precedes their spirits to the Otherworld." She looked at it with dread.

He put his hand on her arm. "It has so many properties, I wouldn't worry about it. It was an accident. Come, show me the treasure. That's what a Viking is interested in." He grinned at her and waggled his eyebrows. "I didn't get this wet for a woman's head wrap."

She slapped his hand off her arm and made a face at him. "You shall look at the shawl because that is worth more than all the treasure in the world."

Still grinning, he stretched out beside her and ran his hand through the fringe of the shawl. The bells were strangely silent. He looked up inquiringly.

She bit her lip. "I don't think you have any right to touch it. It's a sacred object. It won't ring for you."

"It almost got us caught when it rang in the thieves' camp," he reminded her dryly.

He laid it back down but turned one of the tiny bells over in his hand. In the firelight he could see the tiny *ogham fedha* etched inside.

"I wonder if the O'Illands had any idea of its importance," he commented, letting the bell fall back onto the material. He stared at it, his face grave. It had not tinkled.

"No one does," Raven replied. *Not even you,* she thought with a heavy heart. "Melanthe will tell me when the time comes."

Kolby picked up a solid gold brooch, elaborately chased and set with carnelians and lapis lazuli. He was immediately struck by the superiority of the workmanship. He laid it down and picked up a ring. It was big enough for a man's thumb—a ring set with a precious cairngorm—a ring for a high king. Had she made it for her father?

"Did you design and craft these yourself?" he asked.

Raven nodded.

"They're beautiful. The most exquisite work I've ever seen, my lady, and I've seen a great deal of jewelry during my journeys."

"Thank you," Raven mumured. "These were blessed by the ladies of the Shrine of the Great Mother Goddess. I would expect their value to be very high. Vaghn should be pleased with his barter."

Kolby picked up a chain, noting that each link had been forged by hand and polished to a high gloss. The chain dangled from his fingers like liquid. A small gold amulet spun first one way and then the other.

"That's my favorite piece," Raven said.

He held it up to the light. "An apple. Is everything you craft an apple?"

"Not really. But our talisman is the *craebh ciuil*, so many carvings and representations of apples appear in our work. This piece of jewelry is especially blessed by the Great Mother Goddess." She unfastened the brooch at the placket of her tunic and pulled it free from the material. Laying the apple amulet down, he took the brooch she handed him.

"Melanthe designed it for me," Raven said proudly. "I did the casting and setting, but you see how each of us has the goddess in our hearts and minds."

He held it closer to the fire, visually tracing the apple motif. The inset jet stones gleamed as black and shiny as Raven's hair. He had to restrain himself to keep from closing his hand over it and holding it fast. "One of these days," he said lightly, "I'll have to hire you to make me a talisman."

"One with amber," Raven said. "I shall be delighted. Until then, let me give you one now." Picking up the small apple amulet, she pushed up on her knees and leaned across the pallet. "Vaghn doesn't know how much jewelry is in the bag, so I'll give this one to you. I pray it will be a powerful talisman for you." She looped the chain over his head. "I pray that the Great Mother Goddess in her wisdom will lead you to the sacred tree."

The brooch slipped from his fingers as he inhaled her fragrance. Her hands brushed his shoulders. Her face leaned close. Involuntarily he caught her at the elbows. Her eyes widened. Her breath hissed out between her teeth. The tunic—unfastened now— slipped off her shoulder, revealing the creamy upper swells of her breasts.

For the longest time he stared at her skin, her beautiful skin. He wanted to touch it, to taste it. As if dazed, he raised his head and stared into her eyes. They were like dark velvet night shadows. She faced him, her back to the fire. The flames glowed through her black hair, highlighting it in silver-blue. Straight and thick, it flowed over the body. She was the embodiment of the mystery and beauty of the night.

Slowly she pulled the fabric back over her shoulder and drew the placket together with her fist. Without a word, Kolby eased her away from him and rose. When he turned, she refastened the placket with the brooch.

Lifting the edge of the cloak over the entrance, he took a deep breath. "The worst of the storm is over. Pack your possessions. We'd better start traveling again."

He had broken the spell of his own accord. The cave no longer seemed gilded in gold. It no longer embraced them warmly. In an uncomfortable silence, Raven and Kolby picked up their belongings and repacked the horses. He finished sooner than she did and left the cave. She remained behind, making sure she had stowed away everything in its proper place. He still had not returned when she finished.

Finally she walked outside. Moving down the rain-softened pathway, she followed his tracks. She was surprised at how little evidence there was of his having gone this way. Here he had left the path and wound through a stand of trees. She followed. She hadn't walked far when she saw him kneeling, his dirk in hand. A small creature lay on the ground in front of him, struggling and whimpering. It was a fawn.

"Don't!" She ran to Kolby. "Don't kill it." She knelt and took his hands. "It's only a baby."

Kolby jerked his hands from hers and rocked back on his knees. With his shoulder, he brushed a hank of hair from his forehead. "If you had only looked, you would have seen that I was trying to free it from the thorns."

Raven looked at the brambles imprisoning the fawn's hind legs.

"He's tangled up. The more he fights, the more entangled he becomes." He looked around. "His mother's hiding near here, I'm sure. If I free him, he can go back to her."

Raven reached into her quiver and pulled out one of the tiny darts. Not needing her blowpipe, she inserted the point into the fawn's neck and soon it was asleep.

"Will the drug hurt him?"

Raven shrugged. "He'll be a little shaky. That's all."

Then she too pulled out her knife and helped Kolby cut the fawn free. Risking his hands, the Northlander pulled the brambles away. When Raven would have reached for the creature, he stopped her.

"Try not to touch him," Kolby cautioned. "His mother won't recognize him if we leave too much of our scent on him."

Together they walked back to the horses and

mounted. When they circled past the fawn, they saw that it had pushed itself up on wobbly legs. It staggered away as they approached.

In the distance Vaghn saw the approaching storm. Skilled in judging the weather over the loch, he pitied Kolby and Raven on the mountain. He hoped the storm spent its fury before it reached the village. Being stranded here with an ailing woman wasn't to his liking.

He shook his head before entering the hut. Damona rose to meet him. "I'm so glad you came. She's taking a turn for the worse. Nothing I give her seems to help. Her fever's rising."

Melanthe lay on the pallet, tossing and muttering. Her skin was white except for the red flush on her cheeks. Her eyes had sunk in their sockets. Sometimes she opened them, but they focused on nothing.

Vaghn put his arm around Damona's shoulder and squeezed gently. "You're tired, sweetheart. You need some rest."

"Aye, love, but first I need your help. We have to bring her fever down."

"Are you suggesting that we put her in cold water?"

"We must. The stream will cool her."

He shook his head. The treatment was risky. Strong men sometimes died from shock. Still, Damona was a wise woman. He walked to the door and shouted, "Bradach, Durin, Aren."

Shortly, still pulling on their clothing and weapons, the men hurried into the building.

"Aren," Vaghn ordered the young Northlander, "gather wood and build up the fire in here. Make sure Damona has plenty of fresh water and dressings."

The young man nodded and hurried from the room.

"Viking—" Vaghn turned to Durin, who had walked over to stare down at the ailing woman. "The priestess's condition has worsened, as you see. Her fever has risen. Damona believes that if we put her in the stream the cold water will bring the fever down."

"This is madness," Durin objected. "It might kill her. The water is cold. The night air is cold. There's a storm coming. She'll catch a chill for sure. Kolby wouldn't approve."

"He isn't here to ask," Bradach replied. "This is Vaghn's decision."

Damona put her hand on Melanthe's forehead. She shook her head at the heat. "I'm a healer of sorts, Viking. What Vaghn and I are proposing is good. She's too hot."

"Aye," Bradach agreed.

Durin glared at the guide. "What would you know about it? You're one of them. If I were to listen to you, you'd have me believing he was Odin himself come to heal her."

"Nay, he's not an immortal," Bradach said dryly. "But I know him. He was a Druid priest, but he was banished for disregarding a judgment."

Durin looked back and forth between outlaw and guide. His expression clearly revealed that he didn't trust either of them. Kolby had vowed to take care of this woman, and he was Kolby's man.

Damona hurried to his side. "I was accused of being a traitor. They would have burned me alive. Vaghn believed in my innocence and argued for my release. The council wouldn't rescind their judgment. When Vaghn rescued me, he was stripped of his name and clan and banished from the Highlands. We've lived here together ever since."

Tears in her eyes, she turned to Vaghn. "He married me. He's a good man. You can trust him."

"He knows nothing of healing," Durin objected.

"But I do," Damona insisted. "She's very ill, Viking. You can see that for yourself. This may be her only hope."

Durin shook his head. He knelt beside Melanthe and put his hand on her forehead. It was burning hot to the touch. She opened her eyes, but although they glittered, she didn't recognize him. She needed help—but the shock of a cold stream—"She may die as a result of this treatment."

"She will surely die if we don't," Damona insisted.

"Listen, Viking," Vaghn added. "During my travels I've seen physicians pack ice around the ill to bring down the fever, and it has proved successful. Since we don't have any ice, the stream seems the best idea."

Durin capitulated. The woman was so very hot. He had no doubt she was close to death. "She belongs to my liege," he said. "I'll carry her."

Vaghn turned to Bradach. "Since this Viking wants to do it himself, help the other gather fuel. Have towels and clean clothing ready for her when we return."

Effortlessly, Durin scooped Melanthe up in his arms. He was the one who had rescued her when she had first been wounded. He was shocked by how much lighter she was. Beneath the enveloping robes, she must be wasting away. Taking care not to touch her shoulder, he carried her out the door.

Damona and Vaghn followed the Viking to the stream and into the water. The water was so cold it shocked him. Still without a show of emotion, without a sound, Durin moved through the shallows to the deeper water. With the exception of Melanthe's face, he submerged her body. The priestess thrashed weakly, then slumped into a deeper state of unconsciousness. Her teeth chattering, Damona joined Durin on the other side of the Ancient One and gently bathed her face with cold water. Vaghn stood beside her. His eyes were closed; his lips moved in a silent prayer.

Finally the outlaw nodded, and they returned to the shelter. Damona sent the men outside. Then she stripped Melanthe of her clothing and redressed her wound. She wrapped the priestess in warm blankets. She dried her hair with a cloth.

Then Damona herself quickly changed into dry clothes. After she pulled the coverlet beneath Melanthe's chin, she combed the woman's long hair, black liberally streaked with gray.

She touched her hand to the pulse that beat in the priestess's throat. Perhaps the cold water had brought the fever down some, but the heart was beating rapidly and irregularly. She shook her head.

She prayed that Raven would return soon. If she didn't, Damona feared she would not see her mother alive.

The storm had passed by the time Kolby and Raven returned to Vaghn's village. Both were drenched, but after the incident in the cave, neither had suggested they stop.

The central campfire flickered dimly through the night shadows, and lights glowed within the hut where Melanthe lay. As Kolby and Raven rode up the street, Vaghn stepped out of a doorway, a torch in his hand.

He laid his palm on Kolby's bridle. "Did you find the man who attacked the Dryads?"

"Aye." Kolby dismounted. "The treasure is here for you." He took the torch from Vaghn and held it close to Raven, who laid her hand on the satchels slung over her horse's withers.

The outlaw stepped forward and looked at the *craebh ciuil* branded on the leather. "Very good. I prayed that you'd come soon. The old woman is very weak."

Raven swung down from her horse, pulling the satchels with her. Before Northlander or outlaw could help her, she hurried into the hut.

Damona met her at the door. "You've come back."

"Aye, and I've brought the sacred shawl," Raven said.

Damona stood aside. "Vaghn and I have been caring for her," she said anxiously. "We've done everything we knew to do."

Raven stripped off her cloak. She peeled off her gloves and stuffed them beneath her girdle. Then she knelt beside the pallet.

Durin strode into the room. "I have spoken to Kolby, my lady, and he told me to speak with you."

"What is it?" Her eyes never left her mother's wan face. She put one hand on Melanthe's forehead while the other felt for the pulse in her wrist.

She listened while he told her that at Vaghn's instigation he had carried her mother to the stream and held her in the icy water for several minutes. "It sounded like witchcraft to me," he said. "I felt her and she was so hot. I was afraid for her—poor lady— but they persuaded me that they knew best. But I held her. I wasn't going to let her be drowned."

Raven smiled up at Kolby's man. "You did well, Durin. I honor you for your care of her. Thank you so much."

"Then I did the right thing? I didn't hurt the gracious lady?"

She shook her head. "You did well."

As the Northlander left the room, Raven examined her mother. Damona hovered above her, explaining all the reasons for the cold bath. "She rested better for a while. I swear she did. But her fever has begun to rise again."

Raven opened the satchel and pulled out the shawl. Gently she shook it. The sweet ringing of the bells filled the room. But in the next moment there came a sound like singing from the golden bells. Again Raven almost dropped the sacred garment. She shivered. The fine wool flowed through her fingers, seeming to pull toward the Ancient One—the Chosen One among the Dryads.

Raven tucked the garment into her mother's hands. "It's the shawl, Mother. The sacred shawl. I've brought it back to you. Neither you nor the cloister will suffer shame. It's safe. And now you'll be safe."

If the priestess heard her daughter's voice, she gave no sign.

With one hand Raven pushed the cloister satchels toward Damona's feet. "By agreement with Vaghn, the rest of this belongs to you. Golden treasure for trade."

Damona moved the satchels aside. "Perhaps an infusion of tea and honey with a little mead would help your mother. I'll go prepare some."

Raven nodded, and the outlaw's wife hurried out.

Steeling herself, Raven pulled back her mother's bandages. The sight of the wound made her ill. It was horribly swollen with red streaks radiating from it in all directions. The scab over the wound looked as if it might burst open at any minute. Perhaps Melanthe would be better off if it were drained, but Raven feared the shock to her mother's system if she should try to open the wound with a knife. Instead, she set water over the fire and tore fresh strips of linen to dip into it when it boiled. While she worked she murmured prayers to the Great Mother Goddess for the care and love of her faithful priestess.

Damona came and went away to wash the soiled bandages. Left alone again, Raven changed out of her wet tunic into a dry one. When bubbles began to rise in the water, Raven plunged the strips into the boiling liquid and wrung them out. Her hands became blistered, but that was a small price to pay for her mother's health. When she had done all she could, she took a seat beside her mother and bowed her head.

As the fire burned low, and the shadows lengthened, she heard the thud of footfalls. The golden bells in the shawl's fringe vibrated where they lay on the floor.

Kolby came to stand behind her. He stooped and stared down into Melanthe's drawn face. "How is she?"

"I've changed her dressing and put a hot compress on the wound." Despite the discomfort, Raven clasped her hands tightly together. Her fear was eating at her. "Now comes the hardest part—waiting."

"Were we in time?"

"I don't know." She shook her head. Weariness was like a drug on her system. She could scarcely sit upright, but she knew she couldn't sleep.

"Is there anything I can do to help you?" Kolby asked.

"Nay."

He rose, frustrated. His eyes fell on the dwindling supply of fuel. "I'm going to get some more wood for the fire. I'll be back later. Also I'll see that food is brought to you."

She didn't reply. As he left, the bells vibrated again; yet when Damona returned with an infusion in a pewter mug, they made no sound. The outlaw woman knelt beside the pallet. "I'll stay with her tonight. You need some rest."

Wearily Raven shoved a hand through her drying hair, brushing the tangles out of her eyes. "Thank you, but I wouldn't sleep either way."

Vaghn's wife nodded, as if she understood. "Come get me if you need help."

Raven nodded.

Damona left. This time she took the cloister treasure with her.

By the time Kolby returned with the wood and a bundle of fresh oatcakes and cheese wrapped up in a linen cloth, Raven was stretched out on the pallet beside her mother.

He did not disturb her but took dry clothing from his own luggage and stepped over to the hidden alcove behind the bed platform. There he changed his clothes. When he returned, he spread his damp clothes over the end of the platform and sat down beside the central firepit. Taking out his dagger, he picked up a piece of wood and began to whittle.

Staring out through the hole in the roof, Raven touched the soft material of the shawl where it lay beside her mother. Trembling with a powerful sense of foreboding, she drew the fringe through her fingers. The bells sang again. She dropped them as if they had burned her.

"Raven."

She bolted upright and turned to her mother. "Melanthe."

The Chosen One of the Great Mother Goddess licked her dry, chafed lips. Her voice was a whisper. "The shawl?"

"It's here, Mother. It's here. You are wrapped in it." Raven guided Melanthe's frail hand to the fringe. The bells sang softly.

Melanthe's eyes widened at the sound. She closed her hand over them to cease their music. A look of ineffable sadness settled over her face.

"It's your shawl, Mother," Raven whispered. "We found it. Kolby found it for us." She moved the shawl so that the bells sang again.

Melanthe was so weak that she couldn't lift her head. Raven held the shawl up for her to see.

Melanthe caught the edge and pulled it down so that it lay across her body. "I entrust this to you, my daughter. When I am gone—"

"Nay, Mother," Raven interrupted her. She couldn't bear to hear her mother speak of death. To speak of it might bring it closer. "Nothing will happen to you. Rest and get well."

But Melanthe wouldn't be silenced. "See that the shawl arrives safely back at the Cloister of the Grove. No one—absolutely no one—must read the bells. They hold too much magic."

"Aye," Raven murmured. At the same time she cast a sidelong glance in Kolby's direction. He shouldn't be hearing this, yet how could she send him away? She wanted him near her.

Melanthe couldn't possibly have seen her look, but she raised her voice. "The man who rescued us from the attackers—is he here?"

"I'm here, my lady." Kolby moved to the pallet and knelt beside Melanthe.

"Who are you, sir?"

"Kolby of Apelstadt."

"A Northlander," Raven supplied. "A close friend to Gwynneth and Brian mac Logan and a foster brother to the High King Michael of Glenmuir. He is our champion, Mother."

Through this long speech, Melanthe stared at Kolby. Her eyes glowed bright with fever.

"He fought off the outlaws and rescued the treasure," Raven added.

"That is good," Melanthe breathed. For a moment her eyes glowed with tenderness, and she seemed almost like her old self again. "You are a handsome man."

Kolby felt himself blushing. Women had always complimented him. Often their compliments had been a prelude to wanting his body. He paid them no heed. But this old woman's praise made him feel humble. "I thank you, my lady."

"The golden brilliance of the day," Melanthe said excitedly. She let her gaze slide to Raven. "The silver radiance of the night."

It was Raven's turn to look away. "Mother, please."

"I don't think you are truly happy in the cloister."

Kolby stiffened. He looked straight at Raven, who leaned toward her mother, letting her hair fall between them like a black curtain. He could barely contain himself. He wanted to reach across the priestess's body and sweep the hair aside.

"Even if I leave the cloister," Raven argued, "I will be forever under the magical spell of my birth. I shall always be a keeper of the land."

"Would you like to be freed of both?" Melanthe asked.

Raven was painfully conscious of Kolby listening to every word they uttered. "I—I don't know. Sometimes."

Melanthe smiled kindly at Kolby. "My lord, may my daughter and I have a few minutes to ourselves?"

"Aye, madam." He didn't want to leave them, but he honored her wishes.

After he had withdrawn to the far side of the room, Melanthe said, "Mother Barbara and Mother Feich were with me when you were born. The three of us officiated at the ritual in which I dedicated you to the Great Mother Goddess. Through their prayers and magic, you were bound to the land. I doubt there is a spell to reverse the old one. If there is, either one or both women would have it." She clasped Raven's hands, her voice more urgent as it grew weaker. "They are so old, you must reach a decision soon. Once they are dead, you will be forever bound."

Melanthe's eyes closed. Although her lips moved, her voice seemed to come from somewhere far away, to enter the room through the opening above the fire pit. "Among women you are greatly blessed, my daughter. As the Great Mother Goddess, the duality of the earth and the moon, provides for her land and her people, so you are to do the same. As keeper of the land, you are to see that it is strong and healthy."

At first being keeper of the land had been a great honor for Raven. She had considered it her sacred duty. But the more she had come to care for Kolby, the more she wanted to be his lover, his wife, and the mother of his children.

Raven drew her legs up to her breasts and wrapped her arms around them. Resting her cheek on her knees, she stared at her golden warrior standing close to the fire, his face illuminated by the blaze.

Melanthe's trembling hands slid over the shawl, touching the bells and the fringe, then they grew still. Raven thought her mother had drifted off to sleep until she spoke again. "How did outlaws and thieves learn of the sacred shawl?"

"They didn't," Raven replied. "They were not outlaws after our goods. They were O'Illands."

"O'Illands," Melanthe murmured. "They have returned for Gwynneth. Brian should have marched against Triath and killed him."

"We overheard a little of the conversation—a few words only. We suspect that they somehow knew we were returning from the shrine. Triath must be mad. 'Tis ridiculous to seek to exact vengeance for the death of Alba. 'Tis now nine years."

"He lost his son," Melanthe muttered through fevered lips. "He had no other. All he has is vengeance."

"Don't worry about it, Mother. We'll be safe soon. Kolby is going to return us to the cloister tomorrow. When you're well and strong, we'll depart for another cloister, one so far away no one will know about it. We'll be safe there."

"Nay, daughter, you can't do that." Melanthe's voice sank to a bare whisper. "You mustn't run from the O'Illands. Your father and I helped you to do that once. We should have refused you the cloister and refused Alba the hand of your sister. He should have been sent back to Eire in disgrace." Her jaw was set, and a muscle quivered in it. "You will not run away again. Someday you'll have no place to hide.

"I tell you this because I did the same thing. If I had it to do over again, my daughter, I would fight for my husband. I wouldn't have agreed to a divorcement so he could marry another."

Raven gaped in surprise at Melanthe's pronouncement. "You love Pryse?"

"Aye, I always have. I always will." Two tears rolled down her withered cheeks. "I wish I could see him and hear his blustery voice."

Close to tears herself, Raven nodded.

"When I first met him, I was young and proud. I thought he was a barbarian. He was a champion of champions, but he was a rough man, always dressed in the garb of the forest. Like your young man—leather trousers. Leather vest. I was educated in Eire. I had learned the power of words, of stones and herbs. I knew the songs that carried people from this world to the next. I could write the *ogham fedha*." She lapsed into silence, into her memories.

Then she began to hum. Raven stiffened. Her mother was humming the song of the bells. When she spoke again, her voice was infinitely weaker. "I thought Pryse was not worthy of me. I married him and bore you, but then I became convinced I was destined for a higher calling. I took it, but I left the dearest people in the world to me—my daughter and my husband."

"I'll have Kolby send a messenger to Pryse," Raven promised. "He can meet us at the cloister when we return." Tears ran down her cheeks. "You won't have to stay at the Grove. You can go with him. You've years left. Good years. You can be together.''

"Too late," Melanthe whispered. "Too late. I have been entrusted with too many secrets. I cannot leave except to go to the Otherworld." She closed her eyes, although she kept hold of Raven's hand. "You still have time. I don't. Promise me that you'll consider what I have said, Raven."

"I will."

She reached into the basin and wrung out the cloth, gently wiping her mother's face. "Are you in pain?"

Melanthe shook her head—the barest hint of motion.

"Can you eat a little broth?"

Again the shake. For a long time her breath was the only movement about her. Then she roused. "Send word to Gwynneth also."

"I will."

Raven smoothed her mother's hair. She was surprised to find that beneath her hand the skin felt quite cool. Perhaps her mother was rallying. The herbs, the cold bath, the restoration of the sacred shawl had worked a miracle.

Suddenly Melanthe clutched the shawl as if she feared it would be snatched from her again. She touched the fringe and caressed each of the bells. Again, instead of a chime, they made the sound like singing. She brought the hem to her lips and kissed it. Her eyes opened wide. She stared through the hole in the roof just as the first rays of sunlight began to streak across the sky.

"Raven," she called softly.

"Mother?"

"It is time to sing."

"Time to sing!" Raven cried. "Nay, Mother, nay! It cannot be." Her tears, which she had held in check

for so long, fell from her eyes. She sprang to her feet.
"Nay. I won't. You can't ask that of me."

"You must," Melanthe said.

"Nay!"

Pushing away from the wall, Kolby hurried to
Raven's side. "What is it, my lady?"

The Chosen One of the Great Mother Goddess
answered for her. " 'Tis time for me to cross over."

Raven whirled and buried her face in Kolby's
shoulder. It was an instinctive reaction. She sought
comfort from the person who had become the source
of comfort. Without realizing that she did so, she gave
him a part of her burden to share. His strong arms
opened and closed tight around her.

Over her head, the dark eyes of the aged priestess
met the amber eyes of the Viking warrior. An understanding passed between them.

Then Raven broke free from Kolby's embrace. She
dropped down beside her mother and focused on the
pale, hollow face. Melanthe was dying. Her mother.
Not the Ancient One of the Cloister of the Grove, not
a Dryad, not a patient at the infirmary, but her
mother. Raven wouldn't let her go. She couldn't.
Desperately she caught Melanthe's hands and chafed
them.

"We have the shawl," Raven insisted. "You're going to be healed. You'll take your place as a Chosen
One. It is your fate. The Great Mother Goddess—"

"—has brought me here to the forest I love so
much," Melanthe said. "If I cross over here, this is
where I wish to be buried."

Raven whirled around to look beseechingly up at
Kolby. "The Northlander has promised to escort us
to the cloister. He will, Mother. Kolby, say you will."
Without waiting for his answer she twisted back to
her mother. "He'll protect us. He's our champion.
You're going to be better. You really are. We have a

bed here. You'll feel better when the day is full dawned.''

Kolby dropped down behind Raven and put his arms around her. She was trembling so hard, she felt like a captured bird whose heart would break from beating so fast.

"You can't die, Mother—"

"Raven," Melanthe whispered. "Sing for me."

Raven had carried many people across to the Otherworld with the magic of her songs. They were the songs the bells had been singing all the night through. But she couldn't sing for Melanthe. She wouldn't. As long as she didn't sing the songs, Melanthe would live.

"I can't."

She couldn't bear to lose her mother. Melanthe was her dearest and closest friend. She would never see her again, never speak to her again, never hear her words of wisdom and of love.

"You must." Melanthe seemed to breathe the words. "I must cross over, and there is no one I would rather make the journey with than you. It is my right and your duty, my daughter."

Raven pushed out of Kolby's arms and paced the room. All her life she had known that Melanthe would die before her, but she was not ready for this now.

Kneeling beside Melanthe, Kolby thought of Vaghn. Perhaps the banished priest—"Can anyone else sing for you, my lady?"

"Nay."

"Raven," Kolby called. "You have to sing. Don't desert her now."

"Nay."

But even as Raven spoke the word, she was filled with an inner calmness and tranquillity. Strength flowed through her. The word still ringing through the air, she returned to the pallet and knelt. Catching her mother's hand, she twined their fingers together. Soon her husky contralto filled the room.

There is a distant isle,
Around which sea horses glisten
A fair course on which the white wave surges.
Four pedestals uphold it.

Her voice rose from the roof and spread out through the door. Vaghn heard it and Damona too. The outlaw gathered his wife against him and held her tightly. The cloister guards heard it and bowed their heads in grief.

Pillars of white bronze beneath it
Shining through aeons of beauty
Lovely land through the ages of the world,
On which the many blossoms fall.

Aren and Sven and Thorfinn and, last of all, Durin heard it. He clenched his fists that had the strength to deal death with his great battle-axe, but not the strength to hold back death.

Then if one sees the Silvery Land
On which dragonstones and crystals rain,
The trees bear golden apples of surpassing sweetness
They expect neither to decay nor die.

Kolby heard it all as if carried back in time, back to the high grove altar where his beloved had sung the praises of the Great Mother Goddess. He hadn't heard her distinctly that night because of the distance and the soughing of the wind, but tonight the clear, sweet tones touched his heart.

He lifted the apple talisman from around his neck and held it up for Melanthe to see.

"A sacred talisman, my lady, designed and crafted by your daughter and blessed by the ladies of the Shrine of the Great Mother Goddess." He slipped it over her head. "May it go with you into the Other-world."

Melanthe nodded her head. She closed her eyes and began to breathe deeply. Her fingers fluttered over the shawl once more, captured a singing bell, and smiled. Her life went out on the voice of the bell.

Chapter 11

Kolby embraced Raven as the last refrain of the song faded from her lips. She wrapped her arms around his waist and cleaved to him while her tears soaked his tunic. He had told Melanthe that he was their champion, but at this moment he was more. Raven needed his strength and warmth. She needed his friendship. He held her for a long time until her trembling eased and her sobs faded to silence. Finally, after gently putting her away from him, he walked to the door.

"Durin. Aren. Come."

Damona had been waiting just outside the door and entered first. She knelt beside Melanthe's body and addressed it formally. "Holy Mother, I beg your leave."

Then she rose and came to Raven, who stood numb and voiceless. "If I may, my lady, I would consider it an honor to prepare your mother's body for burial. I heard you singing her on her way to the Otherworld." She held out three vials of perfume. "I have these fragrances which Vaghn traded for. May I use them?"

"Aye," Raven whispered.

"We would use one of our tents to fashion into a shroud to inter her in," Damona continued. "We have a green one, only a bit darker than her robe."

Raven couldn't answer. Her throat was too swollen from crying. She nodded.

"What about the shawl?" Damona asked. "Do you wish it buried with her?"

"Nay." When Raven looked stricken, Kolby was the one who answered for her. Gently he loosened Melanthe's fingers and lifted the shawl free. The bells tinkled a sweet and gallant tune, as bells should. Kolby wrapped it around Raven's shoulders.

She shuddered and clutched it fast. "Her robe is ruined," she said. "She'll have to be buried in one of her tunics."

"I have a new robe she can wear," Damona said. "You!"

Damona bowed her head. "I was a priestess many years ago."

Raven wondered fleetingly what had happened to take Damona from her old life, but she didn't have strength enough to ask. "I am deeply indebted to you."

As Damona walked out, Durin and Aren carried the priestess's body after her. Left alone, Kolby led Raven to the fire, sat down on the floor, and held her in his arms. He pressed his face against her hair. Loving the feel of the silken strands, he brushed his hand down her shoulders to the small of her back. Rather than stirring his passion at that moment, her softness and femininity soothed him.

"Our journey was to be uneventful," she mumbled. "An annual pilgrimage to the shrine. Nothing more." She burrowed her cheek into his chest. Kolby enjoyed the pressure and warmth against him. "Nothing more. She died because of me."

"Nay, lady. As a priestess, you know that death is a part of the circle of life. We all pass through it."

"But she was needed in this world at the cloister!" Raven searched his face with tear-drenched eyes.

"You heard her. She loved my father. What am I going to do without her? What can I tell Pryse and Gwynneth?"

Her fresh tears wet Kolby's chest, but he only held her more tightly, stroking his hand over her head and through her hair. He pressed a comforting kiss to the crown of her head. Finally the tears subsided. Every so often, she sniffled.

Raven liked the feel of his hand in her hair, the brush of his fingertips along her scalp. Closing her eyes, she relaxed against him. She rested her palm over his brooch, which she wore as a pendant. Without her knowing, it had become her talisman. At the moment she didn't care who he was or what he was seeking. Neither did she care that she was a high priestess of the largest and most prestigious cloister in all Scotland. She needed and wanted his strength and protectiveness. Beneath her ear she heard the strong beat of his heart, rhythmic and powerful. Kolby of Apelstadt was alive, and she needed life—mayhap now more than ever.

She wanted to bury her griefs in the warmth of their desire, but she couldn't do that. She had the cloister to think about, her vows to it as well as to the Great Mother Goddess. And she owed honesty to herself and to Kolby.

The Northlander piled more wood on the fire. Flames leaped into the air. Sitting down on the pallet, Raven glanced at his wet clothing stretched out to dry beside hers. She saw he had dropped his pack next to the fire pit.

"Are you going to sleep in here?" she asked.

"Aye. Vaghn and the outlaws expect it." He looked at her from under hooded lids. "And I thought you shouldn't be alone tonight."

You're right. I want you with me, she thought. But she didn't speak. Her grief kept her silent.

"I stopped by Vaghn's tent when I went in search

of fuel. He wanted me to tell you that he is more than pleased with the jewelry. He had it spread out on the table before him and was scrutinizing each piece. He's never seen jewelry that equals it in design and craftsmanship."

" 'Twill buy him all the women he and his men want, providing anyone has women to trade," was Raven's bitter comment.

Kolby laid his hand on her mouth to stop the bad thoughts from pouring out. "I also told him that at least one of the thieves was Irish and explained why we think they attacked you," Kolby said. "I let him know they're going to set up winter quarters in the badlands if they don't kill each other first."

Raven nodded. "He has a right to know."

Her gaze fastened on the opened placket of Kolby's tunic. He had worn the apple pendant for only a few hours, yet he looked oddly naked without it.

"Thank you for g-giving my mother your talisman," she stammered. The words were hard to say without pain welling up in her throat. "It eased her journey into the Otherworld. I shall make you another. I promise."

Kolby sat down on the other side of the pallet. "I look forward to it, lady. I shall remind you if you forget. In the morning after the burial," he continued, "Durin and Aren will escort you to the cloister."

She stiffened. Within her a tiny flame sprang to life—the beginning of a resolve. "I no longer have a pressing need to return to the Grove. I was in a hurry for—for the sake of our wounded. Now I have other matters to consider."

"What about the shawl?" Kolby asked. "Don't you need to get it to the cloister?"

"Now that the Chosen One has crossed over to the Otherworld, it shall be returned to the Shrine of the Great Mother Goddess, but again I have no reason to hurry. I can stay here until after the outlaws' forgath-

ering. We can hope that Vaghn will keep his word
and that the man who has seen the sacred apple tree
will be there."

Kolby knew he should send her on her way, out of
danger, but he didn't want her to leave. In fact, he
wanted her to stay. A wild Viking thought had flitted
across his mind more than once. He could kidnap
her—take her away to Northland with him and love
her until she forgot all about the cloister and its
strictures. "I don't know how long I may be," he said
halfheartedly. "It could be weeks."

"It matters not," she replied. Her eyes stared
unfocused into the heart of the glowing coals in the
firepit. She could feel their heat in her blood. She
pulled the shawl from her shoulder and ran the fringe
and bells through her hands, much as she did her
meditation beads. The proof of the magic of the shawl
lay in its silence. Or if it sang, she could no longer
hear it.

Kolby watched her worry the bells, making them
play a jangle of harsh, frenzied music. "Have you
read the incantation?"

"Nay." Raven suddenly crumpled the shawl in her
fist. Fresh tears fell. Her life was so complicated that
she didn't know what to do or where to turn. Her
father was as nothing to her compared to what her
mother had been.

Kolby embraced her, stretching out on the pallet
and bringing her down beside him. He reached for
his cloak and spread it over them. Daylight was
strong in the hut, but neither of them had really
rested in two days and two nights. "Sleep," he
murmured. "I'll hold you."

"I can't."

"Try," he whispered, his hands moving over her
shoulders and down her back.

Gazing at the fire, now a bed of glowing embers, he
held her in his arms. His heart swelled with love for

her. He wanted to protect her from grief and harm. Finally she fell into a fitful sleep.

Kolby relaxed. His eyes too grew heavy, but he was far from sleepy. Raven stirred and burrowed her buttocks into his body, turning his thoughts slowly from comfort and solace to need and desire. As he touched her beautifully slender body, her rounded breasts and hips, he wanted her as a man wants a woman.

He rose and built up the fire. When he returned to the pallet, she had kicked one of her legs out from under the blanket. The tunic rode up her thigh. The lower part of her buttock was bare to him. She rolled over, and he saw the dark triangle of hair at the juncture of her thighs.

The thought of entering her jolted him, but it didn't surprise him. He was hardening, readying. His appetites were strong, and he hadn't satisfied them in a long time. But he wouldn't take advantage of Raven's grief.

Pulling down her tunic, he lay back down on the pallet and pulled her into his arms once again. Sighing deeply, he closed his eyes and held her, praying that they both would find rest.

Wearing a dark green robe, Raven officiated at her mother's burial as the light died in the west over the loch. Torchlight glimmered softly, illuminating the silhouette of the body that lay curled on its side on a wooden bier.

The Chosen One had been prepared for her final sleep as she would have slept in her life. Her green robe had been drawn over her body, the golden talisman hung between her breasts. Her knees had been drawn up to her chest, so she would sleep like a child. She had been wrapped in another piece of green wool cut from the tent supplied by Vaghn and Damona.

On the bier beside her at her hand were flints for her fire, her dagger, and a bowl of apples and one of grain. To everyone's surprise, Rangwald had thoughtfully added a bag of ale, saying with embarrassment that the Otherworld might be a dry place.

Raven had already shed her tears. Now there was nothing left to say. She laid her hand on her mother's shoulder once more in farewell with a promise that they would meet in the Otherworld. Then the ceremony was completed.

Since the badlands had no barrow or tomb in which to bury Melanthe, Vaghn had suggested the cave in which Kolby and Raven had spent the night. In sorrowful procession they bore her body up to it and placed it inside.

Then the Vikings and the outlaws took great pains to close the entrance with stones, to leave no trace that it was the last resting place of a high priestess of the Cloister of the Grove.

Kolby put his arm around Raven as they walked down the trail to the village. "Durin and Aren stand ready to escort you to the cloister. Vaghn has provided a new axle for the cart, so it will be able to move more swiftly and surely. They'll have it repacked and will be ready to move out at morning light. You'll just have to spend one more night in this place."

Raven didn't raise her head. She might not have heard him, so stolidly did she stalk down the trail.

Bradach caught up with him and tugged at his sleeve. "Er . . . Lord Kolby."

The Viking scowled at the guide.

"Er . . . if you don't need my services anymore, you could . . . um . . . pay me and send me back with the priestess. I'd guide them back to the Cloister of the Grove free of charge."

Kolby's mouth twisted in disgust. "I'm sure Lady Raven's cloister guards can find their own way back.

The reason I haven't paid you is that we haven't found what you promised to lead me to."

Bradach's ingratiating smile turned to a scowl. "I led you to Vaghn. He'll show you the way. You owe me money. We agreed—"

Kolby caught the little man by the shoulder and shook him. "You'll be paid when your job is done. Now get on ahead and help pack the oxcart."

"Someone has died." Loping like wolves from tree to tree, the Irishman Donnal and his men watched the burial procession coming up from the village. "They're bringing the body for burial."

"Rich pickings," the thief beside him said with a grunt. "Good. I like the idea of that. The dead don't object when you rob 'em."

"You idiot," Donnal snarled. "There won't be anything worth taking in that chamber. Do you think outlaws would bury anything they could sell or barter? Nay. The old priestess has died, or I miss my guess. The young one is alive. She's the one I'm after. Triath will pay for her, and plenty. She's the one, men. Keep your eye on the village. Things are going to happen down there very soon."

As was the custom, the outlaw women had prepared a small burial feast to celebrate the rising and going to the Otherworld that was occurring in the burial chamber at this very minute. Unable to eat, Raven slowly circled the cart, touching the cargo that the Vikings and Bradach were stowing in it, but not really taking note of it. Finally she stalked away.

"Kolby, I'm going for a walk. I want a little time to myself."

"Don't stray far," he warned. "Night will be falling soon. This is still the badlands." He stood in the street and watched as she headed toward the loch. Then he turned his attention to loading her cart. He and Durin went over the vehicle itself to see that it was properly repaired and would make the trip back to the cloister.

Kolby was saddened by Melanthe's death, but he was more saddened by the thought of being separated from Raven. Still, common sense told him she needed the safety of the cloister. Recreating her life without her mother would be a difficult and painful task for her, but the longer she delayed, the more painful it would be.

He spoke with the cloister guards, including the wounded one. They were all anxious to return. They could be counted on to move the oxcart with all speed and to be diligent in their guardianship.

The moon was rising over the mountains on the other side of the loch when Raven returned. She went directly into the hut where her mother had died and returned shortly, her arms full of clothing.

Aren ran up to relieve her of the load, but she shook her head. He had two bags slung over his shoulders. He turned to Kolby. "Vaghn shared his food with us."

Kolby smiled. "Good lad. Put them in the cart. My lady," he called after her, but she had already entered Damona's pavilion and swung the flap down behind her.

In the background the other outlaws had begun dismantling their tents and packing their horses. Durin checked and tightened the leather straps that held the goods in place. Taking one last walk around the cart, he tapped the wheels and checked the new axle one last time.

"It seems to be in good working order," Kolby said.

"Aye." Durin straightened the lead lines. " 'Tis a waste to wait until the morning meal to begin the trip. We have everything we need. Let's get the lady and be on our way. We have a long journey ahead of us."

Kolby looked speculatively at Damona's tent. He noticed that Vaghn was staring at it as well. As he watched, the outlaw scratched his head. His wife came out and led him away, talking rapidly. Kolby had no choice but to approach. "My lady, 'tis time to begin your journey back to the cloister."

When Raven didn't answer, he pushed aside the flap and entered.

"Raven?"

Her vesture robe lay on the floor. He stooped and grabbed a handful of the fabric. When he picked it up, he held only frayed strips of material. The majority of the cloth remained on the floor. He realized that it had been torn and ripped to shreds. His uneasiness grew as he picked up strip after strip of material. Raven's anger seemed to emanate from each piece.

"You were calling." Raven stepped from behind the hanging cloth that separated the two parts of the tent. From the shadows she stepped into the light, spreading her arms wide. "What do you think of my new clothes?"

His mouth agape, Kolby stared at her. She wore black leather trousers and a vest, a yellow tunic, and knee-high boots. Her hair had been pulled back from her face and fastened with gold pins. It hung in a thick braid down her back.

He gulped. "But that's what outlaws wear."

"This is what Raven nea Pryse wears."

It wasn't the clothing that concerned him. It was Raven's tone, her facial expression, her stance. Gone were the soft brown eyes that held compassion and charity for the world. Her pose was that of a stranger, a hard and bitter stranger. If he had not known her so well, he would have taken her for an outlaw. Kolby was more startled than when the cowl had fallen from her face to reveal that she was the woman of his dreams.

"What about the cloister? Your cloister?"

"At one time I was arrogant and presumptuous enough to believe the cloister belonged to me." Her voice had a touch of iron in it that he had never heard before. "But it doesn't. It belongs to all the Dryads. There is another among them who can guide them as well or perhaps better than I. I won't be returning. I will renounce my vows. I'll leave the cloister."

Still holding the strip of green material in his hand, he shook his head. "My lady—"

"Raven," she said.

"My lady, at the moment you're caught fast in the throes of grief. You're not likely to be making the best choices—"

"I'm not sure that I ever made the best choices," she interrupted.

"This is grief speaking, madam. Return to the cloister. Give yourself time to heal. Then make your decisions."

"I've already given the matter a great deal of thought—"

"Nay, you haven't," he pleaded.

She jerked the wad of material from his hand and tossed it onto the charcoal brazier in the center of the tent's floor. It smoldered for a moment then flamed up. "I've given the matter much thought," she repeated. "Donnal is a cousin of the O'Illands. I know what he thinks. He thinks I'm the softer sister, the one more likely to give them no trouble. You were right when you said I've been running away from life."

"Raven," Kolby protested, "you're—"

She gave him no opportunity to speak. "But you were wrong as to why I was running. I was running from myself, not from Alba. Because of my cowardice, I allowed Alba to bring disgrace and suffering to my entire family. Triath carries on a silent feud between my family and his. Like as not, he sent Donnal. And . . ." She faltered, caught back a sob. "And my mother died."

"You're wrong to take this mission on your shoulders, Raven," Kolby said. "I didn't argue with you, but I am now. The fault doesn't lie with you any more than it does with the sister who took your betrothed, or the father who sent you to the cloister because it seemed the easier way. Even your mother dragged you inside, even though she suspected that you had no true calling."

Raven swung around at him, hand on her dagger. "You'll not blame my family."

"I'll not let you take full responsibility either. You should go back to your father and your sister."

"Gwynneth has done her part to erase the shame on her name," Raven insisted. "Now I must avenge all these wrongs that have been done to Melanthe and me. Our name must be cleansed."

Kolby caught hold of her hands. "You're a high priestess. A woman of peace."

"Who are you to speak of peace, Viking?" She twisted free and threw back the tent flap. Her slim figure in its new tight clothing was silhouetted against the fire that had cooked Melanthe's burial feast. Vaghn and his outlaws still sat around it, as did the other Vikings waiting for Kolby's orders. "I *was* a high priestess. And a coward!"

She stepped out into the night and strode into that circle. She stretched out her arms over the living flames. The smoke rose to the pale moon. "No longer!" she shouted. "No longer. From now on, Northlanders and outlaws, hear me. I shall be a woman of war. Herewith I swear a new oath. I shall be my own champion for vengeance. I am Raven the Vindicator!"

The men stared at her, some in amazement, some in disbelief. The more venal among them eyed her lecherously. The women smiled and nodded among themselves. Damona rose and took Raven's hands through the smoke. "Raven the Vindicator."

Kolby's fists were clenched. His jaw was set so hard that a muscle jumped in his cheek when he joined them at the fire. "It takes more than a declaration to make a champion."

"I was trained to be a warrior," Raven replied. Her color was up, her eyes flashing. "Since my father had no sons, he taught his daughters to defend themselves and their land. He prepared them to become heirs to the high seat of Aliean."

"A blowpipe and a dagger won't bring down enemies," Kolby scoffed.

She sobered instantly. "You're right, of course. I'm not a fool. That's why I ask your help. I can use my dagger to dig up roots and my blowpipe to bring down small animals, but my other skills suffer from ill-use. I need someone to help me regain my proficiency as a warrior. I want someone to teach me how to use the sword and spear, the bow and arrow." She paused. "You're the best I've ever seen. I would like your help."

Kolby shook his head. "I have my own quest. I'll be staying in the badlands until I've learned more about the tree. I could be here all winter."

"Then I'll stay with you and hire your services. What payment would you consider fair?"

He made a cutting motion with his hand. "I don't want payment. I want you to return to the cloister where you'll be safe. When I've found the tree, I'll—"

"Nay. This wound has festered within me for nine years. It must be lanced. If I had come as I should have years ago, my mother would be alive and well today. Listen, Kolby of Apelstadt, I shall do this with or without your help." She looked across the fire at Vaghn's amazed expression. "The outlaws will be more than happy to teach me."

"Their price will be too high," Kolby warned.

"Ask what you will."

"I'll be glad to help you," the red-haired Rangwald yelled. He subsided when Kolby shot him a look that promised killing.

Like a bear baited by wolves, he swung his head from one to the other. Finally he ended by glaring at Raven.

He had to accept that she had made up her mind. Before his eyes she had changed from the sweet, cloistered priestess into a determined avenger. She was a strong woman, strongly resolved to do this deed, but she had been sequestered for nine years. Her strengths and talents that had stood her in such good stead within the peaceful community were useless in the cutthroat world that lay around her. He had to protect her from herself as well as from others.

He couldn't change her mind. He couldn't leave her alone. Her mistakes would be too costly, perhaps even deadly. "I'll train you," he finally agreed, "but you will recognize that I am the warrior. My decisions are final."

She nodded.

Standing in the firelight, the smoke before her, she looked barbaric. He could almost believe she was one of Odin's daughters—a warlike Valkyrie. The leather trousers fit her womanly curves tightly. They clung like a second skin to her long legs. She looked taller and infinitely more desirable. When Kolby finally raised his eyes and looked into hers, Raven smiled.

He felt the strong pull of attraction for her. Oddly, he felt as if he should reintroduce himself to her. He had felt far safer with a quiet and unassuming cloister priestess. This new woman was purposeful and—he suspected—demanding.

He held out his hand to her. She put her hand in his and let her lead him away from the fire.

* * *

They walked together to the stream. Moonlight shone down upon them, gilding his long blond hair with silver. She measured his height against hers. Although tall for a woman, she was at least six inches shorter. Likewise, her body was almost fragile compared to his. His chest, his arms, his thighs. She shivered.

The proof that she had really left the cloister behind lay in the heat that curled in her belly. Her blood was up. The fire that had burned the pieces of her robe, and the smoke that had carried her words to the four corners of the earth, had heated her desire.

"There are no more barriers between us, Kolby," she said.

He dropped her hand and stepped away from her, almost as if he was afraid of her. "I fear there are. It's easy to say you've renounced your vows, but what has your heart to say about the matter?"

She shook her head impatiently. *When would he believe she knew her own mind?* "I am coming to you, Kolby of Apelstadt, as a woman, not as a priestess. I want to be your woman. I want you to be my man."

As soon as the words were out, she wished she could call them back. He would think her brazen. He already thought her crazy with grief. He backed still farther away.

"I wanted to hear those words within hours after I met you," he told her. "I wanted to embrace you and make you mine. I even dreamed of kidnapping you in the Viking way and taking you away to my homeland and loving you until you forgot all about that cloister and those vows."

Her smile was luminescent. "Then help me to avenge my mother and my family and you won't have to kidnap me. I'll come willingly."

"Nay." He put out his arm to ward her off. "You know my situation. I'm not worthy of you, not even if you leave the cloister in disgrace. I am *dicenn*."

"Not if you find the apples. And you will. I know you will."

"Even then I cannot offer marriage."

"I haven't asked for it," she reminded him. "I understand that the basic differences between us haven't changed. You are bound to Northland and I to Scotland. But we can be together until you leave."

Kolby turned his back on her. The stream glittered like diamonds at his feet.

She moved to stand behind him. Laying her palm on his shoulder, she said softly, "I love you, Kolby of Apelstadt. I would do anything to marry you and live the rest of my life with you. Knowing that I can't, I'll take whatever I can have."

Kolby kept his back to her.

"Are you strong enough to accept my love?" she asked at last.

Kolby's great shoulders swelled. He shook his head. Then he spun around and pulled her into his arms. Her breasts were crushed against his broad chest. "Whether it's from strength or weakness, lady, I must have you."

Raven lifted her mouth and he crushed it with his kiss.

"Kolby!" Durin shouted from the village. "Are we leaving or staying?"

Kolby caught her hand and together they hurried back to the dying fire. "Raven will not be returning to the cloister," he announced. "She's going to stay with us in the village and wait for news from Vaghn after the forgathering."

"So you're not returning to the cloister." Vaghn appeared on horseback out of the darkness. He crossed his arms over his saddlebow. The outlaw's tents had been packed, and they were all ready to depart.

"That's right."

The Druid-turned-outlaw shook his head. He studied her clothing with a critical eye. The blowpipe was strapped over her shoulder, the quiver at her waist, the dagger in her boot. "Think well, lady. Once such a choice is made, there can be no returning."

"Have you regretted your choice?"

He looked back over his shoulder at his band gathered at the end of the street. "Nay. The Druid order is a great and wondrous thing, but so is freedom."

"I shall soon find out."

"You're here in the badlands, in my territory, madam," he said. "I know why Kolby is staying behind, but you could seek vengeance with the help of the high king. Why are you staying?"

"I'm Kolby's woman."

Vaghn tossed back his handsome head and laughed. "Ah, so that's the way the wind blows. My congratulations, Lord Kolby."

"He's going to teach me weaponry. I have a debt to settle and I want to settle it on my own."

Vaghn's eyes narrowed. "The thieves who murdered your mother and stole your treasure?"

"Aye," she said grimly.

She motioned to her cloister guards and pulled them aside. While Kolby gave final instructions to his men, she bade hers farewell. "Return to the cloister. Sven and Thorfinn, the Northlanders, will see you out of the badlands and onto the road, which you can then follow on your own. Deliver my message to the good sisters. Tell them that I go to avenge the death of the Ancient One, Melanthe.

"And if it please you to visit the high king's court in Ailean, deliver a like message to my father, Pryse mac Russ. Tell him that Melanthe is dead, killed by thieves with an Irish leader named Donnal. Tell him . . ." She paused as grief warred with her need for vengeance. She swallowed hard. "Tell him that I am safe and shall be home when my task is finished. I'll share the details of my journey when I return."

"We will, my lady." Each of the three bowed in turn. One after another they mounted their horses. "My lady," said the last to climb up. "I'm sorry we failed to save Mother Melanthe. She was a gracious lady and an innocent. The evildoers who did this should be condemned to wander forever."

Ineffable sadness for the loss of her mother, and for a part of her own life, swept over her. Something was passing away with them. She was losing it irretrievably. Nevertheless she patted the guard's shoulder. "My thoughts exactly."

They rode away into the darkness with Sven and Thorfinn riding ahead. Their numbers were reduced to Raven and Kolby, Durin and Aren. Bradach, the Highland guide, skulked in the shadows.

Vaghn regarded them quietly. He thought of the four murderers somewhere in the woods above the loch. He turned to Damona.

"Do you think we should take them with us?"

His wife nodded.

Rangwald plowed a hand through his wiry red beard. " 'Tis not allowed, Vaghn."

"What if they were part of our band?" his chief asked.

"Aye," Damona murmured.

Rangwald pulled his hand down the scar on his face. A crooked smile lifted his ugly mouth. "Aye, that would make it all right." He raked an approving gaze over the Vikings. "It would add four more seasoned warriors to our ranks and give us more bargaining power. The guide and the woman won't eat much."

Vaghn laughed. "No, they won't eat much. And she might come to be fiercer than you, Damona, my wife." He looked to the group for agreement. They all nodded. "Then we'll invite them."

The outlaw leader heeled his horse forward. "My lord and lady, we've taken a vote. We'd like you to join with us, if you're willing."

Raven moved closer to Kolby, clasping his forearm. "'Tis perfect," she whispered. "As an outlaw, you can attend the forgathering. You'll be able to judge the man Vaghn has told you about and decide whether his information is true or false."

Kolby nodded. To Vaghn, he said, "I never considered that you might travel with me."

Vaghn laughed at the Viking's spirit. "Oh, aye, we might travel with you. But I'll be leading the way. Hear me, Northlander, you're closer to finding the sacred tree than you've ever been before. I don't know that the man who's seen it will be here this year, but rumor is that he will be. Seize your moment, man. No telling where he'll be during the next forgathering."

"If he doesn't come, then I'll count on you to return the lady's gold."

"We'll see about that," Vaghn said sourly. "An outlaw might ruin his reputation if he returned someone's gold."

"What about Raven's safety?" Kolby said.

"I guarantee no one's safety," Vaghn replied. "But she'll be in no more danger than the rest of us."

Damona edged her way to Raven's side. "Generally there's a truce that holds good at the forgathering."

"We should go, Kolby," Raven urged. "Let's see what this man can tell us about the sacred tree."

He shot her what he intended to be a quelling look, but she merely smiled. "Yesterday you were trying to persuade me *not* to listen to the outlaws. Why have you changed your mind?"

She hesitated. She didn't dare tell him that she

wanted to go to the forgathering in the hopes that she would see and could kill Donnal. Her lips curved in a smile at the thought of Melanthe's spirit hardly fresh in the Otherworld, being followed by those who had destroyed her earthly existence. What a fitting testimony to Melanthe's worth. How proud she would be when their judgment was pronounced by the Great Mother Goddess.

Raven had to convince Kolby that he should go. "I've given the matter some thought," she said at last. "I was wrong to try to persuade you to go to the Druids for information. They should be your last hope. 'Tis their duty to protect the tree. If they believed your story—and there's no guarantee that they would, even with my recommendation—they would offer to send one of the Chosen Ones to gather the fruit and bring it back to you. They wouldn't allow you to pick it yourself. If there is such a man who knows the location of the tree, then he would probably tell you where it is—for a price."

"Aye," Vaghn agreed. "For a price. Remember, Northlander, all things are achievable if you have the gold."

Kolby took Raven's hand and turned her to face him. "You aren't frightened being here in the badlands?" Kolby asked. "Away from your cloister?"

"Nay, this is where I want to be. In spirit, I have been away from my cloister since you saved us from the thieves. I just didn't know I was."

She realized that she spoke the truth. A few days earlier, Raven couldn't have answered so truthfully. One by one the strictures of the cloister had fallen away. Or had he stripped them away? When she no longer had them to hide behind, she had become herself. She was Raven nea Pryse. She had regained her sense of self.

And this had coincided with her decision to leave the cloister. When she had realized that her mother was dead and gone forever, she had felt the shackles slip from her limbs. She belonged to no one unless she gave herself. And she had given herself, at least for a time, to Kolby of Apelstadt.

"Durin. Aren." Kolby looked at each in turn. "Each of you has a voice in this matter. Shall we join for a time with the outlaws?"

"Aye," Aren said immediately. The idea of riding with a group of outlaws and attending a forgathering where there would be much excitement and many contests of strength and prowess pleased him mightily.

"Durin?"

"I think it's a good thing, my lord," the man with the axe replied. "If you're going to find something that's hidden, who better to tell you where to look than a thief?"

"Then we'll go."

"Have you goods to barter?" Vaghn eyed the cart with a calculating eye.

"Aye," Raven replied.

"Let me see them," Vaghn said. "I'll tell you whether they are worthy of being—"

Raven folded her arms across her chest and shook her head. "Nay, my lord. You'll see them when everyone else at the forgathering sees them. But I'll let you have first choice, I promise."

Vaghn laughed. "From the first moment I saw you, Raven nea Pryse, I knew you would make a good trader."

"We Northlanders have no goods that can be bartered," Kolby reminded Vaghn.

"Ah, but you will protect your lady's." The outlaw leader waved his arm. "Let's travel."

Ready to ride, eager to arrive at the forgathering, the outlaws and Vikings not already on horseback sprang into their saddles. By the light of the moon, the outlaw leader raised his hand and motioned them forward. In silent procession they moved through the forest. Bells tinkled. Saddle leather creaked. Horses' hooves struck stone.

Kolby and Raven fell in at the back of the train. Behind them rode Durin and Aren, the latter excited beyond belief that he was actually joining an outlaw band, if only for a time.

As the moon began its course down the sky, and stars began to fade in the graying light, Raven felt as if she were riding into an unknown land. Like her mother, she was entering the Otherworld. Having known only the king's village in Ailean and the Cloister of the Grove, she was on her first grand adventure.

Always she had cast herself in the role of the older sister, the caretaker. Gwynneth was the one to sail the high seas and lead a life of daring adventure. Now Raven realized she could also. The choice had always been hers.

Chapter 12

By early afternoon of the next day, the company entered a clearing canopied by thick forest foliage. Charred remains of previous fires attested to its frequent use as a campsite. Nearby Raven heard the rush of a swiftly flowing brook.

"We'll spend the night here." Damona slid out of her saddle and stretched her cramped limbs. "And we'll leave on the morrow after the morning meal."

Raven also dismounted, always glad when she could give her hips and buttocks a rest. Spreading her thighs over the back of a horse was something she hadn't grown accustomed to as yet. Nevertheless, she was impatient to get on with her quest. "There are several more hours of daylight during which we could travel. Why don't we ride on?"

"We don't need to," Damona said. "We've allowed plenty of time for travel to the forgathering, and we want to be rested when we arrive."

The evening breeze caught tendrils of hair that escaped Raven's braid and blew them across her face. She snagged them with her fingers and tucked them behind her ears. She hadn't yet become accustomed to her hair being free from the cowl and wimple.

Damona gave her horse's reins to one of the outlaws and motioned for Raven to do the same.

241

"Walk a way with me. You'll soon understand why we chose this spot."

Raven followed her up a narrow, winding path to the brook. The water was pure, almost crystal-white in places, ice-blue in others. It danced along, rippling and splashing, spraying over rocks, sweeping around others. Raven knelt and cupped her hands to drink. It was so cold it made her teeth ache.

The women walked across fallen leaves that carpeted the path in rich autumn colors of gold, scarlet, and orange. Heather climbed thickly between the rocks on the steep inclines. Finally they reached a secluded area surrounded by huge gray boulders and flanked by trees.

Damona slipped through a space between the granite monoliths into a tiny clearing. Like a roofless cave, the boulders surrounded an area where a mixture of sand and clay had created a floor.

"What a beautiful place," Raven exclaimed. "No one would ever know it was here. How did you ever find it?"

"Vaghn found it years ago. It's where he and I usually sleep." Damona's fair skin pinkened as she smiled. "Tonight you and Kolby may have it."

Raven's eyes widened. She looked around her with a timid smile curving her lips. "It's so lovely that I—I won't be impolite and say you shouldn't, but are you sure?"

"Vaghn and I have discussed this. We want you to have this place for the night. Please accept our hospitality exactly as you would if you were visiting in any other territory, my lady."

"I will, Lady Damona." Raven inclined her head.

Damona laughed and waved her hand in the manner of a queen bestowing a favor. "Thank you, Lady Raven. Just because we're outlaws and outcasts doesn't mean we have abandoned civilization altogether."

"Indeed."

Damona took her hand. "Then that's settled. Have your men carry your packs up here. They can spread your pallet and lay your fire."

The thought of what lay in store for her and Kolby that night brought heat to Raven's cheeks. At the same time she felt a thrill of gratitude, almost as if this outlaw woman had taken a mother's place to provide for what amounted—in some strange way— to Raven's wedding night.

They arrived back at the clearing to find it abuzz with activity. A central fire blazed. The men had set up a metal tripod over it and the women were adding ingredients to a cauldron hanging from it.

Torches had been lit and stuck in the ground at the corners of the camp. Pallets were being laid out around them.

"Tonight we'll have a hot meal," Damona explained. "And a little diversion."

Raven watched as one of the outlaws seated himself under a tree and began to tune a musical instrument.

"A harp!" she exclaimed. "We're going to have music."

"Aye, tonight we'll sing and dance. After the forgathering, winter comes on fast. Life is hard enough for those with roofs over their heads. For such as we, it is a struggle that we sometimes lose."

Raven shivered as she nodded. Highland winters were a struggle for everyone. She looked across the camp and saw Kolby talking with Vaghn among the trees. Kolby's eyes met hers. She realized he must have been waiting for her to look around and see him. She smiled.

He spoke to the outlaw and the two men came toward them across the clearing.

"Isn't this wonderful?" She gestured toward the changing colors of the forest that surrounded them.

"And to think only a few days ago I was frightened of the forest."

"It can be a fearsome place, lady," Vaghn warned. "We never underestimate it. Always we are in awe of it. And the beasts are not our major concern. Dangerous people hiding in it can be upon you before you can draw sword."

"Aye," she murmured. These people were being so kind to her she could almost forget that she and Kolby were traveling with outlaws. "Damona has shown me the place where we are to spend the night. Thank you both for thinking of us."

Vaghn smiled. "We thought it would make up in some small measure for the earlier unpleasantness."

"Aye," Damona said slyly. "The two of you have had very little time together."

"My lord," Raven said to Kolby, "would you have one of the men follow me with our packs? I'll lay a fire and spread our pallets for the night."

Kolby captured Raven's hand in his. "I've already sent one of the men to perform those offices. I'll carry whatever you want when we go up together."

"But not too soon," Vaghn protested. "We will have games tonight. I want a chance to win back what I lost to your bow."

"Set them up, outlaw. But be prepared to lose. My men and I will win easily."

"Ah, the boast of a hero. But can you live up to it?" Vaghn laughed. "I think it will be harder this time."

Laughing, the two men parted company. Vaghn and Damona returned to the central fire. Kolby and Raven walked toward the brook. The Viking caught her around the waist and swept her up onto a gray boulder. She laid her hands over his and stared down into his upturned face. They were aware of each other as never before. Their bodies had known their desires for so long. Now their hearts and minds were also in tune. Now the time had come to enjoy the sweet pleasure of passion.

"Raven, do you fully understand what is about to happen?"

She dropped her eyes before his intense amber gaze. "It already has."

"Nay. More will happen tonight than you could ever dream. It's still not too late. Say the word and I'll leave you to sleep alone. But understand clearly. If I go up to Vaghn's place, I'll go as your man. And you can never return to the cloister."

"Aye. I don't have the heart to."

A muscle flickered in his jaw. He put his hand around her waist and brought her down against him. His mouth swooped down and he kissed her with lips and tongue and teeth. Desire flashed through her like lightning over the loch.

At last he raised his head. "Then 'tis agreed."

Together they walked up the trail.

"I wish we had already attended the forgathering," Raven said mournfully. "Damona told me about the beautiful clothing they barter for. I would so love to have a new gown."

"I'll buy you one," Kolby promised.

"Aye, but not in time for tonight's celebration." She smiled. "I want to look beautiful for you. When I was going to marry Alba, my father arranged for such beautiful clothes to be made for me. And jewels to deck them. And fine linens for our marriage bed."

Kolby's face fell. "This is all wrong—"

"Nay. Nay. This is right. We will be very, very happy. All the beautiful clothes and jewels in the world did not make my sister happy on her wedding night."

"Our first banquet together will be a meal prepared by outlaws in a camp." Kolby clenched his fists. "I should be ashamed."

"Never." She and Kolby were to share an intimacy

she had denied herself when she entered the cloister. She was thrilled at the idea of being part of a couple. She would walk beside him and sit beside him and later she would lie beside him. "Neither one of us should feel shame about the other." She spread her arms wide and twirled around. "Oh, I'm so excited."

Kolby chuckled. He caught her by the waist and pulled her against him. "The festivities excite you, do they?"

"Aye, it's been a long time since I've been to a banquet outside the cloister." She gazed into his beautiful amber eyes. "And I have never attended one in the company of a man."

"This will be your first?" he asked incredulously.

She nodded, warmed by the awe reflected in his face.

"I'm glad it is with me, lady."

"Me too. Everything is so much nicer when I can share it with you."

He hugged her tighter, his cheek brushing against her hair.

"They're going to have music and dancing, Kolby."

"Can you dance?"

"Aye, Pryse made sure I acquired all the graces a woman should have to be a good wife. Can you dance?"

"Aye, 'twas part of my training as a warrior."

She was quiet for a little while, kissing his neck, touching her lips to the lobe of his ear, squirming when he tormented her in the same way. Then she pulled away. "I shall miss the cloister festivals, especially the apple festival."

Smiling, Kolby watched her smooth her hair and regain her composure. Then he put his arms around her again, as if he couldn't keep his hands off her. "'Tis fitting that the apple is your talisman. 'Tis what brought us together. If Ura hadn't lost his orchards, I'd never have come here searching for the tree."

He brushed his fingers over her cheeks. Callus-hardened hands, which wielded weapons with deadly accuracy, touched her with infinite tenderness. "Skin the same soft color as the apple blossom, as smooth as petals."

Delicate color shaded her cheeks.

He was finished with daydreaming. She had divested herself of cowl and robe. She wanted to mate with him. He was glad all the barriers had been removed. She would receive him with joy. He would love her in return.

"The apple itself is delicious," he murmured against her cheek. "I would taste it."

"Aye, my lord. 'Tis past time."

He cupped the back of her head and pulled her close. Their mouths touched, warmly at first, then hotly.

She parted her lips. Kolby answered the invitation by sliding his tongue into the moist sweetness. She inhaled deeply as he explored her mouth, kissing her thoroughly and satisfactorily. She pulled away from him and stroked her hand over his face and lips. She outlined his eyebrows.

As they looked at each other, her eyes darkened until they were swirling with passion. So dark, they looked like jet rather than brown. But they were alluring, compelling. They drew him to her. They called to his soul.

"You set me afire, my lord. I can hardly wait for us to mate."

"Nor can I," he murmured.

They could still hear the talk and laughter grow louder as outlaws and Vikings settled down in camp to wait for the evening meal to be served. Gradually the noise faded away. Raven and Kolby entered a magical world that belonged only to them.

He put his arms tight around her waist and lifted her against his chest. Beneath his breastbone, she could feel the pounding of his heart. Against her belly his male organ hardened and throbbed.

She took his lips. With a low sound, he deepened the kiss. He let her slide down his body until she was standing on her own feet. But she was not standing on her own strength. She clung to his shoulders and pressed against him. Every nerve in her body ached for him with a sweet pain. She sucked in a shuddering breath.

"Will you always have this effect on me?"

"I hope so, lady."

She pushed away. Hands entwined, they approached the entrance to their bower among the rocks.

A fire blazed and their bed had been made. Bright and beautiful clothes had been laid across the pallet. A red tunic for her. Dark brown trousers and a forest-green tunic for him. Boots for both of them. Ribbons and girdles were scattered about. Jewelry.

She gasped. "Where did these come from?"

"From Vaghn. I bartered for them," Kolby replied.

"Oh, Kolby!" She threw her arms around him and hugged him tightly. "For us. For tonight."

"Aye."

"I don't know when I have been so excited."

She danced over to the pallet. Kneeling down, she picked up her tunic and brushed the material through her hands. She ran her hand over the Norse braid that decorated the neck placket. She touched the ribbons one by one, pausing at a red one, discarding it for another, moving to another. Finally she selected a gold one as the one she liked best.

Then she examined the jewelry piece by piece. The last piece she picked up was an armband. It was old, simply designed, but elegant. She ran her fingers over it. Finally she clasped it over her wrist. She held her hand out, twisting her arm and admiring the bracelet.

"Do you like it?" he asked.

" 'Tis the most beautiful and unique piece of jewelry I have ever seen, my lord. I have not seen many of such high quality. From whom did you purchase it?"

" 'Tis an old one, lady," he replied. "I collected all the other pieces as part of my warrior's booty," he replied. "This one has belonged to me for as long as I can remember."

"Was it your mother's?" Raven murmured.

He shrugged. "I want to think so. I was wearing it when Ura bought me to his stead. Because the bracelet was plain, my former owner attached no value to it. When Ura questioned him about it, he said I was wearing it when they stole me. Ura and Nanna always believed it belonged to someone in my family—perhaps my mother."

"I shall wear it forever," Raven promised.

Leaping to her feet, she planted kisses on his lips, his cheeks, his chin. In between kisses, she said, "Thank you, my lord. You have made me so happy."

Her face glowed. Her smile dazzled him. Her eyes sparkled.

"In making you happy," Kolby confessed, "I'm also happy."

" 'Tis the same for me." She bent, picked up the tunic, and held it in front of her. She rushed over to the stream and leaned over to look at her reflection. "You have given me such beautiful treasures."

"A few," he admitted. "Since they give you so much pleasure, I'll have to make sure I give you many more in the future."

Still clutching the tunic to her chest, Raven looked up at him. "I love the clothing and the jewelry," she said softly, "but I was thinking of the most important gifts you have bestowed on me, my lord. Love and happiness."

Sitting down beside her, Kolby caught the tunic by the shoulder and gently pulled it from her hands. He laid it aside. He drew her to him and kissed the tip of her nose. He pressed his lips to each of her eyelids in turn. He whispered kisses along her jawline, up her temple.

"You shall be the most beautiful woman at the forgathering, my love, no matter what you wear—or do not wear."

"And you will be the most handsome man, my love."

"Ah, lady." He chuckled richly. "You're making an assumption. I'm not. Yet I've seen you naked."

Her smile turned into mischievous laughter. "I make no assumption, my Viking warrior. Did you think I would allow you to see my nakedness without seeing yours?"

He drew back. "When? Where?"

"I spied on you as you swam and bathed during the time we tracked the Irish thieves."

"My little priestess, you are quickly becoming a wanton."

"Aye, my lord, I am, and I find it most enjoyable."

Without touching her anywhere else, he brushed soft kisses over her lips, pressed them to the corners of her mouth.

"Will you mate with me?" Raven asked.

"Aye."

"Are we going to do more than we did last time?"

"Do you want me to?"

She cupped his head in her hand and pulled his mouth against hers. "Aye."

When he pulled back, his hand so big and strong, began gently to stroke recalcitrant tendrils from her face. He turned her around and patiently untied the ribbons in her hair and combed her long tresses from their braid.

"I've always dreamed of doing this," he said.

In the fading sunlight her dark hair glistened a silver-blue.

"And this."

He reached around her and unfastened his brooch from the neckline of her tunic. He brushed his lips down the side of her neck and planted a kiss on the point of her shoulder. Desire burned through Raven, flaming, sensitizing her. She quivered.

"You grow more and more delectable," he murmured thickly.

When she felt the abrasive caress of his callused fingers on her breasts, she moaned softly. He dropped his hands, and the material of the tunic slid farther down, revealing her hard nipples.

With a growl, he spun her around in his arms. The power and ferocity of his movement frightened her. His mouth closed over her breast and sucked the nipple up into his mouth. She cried out as his tongue found the tip and curled around it. He unleashed such tormenting pleasure that Raven quivered anew.

Marshaling all her strength, she moved away from him. She enjoyed his caresses, but she wanted to caress him also. She pulled open the tunic placket and felt the garment fall over her shoulders and down her body. As if the yellow fabric at her feet were the brilliance of the moon, Raven stood as imperial and majestic as the lunar goddess herself.

His body responding to her sensuality, the evidence of his arousal thrusting against his trousers, Kolby stared in mesmerized fascination. "If you don't undress faster, I shall be tempted to rip your clothing off you."

"Your threat excites me," Raven confessed. "Doubly so when you claimed at one time not to be interested in what lay beneath my cowl."

"But I was. You infuriated and intrigued me. I immediately fell in love with the lady of winter."

He stepped closer to her, to touch his mouth to the brooch that hung between her breasts. She felt the smooth pressure of the gold against her skin, the brush of his lips as he moved his kisses up the delicate chain to her earlobe. He caught the chain and removed the pendant, dropping it on top of her tunic.

Clad in her trousers and boots, she walked over to the pallet, bent and carefully removed the clothing Kolby had bartered for. Sitting down, she removed her boots and unfastened the footlets on the bottom of each leg of her trousers. She stood and unfastened her girdle. As the leather parted, the trousers slid down her legs.

Kolby stared at the short, white braises that fit snugly from her waist to the top of her thighs. The underpants cupped her hips tightly and showed the full length of her legs.

"Men's braises have never looked so appealing."

"These are women's braises, not men's." She grinned mischievously. "Since the outlaw women wear trousers, they sew these for themselves."

She stepped out of the trousers, kicking them closer to her tunic. She untied the drawstring of the braises, pulled the material apart, and stepped out. The white linen fluttered to the ground.

Mesmerized, Kolby stared as she lay down, her movements deliberately sensual. She stretched out on the pallet. Kolby's eyes grew darker. His chest heaved with the effort to control his breathing.

"Who is being too slow about undressing, my lord?"

Never taking his gaze from her, Kolby began to undress as methodically and as deliberately. He removed his weapons, his gloves, and his wrist guards. His tunic came next. He pulled it over his head and let it drop on top of hers. "They can keep each other warm," he said softly.

Sitting on a boulder, he removed his boots, then rose. He waited, letting Raven look at him as he had looked at and appreciated her.

She visually touched every feature of his face, his

chest covered with the mat of golden hair, his lean, hard stomach. He was all sun-bronzed skin and muscle. He was hers to love.

She caught her breath as he unfastened the first lachet of his broad leather belt. The second. The third. He pulled the leather apart. He shoved the belt, trousers, and underpants over his hips in one smooth motion. He straightened, and she stared at the thatch of golden-brown hair from which his manhood sprang, aroused and throbbing.

He was hard and ready for her.

For a moment a tremor of primitive female fear raced against her excitement. After mating with Kolby, she knew she would not be the same, physically or emotionally. In their coming together, she would be giving Kolby a gift that was far more precious than her virginity. She would be giving him her heart. She had done that for no man, but she wanted to do it for Kolby. Nothing would stop her now.

He drew in a deep breath. His chest expanded, his lower body throbbed. His voice was hoarse. "Are you sure, Raven? Be very, very sure."

"Aye, Kolby. I'm not renouncing my faith in my gods. I'm merely changing the way in which I worship them." She held out her hand. "Come, my love, this is what I want."

" 'Tis what I've wanted all my life," he murmured.

He moved onto the pallet where he lay down, straightening his length alongside hers. Their bodies whispered seductively against each other. He bent his head and slowly kissed the soft, vulnerable curve of her throat. She twisted, trying to get closer to him, wanting more of the wondrous sensations that struck like lightning through her body.

His soft, warm lips brushed hers. They kissed again and again. He teased and tormented her with light, brushing strokes, with soft endearments, until finally he claimed her mouth.

In between kisses, Raven murmured heatedly, "I fell in love with you the night I saw you at the high grove altar. When you rescued me, I knew life wouldn't be the same again. I couldn't let you go."

"That's the way I felt about you," he whispered. "I have searched as diligently for you as I did for the sacred tree."

She captured his mouth in a hot, demanding kiss that precluded talking. He flattened his body against hers; his chest rubbed against her sensitized nipples, his stomach against hers. His manhood teased her femininity, promised her deeper pleasure. She played her fingers through his chest hair and found herself entranced by the hard, muscled contours of his body.

As they kissed, Raven caressed his buttocks; she kneaded the sinewy flesh. She ran her hands up his spine and across his shoulders. Her fingers tangled in his hair. Their kisses grew hungrier and more devastating. Dark passion flowed through them. The force of his tongue, the hard length of his body, bore into her with a fierce urgency. She welcomed him with the same urgency.

She writhed beneath his loving ministrations. "Kolby!"

"Aye, my love, we're getting ready."

"Not getting ready," she almost panted. "I am ready."

He kissed her breasts, her midriff. His tongue drew erotic designs all over her stomach and around her navel. Her fingers furrowed in crisp golden hair, and she pulled his head up.

Kolby loved her with his mouth and with his hands. They traveled down her stomach to the downy triangle. His fingers slid through the softness, finding the place he hungered for.

When Raven felt his hand between her legs, she shuddered. She remembered the pleasure he had given her the day Vaghn had forced him to authenticate his claim. Her eyes closed. Soft sighs whispered between her lips. As he laid his palm over the mound of her femininity, his teeth grazed her breasts, moving from the fullness of her nipples and back again.

The pleasure was so great that Raven cried out. Still she wanted more. She had to have more! The tormenting longing raced through her. Her hips moved against his hand. When she felt his finger slide slowly inside, she stopped breathing altogether. Then she inhaled sharply. He was making love to her as he had done the first time.

She turned her mouth to his. "Kolby."

"It's all right, my love. I shall take you all the way this time. I promise." He sealed his word with another kiss.

Caught up in the pleasure he created in her, she arched her body. She begged for release.

"You want me to teach you how to become a warrior, my lady love," he murmured, his voice thick. "I'm also going to teach you how to be a lover."

At the same time that he slid his tongue into her mouth, he pushed a second finger into her. Raven moaned as he stretched her slowly, opening her completely to his touch, preparing her for his entry. A strange, pulsing tension built in her. She enclosed Kolby in her arms and clung to him. He moved only his hand to find just the right place.

All Raven's feeling was centered in the pleasure point under Kolby's hand. Suddenly it exploded, and she arched her body as it convulsed around his probing fingers.

"Kolby. Kolby. Kolby." She whispered his name over and over.

She wilted in his arms, her head rolling to the side, her breathing ragged. Kolby rubbed the length of her back in a soothing movement. Raven felt so weak she could hardly speak.

She ran her hand down his chest to his stomach

and lower. She touched him. He was fully aroused. She heard his intake of breath.

She leaned over him, her hair trailing over his chest. "What about you?"

He chuckled. "We have only begun, love." He pushed up, caught her by the shoulders and laid her on her back.

His mouth lowered to hers, and she welcomed it and his tongue warmly. Her body molded to his as she wrapped her arms around him and ran her hands down his sweat-slickened body.

He lowered the weight of his body over hers, his knee spreading her legs apart, his hand stroking her inner thigh. This time she knew beyond a doubt that he would make love to her in a different way. They would consummate their coupling. She felt his hardness as it touched her maidenhead. A shiver of pleasure slid through her, and she inhaled deeply.

He lifted his lips from hers. His eyes were luminous with emotion. "It will hurt for a moment. After that the pain will be over and the pleasure will begin."

"Having you can't hurt nearly as much as not having you," she whispered. "I want you inside me, my love."

He lowered himself into her with a slow, tender thrust.

She received him completely, wincing momentarily when he ruptured her maidenhead. As he pushed her open, as he filled her femininity, wondrous sensation flooded through her.

"You are so tight, my lady," Kolby whispered. He lay still, braced on his hands above her, as their bodies accommodated each other. "I'll be gentle with you."

"Nay." Her voice was thick with passion. "Mate with me."

"I will."

"Love me."

"I do."

He pulled out slightly, then entered again. Raven could hardly believe her body could contain him. She loved the feel of him inside her, growing, throbbing. She loved the weight of him upon her, his body stroking her until she was ablaze with passion. She was effused with hotness. She thought of nothing else but reaching ultimate satisfaction with him.

He thrust into her. She arched to receive him. Higher they climbed. Faster they moved. New, quivery sensations spiraled from her lower body; she dug her fingers into his shoulders.

"Kolby!" she cried.

"Aye, my lady love."

"I love you." She tensed, then convulsed around him.

"I love you."

He thrust again and again, his body stiffening as he savored his own release. He cried out his pleasure, and she received his seed into her womb. A feeling of awe rushed through her.

He wilted on top of her. She held him. When he went to move off her, she refused to let him go. For a long time he lay there. Finally he rolled off and pulled a cloak over them both.

Still keeping her in his embrace, he nuzzled her throat and shoulder. "I love you."

"I love you."

They lay for a long time, arms and legs entwined, bodies breathing in perfect rhythm.

Then the lur-horn sounded.

"Festivities are about to begin," Kolby said.

Raven gave a wry laugh. "They have already begun, my love."

Chapter 13

Basking in a joy they had never experienced before, Raven and Kolby made love again. Then they bathed in the stream together and washed each other's hair. They teased and laughed and kissed—mostly kissed—as they dressed each other for the banquet. Raven couldn't remember when she had been so happy.

In the distance she heard laughter and gaiety coming from the camp, and it infused her with new life. Temporarily she pushed aside the thought that her mother had crossed to the Otherworld, that she and Kolby were traveling with outlaws, that they would be meeting with even more outcasts of society. A few days ago Raven would have thought this a horrible incident rather than an adventure. Now she was seeing the world through new eyes.

After she slipped her new tunic over her head, Kolby clasped her hands. "Red is a beautiful color on you."

"'Tis one of my favorites," she replied. "For years after I went into the cloister I missed it. Now I can wear it again."

He picked up his brooch, which she now wore as a pendant, and slipped the chain over her head. He brushed his fingers around it and up the chain.

"I would be perfectly content to be this brooch," Kolby confessed. "To lie here, my lady, on your beautiful creamy breast."

She shivered with delight. "While I like the brooch and shall keep it always, I much prefer to have a man at my side—"

"Your side?" he teased.

"In my bed."

He kissed her and murmured, "Aye. In your bed."

Laughing, exhilarated with life and love, Raven twirled around so that he could fully see the tunic on her.

"You are a vision, my lady. I'll be the envy of all the men tonight."

She grinned. "Do you really think so, my lord?"

"I know so."

"I must confess, my lord, I find trousers much more convenient to wear than a tunic."

He hiked a brow. "Are you going to be wearing only trousers from now on?"

Raven laughed. "Nay, only when I travel."

She walked around their sleeping area and picked up their clothing. When their garments were in order, she picked up their weapons. As she handed Kolby his, she looked critically at her own blowpipe and dagger.

"Did Vaghn have any weapons to barter?" she asked.

"Some."

"I shall have to speak to him about a sword," she said. "Until I can craft my own, I will need one for practice."

The need for weapons and revenge brought thoughts of her mother to mind. They haunted and saddened her. Even if Raven personally had had no score to settle with the thieves who had attacked them and stolen their goods, she had one to settle for Melanthe.

"Raven," Kolby began, "there is no need for you to—"

"As you must search for the sacred tree," she interrupted him, "I must avenge the shame heaped on me and on my house. I would like you to begin instructing me tomorrow evening when we stop for camp."

"Vaghn may not have a weapon suitable for you," he argued, desperate to put off this training. He feared it would set her irrevocably on a path that could lead to her death. The thieves' leader Donnal was a thoroughly ruthless man. He had killed without compunction. The other thieves had cared no more for their fallen comrade than for the fall of a leaf. "You don't have the strength of a man. You need a special weapon—one made for your hand. Otherwise you won't be able to use it properly."

"If Vaghn has weapons for Damona and for the other outlaw women," she said confidently, "he'll have one for me."

"When are you going to return the shawl to the shrine?" Kolby asked. Anything to get her back to the religious sites that had been her home. Anything to turn her from this dangerous course.

"Eventually." Raven remembered with a thankful heart how he had retrieved the shawl from her mother's hands and wrapped it around her shoulders. "It's safe with us for now. No one knows its true value."

"Not even me, my lady," Kolby pointed out.

She flushed, unable to meet his gaze. She longed to tell him the secret, but she knew she wasn't entitled to. Moreover, if someone besides a Chosen One tried to read the inscriptions on the bells, the shawl might not give up its secrets. "Its value is mainly to the shrine and the cloisters. After we've attended the forgathering and you have spoken with the man who is said to have seen the tree, I shall send a runner to

Pryse and Gwynneth. I want them to meet me at the cloister, so that I can grieve with them over Melanthe. At the same time we can return the sacred object as a family. And you shall be a part of it, I swear."

"You would include me?" he asked incredulously. Her last statement had shocked him and touched him deeply. He had never been part of anyone's family. Would loving Raven nea Pryse bring him into a family?

Raven caught the expression in his eyes. She smiled. "Of course." She inhaled. "Come, love, 'tis time we joined in the other festivities. The evening meal smells so good. It's been a long time since I've had a freshly cooked meal."

The main camp was ablaze with fire and torchlight. The first fire had become a larger fire pit. A huge wrought-iron rack had been set over its length, and food was being cooked in cauldrons, baked in ashes, and roasted on spits. The camp was also ablaze with brightly colored clothing and other signs of revelry. Furs had been spread and warriors lounged about, talking and laughing. One pair played fox-and-geese with crudely carved bone pieces on a painted board.

"Start the festivities!" one of the outlaws shouted happily.

A horn blared. Cymbals crashed. A piper and a harpist spun out a melody. A hand drum provided the drone beneath.

The outlaws began to clap in time. From their place beside the campfire, Vaghn and Damona leaped to their feet. Both wore green tunics and black trousers. Once, Raven would have described them as garishly dressed, but not anymore. Their bright clothes captured the essence of their free and easy natures. They had been sent to the badlands to die, but their struggle had made them strong and confident. They had defied fate and survived.

Vaghn raised his arms and shouted to the group. "What would you have us do?"

"The pole dance! The pole dance!"

The outlaws formed lines between the torches. Four warriors, two on either side of the area, held two long, slender saplings parallel to the ground. Hands on their hips, Vaghn and Damona stood poised between the two poles. As first the pipers and harpist played, the couple danced with slow steps, measured and graceful. Then drums and a horn joined them and the tempo increased. The warriors moved the poles up and down. Lastly the cymbals crashed. The warriors clacked the poles together, as man and woman, without missing a step, jumped over them, in between them, and around them.

Their audience cheered and called out encouragement, for the poles never touched either dancer. Vaghn caught his lady at her waist and lifted her above his head. Laughing, she spread her arms out and let him spin with her in the center of the moving poles. All the musical instruments came together in a great crescendo. Then silence.

The group burst into excited applause.

Vaghn lowered Damona's feet to the ground and together they bowed.

"Viking. Raven." Vaghn shouted. "Come join my wife and me at the seat of honor." The outlaw's color was high. He looked as happy as any man Raven had ever seen in her life. How could outlaws be so happy when many good men and women in the cloisters were not?

Kolby and Raven stepped up to the soft furs and brightly colored blankets that covered the ground. They sat down on them and leaned back against saddles. Kolby saw the tip of a board game protruding from beneath one of the blankets. He knew what was in store for him and the outlaw leader later in the evening.

When they were seated comfortably, Vaghn offered them a cup of ale. "'Tis of the finest quality."

Kolby took a sip and savored the taste of it. "Aye, my lord, 'tis."

The pipers and harpist began again and a slower, less strenuous dance began.

Damona leaned across to Raven. "Your tunic fits you well, my lady, and the color enhances your beauty."

"Thank you." Raven smiled. "I find trousers to be much more comfortable than tunics. I can understand why you wear them."

"Aye, and much more practical," Damona agreed.

Damona and Raven talked a little longer about clothing, then Raven turned to Vaghn. "My lord outlaw, do you have a sword I can barter for? I should like to have one so that I may begin practicing."

"Aye." Vaghn looked at her in a calculating fashion. "I have one that might fit you right enough. But the price will be high. It's an extremely fine weapon."

"Stolen from the finest swordmaker, no doubt," Kolby remarked dryly.

Vaghn shrugged. "Only the very best is worth the risk."

"Let me see it," Raven said. "Then we'll haggle over the price."

"Rangwald," Vaghn called, "get that blade with the silver-chased hilt."

While they waited, the outlaws kept the ale flowing. A group of them were engaged in a game of dice, gambling over each throw. The losers groaned and the winners cheered. Sven and Thorfinn drew near and were invited to join in. The Highlanders welcomed the opportunity to try for the Vikings' purses.

Vaghn poured Kolby ale. "What if the thieves who stole from the ladies attend the forgathering?" Vaghn asked.

"You said they couldn't without permission," Raven countered.

"Perhaps they already have permission," the outlaw chief replied. "Even their leader, whom you say is an Irishman, may roam the badlands. In that case the council will take no action. Whatever grievance you have must be settled between you."

"If I see them, then that's how I'll settle it." Raven's voice was low. It rang with determination. "I'll recognize them, but they won't know me. They've never seen my face. They know only a high priestess, a woman clad in a dark green robe and a cowl."

"They'll recognize Kolby and his warriors," Vaghn pointed out. "They're the ones who rescued you."

"They won't suspect I'm the woman they're searching for. I've sworn to avenge the honor of my name and my family, Lord Vaghn, and I shall."

Vaghn looked skeptically at her and then at Kolby. " 'Twould not be to your advantage, or mine, for the outlaws at the forgathering to learn who you really are. They would feel that I had deceived them by bringing strangers among them. Your tents should be set up behind ours."

The Viking shook his head. "We'd appreciate your taking us among you. If Donnal finds her—"

"You'll be hard put to protect her," Vaghn finished for him.

Raven could feel her anger building. "I ask you both to withhold your judgment. We have almost a week before the forgathering. I'm willing to do all I can to regain my skills."

Kolby rolled his eyes in disgust. "I may not be able to teach you enough."

Vaghn took a deep draught of ale. "If you're determined to kill these men while you're in the badlands, my lady, remember. The fight must be fair. No one cares who fights with whom as long as he gives him an even chance. It is our one law, and it applies to all. Lord Kolby's right. You may not know enough to win."

"Either way, the fight will be fair," Raven promised. "Like you, Vaghn, I've been trained to be a Druid. It is our duty to settle all disputes and questions of honor. If any crime has been committed or murder done, we must decide the guilt or innocence."

"Aye, lady. So you must."

Rangwald returned bearing a thick bundle wrapped in cloth. He laid the bundle on the blankets between Kolby and Vaghn and unfolded the fabric to reveal not one but five swords.

With a toothy smile Vaghn waved his arm across them. "See which one fits you best, my lady."

Raven picked up each one, flexed her hand around the hilt, and swung it through the air. All five were crafted for warriors, so they were equally massive and cumbersome. She wished she had the one her father had had crafted for her years ago. She needed a sword whose pommel fit her hand, whose length from hilt to point was the same length as her arm.

She noted the inscriptions on the weapons and their names. No warrior wanted another man's weapon unless its previous owner had distinguished himself and the weapon in battle. When that happened, thereafter it carried great magic. She rather doubted the proven valor of these weapons. How had the outlaws come by them if not because their previous owners had been defeated and the swords proven weak?

Reminding herself that this was only for practice, Raven selected the one sword that seemed the lightest. It was also the best crafted. A large red jewel twinkled in the hilt. By the runes carved into the blade, she could read that its name was Wolftooth.

She handed it over to Kolby for his inspection. He took it from her and nodded. His hand was too big for the hilt. It covered up the jewel. He ran his fingers along the blade and studied the bluing to be sure it had no detectable flaw.

"The weight is good for me," Raven said. "And it seems well-balanced."

He nodded. "'Tis a good one, lady."

She looked at Vaghn. "Of course, it is a poor thing. Worthy only for practice. I will look elsewhere for a well-crafted blade with magic in it. Wolftooth's owner must have been a poor swordsman who slipped and lost his life."

Acknowledging her as an able barterer, Vaghn grinned like the wolf whose tooth he sought to trade. "Nay, lady. He was the greatest of warriors. He slew many men with this blade. It has drunk the blood of Gauls and Irish. He who owned it died of a lung fever, and his wife sold it because it made her weep to see it lie unused."

"He must have been the smallest of men," Kolby put in, joining the barter with some amusement. "Perhaps he was a little dark man from the lands far to south."

"Nay, he was a huge man," Vaghn denied. "He used this for a dagger. His great sword was twice as long as this. Come. What have you in your poor store that is of equal value?"

Raven smiled. "I have a tapestry woven by the ladies of the shrine." She ran her hand over the cloth they sat on and shook her head. "Not such poor stuff as this, but rather, notable goods that would serve as a seat of honor for an outlaw high king. It is much richer than these, outlaw."

"But only one." He shook his head. "What about my lady? She must have a tapestry as well. She would weep and wail and chastise me daily if I did not think of her."

"I would," Damona agreed. "I have to have the same as my husband. My rank demands it."

"They are probably poor quality, wife," Vaghn argued.

"The best," Raven assured him.

"How many?"

"Two. People at the forgathering would take notice. I will be robbing myself to give all this for a practice sword." Raven looked disgusted. "You should be willing to give it to me to take such a poor thing off your hands."

"It has a ruby in the hilt," Vaghn countered. "Rubies bring good luck. Your life would be protected by its magic."

"I doubt it's a ruby. Mayhap a garnet or a piece of red glass," Raven remarked to no one in particular.

"It has great magic," Vaghn insisted, ignoring her comment. "It will shield you while you learn, lady."

"There is no magic in a sword," Kolby sneered. "The man who wields it has great prowess and a little luck when he is young. He learns more by staying alive."

The three of them looked at him aghast. All three believed implicitly in the magic that attached itself to the blade of a hero.

"I will give two tapestries for it," Raven declared, slapping the ground on which she sat. "Although I have been robbed by doing so."

"I will allow the sword to pass into your hands for that poor price for the sake of my wife whose dear friend you are." Vaghn slapped the ground in turn.

"Done."

"Done."

Kolby shook his head in disgust. "Aren, get the tapestries for my lady since she is determined to exchange quality goods for inferior trash."

As soon as Raven told the youth what to search for, Aren dashed to their sleeping area. He returned shortly with the tapestries rolled up in another blan-

ket. He unrolled them on the ground in front of the
outlaw.

"Bring torches!" Vaghn yelled.

Outlaws crowded in and held torches closer to
the fabric. Silver and gold threads were reflected
in the light. Vaghn and Damona ran their hands over
the precious fabric.

Damona's eyes lit with pleasure. "They're beautiful, husband."

"Aye, wife, they are." Vaghn looked at Raven, his
own face alight. "You have traded me wonderful
things. I swear to you that the sword is a good one—
though it did not belong to a man who used it for a
dagger."

Everybody laughed.

"Now, my friends, we shall celebrate."

They ate, they drank, they talked and laughed. One
after another they told each other riddles. Then the
games began.

They wrestled. Rangwald was easily the strongest
among the Highlanders until big Durin of the Vikings
accepted his challenge. The men stripped off their
tunics and trousers. In their breechclouts they grap-
pled with each other.

Rangwald was wiry and agile, but Durin was burly.
His great shoulders and massive thighs overpowered
the other man. After much grunting and straining,
Durin suddenly dived low and swung the outlaw up
in his arms. While the other Highlanders groaned
and cursed, Durin slammed the red-haired man to
the ground and pinned him.

A howl of anguish went up as the champion fell,
but almost immediately the outlaws hailed the new
champion with good spirit and threw pieces of jewelry to him. He was named in toast after toast.

One after the other, the warriors challenged each
other with spears and daggers and darts and hand-
axes. They threw their weapons at targets to see who

could get the closest to the center. They laid wagers. They celebrated the winning and the losing.

Only when the fires died and the ale had clouded their senses did they find their furs and curl up for the night.

Vaghn lounged lazily on his new tapestry. "What about you and me, Viking? We haven't tried each other's strength."

Kolby pointed. "Is that a game I see tucked beneath that blue bolster?"

Vaghn's teeth flashed. "Aye, but you couldn't play it, my friend. It is from the distant East and very difficult to master. It is the art of war between kingdoms. This game has traveled over hundreds of miles and passed through many hands to get to me. There may not be another one like it in all the islands."

"A game of war." Kolby was intrigued.

"Aye, with high kings and queens, thanes, and Druid priests, and soldiers, and the most amazing thing of all, elephant commanders."

"Show them to me." Kolby leaned forward eagerly.

Vaghn brushed the pillow aside and pulled the lacquered board to the center of the blankets. He emptied two pouches and set up the playing pieces. At one end of a checkered board, such as one might play draughts on, he arranged gold pieces inset with red stones. At the other end he arranged pieces inset with blue stones.

Raven leaned down to pick up a tall piece with a crown carved on top to represent a high king. " 'Tis exquisite."

"I can teach it to you," Vaghn said to Kolby, "but don't expect to win. Because you haven't played it before, there will be no wager."

Kolby ran his hand over the board. He too picked up one of the playing pieces—a block carved with legs and a strange long piece in front like a very long nose.

"An elephant," Vaghn told him. "None has ever seen one. I suspect it to be a fairy beast."

Kolby snorted at the idea of such and set it back. He looked at Raven. "Which color, my lady?"

"Red," she promptly replied.

"Red, it is." Kolby tilted his head to one side and stared at Vaghn. "What's your stake, outlaw?"

"You'll lose," Vaghn warned. " 'Tis a difficult game."

Kolby shrugged. "To play without a stake is to waste time."

"Very well. Your longbow and arrows if I win."

Kolby glanced down at the board. He had seen the game once before on a voyage across the Baltic and into the heart of Russ. He had played it once, but he had lost badly. Still, he was older now and more experienced in life and the strategies of war. The outlaw might win, for he was probably proficient. On the other hand, he might not have played as often as he would have liked because he might not have had opponents to play against.

Silence had fallen over the group as they watched the leaders. All sensed that the winner of this game would win great respect and honor. Kolby picked up several of the pieces and studied them as he remembered their specific moves. He was exceptionally fond of his bow and didn't relish losing it. But he couldn't refuse the challenge.

"Done." Kolby slapped the ground. "Aren. Bring my bow and arrows. And what will you wager?"

Onlookers smiled approvingly and murmured among themselves as they laid their wagers.

"Ask." Vaghn spread his arms magnanimously, sure he would win.

"Six of your horses—of my choosing—if I win."

"Six of my *scrawny* horses. I didn't think you liked them."

"I can always use extra mounts for the six of us. Besides, these animals are bred to the clime. They can cross over bogs as easily as they can climb a mountain." He grinned. "When I win them, I'll have something to barter back to you for the cloister treasure."

"Six horses." Vaghn agreed. He laughed and slapped the ground in front of Kolby. "Done!"

Raven inched closer to Kolby, Damona to Vaghn. All four of them stared at the board. Outlaws and Vikings closed in around them. Two heads bent low as they contemplated the game pieces.

"You may have the first move," Vaghn offered generously.

Kolby moved the high king's man two spaces forward. Vaghn's eyebrows shot up. He bared his teeth in a snarl as he realized his opponent had played the game before.

From then it was attack and defend as the men slid their pieces across the squares. Vaghn played with surety and confidence which gave testimony to his skills. Kolby played tentatively, cautiously. Still, he managed to surprise Vaghn with his open formations.

The outlaw was a veteran and a ruthless one. One by one, he attacked Kolby's pieces and removed them from the board. However, Kolby was able to give almost as good as he got and defended himself, so Vaghn lost nearly as many pieces.

Then they reached an impasse and the game slowed. Each pondered his next move. The outlaws and Vikings who had been watching drifted away to their blankets. Only Kolby and Raven, Vaghn and Damona remained.

Kolby stared at the playing pieces that represented the elephant commander. According to the people of the Middle Eastern countries, who fashioned the game after their military strategy, this player was the most important and second only to the high king. For this reason, when the high king was threatened with capture, he could change places with the elephant commander and so escape.

"You're about to lose your elephant commander," Vaghn cautioned Kolby. "The high king will have nowhere to move. On the next move he'll be captured." He moved the Druid piece to threaten other pieces on a diagonal. Damona nodded her approval.

Kolby leaned back and studied the board. The outlaw had successfully captured his most powerful warrior leader and had cut his forces out from under him. Only the king's thane and a couple of men remained to protect the high king. Kolby's king was closer to the outer perimeter of the board than Vaghn's, but Vaghn was closer to winning the game.

"You are hemmed in, Viking, with no way to escape," Vaghn said as he used his Druid to knock Kolby's elephant commander from the board. "Do you surrender?"

"Nay."

"Without their leader, warriors have a tendency to scatter," Vaghn taunted.

"My warriors won't," Kolby said. He pointed to his high king piece. "They have their king yet and his thane."

Vaghn leaned back on his elbow and looked at Kolby, a smile on his lips. Ignoring the sardonic gaze, Kolby concentrated on the board and on his remaining game pieces. There had to be a way to escape. If he were to save his forces, reach the other edge and win the game, if he were to save his bow, he must sacrifice the warriors.

Kolby didn't mind losing a game, but he didn't want to lose his most highly prized weapon. As he stared, he heard the flap of strong wings. Midnight

Wind came like a messenger from Hel herself and landed on his shoulder.

Vaghn started. For a few seconds fear blanched his cheek. He couldn't believe it. Ravens sometimes bore messages to the Druids from the Otherworld. That the Viking should have such a creature land on his shoulder troubled him. When he realized the creature was a pet, he relaxed, but in that time Kolby had moved a piece—the high queen's thane.

Vaghn stared. The high king stood alone, unprotected, vulnerable.

Surprised, the outlaw frowned. "Are you sure you want to do that, Viking?"

"I'm sure."

Vaghn slid one of his men to take Kolby's sacrificial piece.

Raven sighed. Damona smiled.

Kolby picked up one of his high queen's Druid priests and swept him across the board. He swept away Vaghn's elephant commander and left the high king totally exposed. Vaghn had no warriors to throw between the Druid and the high king. He could not move his high king into the line of Kolby's thane. Kolby held up Vaghn's high king so Raven and Damona could see.

"As you said, Vaghn, only one can win." And Kolby had won. Victory tasted sweet!

Raven flashed him a big smile and clapped him on the shoulder.

Vaghn stared dazedly at the game piece Kolby held in the air. He looked back at the board where Kolby's high king sat in solitary splendor.

"The Viking wins," Vaghn finally conceded. "According to our challenge, you may choose any . . . er . . ." He cleared his throat. Kolby held up six fingers. ". . . six of my horses you wish."

"I accept the horses with deep gratitude." Kolby bowed in mockery.

"You won them fairly. You played the game with great skill," Vaghn acknowledged. "You deserve the horses. They will serve you well in your search for the tree."

He picked up Kolby's bow and ran his hand appreciatively over its curve. " 'Tis a fine weapon. I wish it had been mine."

"One of the best," Kolby agreed.

Vaghn returned it, and Kolby slipped it over his shoulder. He rose. "Now, my lord, by your leave, my lady and I should like to retire."

Vaghn waved them away and had Damona refill his tankard. "On another day, Viking, I shall win the bow from you."

"I'll give you the opportunity," Kolby promised. He guided Raven through the camp.

As they walked, Raven said, "I thought surely you were going to lose your bow."

"So did I," Kolby admitted. "If I were a superstitious man, I would say that Midnight Wind brought me directions from Odin on which piece to move."

"Perhaps he did," Raven said.

"Nay. I heard nothing. My mind told me the raven would distract the Druid from his plan."

When they reached the top of the incline close to their sleeping area, Raven looked up at the sky, aglow with starlight. "Tonight has been wonderful. I wish all our days could be as happy as this one."

They walked into their camp, the fire nothing more than golden-red embers. Kolby fed it until flames curled upward and lighted their faces. He and Raven undressed and slid beneath his cloak.

"And all our nights as wonderful as this one," Kolby murmured, taking her in his arms.

Durin pulled Kolby aside the next morning as the thane came down to the central gathering area to break his fast. "Bradach decamped during the night."

Kolby raised one wary eyebrow. "Without his money?"

Durin took a few choice words to describe Bradach's ancestry, in particular his mother's relationship with his father. Then he continued, "He took Aren's horse and helped himself to items from several of our packs."

"Did he get anything of great value?"

Durin snorted. "We didn't have anything of great value but our pride. Shall we hunt the cur down?"

Kolby shrugged. "Nay. Let him go and good riddance. Aren can have two of the horses that I won last night. With those he can trade for a fine horse at the forgathering."

For ten mornings, after consuming meals of oatcakes sweetened with a little honey, the company moved on. As they traveled farther down the southern shore of the haunted loch, Raven felt Kolby's excitement growing. So far they had not passed any other bands of outlaws, but sometimes the sound of horses' hooves and the squeak of harness alerted them that others were making their way by different routes to the forgathering.

Each day Raven dressed in trousers and tunic. She plaited her hair in a single braid, and wore a leather headband around her forehead. She had practiced with her blowpipe until her mouth and tongue were sore from having used them so much. She had also polished her skills with the dagger.

Kolby had wrapped her sword in cloth to protect her skin from the edges. Then he made her swing it for an hour each morning and afternoon to get accustomed to its weight before they started practicing as opponents. Each day she gained new strength and confidence, but so far Kolby had not actually engaged her in mock battle.

She was also becoming a woman obsessed. Her

only thought was to avenge the shame brought on her name. Kolby could not fault her for this, for she had accepted the warrior's creed. Now she lived by it.

Their days were filled with traveling; their evenings with practicing; their nights with wild love. With each passing day Kolby and Raven fell more deeply in love. And the deeper in love they fell, the less they talked about their future—the more they lived for the day. They gave to each other. They took for themselves.

Away from the rest of the camp, Kolby and Raven lay beneath a cloak on their pallet. Since the nights were getting cooler with each passing day, both of them now slept in their tunics and undergarments.

The air was brisk, but the sky was clear and full of stars. Bramblemoon month was the loveliest time of year, Raven thought. Frost had changed autumn leaves to their full color. She loved it.

Both she and Kolby were tired. Since they would be arriving at the rendezvous spot for the forgathering on the morrow, Vaghn had pushed farther tonight than usual. They had eaten a cold meal, then relaxed around the fire. Raven and Kolby had gone directly to bed.

"On the morrow, we arrive at the forgathering," she said. Turning over, she leaned against him. "Are you excited?"

"Aye. And fearful," he admitted. "I wonder if this is another trail that will lead me nowhere."

Raven thought about the shawl in the cloister satchels. Many times she had been tempted to tell him what the inscriptions on the bells meant. Even if she could not read them, they could find someone who could. She couldn't bring herself to do so. Even though she had taken off the cloister vestments, both physically and emotionally, she hadn't shed her integrity. She would not violate a sacred oath.

"Perhaps the man who knows where the tree is

located doesn't exist at all. He could be one of Vaghn's schemes," Kolby said. " 'Tis very prestigious for Vaghn to appear at the forgathering with warriors of quality like my men. And he knows we are not outcasts, that we do not live by their code. Therefore he can trust us. I'm not sure we can trust him."

Privately Raven also doubted the existence of the man who had seen the sacred tree, but she didn't believe that the outlaw leader had lied to them for his own prestige. "We have to believe Vaghn. He has given us no reason not to."

"Nay," Kolby muttered, but he sighed.

"If you don't find the tree, will you keep searching?" Raven asked. "For how long? Forever?"

"Nay, Michael and his father have been sailing back and forth between Glenmuir and Northland with some regularity. They keep me informed as to Ura's health. When he dies, my mission, even if I never complete it, will be finished."

Raven bit her lip. She threw her arm across her eyes. "Are you eager to return to your homeland?"

He held her tight. "I wish only to remain with you, lady."

He turned on his side. Their foreheads touched. In one twisted, cruel stroke, destiny had thrown them together, but had guaranteed their ultimate separation. As long as they rode through the badlands with outlaws, they could pretend. But the day would come when they would ride out of the dark forest, around the haunted loch and back to their homes. Their destinies would take them in separate directions.

Kolby pulled her closer to him and inhaled her womanly sweetness, letting it fill him, letting it ease his heavy heart. His lips touched hers, and she received him hotly, demandingly. She opened her mouth and took his tongue into hers. She gently closed her teeth around it. He trembled in her embrace. She released him.

"Mate with me, my love," she whispered.

Alerting him to her need, she slid her hands around his buttocks and pressed him against her belly. Kolby groaned. His hands shifted on her body, finding and stroking her breasts through the tunic fabric to send rush after rush of pleasure through her, to create a fevered wanting in her.

His lips moved in a hot trail over her breasts, up her neck, and finally claimed hers once more in a hard and searching kiss. His tongue did wonderful things to her as it stroked the inside of her mouth. He had possessed her completely when he had ruptured her maidenhead. Now in a simple kiss he promised to take her soul.

Turning her face from his, yet feeling the heat of his mouth, Raven drew in ragged breaths. She had resisted the sacrifice of maidenhood, but that had been only a tiny membrane. Now he asked for her soul, and she willingly gave it to him.

Kolby's lips moved over her cheeks as his hands moved over her breasts, his callused fingers kneading and stroking until her nipples crested. When he rolled them gently between his fingers, Raven became trembling sensation from the top of her head to the bottoms of her feet.

"Each day you grow sweeter. Hotter," Kolby said. "I can't live without you."

She opened her eyes and stared at him.

"Sometimes I feel you are a potion and I'm addicted to you," he confessed. "Truly you are magical, my lady love. The lady of winter. My lady of the night."

"Nay, if I had magic powers, I would cast a spell that would solve all our problems," she murmured. "One that would allow us to be together always."

His hands moved once more, light, gentle strokes from rounded buttocks to her shoulders and back to her hips. She gladly followed when his hands pressed her hips against the hard heat of his sex. She smiled and purred—pure satisfaction from deep within.

She rotated her hips against his arousal. He groaned, and his arms tightened, locking their bodies together. They moved each for himself, each for the other, their pleasure one.

His tongue trailed fire along the side of her neck. "I want to be inside you again."

"Aye, my love, I want it too." She arched her hips against him.

Burning with desire, Raven gave him what he wanted; she took what she wanted. The kiss was deep, wet, and passionate. She didn't want tenderness. She needed an urgent joining. Her arms locked about his neck, she clung more tightly to him. When he finally ended the kiss, he raised his head.

He touched the taut nipples that pressed against her tunic, and again sensations curled sweetly through her body. He bent down to her breasts. He touched them. Through the material she felt the moist warmth of his breath.

When his teeth closed delicately around one nipple, she cried out her pleasure. One hand curled around his neck, and she brought him closer to her. She locked his body to hers.

"Undress me," she whispered. "Make love to me."

His hands moved to her waist. A few tugs and her tunic was gone to reveal her breasts, swollen and throbbing with need. His hands possessed them, and again Raven felt the fiery burst of need. Every touch to her body reminded her how empty her life had been without him, how much she wanted him.

Before he knew what he was doing, Kolby was kneeling over her. He unfastened her underpants and slid them down her legs. She felt the rush of air against her skin.

Kolby clasped a foot in each hand. She had marveled at how big his hands were, but as they held her feet, they looked even bigger. With his thumb he drew designs on her skin. She cried out with pleasurable surprise, not realizing until that moment that her feet and ankles were so sensitive. The strokes continued, whetting her desire. She whimpered and writhed.

"Sweet, sweet Raven," he whispered.

When Raven thought she couldn't endure the pleasurable torment any more, he brought the foot to his face.

"I love every bit of you, my lady."

He trailed kisses along the bottom of her foot, then lightly rubbed his beard-stubbled cheeks and chin against her instep.

She breathed raggedly. She shivered. She arched against him. With the tip of his figners he traced a line of fire beneath her arch. Her pelvis burned with need. She felt an emptiness, an emptiness that only Kolby could fill.

"Kolby—" She tangled her hands in his hair. "Now."

He released her feet to straighten and to kiss up the length of her legs to her waist, over her breasts and up her neck. He brushed his mouth over her lips, the pulse at the base of her throat, and the tips of her breasts. She moaned softly.

His lips touched hers, and she cupped her hands behind his head to hold him firmly to her. As his tongue had penetrated her body only moments before, hers penetrated his now.

She insinuated a hand between their bodies to touch his belly. She felt the brush of crisp hair against her palm as she slid it lower to unfasten the waistband of his trousers and to slip her hands through the folds of the material. Her fingertips caressed and traced hot satin skin that surged within her grasp. As she reacquainted herself with the contours of his hunger, she felt him tremble.

"You've given to me, my love, she murmured thickly. "'Tis time I gave to you."

She lowered her face and circled his nipple with her lips. She swung her head so that her hair brushed against his torso. She began to caress his other nipple with her tongue. One hand spread through the thick hair of his head while the other gently touched his most intimate parts.

"I've wanted to touch you like this," she murmured, "since that morning I saw you bathing."

As Kolby breathed more heavily, Raven lowered her head. Her hair and her lips brushed caresses down his abdomen. Her tongue flicked against the taut stomach muscles. She trailed her fingers up and down his thighs. Raven straddled him, lowered herself on him, and pushed back on her knees. Swathed in star glow and moonlight, she let Kolby look at her.

"Raven." His voice was thick.

She sheathed his erection with her moist warmth. When she leaned over him, balancing herself on her palms, she ran the soles of her feet down his legs, stretching her body along his.

Kolby captured one of her nipples in his mouth and began to tug gently. He caught her buttocks with both hands. He settled her on top of him and began to arch and thrust.

Wanting to please him and wanting to be pleased, Raven worked with him, their bodies moving in matched meter. As they neared their climax, Raven gasped for breath, but she didn't release Kolby's mouth. Rather she cupped his buttocks with her hands as he cupped hers. They made the last arch and thrust together. Spent, Raven collapsed on him, breathing heavily. She closed her eyes and reveled in the sweet aftermath.

Kolby pushed dampened tendrils from her face. He traced the outline of her ears and breasts. He tickled her buttocks.

She lay there with her head on his chest. "I'm so glad I have you with me," she murmured. "I don't know how I would have endured Melanthe's death without you."

"You would have," he said. "You're a strong woman."

"I would have," she admitted, "but with more difficulty."

After a few wonderful moments in which she listened to his breathing, to his heart beating, she whispered, "Good night, my love."

He whispered the same words to her.

Chapter 14

Bradach squirmed and squealed in terror, antici-pating the agony to come. "I tell you the old priestess died. The old one. Her guards went back to the cloister. Don't—don't—"

His protests rose to a scream as the point of Donnal's blade penetrated his clothing and drew blood from the taut skin of his belly.

"But the young one didn't go with them, did she? That's right, isn't it? Isn't it?" The Irishman twisted harder.

Bradach rose on his toes, bracing his back against the tree. He could feel the blood trickling down his thigh. Desperately he looked from one vulpine face to the other. No mercy anywhere. The pair holding him and the one standing behind Donnal might have been looking at a rabbit that Donnal was about to skin for supper.

"Yes. Yes. Yes! That's right! That's right!"

"So she's spreading her legs for the Viking?"

"No. Yes!" Bradach didn't know which answer the man wanted. The knife point twisted and he howled again.

Donnal grinned. He spared his men a swift grin. "Then we can have a turn with her before we take her back to Triath."

Heat kindled in their eyes. Only one of them looked skeptical. "He's a big one—that Viking."

Donnal snarled. "Coward." He returned his attention to Bradach. "Where are they bound?"

Bradach saw his chance. A slim one, but a chance. "I'll take you there," he begged. "I'll take you there. Free. No charge. I can guide you right to them. That's what I—I—"

"Where?" Donnal punctuated his question with a twist of the knife.

"Ow! The forgathering. The outlaws' forgathering. I'll take you there. I swear I can lead you—" He never finished his sentence.

Donnal drove his knife upward into the Scotsman's heart, twisted, and stepped back out of the way as the lifeblood followed the blade out onto the ground. He and the others had turned away and headed for the horses before the body stopped twitching.

Vaghn led his troop toward a tumbled gray crag that lay athwart the cut in the mountain range. As Kolby rode up beside him, the outlaw pointed to the narrow keyhole entrance that they would soon be riding through. "That's the entrance. On the other side is the hidden glen."

Kolby looked at it in wonder. "How did you ever discover such a place?"

Vaghn shrugged. "Mayhap the first outlaw who fled into this land found it. Mayhap it was found later. All I know is that it has become the place for the forgathering. No one comes through here but outlaws."

As if to prove the truth of his statement, a bearded man reared his head from amid the boulders that lay atop the slanted crag. Sharp eyes scanned the faces riding single-file toward him. In his hand he held a mighty bow, trained on Vaghn's heart.

Vaghn raised his hand. "Greetings, Pebyr. All is well?"

"Greetings, Vaghn. All is well. You've new men with you, I see." Pebyr's eyes narrowed as he studied each face in turn. His stare returned to Kolby, who was riding directly behind Vaghn in the narrow passageway.

"A few. A few," Vaghn said easily. "A high king didn't take kindly to some Northlanders cheating him."

The guard gave a bark of laughter. "High kings do take a dim view of that." He looked hard at Kolby, then at Raven, and then at Durin, Aren, Thorfinn, and Sven. The moment was highly charged. Then he nodded. "Pass on."

One by one they rode through the narrow cut, their knees almost brushing the sides of the granite.

"How do they get carts through here?" Kolby wanted to know. "I thought you said this was a trading fair."

"There's a wider cut down at the south end of the glen," Vaghn said. "And a strip of beach on the north side where it fronts the loch. But only the most daring bring goods in by water."

Raven leaned forward to whisper for Kolby's ears only. "They know to be afraid of the kelpies."

The Viking grunted and hunched his big shoulders, as if he were trying to ignore a buzzing insect.

Vaghn's horse pulled against the rise, crested it, and started down the other side. "Break out the banners!" he shouted jubilantly. "Let them see us coming!"

The sight that spread before Raven was pure magic. In amongst the dark green trees on the shore of the gray loch, a temporary village of brightly colored tents and portable lean-to shelters spread along the glen. Standards rose in front of the tents as gay as any that she had seen at fairs in Inverness or Forres.

Beneath Vaghn's own red, gold, and black banners the troop made a gallant entry through the center of the forgathering. The former Druid and his wife seemed in their element, exchanging greetings with familiar faces, issuing and accepting challenges from the leaders of other bands, and generally letting everyone know they had arrived.

Down the glen they rode, wending their way through spaces left between the various tents where goods could be sold to all comers, people could parley and haggle among themselves, and livestock could be corraled. In front of the tents, small fires burned. Over every one of them were iron racks and cooking spits. Delicious smells filled the air.

Raven had to swallow hard; she had eaten nothing since they had broken their fast early in the day. Though she looked longingly when one vendor held up several sticks with roasted meats sizzling on their ends, the troop trotted smartly along. The magnet that drew them was the only permanent building in the area—a huge mead hall.

A large fire blazed in the space that had been cleared in front of the building. Vaghn held up his hand. Rangwald leaped down and made a show of taking the outlaw chieftain's bridle so that he could dismount in grand style.

Out of the door of the mead hall came several men of Vaghn's stamp, dark men with the eyes of hawks. Though they grinned and clapped Vaghn on the back and clasped his hand in hard grasps, Raven had the feeling that none of the camaraderie was real. In their hearts and minds, they walked alone, each separate, a law unto himself.

As she edged her horse nearer, Kolby reined his stallion to cut her off. "Don't," he bade her. "Keep your head down and draw your cloak across your legs. I don't want to have to fight the entire lot for you."

She flashed him a defiant look, but then realized that several of the outlaw chieftains, their greetings finished, were scanning Vaghn's troop with particular attention to the women. Without argument she drew the edges of her cloak up over her knee and backed her horse into the middle of a square formed by Kolby's four Vikings.

"Your place has been reserved for you, Vaghn," she heard one of the men say. "But before you go, come in and drink with us. Tell us all." The outlaw motioned to Kolby to join him and the whole group entered the mead hall. Rangwald led the others away to the appointed spot.

The odor of food was always in the camp. Men were constantly going out on hunting expeditions and returning with freshly killed game. Others spent hours beside the loch catching fish. Their women had brought sacks of turnips, onions, and oats with which to prepare stews and soups, as well as casks of cheese and butter to enrich the dishes.

At least four brewers had been invited to attend because their ales and beers were popular with the outlaws. Huge kegs were set on the tails of carts and men brought their own tankards to fill for a price.

Most of the outlaws had spread items for sale or trade on trestles or on groundcloths in front of their tents.

Raven wondered at the variety of their wares. She had never seen their like before. " 'Tis amazing," she remarked as Aren presented himself to be her escort for the day. "The craftsmanship is truly remarkable on some of the items. On others it's very crude. And yet the goods are displayed side by side."

The Viking lad concealed a smile. He felt infinitely older and wiser than the innocent lady from the

Cloister of the Grove, who didn't realize that almost everything for sale here was stolen. Instead he struck a pose in front of her. "What do you think of my new clothing, my lady?"

With a smile she looked him over from head to toe. The lad sported bright blue trousers, cross-gartered with yellow strips of hide, and a red silk tunic. His headband was also red. When Vaghn had suggested that the Vikings adapt the outlaw's mode of dress so as not to draw attention to themselves, Aren had taken his advice with enthusiasm. "I think it very fine." She refused to hurt the boy's feelings, but she tempered her compliment with her next question. "Has Lord Kolby seen you?"

Aren grinned and winked. "He rolled his eyes. No doubt he's envious because he couldn't find a red silk tunic to fit him."

"No doubt," Raven agreed. "You do look like an outlaw. No one can accuse you of being a Viking."

"I'm a member of Vaghn's outlaws." Aren strutted around in a circle. Then he dropped his pose and looked around more seriously. "Where would you like to go, my lady?"

"I'd like to find a swordmaker."

Aren shook his head. "I don't know about that. Maybe a sword seller."

"Then we'll see what he has to offer." With her hand wrapped around Wolftooth's hilt, she allowed Aren to lead, and in some cases clear, the way. She hadn't yet decided whether to trade for a smaller sword. Ten days of practicing had given her confidence and increased her own strength. The weapon did not seem nearly as large or cumbersome as it had originally. Still, she wanted to look.

Her desire for revenge burned hotter with each passing day as she remembered Melanthe's goodness and thought about all the wonderful things she would have done as a Chosen One of the Great

Mother Goddess. Sometimes Raven woke up in the night trembling with sorrow and anger.

The two walked along until they came to a tent that was larger than most of the others around it. Banners divided diagonally into fields of blue and red hung from standards attached to each corner. A swarthy man with a hard face sat on a stool beside a collection of swords and daggers spread out on a dark cloth. Through the tent opening, Raven could see a couple of men with his same dark looks seated in front of a board game.

As she hefted each weapon in turn, the seller looked her over with a calculating eye that made her uncomfortable. One sword was definitely smaller than the rest, with a handsome gold-chased hilt that fit her hand well and a blue-steel blade that sang through the air. She could see no flaw in the weapon anywhere.

She tilted her head in her youthful escort's direction. "What think you, Aren? How much do you think it's worth?"

His whisper barely reached her ears. "As much as you are willing to pay, my lady. Remember, everything here is probably stolen."

She looked at him in astonishment. That thought hadn't occurred to her.

At that moment the swarthy man barked out a question. "Do you want it?"

"I'm—I'm not sure." Suddenly the rippling banners and tents and the throng of people seemed less gay. The day seemed darker and uglier.

" 'Tis a good sword for a woman," the tradesman urged. "Fit to her hand. And so sharp a man wouldn't know he'd been cut until he saw his own blood."

Raven shuddered. Revenge was the scavenger of the soul, or so she had been taught. So she did believe. It had brought her down to deal with the lowest of the low. Then she remembered Melanthe.

Donnal had spoken of Triath. Her family must be rid of the O'Illands forever. She would worry about the condition of her soul later.

"'Tis such a small piece, it must be worth very little," she remarked, laying the sword down.

The swarthy face remained impassive. He spread his hands. "You're welcome to look elsewhere, but mark me well. If another woman comes by and wants it, it goes with her."

"I will trade you the sword that I have." She drew the outlaw's sword from its scabbard. "It is of greater worth because it is a better size and should be easier to trade."

The swarthy man spat on the ground. "'Tis worth nothing. You got it from that weasel Vaghn. I know the man who made it. His swords are flawed. It will break on you in battle."

She shook her head. "You lie."

"I don't lie." Smiling like the evil one, he took Wolftooth from her and lifted the smaller sword. With the ease of long practice, he struck them together above the cloth. Steel clanged against steel, but one did not ring true. Indeed, the sword that she had bargained for, the sword that Vaghn had sworn was a true blade, snapped in two as if it were a twig.

Both she and Aren stared dumbfounded as fully half the blade fell to the cloth. The tradesman used the tip of the smaller weapon to flip the shattered piece off the cloth. Contemptuously he tossed the hilt after it into the weeds.

With a mocking grin, the swarthy man whirled the victorious sword above his head, making it sing like a lyre. Then he bowed knowingly. "You would have died, woman. In your first fight."

Ferocious anger boiled in her. She was Raven nea Pryse, daughter of the high king of Ailean. Vaghn had cheated her. The proof lay in the weeds. For all she knew, Kolby had let him do it when the Viking had picked up the sword and pronounced it sound. She preferred to believe that Kolby had also been fooled. Surely he hadn't planned that when they started practicing together he would defeat her easily and make her turn from her quest. She clasped her hands together as high color burned in her cheeks.

The men inside the tent came to the opening to grin at her.

"My lady." Aren laid a hand on her arm. "Come away."

She shook her head. "How much for the sword?"

The swarthy man grinned. "What do you have to trade?"

She had almost nothing. Her gold had been traded by Kolby. Then her hand flew to the brooch—his brooch—at the placket of her tunic. If he had encouraged her to buy a flawed blade, then he could pay for her new one. "This."

The swordsman looked at it.

Aren tugged harder at her arm. "No, lady," he whispered. "'Tis Lord Kolby's. 'Tis very valuable."

The man heard him. A slow grin spread over his face. "The brooch for the sword."

She looked at the blade. "I want an inscription on it."

He motioned one of his companions forward. "Many do. Something fierce. Canilis can do that for you."

She pulled a square of leather from inside her tunic and knelt to unfold it on the cloth.

The men bent over it. Almost immediately the one called Canilis straightened away, his eyes wide. He shook his head. "The *craebh ciuil*," he muttered. "You want the *craebh ciuil*."

She raised her head from her design of branch and apples. "Aye. And I have the right to carry it."

He continued to shake his head, but the sword seller slapped him on the side of the head and cursed him for a fool. At last the man whined that he would do it. The tradesman held out his hand. "The brooch."

"When the sword is delivered."

He slapped his palm. "I can't sell it after it's inscribed with that name of yours."

Still she hesitated. "How do I know you won't leave?"

Angrily he threw up his hands. "Do you think you're the only one who'll buy from me? Be off with you unless you want to buy them all. I've got a business to run here." Beside himself with exasperation, he hooked his thumb toward the weeds. "Take your broken sword. Mayhap you can find a smithy to mend—"

She tore the brooch from the placket and flung it down. "In three days," she demanded. "In three days."

The two men exchanged looks. Canilis hung his head. "In three days," he muttered. "In three days."

She strode away, her hand clasping the placket of her tunic, Aren at her heels. The two of them skirted around a man who was moving three small walnut shells around and around the top of a table. Men were lined up to place bets on which shell covered a small red rock. "Do you know where Kolby is?" she asked.

Aren gulped. "In the mead hall participating in the games. Vaghn has placed huge wagers on his strength."

They walked past tents where traders hawked their wares, but Raven no longer paid attention. Her ears were burning with anger. She could feel the breath hot in her throat. She strode into the mead hall.

Just inside she was forced to stop. The room was so crowded. Outlaws flanked the trestle tables, drinking and exchanging gossip, boasting of their great deeds. They roared with laughter and shouted with anger.

The game master walked up and down among them, taking the wagers and wielding a mighty cudgel as he threatened those who disagreed too loudly.

"Do you see him?" she asked Aren.

The young man looked around. A slow grin spread over his face at the sight of all the gaming men. "I'll search for him."

She saw he was eager to be among them. "Go and join in," she advised. "I'll be safe here. I can take care of myself."

Before he left her side, Aren looked at her curiously. "Who are you searching for, my lady? Vaghn or Kolby or the Irish thieves?"

Her face was winter-cold. Her eyes glinted like ice. "All," she said. "I have many scores to settle."

Aren gulped. "Any sword may be flawed, lady. The eye can't always tell."

She managed a small smile of reassurance. "Do you see Lord Kolby?"

"Aye."

Shoving people aside with his shoulders, Aren led the way through the throng. At the foot of the dais in the center of the mead hall, Kolby was seated on a stool at a trestle table. Across from him sat a huge man. His upper arms were like tree trunks. His forearms were like huge hams. His red face glared out from a tangle of wild hair and beard.

All around them men were making bets. A great deal of money lay on the table. Vaghn was bragging loudly that Kolby, whom he called the "Golden Viking," was his man.

"My lady." Kolby rose when Raven came to his side. When he clasped her hand, he ran his finger over the bracelet he had given her. He did not seem to notice the absence of the brooch. His Viking blood was up. "I'm glad you're here. Have you a token to give me for luck?"

"You'll be needing it," a rough voice yelled. "Gare broke two men's arms at the last forgathering."

Raven couldn't believe the size of the man. Beside him, Kolby's arms and shoulders, which she knew were as strong as iron, looked like a boy's.

"Five times champion," yelled another.

Raven watched Vaghn taking bets. He stood to make a great deal of money. She wondered if he bet with Kolby or against him. She couldn't doubt that the outlaw chieftain had at least suspected the sword was flawed. She promised herself to confront him and demand a reparation.

For now she looked up into Kolby's golden eyes. They were confident. He smiled, though the tension in his body was apparent in the flexing of his muscles.

She looked at Gare. He was powerful and fearsome, but he had a certain dullness of eye. She turned to the assembly and raised her arm. "My man shall defeat him!"

While the Vikings and Vaghn's outlaws cheered, she took off her headband and laid it across Kolby's shoulder as a token. Then she covered it with her hand. So far had she come from her cloistered life that she thought nothing of touching him in public. Still, she didn't hang around his neck and kiss him as she had seen some of the other women do to their men. "A talisman."

His hand covered hers for an instant. "No apples?"

"No apples, but a great deal of magic."

He dropped down on the bench and took his position.

"The game's about to begin!" the master shouted. "Come all! Make your bets now."

"Double on the Viking!" Vaghn shouted.

Above the roar of the excited men, the master called out the instructions. Both men braced their elbows on the table, right hand clasping right hand.

The object of the game was to force the opponent's hand to the table by the weight and strength of arm and shoulder alone. While it looked simple enough and relatively safe, men's arms had been known to snap like dry sticks, wrists had been broken, and hands had been crushed.

"Begin!" the master shouted.

The crowd's roar rose to pandemonium.

With the first flex of his rippling muscles, Gare forced Kolby's hand to the left. Kolby's face turned red. The veins in his arm bulged as the muscles swelled. Clenching his teeth together, he grunted and pushed against Gare's hand. The outlaw was tough and determined to win.

Gare's companions standing behind him laughed and made comments about limp-wristed Vikings.

Grinning confidently as he looked around at his supporters, the outlaw took a tankard of ale in his free hand and drained it in one gulping swallow. The cheers of the crowd shook the mead hall's powerful beams.

His face darkening with the effort, Kolby swung the outlaw's arm back up. Gare's tankard tumbled to the floor. The man snarled, heaved, and pushed Kolby's arm down once again. It trembled dangerously close to the table. The game master squatted and looked, but the back of Kolby's hand did not quite touch.

Raven held her breath as the outlaws began to mutter among themselves. Until today Gare had been the champion arm wrestler. No one had ever opposed him for so long.

Then, slowly, Gare's arm began to rise. Slowly. Slowly. Sweat streamed from both men's faces. Kolby's jaw knotted with effort. His men began to grin.

"Do it, Kolby!" Durin called. "He's a slab of blubber and half-drunk besides."

"Do it!" Aren yelled.

The arms were upright again. Then slowly, slowly, Kolby pressed Gare's backward. Now it was the outlaw who was red-faced. He drew in a breath, his brown, uneven teeth exposed. He pushed against Kolby's hand, but his strength was depleted. Kolby kept the pressure steady. Gare's expression changed to one of desperation.

The game master moved to Gare's side of the table to check when the back of Gare's fist touched down. The crowd had grown silent except for the gasping and groaning of the combatants.

With a mighty shout, Kolby forced the outlaw's hand to the table and held it there. The game master hit the table with his hand to signal the contest was over.

"Vaghn's man has won!" he shouted.

Kolby rose amid the cheers of his men and the cries of disappointment from the outlaws. He raised his victorious arm aloft. Aren raked in his winnings. Vaghn's outlaws and the Vikings began to collect their bets.

Turning to Raven, Kolby swept her a low bow. "Because of you, my lady."

"Hardly, my lord." She laid her hand on his upper arm. "Because of your prodigious strength."

Suddenly Kolby's expression changed. He stared at the placket where her tunic gaped. She lifted her chin, her eyes daring him to say something.

She was spared an explanation when Vaghn clapped Kolby on the back and turned him around. "You've made us all rich," he declared jubilantly.

Kolby's eyes narrowed. "Now find the man, Vaghn. We've been at this place two days now and still I'm no nearer the tree."

Vaghn's smile slipped. "He's late," he protested. "He's a hermit. He doesn't like crowds."

Kolby's big arm, the arm that had defeated Gare,

wrapped around Vaghn's shoulder. His big hand squeezed. "Find him. Or you'll be very, very sorry."

The outlaw sucked in his breath. His black eyes darted about the crowd, but no one else noticed that he was in distress. Finally he nodded, but with a certain lack of conviction.

Kolby released the man and stepped back. One more long look and he turned his attention to Raven. "Where is your brooch, lady?"

Rather than answer Kolby, Raven caught hold of Vaghn's cloak before he could slip away. "Vaghn, you sold me a flawed sword."

The outlaw started to shake his head, but she held up her hand. "One blow, Vaghn! One blow from a smaller sword and the blade snapped."

"I swear—"

"You're a thief," she interrupted. "I should have known better than to buy anything from you, but my need was great. It still is." She let her anger shift to Kolby. "Did you see the flaw on the blade?"

He crossed his arms before his chest. "I told you there was no magic in it."

His answer set her blood on fire. He had neither denied nor confirmed her accusation, but she was fairly certain he had seen something on the sword to make him doubt it. Still he had let her trade away precious tapestries for false goods. And he had traded away her gold for his own information.

And now he wrestled and played with these outlaws as if he were one of them.

She turned on her heel and began to force her way through the crowd.

Kolby threw Vaghn an angry look. The outlaw shrugged as if to say he had no morals, nor any responsibility if someone felt himself cheated. "I don't make the swords. I sell what I steal."

Intense frustration swept Kolby. Would this foolish

quest never end? He had taken the cloister gold to buy information that would probably be useless when he finally got it—if he ever got it. His lady love's mother had died and she could have been endangered by a flawed sword. She had every right to be furiously angry with him. And here he stood, engaging in stupid games while all around him the scum of the earth rioted and reeled, yelling, drinking, sweating, stinking.

He motioned to Aren. "Use whatever you have to from that pile of coins you raked in to get back her brooch."

"Aye, Lord Kolby." The lad darted away.

Durin came to his side. "Trouble."

"Nothing but," the Viking replied. His friend nodded. "Ura never knew what he asked me to do. The price of my name may be too high to pay."

His friend nodded sympathetically.

Sick to his stomach, Kolby plowed his way through the mass of humanity that kept him back from the door of the mead hall.

Raven returned to the tent Kolby had traded for. How she longed for Melanthe's counsel. For the first time in her life, she felt truly alone. Dropping to her knees, she opened the satchel and drew forth the sacred shawl, her mother's most treasured possession. The bells tinkled tender music as she swung the soft blue wool around her shoulders and wrapped it over her arms.

She knelt there for a long minute, trying to calm her thoughts, but the camp noises intruded on her meditation. She needed to be away. She had to get away. Her body trembled and her breath came fast. After nine years in the peace of the cloister, the shock of so many people was robbing her of the ability to think.

The shawl enfolding her from shoulders to just

above her knees, Raven hurried away between the tents. Careless of where she walked, she paid no heed to the outlaws trying to tempt her with their tawdry wares. Head down, her hands buried beneath the soft blue folds, she fled to the peace of the forest, anywhere she could be alone. Along the way, people jostled her, and here and there a dog ran out to bark and snap at her.

Then she passed the last row of tents. Out in the open air, she took a deep, clean breath before she plunged into the forest. After the smells of humanity the air was sharp and clean. After the motley colors of the tents and dress, the dark green was soothing. After the noise of hundreds of voices, the quiet fell over her like a balm.

She stopped and leaned her shoulder against a tree. After the tumult of the forgathering, the peace was blessed. She closed her eyes.

A hard arm encircled her waist. A hand clapped her across the mouth.

"Got you," a masculine voice growled as Raven was dragged away from the tree, deeper into the forest. "'Tis the priestess. Who else would wear the shawl with the bells? It came from the cloister satchels. We have her, Donnal."

Raven struggled. She kicked backward and punched, but the shawl, its bells jangling wildly, entrapped her arms and she couldn't see behind her. Besides, the man was strong. She landed a lucky kick on his shin. He grunted. Then his arm around her waist tightened so she couldn't draw a breath. She could feel her ribs bending under the force. Her vision began to fade. Was he going to crush the life out of her?

"What've you got there, Ulad?"

"'Tis the young one that the Scotsman told us about. I swear." As he spoke, the one called Ulad eased his arm around her waist.

From beside a swift-running stream, a figure rose and stalked toward her.

Raven sucked in a desperate breath and let it out in a cry of terror. The Irishman stood before her. Not with a hood concealing his features. Not in the dark of night. Not from a distance. But so close she could lay her hand on his chest.

A nightmare come to life. For a moment she thought she was dreaming. He looked like Alba O'Illand. How could such a thing be? Alba was dead. She had been told he was dead. Moreover, before he had died, her sister's wildcat had clawed his face. This couldn't be Alba.

Even in the darkness of the forest, his blue eyes glowed brightly above his sharp cheekbones. His high white forehead was just as she remembered it, with a mass of auburn hair curling around it. He was as handsome as ever—and as evil.

"Raven nea Pryse."

"Donnal?" she whispered.

He nodded. His fist lifted her chin and turned her face upward. His eyes scanned her. "Greine o Donnal. Alba's cousin. Heir to the house of O'Illand unless you spoil it for me. But I don't think you will. So this is the sister that Sligo's high king has sent us for."

"Why have you come for me?" she demanded. "Why come all this distance and kill so many people?"

"Triath." He stepped back. "The old man wants a child of your body. He wants to father a son to replace the two he's lost. He'll never do it."

Raven shuddered at the flat intonation of his voice. She remembered the night he'd killed his own man with no more compunction than one would kill a rat. She remembered her guards murdered, good men, competent men, but no match for merciless killers. Above all, she remembered her mother, an innocent, a truly good and kind woman, dying in fever and pain. Clearly, this man was pure evil.

"Let me go," she said. "Tell Triath you couldn't find me."

"It's a thought." He laughed. His hand slid down her neck and into the gap in her tunic. He closed his fingers over her breast. "But you're a pretty wench, and spirited."

Raven had worked her own hand free of the shawl. Like her sister's wildcat, she clawed at his hand where he presumed to touch her body. Donnal caught her wrist with his other hand and slapped her cheek.

"Pretty and spirited." His hand closed over the bracelet Kolby had given her. With a twist he pulled it off and held it up. "Gold. Good. But not nearly enough. If you have the shawl, you must have the gold as well. Where's the rest of it?"

"Where you'll never get your hands on it."

He looked over her head at Ulad. "Bind her. She can entertain us as we travel." He leaned close until his hot whisper brushed her cheek. "We can always drop her overboard off the Irish coast."

A sweep of his leg tripped her up. Leather thongs bit into her wrists and then her ankles. They had her trussed and helpless while she was still trying to recover her breath.

Donnal mounted his pony. Ulad hesitated before handing her up to the Irishman. "Your mount's already got a bowed tendon," the thief warned. "Light though she be, she's still extra weight."

"She rides with me," Donnal growled. "Nothing happens to her until I say so."

With a shrug, the thief tossed her over the saddle bow. Raven groaned as the weight of her body knocked the breath out of her again. She was going to have a painful ride. The jangling of the bells sounded like weeping.

Night was coming on. No one knew she'd been

abducted. Moreover, Kolby might not come after her anyway. He was undoubtedly angry that she had bartered his brooch for a sword. He might leave her to pursue his quest. Her only salvation might be her strength and craft—and the one small dagger strapped to her thigh.

Then she remembered the night she had watched Kolby track these very same men by the light of the moon. He and his raven had a special love of the night. She was a fool to think he wouldn't come. He was her champion. As a matter of pride, he wouldn't let her be taken away from him. She composed her mind to pray to the Great Mother Goddess for help and strength and—above all—forgiveness.

As the thieves rode away down the narrow glen, her fingers moved in the darkness, closed around one of the jingling bells—and ripped it from the sacred shawl. Praying most earnestly, she let it fall.

Chapter 15

Pushing aside his tankard of ale, Kolby squirmed on the bench and craned his neck to see through the throng of people gathering in the mead hall. The ceremony was about to start. All the outlaw leaders were together here tonight to elect from among them the one who would be their leader for the coming year.

Where was Raven? She should have recovered from her anger. He had sent Aren to retrieve the brooch and incidentally to pay for the sword. The boy had returned promptly with the information that since the great golden Viking was purchasing it, it would be ready with the inscription complete on the morrow.

Kolby relaxed. Raven would be pleased when she returned. Everything would be good again.

Why didn't she come? This running away like a child who's been denied her way was bad enough. She shouldn't stay away and pout. Things were definitely not going to suit him.

The lurhorn sounded.

Vaghn pushed through the crowd and climbed onto the dais. The tapestries he had taken from Raven for the flawed sword were draped over two chairs set side-by-side toward the middle. From what Kolby could see, the election of the next outlaw high king was a mere formality.

Vaghn looked around irritably. Seeing Kolby so close, he lifted his tankard and toasted. "It looks as if both of us are suffering from the same malady."

Kolby looked at the outlaw chieftain, clad in the brightest garb he could patch together, with a heavy gold torque about his neck and at least two rings on every finger. He looked down at himself, clad in the simplest of clothing with only an armband for decoration.

"I mean that our women are not here," Vaghn said. "When the other men appear, the ceremony will start, whether my wife is here or not." He lowered himself into his chair, careful not to wrinkle the magnificent tapestry, and held out his tankard to be filled by a passing youth. He drank and then belched. "We still have time. The lurhorn hasn't sounded for the third time."

Kolby sipped his ale. His gaze returned to the entrance. Finally, he saw Damona arrive and push her way through the crowd. For the first time since Kolby had met the woman, she was wearing a gown. Obviously expensive, it was made of deep blue wool—not the cheap blue woad of the native clays, but the expensive darker purple-blue from France. It was embroidered at neck and hem with fine silk floss. Her arms were heavy with bracelets that he recognized as part of the cloister treasure. A gold replica of an adz lay between her breasts suspended from a gold torque around her neck. Every finger was encircled by a ring. Gold combs pulled her hair to the crown of her head and anchored it in a thick coil.

Rather than taking her seat immediately on the dais, she stopped in front of Kolby. "Have you seen Raven?"

He shook his head.

"She was going to loan me the blue shawl, but I couldn't find her anywhere." She frowned. "I thought she might have brought it with her."

"She . . . er . . . went for a walk," Kolby said. "She should be back at any minute."

"I've searched the entire gathering and I can't find her anywhere," Damona said. "Someone saw her going toward the stream. But by that time I was late." She smiled at Vaghn. "I wouldn't want to miss tonight."

He held out his hand and she mounted the dais like a queen.

Without a word Kolby rose and strode across the Great Hall. At the door he pulled one of the torches from the corbel and pushed through the opened doors. With Aren following, he wended his way among the various tents and stalls until finally he left the clearing.

"What happened?" Aren wanted to know. "Has something happened?"

"I'm not sure."

"She just went for a walk. I recognized her from the back because she was wearing her mother's shawl," the boy defended himself. "I didn't think anyone would bother her. Everybody's obeyed the rules."

Kolby didn't answer. Instead he concentrated on the tracks. He stopped beside a huge tree. The sight of the torn sod chilled his blood. "I think she's been abducted." He pointed with the torch. "See. There was a struggle here. Raven's footprints are here, and someone else's. Someone must have dragged her. See how her heels dig in."

He followed the heel marks down to the stream. There he knelt and touched the ground with his hand. His index finger traced a mark. A notched hoofprint. "The Irishman."

"The men who attacked her and Melanthe?"

"The same."

"But she said they wouldn't know who she was. She was always dressed before in a robe and cowl."

"She was wearing the shawl," Kolby pointed out. "They must have recognized it." Kolby twisted his hand into a fist. The garment was at the root of all their problems since the beginning. "I should have let her bury it with Melanthe. Instead I put it around her shoulders myself."

The rustle of leaves made him raise his head.

"Kolby," Durin called.

"Over here," he replied.

The Viking, wearing the garish costume of the outlaws, strode out of the forest to the shoreline. "Vaghn sent me to find you. He wanted you to know that the Old One, Ovar of Wicke, is here. He's the man Vaghn brought you here to meet. He should be arriving in the mead hall before the banquet ends tonight."

"Ovar?" Kolby shook his head. His eyes searched the ground beside the stream. Which way had the thieves taken Raven? His skills mustn't fail him now.

"Kolby?" Durin put his hand on his leader's arm. "Kolby. Did you hear me? The man who has the information you need. You'll be face-to-face with him within the hour."

Kolby swung around. Suddenly Durin's words registered on him. His whole soul cried out, but he couldn't forsake Raven. She was in danger. He nodded curtly.

"Vaghn wants you in the mead hall now, to sit beside him on the dais. Let's go, Kolby."

"Raven's missing," Kolby replied.

Durin whistled through his teeth. "Send one of us to hunt for her then. You are Vaghn's honored guest. To miss the banquet would shame him. He might not introduce the man to you."

"I think she's been abducted."

"By the Irishman?"

"I believe so. Return to the village. Get our ponies. Yours, mine, and Aren's."

"What about Ovar of Wicke?" Durin asked.

"I shall have to talk with him later."

Durin slammed his fist into the palm of his hand. "This is the whole purpose of our trip, Kolby. You can't turn away now."

"I can't desert her." In that instant Kolby cared not a whit about Ura or the twenty magic apples. The only thing that mattered to him was Raven. "Hurry, Durin, bring the horses after me. I'll follow the trail with the torch."

Earlier, Kolby had been thinking about the changes in Raven. Now as he followed the trail in the dark, he marveled at the change in himself. When he had rescued her and Melanthe from these same men, he hadn't forgotten his purpose in being here. Always it had loomed large; all his decisions were based on his need, not hers. Now he had pushed his aside. She was his purpose for living.

"I must save Raven." He motioned to Aren, who had followed in his footsteps. "Go back and get Sven and Thorfinn. I'm going to need all of you. No wild berserker fighting. This time we must save the lady at all costs. We won't be outnumbered. And we take no prisoners."

"Aye, Lord Kolby." The young man dashed away.

Raven's stomach was a solid bruise where she was bounced against the wood and leather saddle. Her ribs ached. Her pounding head felt as if it would burst. The night had grown cold as they skirted the black loch. She wished she had one of Kolby's fur-lined cloaks. She wished she had Kolby's brooch to pin her gaping tunic together across her breasts. She wrapped her fingers around another bell and twisted it off the shawl.

"Great Mother Goddess, forgive me in my sore need," she murmured.

The terrain was rocky. Stones constantly turned under the ponies' hooves. They had to turn from side to side to ride around boulders. Then Donnal's pony stumbled badly. Head down, sides heaving, it balked. The Irishman cursed. Drawing his dagger, he pricked the animal's haunch. It tossed up its head and plunged forward.

Everyone heard the snap of its foreleg. The plucky animal screamed like a woman. Only Donnal's strength in hauling back its head kept them all from falling.

One of the thieves climbed down and hurried to kneel beside the mount. "Its leg is broken," he reported when he stood up.

Donnal cursed. He swung down and pulled Raven down against him.

"I told you." The man called Ulad sat his horse behind them. "You should have stolen a horse for her—or made her walk."

Raven felt her captor stiffen. His hands were like iron as they set her aside. "That you did," he said in an affable voice. He turned from her and walked back a couple of steps to the henchman. "Now you're the one who's sorry I didn't."

The dagger with which he had stabbed the pony was still in his fist. With his left hand on Ulad's saddle bow, he stabbed upward. With a gurgling scream, the thief struggled briefly, but Donnal drove the blade deeper and deeper. Suddenly the struggle stopped. The thief slid off on the other side of the saddle.

Raven moaned in terror. The madness of Alba was increased tenfold in this cousin. As if nothing had happened, Donnal stalked back to her. He bent and cut the bonds at her ankles with the bloody knife. "I think you can ride astride after this," he said. "You won't try to escape, will you?"

She shook her head.

To the man holding their horse, he said, "Leave it. We've got another couple of hours till daylight."

"Do you know where we're headed?" the other asked cautiously.

"Nay," Donnal replied. "I'm trying to get as far away from the forgathering as possible. There's no sense in fighting with the Viking if we don't have to. And we don't know what the outlaws will do when they find that dead guard at the moutain passage. We can only hope we're not being followed."

Back in the saddle, their numbers reduced to three, Raven doubted that she would see the end of the glen, much less Eire. One part of her prayed for Kolby to come soon. Another part prayed that he wouldn't. Donnal was capable of terrible cruelty and cold-blooded murder. Kolby would be risking his life to come after her.

She wrapped her hand around the next bell, then released it. No need to drop it at this point. The dead man and the crippled horse marked their trail.

The Vikings rode in a single column.

"We need to stop, Kolby," Durin called out. "It's too dark to see, and we're liable to lose the trail."

If Kolby heard, he gave no sign. In a pocket in his cloak were two golden bells from the sacred shawl. She was leaving a trail for him. She depended on him. He was her hope. He wouldn't disappoint her.

He lay along his horse's neck, his burning eyes trained on the ground. A man obsessed, one deter-mined to find and rescue Raven, he rode on. His men drooped in the saddle behind him. A preternatural obstinance gripped him. As long as he continued to ride, he controlled his destiny and hers. If they stopped, it would be taken from him.

The trees grew thicker, the ground rougher as the wall of the glen rose upward out of Loch Ness. He worried anew about Raven. Was she warm? Was she hungry and thirsty? Was she being abused?

Under his breath he vowed that Donnal would leave this life with the blood eagle on his back if Raven was harmed in any way. In his mind's eye he could see the cold-blooded murderer gasping out his life with that most cruel of Viking punishments—his lungs pulled through his ribs at his back. A fitting end for such a one.

Durin urged his horse up beside his leader. "'Twould be better to take a short rest, Kolby. The horses are exhausted. An hour only. A fresh start. Give the moon time to rise."

Kolby didn't answer.

Durin looked over his shoulder at the others, then back at his friend. "Lord Kolby. If we don't stop, I'll be obliged to ask for a show of hands."

Kolby sighed and sat up. Rubbing his hand over his face, he blinked owlishly. "Aye," he muttered. "Aye, you have that right. But will you exercise it?"

"Nay, I want you as our leader, but I want you to exercise some caution and wisdom, as a leader should." Durin waited. When Kolby didn't reply, he added, "You're too close to this woman to make a good judgment. If you exhaust yourself and us, then how will we fight when we catch up to them?"

Kolby heaved a sigh. Looking over his shoulder, he saw Sven drooping in the saddle. Thorfinn actually had his arm around Aren to keep the youth from falling. "Aye, Durin, you speak the truth. We'll rest."

They stopped for the night. Refusing themselves the comfort of a fire, they wrapped in their fur-lined cloaks and slept.

Stiff, his joints aching, Kolby rose before first light. So did his men. With little conversation they took care of their personal needs. Kolby strode into the woods, then to the stream where he washed his face and hands.

When he returned, Durin and Aren were hunched together.

"Looking at the tracks?" Kolby asked.

"Aye, the notched one." The man with the axe pointed. "They're moving in that direction."

"I was following that last night," Kolby informed them. "We won't lose them."

Quietly they mounted and headed out. In the daylight, set on the course, the Vikings trailed the Irishman with ease. From time to time they came across a golden bell, which Kolby added to his pocket. Their music was muted against his thigh, yet the sound comforted his heart. It was as if Raven were singing to him.

They had ridden a good ways when a black shadow sailed across their trail. Midnight Wind swooped down and landed on Kolby's shoulder.

"Hail, old friend." Kolby smoothed the feathers that covered the glossy back. "I thought you had flown away for good this time."

The raven cawed.

"I'm always surprised at the way that bird keeps up with you," Durin said.

"The other Raven would say he's magical," Kolby answered. "If I believed that, I would believe that Odin sent him to me to whisper in my ear. He would be a part of the search—my eyes above the treetops. What say you, friend?"

The raven flapped its wings and flew away.

Morning came and went, but Kolby didn't stop for food. All he thought of was Raven. He loved her and couldn't live without her. He had thought nothing was more important to him than acquiring a name, belonging to a family, and becoming lord of a steading. But all that paled into insignificance if he did not have Raven. She was the most important thing in his life, and he would give up honor and prestige for her.

Midnight Wind appeared again, sailing in the sky, circling, cawing hoarsely. He dropped down on Kolby's shoulder, flew away, soared, returned, and flew off again. He tried to land on the head of the pony, but only succeeded in frightening the beast so that it whinnied and half-reared.

"Something is amiss," Durin suggested.

"Aye," Kolby agreed. "Odin's eyes indeed. Perhaps we're getting close to the abductors." He stopped at a small crossing, let the ponies drink, and knelt to study the hoofprints. Then he led his horse across the stream and knelt to look again.

Shaking his head, he came to his feet. Fear clutched at his heart. Slowly, more carefully, he searched the area again and again. "Something has happened," he told them. "I can't find the notched hoof."

His men got down off their horses and began to search too. "I think there are only three horses now," Durin said at last.

"Spread out along the banks," Kolby ordered in a hoarse voice. "Find that fourth horse. We can't go on until we find it."

Durin stared at his leader. Kolby's face was drained of color. His mouth looked as if it would never smile again. Durin had sailed and ridden with Kolby for many years. For the first time he saw his leader a victim of his own emotions. Durin had known that Kolby was attracted to the priestess; he would have to be blind not to. But he hadn't realized how deep his feelings went.

He swung round and clapped Aren on the shoulder. "Search hard, lad. For our lord's sake."

Less than a half-hour later, with Midnight Wind to help them, they found the horse. Head down, eyes closed, it stood on three legs fifty yards downstream in a dense copse.

"Kolby!" Aren called out. "Its leg is broken. What shall we do?"

The older men exchanged looks. Durin put his arm around the young man's shoulder.

Before he could lead him away, Sven shouted from the rocks. "Over here."

There, lodged between two boulders, was the cold, limp body of one of the thieves.

"What happened?" Aren walked behind a tree, so he wouldn't have to look at the murdered man.

Kolby shrugged. "There is no honor among these men, Aren. Just as there is no honor among Vaghn and his troop, although they are better than most. My guess is someone's horse broke its leg, and so this man was gutted for his."

"But—"

"Come, lad." Over his shoulder he made a cutting motion across his throat.

Thorfinn nodded soberly and started back to end the crippled pony's suffering.

Back on the trail once more, the five set out with grimmer purpose. Death in battle the Vikings could understand. And honor to the victor. But murder and cruelty they could not abide.

"Move as silently and swiftly as possible," Kolby ordered. "They'll have to move more slowly. I count only three horses now. Unless the Irishman has killed another of his men, he'll be riding double with Raven."

"We should catch up with them easily."

"That is," Aren replied, "if we find their tracks again. It's getting harder. That vine that hangs from the trees brushes away the tracks when the wind blows."

"Aye, and the forest is growing thicker," Durin grumbled.

"And darker," Thorfinn added.

Leaves rustled about them as the wind strengthened. The tracks were wiped away in front of them. Kolby was ready to call a halt when he heard a tiny jingling sound. He sprang off his horse and led it forward. There among the blowing leaves was another golden bell.

He snatched it up and held it for the others to see. "My lady is leading us to her," he called.

Mile after mile fell behind them, and they continued to follow as best they could. But the farther they traveled, the less obvious the tracks became. They had to stop more frequently and study the ground; they had to search for impressions. Finally they lost them altogether.

At Kolby's command, each of them fanned out in a different direction, circled around, but found nothing. Kolby didn't know which way to proceed. He and his men had memorized their landmarks so they could return to the forgathering, but he had no idea what lay ahead of them.

At that moment Midnight Wind dropped down on the lower limb of a tree and looked around, his amber eye glittering. Suddenly, with a hoarse chortle, he bobbed his head two or three times and sailed down to the ground. He rose with something in his beak. Circling once, he dropped it to the ground at Kolby's feet. It fell with a soft ping and rolled.

Kolby swept it up. "Another bell," he exclaimed. "This is the way. This is the way." He looked at the bird where it sat on a limb preening its feathers. "Odin's eyes."

He shook himself, then stood for a moment thinking. Finally he said, "All of you came a-viking with me in quest of the sacred apple tree. Last night I abandoned the quest to search for Raven nea Pryse. We are close to finding her. I think we are very close. But there could be danger."

His gaze skimmed the faces of his men.

"As with all adventures, trading and war expeditions, you have a voice. I shall continue to ride after the woman. If you want to join me you may—and welcome. If you wish to return to the mead hall, you may do that also. I will bear no hard feelings toward you, whatever your decision."

Durin stepped forward. "I ride with you, Kolby."

"And I." One by one, the others stepped forward. Quickly they remounted, spread out, and rode slowly. Constantly they searched for the tracks, for the scrapes on the rocks, and, most importantly, for the glint of bells.

The deeper the thieves moved into the forest and the farther away from the forgathering, the more fearful Raven became. The Irishman's two remaining men exchanged glances from time to time and gradually began to lag behind. Donnal muttered threats at her shoulder, but he seemed more nervous about the thickness of the forest, the strange vines that clutched at their shoulders, and the lack of sound.

Raven realized she was riding with a madman into a forest from which Vaghn had said men never returned.

Again and again she prayed to the Great Earth Mother. During the ride, she had managed to tear the bells from the fringe, one by one, and drop them on the trail. They were almost all gone, but the jingling was as strong as ever. *Magic*, she thought. *I am surrounded by magic.*

Finally the Irishman stopped for the night. It was so dark and they were so deep in the forest, Raven had no idea where they were. She heard no water to indicate a brook or a stream.

One of Donnal's men left her feet bound, but untied her hands. Gratefully she drank the water he gave her while the other built a small fire. Although Raven was too far away to benefit from its warmth, she could see the men better by its soft glow.

Exhausted and sore from her ride across Donnal's saddle, she was fast sinking into sleep when Triath's cousin arose and strolled toward her. She shuddered as his resemblance to Alba reinforced itself in her mind.

With a pack slung over his shoulder, Donnal knelt beside her. He stared solemnly at her, his expression chilling. His eyes crawled over her flesh, and she was sure he was assessing her body beneath her clothing.

"Very nice," he murmured. His hard fingers slid into the opening of her tunic and found her nipple. Watching her reaction carefully, he pinched it. Despite her determination to remain still, she squirmed in pain. "So sensitive."

Biting her lower lip, she turned her head away and braced herself to endure.

To her surprise, he drew back his hand. His voice was perfectly normal, if a bit gruff, when he asked, "Are you hungry?"

She didn't want to eat. Food was the furthest thing from her mind at that moment, but she knew she had to keep up her strength.

Without waiting for her answer, he slipped the pack from his shoulder and handed her some dried meat and a chunk of bread. She washed the food down with a swallow of cool water. She didn't drink more because she wanted to delay having to take care of personal business in front of them for as long as possible.

When she finished, he nodded and rose. "You might just make it to the Irish coast."

He returned to the fire. She wrapped the shawl around her shoulders and listened to the conversation from the fireside. The men were arguing about the direcion they should travel on the morrow. Two of them disagreed on the landmarks they had passed.

They were lost!

Lost in a forestland. It was so dark, the night seemed alive and deadly. The animals were its eyes, the tree trunks its many and varied faces, the branches its clawing hands. She couldn't see beyond the circle of the campfire. They were lost and she was lost with them—utterly forsaken and alone.

Her wrists were raw and scabbed where the thongs had bitten into them. She imagined her ankles were the same. When she was unobserved, she worked at untying them, but she couldn't loosen the knots. The Irishman had twisted them in a complicated pattern that defied her fingers.

The two thieves rolled up in their blankets to sleep. Donnal settled down against a stone. He sat across from the fire, his eyes staring in her direction. Could he see her? Somehow she doubted that he could. But he didn't need to. He knew what he wanted to know about her.

Deciding that whatever she did would be best done in the morning, Raven finally settled down for the night. She had dropped all the golden bells but one. They were so small that she feared Kolby would not think to look for them.

In the cold morning hours, she faced the fact that she might never see Kolby again. Her thoughts were bittersweet. She thought of things she should have told him. She should have revealed the secret of the shawl. Now its magic was destroyed to no avail.

If she had a chance, she would cleave to his side forever. She knew now that should the other two Dryads who had accepted her into the order be unwilling to release her from it, she would go with Kolby anyway. She would go and live in the Northland with him. She loved him so much she would willingly risk her hope of life in the Otherworld for him.

As matters stood at the moment, she was not his liege's choice for Kolby's wife, but perhaps if she went to Northland with him, she could appeal to Ura. Perhaps she would even find favor in his eyes. After all, she was the daughter of an affluent and influential high king. She would give Kolby healthy children. Most of all she knew how to plant the apple orchards and tend them and how to brew the magical apple wine. Ura would be a fool not to accept her as Kolby's wife.

Closing her eyes, she slumped against the rock. Even in her exhaustion, she dozed fitfully until light began to line the eastern sky. She heard a bird caw and opened her eyes to see a huge black raven circling overhead. Still half-asleep, she didn't move.

Was it Midnight Wind? The raven circled as Kolby's bird had done when Vaghn and his men were riding toward the village.

She tensed as hope surged through her. *Great Mother Goddess,* she prayed, *let it be Kolby's bird. Let Kolby find me.*

She sat up, her heart beating erratically. Blood rushed through her body. With every sense she listened. For a long time she heard nothing but the heavy silence. She glanced up, but the bird was gone. Had she imagined it?

Then she heard the chirrup of another bird—a strange call, unlike any bird she had ever heard in the Highlands. But she recognized it. She had heard it once before when Kolby and Aren had used it after they crossed into the badlands. An answering call chirruped from somewhere on the right. Another one. A fourth. Quickly followed by a fifth.

The thieves' camp was surrounded. And she knew by whom.

Five! Kolby and his four Vikings!

They had come to rescue her. Cautiously she drew her knees up to her chest and worked again at her bonds. She wanted to be ready to run toward help. Again she could not budge the knots. Her hands were clammy with perspiration.

Even though she had heard the calls, she was not

prepared when the air was suddenly split with blood-curdling battle cries. They came from every side, dinning in her ears. They frightened even her who knew who made them. Terrorized, the Irish outlaws leaped to their feet.

Taking advantage of their bewilderment, Raven rolled over and began to drag herself away.

"Nay, wench, you'll not be doing that!" Donnal shouted. He launched himself through the air and landed hard on her body, driving the breath from her lungs. Wrapping his arms around her, he hauled her to her feet and tossed her over his shoulder before making a run for the horses.

"Raven!" Kolby's deep voice boomed from behind the thicket of vines. "Raven, where are you?"

"Kolby!" she shouted. "Over here!"

Donnal tipped her off his shoulder and slapped her face. "Shut up, bitch!"

Her cheeks stung from the blow. Her ears rang. Donnal bent and slashed the bonds that held her ankles. Gripping her by the thigh, he set her on the pony's back and climbed up in front of her. A quick twist of the reins had her wrists securely tied around his middle. They set off at a gallop.

"Kolby!" she screamed again.

Donnal laughed. "Better pray that he doesn't follow. If your Viking tries to shoot me, he'll shoot you instead. If he comes too close, I'll kill you myself. Triath will have to believe that you died at the hands of someone else."

"Better that you drop me here and tell Triath that you couldn't find me," Raven argued. "You can escape unharmed. If you take me with you, Kolby will see that you don't escape these shores."

Sure enough, they heard a pony galloping after them.

"'Tis Kolby," Raven said. "He won five of the best

ponies in all the badlands from Vaghn, the outlaw chieftain. He'll ride you down.''

With no thought to the danger, his only purpose to rescue Raven, Kolby chased his quarry into the dense forest. He twisted around trees. He wound past brush and bushes, around jutting rocks and small dirt mounds. He threaded his way through the huge vines that hung in profusion.

Though day had dawned, the forest was still too thick for light to penetrate. Through murky darkness Kolby pushed on. Wisely he allowed his horse its head. He couldn't see how the forest could get any wilder, but it did. Bushes swiped his calves and thighs. They snagged his mantle. Thorns an inch long tore the material and his flesh underneath. Kolby's entire body burned from them.

Still he didn't stop, didn't even contemplate stopping. Eventually he saw the horse with two silhouetted riders on it. He urged his pony onward, encouraging him, begging him. He pulled his bow off his shoulder and nocked an arrow.

''Raven!''

Both riders turned their heads, but Kolby knew his love by the way her hair whipped around her shoulders. The coward had placed her behind him. The Viking had no choice but to thrust the arrow back into the quiver and ride on.

He could see the Irishman lashing the pony across the withers. The mount picked up speed and then plunged through a canopy of vines.

They were out of sight for only a few seconds, but when Kolby's horse plunged through the same vines, they were gone. Disappeared. He had lost them.

Kolby couldn't believe what he had seen. Where had they disappeared to? What sort of place was this long glen above the black Loch Ness? The hair rose on the back of his neck. Had he been chasing a kelpie? The bells in the pocket of his cloak jangled.

He urged his mount forward and upward. Until suddenly they emerged from the timberline. The pony slowed.

It was dark. Black night. Yet he knew full well he had made his attack on Donnal's camp in daylight. He had planned it so there would be no risk of sending an arrow into Raven by mistake.

Kolby slipped out of the saddle and walked cautiously forward. A ravine yawned before them. He saw the white glitter of rocks in the depths below. How could rocks glitter when there was no light?

He listened. The only sound was the wind soughing through the trees behind him and the lapping of the waters from the distant lakeshore. At least he thought it was the lapping of waters. He turned to retrace his steps. Somewhere in the ravine he heard the tinkle of bells.

When he twisted around, the bells in his own cloak answered with a sound like laughter. He could no longer doubt that something beyond human ken was at work around him. He should go back if he valued his life.

But he did not value his life as much as he valued his love. He had no choice if he were to find her. He remounted and let the pony carefully pick its way down the steep incline.

The closer to the glittering rocks he came, the thicker the thorns grew. Like knives they cut his clothing. The very vines through which he rode were also thorny. They scratched and tore at the leather gloves on the reins. Like daggers they impaled his cloak and tried to tear it from his shoulders. The bells jangled with every step.

He was riding into a bramble thicket—a deadly thicket. He had never seen one, but he had heard of them, where vines could grow as thick as the trunks of young saplings. Many of the thorns were large and strong enough to be used as tent stakes. They glittered like the rocks.

Raven screamed.

The pony stopped, and Kolby realized he had somehow passed into the brake itself. He was surrounded by it. A look behind him showed him that the pathway he'd been following had disappeared. He felt his pony shivering. He swung down to examine it. To his amazement, it seemed to be unharmed, without a single scratch.

"Raven!" Kolby shouted.

No answer.

It was strange, but despite the thick brambles and the encircling darkness, the brake and the thorns that surrounded it were light. Shining. Shining like glass.

Dismounting and unsheathing his sword, he began to inch forward, hacking a pathway through the thick growth. No matter how carefully he proceeded, the thorns imprisoned his trousers. They slashed his flesh.

"Raven?" he called desperately.

No answer.

He kept cutting. "Raven."

"Kolby," came her weak reply.

He stiffened. "Where are you? Answer me so I may find you."

"Over . . . here."

He swung a quarter round and sighted with his sword. With renewed energy and fervor, he slashed and slashed, moving slowly forward.

"The thorns," she whimpered. "The thorns. I'm caught in them. I can't move. Oh, hurry, Kolby. Hurry."

"I'm coming, my love. I'll be there in the blink of an eye."

"I knew you would come. I prayed to the Great Mother Goddess."

"Where is the Irishman? Where is the murdering thief?"

"He threw me from his horse and plunged out of the thorns without me."

At last Kolby found her. He could see her body through the thorns. He feared the worst. "How badly are you hurt?"

"Cuts mostly. Bruises."

He chopped his way through the brambles, but as soon as he had taken a step, they seemed to close ranks behind him. He was quickly becoming their prisoner just as she was. Thorns dug through his cloak and tunic and his leather trousers. They sank into his thighs. Even his calves and feet with their heavy leather boots were no match for the vicious darts.

Bleeding and torn, he reached her. She lay on her back, entangled in the vines that glittered like crystal in the darkness. From head to foot, she was bloody. Her tunic and the sacred shawl were in shreds. Even her hair was entangled in thorns. She couldn't even move her head. Yet she was the most beautiful, certainly the most precious sight Kolby had ever seen. He knelt close to her and caught one of her hands. He tried to hold her gently, but she clutched him.

"Hold me, Kolby. Just hold me."

He saw the cuts at the corner of her mouth, her swollen lips, the shadow of a bruise on her face where her captors had hurt her. He hated the Irishman with a killing hatred. If the man still lived, Kolby knew he would kill him. So he vowed.

"I didn't know if you would find me," she whispered. "The bells?"

"Aye, the bells. We followed the bells." As if in

agreement the golden lilting sounded all around them.

"The other thieves?" she asked.

"I'm sure my warriors have them. There were naught but two left. Donnal is a cruel master."

"Aye, he is that." She seemed exhausted. Slowly he began to cut the brambles away from her. He winced with pain himself when he had to pluck a thorn from her flesh.

"A little while, my love," he crooned. "Soon you'll be free."

"Hurry," she whispered. "This place frightens me." Without stopping for a breath, she said, "They were lost, you know. The thieves had no idea where they were. But they kept riding blindly, driven by Greine o Donnal. He's mad. As mad as his cousin Alba."

"Don't think about him," Kolby said. "He'll never bother you again, I swear."

"Do you know the way back to the forgathering?"

"Aye, all of us memorized our landmarks." Even as he spoke he realized he had no landmarks in this dark place. The killing thorns were everywhere. If he were a praying man, he would pray now.

Gently he touched her leg. "There are three thorns embedded in your thigh. Two small ones and a fairly long one. 'Tis like an arrow shaft, my love."

She nodded and drew in a deep breath. "Did your man ever arrive at the forgathering?"

"Aye." He pulled out the two smaller thorns.

She winced. "So Vaghn was teling the truth."

Kolby leaned closer and caught the end of the large thorn. It was deeply embedded. It was going to hurt when he extracted it.

"What did he say about the tree-ee-ee?"

Her question ended in a small scream as Kolby yanked the hideous thorn from the wound.

"I haven't talked to him yet." Kolby held the thorn

up. " 'Tis the size of a hunting spear, barbed to make the removal painful if not impossible."

"You didn't speak to him?" She tried to rise, even thrusting aside the brambles to reach up to him. "You didn't speak to him?"

"Not with you in danger." Kolby pressed his hand against the wound to stop the blood that ran freely from it.

"Oh, Kolby. It is what you have waited for, searched for two years to find." She sank back and threw an arm across her face. "Ever since you met me, I've caused you delay after delay in your search for the tree. Now when you are so close to achieving your goal, you turn aside to come after me."

He chuckled lightly. "You said the price of protecting you would be high, madam. And it has been. But I willingly pay the price, and would pay more besides."

He brushed the tangled hair from her cheeks and pressed a light, sweet kiss on her forehead.

"One more thorn, my love, and a couple of bramble vines, and I'll have you out of here—"

Dead leaves on the ground crackled. Some of the bramble vines vibrated. Kolby glanced around. He saw nothing.

Then he heard the slither, the hiss. He looked again. A shining snake slid over and under the brambles as it undulated toward Raven. Its tongue flickered ominously.

"What is it? Oh, Kolby—"

"Don't move," he whispered. He obeyed his own command, hardly daring to breathe.

The brambles protected the creature, and there was no way Kolby could kill it. He would have to bide his time and risk their lives—Raven's life.

The snake reared its head. Its scales glowed with unearthly light. It pinned its beady eyes on Raven. Taut as a bow string, it coiled, ready to strike. Fangs like the tiny darts she used in her blowpipe glistened. Venom gathered on the tips.

Kolby broke out in a cold sweat, but he didn't take his eyes off the reptile. At the same instant that the snake moved to strike, Kolby thrust his hand through the brambles. The thorns cut like knives through his leather gloves, but with one hand he grabbed the snake at the base of its head. With the other he caught hold of the lashing tail. He leaped to his feet and whipped it around his head. With all the strength of his mighty arms he pitched it far, far out of sight.

"You killed it!" Raven cried out. "You killed the snake, Kolby."

"Aye, my love. Or at least sent it so far away it can't bother us again."

"It's dead. I know it's dead. Oh, Kolby."

"It's dead," he reassured her.

Like a berserker, he worked to free his lady. Regardless of the pain to himself, he drove his hands through the brambles. He chopped when he could. He caught the vines with his hands and yanked them out. When he had finally freed her, he held her close, their blood intermingling as they clung to each other. By Odin, he couldn't live without her!

She caught his hands and pulled the shredded leather aside to look at the deep cuts in his palms. Tears flowed down her cheeks.

"For me," she whispered. She brought his hands up and gently pressed her lips to his palms. "For me."

Chapter 16

Relieved that she was alive, Kolby hugged her tightly. "I almost lost you," he murmured. "First to the Irishman, then to the brambles, then to the snake."

His grip tightened as he imagined never holding her again, never seeing her smile. She cried out and he pulled back.

"The saddle," she explained. "It bruised my stomach."

She laid a bloody hand against his beard-stubbled cheek. "But you didn't lose me. You saved me. My champion."

Kolby swept his precious woman into his arms and carefully picked his way through the bramble thicket. This time the brambles seemed to move magically out of the way. They almost seemed to part so that he could walk through them. The closer he came to the edge of the brake, the lighter the sky grew until he stepped out into the clearing in broad daylight with a bright sun shining overhead.

He swung around. The brambles had closed behind him, the thick black vines closely intertwined.

He climbed up the incline, out of the ravine until he found a place for a camp near a small pool of clear water. Still holding Raven, he used his feet to rake a

327

large pile of leaves together. Gently he laid her down on top of them.

"Give me a little time," he murmured, "and I'll tend your cuts. I need to get a fire going and find my pony."

"I'm all right," she murmured, her eyes closed. "I'll be up and about after a little while." But the dark hollows beneath her eyes and cheekbones, and the pallor of her lips, betrayed her lie. She was not going to be all right for a long time.

"Just rest." He arranged her pitifully wounded hands across her midriff and hurried away to search for his pony. Because of her injuries, Raven was going to need the beast for the return trip.

Much to his surprise, Kolby found the animal standing docilely at the edge of the brambles. It nuzzled him almost as if it were glad to see him, and kept a loose rein as he led it back to camp.

He tethered it, untied his roll from its saddle, and dropped it close to Raven. Then he concentrated on building a fire. As soon as the flames were blazing, he shook his pallet onto the ground and took an inventory of its contents. A pewter tankard, an extra knife, some oatcakes, and a small packet of spices wrapped in a linen cloth, a half a dozen arrows, and a wool tunic. He looked from them to Raven's pale face. His fear grew.

After stripping off his own clothing, he undressed her, scooped her up into his arms, and carried her into the flowing stream. He waded in until they were both fully submerged. Setting her on her feet, he gently washed the blood from her face, her neck, her shoulders. Shivering, she clung to him.

"It's all right," he assured her. He spared a fleeting thought to himself, the Viking warrior, holding a naked woman close in his arms and thinking only of her health. It was a mark of his love for her. "You're going to be fine. I'll take care of you."

"The cuts aren't bad," she said between chattering teeth. "There are just a lot of them."

"Too many," he agreed, scowling.

Her own eyes slid over his naked body. Again he knew a rush of love. Even in her pain, she cared enough about him to want his body to be well. "What about your wounds?" she asked.

He shrugged. "Mostly cuts on my arms and hands," he said. "I'll be fine."

When he began to wash her thighs, tears burned his eyes. The puncture wounds were deep, the skin bruised and discolored. Already her flesh had begun to swell.

"If we're not careful, these could become inflamed."

She looked down at herself and shook her head. "We're even farther from the cloister than when Melanthe was hurt. We must hope that the clear water will do its work."

When she was clean, he carried her back to the campsite and stood her on her feet again. Quickly he dried her, squeezing as much of the water out of her hair as he could. He tore the piece of linen into strips to bandage the worst of her wounds. Then he picked up his clean tunic, shook it out, and slipped it over her head.

He spread his pallet over the leaves and laid her down, covered her with his fur-lined cloak, and pulled on his own clothing. When he had her tucked in, he put more wood on the fire. After taking his tankard out of his pack, he walked to the pool and filled it. When he returned, he set it on the fire.

"I'm going to check the area," he said. "The Irishman is probably a long way off by now, but we don't want to take any chances."

As a measure of her weariness, she barely nodded as he strode out of camp.

* * *

Her thigh had begun to ache, a deep ache that spread slowly through her body. Her eyes burned, her lids so heavy she couldn't keep them open. She felt so bad, she couldn't think. She didn't want to think. She sought the oblivion of sleep. Curling into a ball, she snuggled into Kolby's tunic. She inhaled and brought into her the fragrance of the man. She felt safe and protected.

She was dozing when she heard Kolby approach. His steps were light; still she heard him. He knelt beside the pallet.

"Raven," he said softly.

"Aye."

"I'm back. I've made a circle around the entire area. There's no sign of Donnal."

She sighed. "I suppose it's too much to hope that he's dead somewhere. He was going to drop me overboard in the Irish Sea."

She heard Kolby growl. When she managed to get her eyes open, he was standing beside her, his fists opening and closing as he breathed. His amber eyes scanned the trees and brambles, willing Donnal to appear so he could kill him.

She laid her hand on his ankle. "You've driven him off, my champion. Let's not think about him anymore."

He squatted down beside her again. "How do you feel?"

"I feel as if I've been through a battle," she murmured. "I can only imagine how you must feel. Whether you wanted to be my champion or not, my lord, you've been forced into the role. You've had to fight off thieves, abductors, outlaws, and a storm. I just may hire you to challenge Triath, High King of Clan O'Illand of Sligo."

"I will gladly challenge Triath for you, and any warrior he would pit against me. He won't touch you or your family again, lady. This I swear."

"Thank you," she whispered, and smiled as much as her swollen lips would allow.

Taking the hot water that was left, Kolby brewed her a tea using the bark of cinnamon from his packet.

"I don't have any victual bags with me," he apologized. "Just a couple of these everlasting oatcakes. Later I'll hunt us up some real nourishment."

Gratefully she accepted the tankard and sipped the hot drink. He laid the oatcake within easy reach and went to take care of the ponies.

When he finally sat down, she handed him the half-empty cup. He noticed she had not touched the oatcake.

"Nay, you drink it." He pushed it back toward her, but she shook her head and turned her face away. He could not miss the faint flush on her cheekbones. "You need the nourishment, love, far more than I do."

She did not answer. In a minute she looked at him again. "I hope the man will wait for you to return," she said. Then suddenly anxious, she half-raised her head. "The shawl . . . the bells."

"The shawl was ruined." He pointed to a pile of blue material. "What's left of it is over there with the remains of your tunic."

"Oh." She sank back and closed her eyes. The sacred shawl destroyed. *Dear Great Mother Goddess, understand and forgive.*

"As for the bells." Kolby reached across her to locate the pocket of his fur-lined cloak and pull out a small pouch. "All I found are in here."

She took the pouch from him and rubbed her fingertips over the soft, worked leather. "Do you think we should return to the forgathering now rather than stay out here?"

"I wish we could, lady, but my pony needs to rest before I can ask it to carry double so far so soon. I pushed it far beyond its strength to find you."

Raven tucked the pouch beneath her chin and lay back down.

"You need to rest also." Kolby touched his hand to her forehead. "You have a fever. I don't like it. Let's see if we can lower it and stop the bleeding before we travel on."

"You may miss the man," she fretted.

"I'll find him again." He patted her hands. "As long as I know that he exists, he won't get far from me."

Abruptly she sat up. Though her head reeled, she was determined not to cost Kolby his one chance. He had saved her. She owed him her life. She owed him his name. She lifted the pouch of bells. They were silent, as if they listened rather than sang.

"You don't have to find him again. Your quest is over, Kolby Urasson, Lord Kolby of Apelstadt."

He rocked back, encircling a bent leg with his arm. "You know the way?"

"No." She leaned forward and caught his hand. Placing the pouch in it, she closed his fingers over it. The bells sighed with a sound like singing. "The directions are inscribed in the bells."

He looked at her wonderingly. "That's the magical incantation," he guessed.

"Aye." She closed her eyes as shards of pain split her vision into bands of light and dark. She didn't want to see the disappointment or anger in Kolby's face because she hadn't told him sooner. But the darkness of her mind brought still more pain. She remembered her delight and Melanthe's happiness when her mother became one of the Chosen Ones. Melanthe—dead within a fortnight of her crowning glory. Raven swallowed hard.

Were the bells singing the death song again?

As if from a long way off, Kolby's voice reached her ears. "You've known all along."

She opened her eyes to meet his angry gaze. Never

had polished amber looked so hard. "I wanted to tell you," she said, "but I couldn't."

"Because of your oath to the Great Mother Goddess?"

"Yes. Because of my oath."

He opened the pouch and poured out the bells. Each one spoke with its own voice as they rolled over the cloak. Holding each one up, he looked at the writing inside their golden throats. It did him no good. He couldn't read the *ogham fedha.*

"I can read them," Raven assured him softly. "It would be easier if they were still on the shawl because they would be in the correct order."

"They served a greater purpose when you threw them on the path for me to find." He scooped them up in his hand and returned them to the pouch. Dropping it on the pallet beside her, he tucked the cloak around her and rose. "I'm going for a walk."

"You're angry," she called after him.

"No. I'm surprised and frustrated." He stopped, his fists clenched at his sides.

"But also angry?"

"Aye. Angry. At the way Fate has played with us. Angry that you did not trust me enough to tell me the truth until today. You know that I wouldn't have expected you to violate your sacred oath."

"My reasons are very complicated. As long as I held the truth close within me, I could keep it. If I once told you that I knew it, I didn't trust myself not to betray it."

Without another word, he strode off, his footsteps heavy. He was gone for so long that Raven began to worry. An early darkness settled over the forest, and the fire burned low. But she felt too exhausted to add more wood to it. She wrapped her hand around her arm and discovered to her horror that the bracelet Kolby had given her was gone. She remembered when the Irishman had taken it from her and slipped it into his bag. It was in his pouch. Kolby's bracelet had been stolen. The only thing he had of his childhood.

Weak though she was, she pushed herself up on her feet. Unable to reason, she was so distressed that she actually took several swaying steps before Kolby came running toward her.

"Raven!" he shouted.

She was so distraught, she staggered on. "My bracelet," she muttered. "My bracelet."

"Raven." Kolby caught her by the shoulders. "What's wrong?"

"My bracelet. My bracelet. He stole it. It's gone. The bracelet you gave me. Your heritage bracelet."

His smile was like warm sunshine on a cold day. "Calm yourself, love," he said. "It's only a bracelet. I want you. I have you."

"You have me," she murmured.

"Aye." He walked with her back to the pallet, laid her down, and tucked her under the covers. "All will be well," he promised. "I've found something for our evening meal."

He produced a headless snake, the twin of the one he had slain among the brambles.

"That?" She scowled.

"This." He dressed it and cut it into small pieces, which he wrapped in leaves and strung together with small twigs. "It may not be the tastiest food you've ever eaten, but it will stop the bite of hunger."

Using a stick, he shoved the leaves into the glowing embers of the fire. While the food cooked, Kolby hobbled the pony and allowed it to graze afield. Raven watched his proceedings for only a minute before she drifted off to sleep.

Several hours later, she slipped into delirium. Thrashing about on the pallet, she gazed at him without recognition. She was hot and cold by turns—

sometimes burning with fever and fighting the covers, sometimes shaking with icy tremors, her teeth chattering. When one particularly bad bout of chills went on and on, Kolby crawled beneath the cloak and held her in his arms, using his body to warm her. But largely he was helpless. Nothing seemed to do any good. Her condition worsened. Gradually her shivering slowed and finally ceased altogether, but she was hot, hot, hot.

Kolby lay there, wondering what to do, how to save her. Now he understood her desperation when her mother was ill, her feelings of acute helplessness.

Vaghn and Damona had submerged Melanthe in cold water to bring down her fever. Kolby would do the same for Raven. Sliding out from under the cloak, he undressed himself for the second time and slipped the tunic off her. After wrapping her in the cloak, he walked to the pool, dropped the mantle on the ground, and waded out into the water. He held her there until she was shuddering convulsively and her teeth were chattering.

He returned her to the pallet, dried her off, and redressed her. He slid beneath the cloak and brought her into his arms. He tended her all night.

Raven awakened to feel Kolby's warmth and strength wrapped around her.

"How are you feeling?"

"Sore and weak," she replied. After a moment, she asked, "Did you carry me into the water again?"

"Aye, my lady. We almost spent the night there. I bathed you first, and later carried you back several times because you were fevered and delirious."

"Had you observed this custom during your travels?" she asked.

"Nay, I remembered what Durin and Damona did to try to bring your mother's fever down."

He traced his fingers across Raven's cheekbones.

The hot flush that had been there for so long had faded to a more natural color. "Your fever is down. With any kind of luck, it won't come back. Your wounds should be washed clean of all infection now."

He couldn't resist his impulse. She lay looking up at him with her brown eyes so full of love, they made his heart turn over. He pressed his lips to her forehead, her cheeks, and finally her mouth, which trembled and opened for him. He drank from her as from the cup of life.

He wanted her, but he sighed and lifted his head. "Are you hungry?"

"A little."

"I have something to eat."

"The snake." She wrinkled her nose.

"It will keep your stomach from roaring its discontent and will give you strength."

He put her hand under the cloak and tucked the garment around her. As soon as he'd risen, he walked over to Raven's torn clothing and picked up what remained of the shawl. "What shall we do with this?"

She felt as though her heart were being torn from her chest. "Burn it."

"Are you sure?"

She nodded. Steeling herself, she watched as he dropped it on the fire. This was the second holy garment that she had burned. The first had been her robe. She was grateful for all she had learned during her years in the cloister, but that phase of her life was over.

As if in affirmation of her new life, smoke billowed into the air. The material blazed up, then nothing remained except a thin sheet of ash. An errant breeze soughed along the ground, picked it up, and scattered it across the gray rocks, where it disappeared completely.

" 'Tis gone," she murmured. "It has returned to the

Great Mother Goddess." After a while she asked, "Will your warriors search for us?"

"Not soon. First they will take the slain and the prisoners to the forgathering. Don't forget that this is outlaw territory. The badlands. Offenders belong to them."

"I can't imagine Vaghn or any of his lot being lenient with them," Raven said.

"Nay. They are outsiders who have violated their code."

Kolby lifted a small branch to poke it more deeply into the fire. The singed edge cut into his open scratches. He winced.

"Let me see," she said. "Your hands. Have you doctored them?"

He grinned. "Aye, my lady." He laid the dagger down and turned both hands over so she could see the scratches on his palms. "I was wearing leather gloves that protected me."

She brought his hands to her face and kissed them, in a gesture reminiscent of the night before when he had dragged her out of the brambles. "Thank you for taking care of me." She heard a whinny and looked around. "How is your pony?"

"He should be able to travel tomorrow."

"And so should I," Raven said.

"You won't if you continue to go without food." Returning to his chore, he quickly cut the snake into bite-sized pieces.

Reluctantly, with much grimacing, she swallowed the first bite. " 'Tis not so bad, Kolby. Probably the most distasteful part is the thought of eating it."

"Aye." Piece by piece he fed her.

"I gave the bells a great deal of thought last night," he said at last. "I don't want you to interpret them for me. I want to know where the tree is, but I don't want you to break your sacred oath."

"You don't believe in the Great Mother Goddess,"

she reminded him. "What difference if I break an oath to something that isn't real?"

"I don't believe in either her blessings or her curses," he agreed.

"Then why?"

"*You* believe in her."

"Aye, I believe in her," Raven replied. "Like the brambles, these oaths have wrapped themselves around me until I've allowed them to strangle me. Your purpose is good and true. The Great Mother Goddess will give you her blessing—whether you believe or not."

"Then, lady, it is her prerogative to lead me to the tree itself."

"Perhaps she will," Raven replied softly. "You met me. I had the shawl with the bells. Everything that has happened so far, Kolby, has brought you closer to the tree than you were before."

"We can also look at the situation in a different light, madam. You have never been so close to death as you have been since I rescued you from the abductors."

"I am going to interpret the bells," Raven declared, sitting up and holding out her hand to take the pouch. "Whether you use the information or not is your choice. It will take me longer because they are mixed together, but I shall read them."

Lowering her head, she opened the pouch and spread the bells over the ground. Kolby left her to her chore. Getting his bow and arrow, he went into the forest and shot some game. He returned soon with two rabbits. He tossed them on the ground, then built a rock grid over the fire. He stripped a large piece of bark off a fallen log and set it on top of the rocks. As soon as he had dressed the rabbits, he cut them into pieces and dropped them onto the bark. He added a few spices and water and cooked them. When they were done, he set the bark bowl between him and Raven.

"Oh, Kolby." She sighed. "This smells so wonderful."

Using his dagger, he stabbed the first bite and offered it to her.

"It's hot," he warned.

Gingerly she pulled off the meat with her teeth. It was tough and stringy, but nothing had ever tasted so good to her.

Bite by bite they devoured one of the rabbits, leaving the other for the evening meal.

"Did you see anything unusual when you walked through the forest?" Raven asked.

Kolby leaned back against the boulder, stretching out one leg, drawing the other up and circling it with an arm. "Like what?"

"From what we've heard, we know the tree is in the dark forest. We're in the dark forest. And it's protected by a bramble thicket. And we've been in a bramble thicket."

"Aye," he confessed, "I looked for the tree myself today. But it would have to be magical to survive in the middle of the brambles. Nothing grows in there but more brambles."

"Yet there are pathways through them," Raven reminded him.

"I thought so last night when I walked out with you," Kolby told her, "but I saw no sign of any today."

"There have to be," Raven insisted. "That's the way the Chosen Ones get through to the tree to take care of it. Let's walk around the thicket now, Kolby, and see what we can find."

"Do you think you should be walking?"

"I'll have to move a little slower than usual," she replied. "But I'll be all right.'

With his sword, he cut them each a walking stick. Step by step, they traversed the incline, and soon they were walking along the edge of the bramble thicket. Black and brown, the bramble vines seemed to surge into the air, so high Kolby couldn't see over them, so thick he couldn't see through them.

No matter where Raven and he polked or pulled, how far they walked in either directon, they found no pathway through the brambles. Raven shivered when she saw the size of the thorns, the thickness of the vines. Kolby pulled her to him.

" 'Tis so ugly," she whispered.

"Aye."

"How could it hide such beauty as the sacred tree?"

"I have been wondering that myself." He paused. "But last night, I would have sworn there was something magical about it."

She swung around to face him and took his hands in hers. "I too. The farther we rode, the darker it became and the more I felt the magic."

"I've never seen moonlight as radiant as that which shone down on us."

"Not on Donnal and me," she whispered. "It was as dark as the grave, and cold. And horrible."

"Perhaps it is just a legend," Kolby went on. "Perhaps at one time apple trees grew here, but the brambles overtook them one by one, until finally only one tree survived. People traveling through the forest reported the stories of the tree. In the retelling the tree became sacred. Somehow it became the magical tree of the gods."

As he talked, Raven was compelled to believe. How could something as lovely and wonderful as the sacred tree live in the middle of such desolation?

More than ever Raven was determined to interpret the message on the bells. She was frightened of the curses of the Great Mother Goddess, and she regretted that she must go against a promise she had made to the cloister, but she vowed that Kolby should have his ultimate wish—his name, his family, his clan. The answer was in her power to give, and she was going to give it.

When they returned to the camp, she cleared an area of ground, found a stick, and began to transcribe the letters from the bells to the earthen table. By evening she was exhausted and still had not begun to make sense of the *ogham fedha*.

Walking back from the pony, Kolby announced, "He'll be ready to ride on the morrow. We'll leave at first light."

"At first I hated being here," Raven said. "Now I hate the thought of leaving. We're close to the tree, Kolby. I know it. I can feel it."

It worried Kolby that Raven was continuing to try to interpret the bells. Several more times he had tried to dissuade her, but she refused to give up her study. When she rose and disappeared into the woods, he walked over to where she had been working and knelt.

The shawl was gone, burned. The ashes had returned to the earth from whence they had come. The Great Mother Goddess had reembraced them. Kolby never gave the ritualistic side of religion much credence, but from what he had heard about this great goddess, he guessed she would gratefully receive the bells to protect her tree.

With a sweep of his big arm, he erased the letters Raven had been painstakingly transcribing in the dust. As his hand closed over the bells, they tinkled softly. He dropped them into the leather pouch and walked to the edge of the brambles. Pulling the drawstring, he opened the pouch and tapped the bells into his palm. He looked at them for a long time. They were beautiful things. Solid gold, with an intricate design on each of them. And inside cryptic letters. Letters that could lead one from the world of the real to the world of magic.

He reconsidered taking them back to camp and letting Raven try to interpret them again. But he couldn't. He knew deep in his heart that he would never find the tree with these bells, and he feared that Raven would be hurt because of them.

For the first time in his life, he spoke to a being whose presence he could in no way sense, to a being in whose power he would never fully believe.

"Great Mother Goddess. You appeared to my liege and benefactor in a dream and gave him instructions on how to save his life and his land. For two years I have searched for the sacred tree and have not found it. But I will not let Raven violate her oath to help. I return your secret to you."

One by one, he threw the bells into the thicket.

When they were all gone, he returned the empty pouch to his cloak. "Your secret is safe, Great Mother."

"Now you may never find the tree," Raven said softly from behind him.

He whirled around. "I didn't hear you coming."

"Nay. You were preoccupied."

He spread his hands wide, asking for her forgiveness. "I couldn't let you do it."

"Why not?"

He folded his arms across his chest and looked away into the distance. "Because—"

"Why?"

"Because—some things are magical and holy."

"Oh, Kolby." She went to him and put her arms around him. "And this is one of them?"

"Aye."

Although Raven was saddened by the thought that Kolby might never find the tree, she hid her smile against his chest. She remembered the night when she had first stared into the amber beauty of his eyes.

She had thought he lacked a sense of reverence. Now she knew better. He was a man with deep, heartfelt emotions and convictions.

He sought honor, but all the time he had more honor than any other man she knew.

Durin, Aren, Sven, and Thorfinn returned to the forgathering with two prisoners. They pushed the thieves in front of the outlaw assembly in the mead hall. The building was overflowing with people.

Although this was the eighth day, none of the tents had been taken down. No one had gone home. Curiously they awaited judgment.

Sitting in the high seat, Vaghn stared distastefully at the two. "You have brought disruption to our assembly and to our land."

Other outlaws on the dais nodded. Growls of anger rumbled from hundreds of throats. The thieves cowered against each other. One sought to protest, but he was shouted down.

A wizened old man, wearing a long gray tunic and sandals, sat to the right of Vaghn. If the badlands had a high counselor, it was Ovar of Wicke. He had lived in the area long before it was called the badlands and long before it became the home of outcasts.

He and Vaghn had forged a friendship. With their wisdom and skill, they had maintained a tenuous order in the land below the loch. To keep others out, they made certain that rumors circulated of a loch haunted by monsters and magic horses and a treacherous dark forest from which no man ever returned.

Ovar's last tooth had long since slipped from his head, and his white hair was wiry and thin. It stood out from his head like the hackles of an aroused animal. Now his disgust and anger were palpable as he stared at the hapless creatures whom Durin had pushed to their knees.

"Never in the thirty years I have lived in the

badlands has a woman been abducted during for-gathering," Vaghn said.

"She stole the shawl from us," one of the thieves protested. "It was ours."

"But you stole it from her to begin with," Vaghn countered.

The two looked at each other with real fear. "Nay. We stole it from two priestesses."

"Priestesses!" old Ovar thundered. "What sort of men are you? Have you no shame?"

The one who had not spoken began to weep noisily.

"Aye, and you killed one of the priestesses," Vaghn continued. "This one lived and joined my band of warriors."

The thieves stared at him, then at each other.

At last one shrugged. "'Tis true. She is the high priestess, Raven nea Pryse. She belongs to the High King Triath of Sligo Bay in Eire. He sent his kin to fetch her back because she dishonored him. When he got her back, we were to receive a great reward." He looked at Vaghn's thunderous brows. "Mercy, my lord, mercy. We're thieves, just like the rest of you. You'd think nothing of this if you'd done it your-selves."

"That may be so outside the forgathering," Vaghn said. "But you acted in violation of our laws. You entered our forgathering and stole one of my outlaws—because Raven nea Pryse was one of my band. You disobeyed our laws. Punishment is what you deserve. And punishment is what you'll get!"

"Aye!" The assemblymen shouted in unison, slap-ping their palms against the tabletops.

The outlaws raised their voices in agreement. The mead hall rang with their cries.

"Torture. Slow and painful!"

"Aye!" resounded from every throat.

When the tumult had died down, Ovar leaned forward, his eyes piercing the cowering men. "How far into the forest did you travel?"

The men shook their heads disconsolately. "We don't know."

"Cite a landmark."

"It was too dark. We saw none. We were lost as soon as we rode away from the stream with the woman," one explained. "We were in a frightful forest with no pathways and no sign of people."

Vaghn waved his hand. "Rangwald. Away with them."

"No! No!"

But Rangwald grabbed each of them by the scruff of his neck and flung them ahead of him from the hall.

"Let us drink!" Vaghn shouted. The outlaws cheered lustily. Dispensing justice was always thirsty work.

A pitcher of ale in hand, Damona refilled Ovar's tankard first, then Vaghn's other women moved through the hall doing the same for the warriors.

Setting his tankard down, Ovar bridged his hands in front of his face. "Fifty summers ago, Vaghn, I chose to come here to be a recluse and to guard the tree against evildoers."

"You have performed your task well."

"In all those years, I have seen the tree only once, but I know where it is. Even if I lead this Viking you've told me about to it, I can't guarantee he will see it. 'Tis magical. All behold it, but few see it."

"Aye." Vaghn sighed regretfully. "I have gone to the spot many times myself, but I have never seen it."

"You say this man is worthy of its fruit."

"Aye, and so is the woman. If anyone can see it, they can."

"Then, my friend, perhaps I won't have to divulge

any information at all. Perhaps the Great Mother Goddess will guide them to the tree herself."

Darkness settled over the campsite as Raven and Kolby lay together on the fur-lined cloak. Their fire burned brightly, and golden shadows danced over them.

"Are you sure you have recovered enough to begin our journey tomorrow?" he asked.

"Aye," she answered. "I hope the man is there, and we can talk with him. We are close to finding the tree, Kolby. I can feel it."

"I've felt that way many times," he said, "and I've always been disappointed."

"This time you won't be," she prophesied confidently. "We're going to find it."

He raised up and leaned over her. "Sometimes I wonder what it will be like when you and I are released from our oaths. What would our lives be like if we had only ourselves to consider?"

He ran his hands gently, tenderly over the curve of her shoulders. He dropped soft kisses on each wound where a thorn had pierced her flesh.

"I have thought about it so much," she confessed. "How would we feel if we could give to each other freely, without the thought that someone may be hurt."

He cupped her face and brought her lips to his in an infinitely sweet kiss, devoid of passion but full of promise.

"The more I'm with you," she said, "the more I want to be with you. I can't imagine my life without you. What will become of me if I cannot be released from my vows?"

"Aye, as matters stand, the future looks very bleak. I am bound to Ura by blood oath. I must continue to search for the holy tree and return to Northland with the apples. Even though Durin has advised me to make this the last trip, whether we find it or not, I . . ." He shook his head.

"You cannot dishonor your liege," she finished for him.

He laid his cheek against her shoulder. "You are no longer a cloister priestess. You are the daughter of the high king, and your child will be heir to the high seat. Your vengeance against Triath will be taken by your father. Your duty is to marry where he commands. He will select an honorable man."

"No man is more honorable than you."

Both moved at the same time, and their mouths met in a hot and desperate kiss. She ran her hands down his back, stroking and kneading, moving up and down the indentation of his spine. After a long, hot, and demanding kiss, he raised his head.

"We must be careful." He gazed at her swollen lips. "Your injuries."

"The only injury I suffer," she said, "is to my heart."

She touched his face, guiding his mouth to hers at the same time that he touched her breasts. She gave herself over to the richness of his touches, to the promise of ultimate possession.

When he lifted his lips from hers, he pulled back to look at her, cherish her. The firelight reflected her facial features filled with passion. Dark lashes caressed her gilded cheeks. Kolby's manhood hardened.

"Long ago, my love"—Raven sat up and captured Kolby's head in her hands—"I asked if you were strong enough to mate with me, knowing that we could not be together for long."

"Aye."

"You replied that you didn't know if it was because of strength or weakness, but you must have me."

He pressed her head against his chest and buried his cheek in the silky strands of her black hair.

"Now, my lord, I know when the strength is going to be required. When we can no longer be together."

Raven claimed his mouth in another desperate kiss. "Though I may never have you," she whispered, "I'm going to touch as much of you as I can. Your body."

She spread kisses over his face.

"Your heart."

She laid her cheek against his chest and listened to the pounding cadence.

"Your soul."

She lifted her head. He lowered his and their lips touched. They kissed long and hard and searchingly. When at last Raven released his mouth, Kolby was trembling with intense arousal. He caught her hand and curled it about his throbbing staff. She sighed, loving the pulsating warmth of him.

"Aye," she whispered.

His chest brushed against her breasts. Careful of her wounds, he extended his legs the length of hers and pulled her into the tight, warm circle of his arms.

Her scent filled his head and the fire of her passion became one with his. She touched him; he touched her. Each rediscovered the sensitive areas on the other. They writhed beneath their love strokes.

He eased her up, lowered his full weight on her. Gently he urged her legs apart and touched her femininity with his firm virility. Raven opened her legs further and arched her hips to receive him.

Kolby thrust slowly and deeply, then stopped to let her warm flesh open and pulsate around him. His lips captured hers in a long, deeply satisfying kiss as he began to stroke gently. Raven moved with him.

Kolby heard her moans and whimpers. His need for release increased. Spurred by her cries and thrusts, he plunged deeply, rapidly, and fiercely. They trembled in an uncontrollable blaze of passion.

Kolby's entire body ached with the need to release the burning desire that licked through him. He heard her gasp and the soft flesh that surrounded him quivered. He cried out and buried his face in her sweetly scented hair. She gathered him close and rocked back and forth with him as they gently floated back to earth.

Afterward they lay together. Raven laid her head on Kolby's chest. He drew his hands through her hair.

"I love you," she murmured.

"I love you," Kolby whispered.

He had found his soul mate, the only woman who had ever touched his heart. He loved her, and she loved him. Why wasn't that enough?

Strangely regretting their imminent departure from the dark forest, Kolby lay awake for a long time, holding Raven as she slept.

First light speared grayly through the early morning darkness, followed by dawn's softer colors, which washed the sky in lavender and blue and pink, and finally gold.

Gentle autumn winds blew through the forest. In the melodious rustle of leaves, he could swear he heard the tinkle of the cloister bells. But that couldn't be. Still he tensed—listening.

Gold. Gold was everywhere, gilding every rock, every tree, every thorn, every bramble. He raised himself on one elbow and looked toward the east. Never had he seen a sunrise the equal of this one.

"Raven." He shook her. "Wake up."

Wiping the sleep from her eyes, she sat up. "Is it time to go already?"

"Nay. Look at the sunrise."

Raven stared upward into a sky washed in sunlight. She raised herself to see a forest lush and colorful. "What is it? What's happening, my love?"

"Look." He pointed to the brambles.

Somehow, their thorns tipped with gold, the brambles looked warmer, softer, less menacing. Astonishment on her face, Raven slowly pushed up. The cloak slid to her midriff.

"The bramble thicket," she muttered. "It looks like a nest of gold."

"Aye, I see it."

Even as they stared, the sound of bells reached their ears. Mesmerized, both of them gazed as light flowed over the thorns, flowed farther, faster, until it crashed into a great trunk. Before their astonished eyes a huge tree appeared, rising from the middle of the brambles. A tree with purest silver leaves and golden apples hanging from its boughs.

"It wasn't there before," Kolby whispered. "I swear."

"No," she agreed. "By magic it appears. I know it. Don't you hear the bells?"

He did indeed—a sound like none other.

A ray of light like a golden spear shone through the brambles. Keeping his eyes on the light, Kolby pulled on his leather trousers and then his boots.

Beside him, Raven rose from the pallet, gathering his fur-lined cloak around her nude body. Her hair hung down her back in a silken veil.

"The tree, Kolby," she whispered in awe. "We've found the tree."

"We've seen it," he corrected. "Now we have to get to it."

Unafraid, she stepped off the pallet. If the ground was rough or painful beneath her naked feet, she made no sound. Like a priestess walking the path to the altar, she followed the light and he followed after her. He caught up to her, and hand in hand they traversed the brake. As they came closer, the light pointed them to a narrow pathway.

"Kolby!" Raven cried out. "Look!"

Together they stepped onto the pathway. A hissing filled their ears, as if snakes waited in the brambles.

Beneath the golden tips of the thorns was blackness, awful and terrible. Moreover, the thorns seemed to grow and turn and twist and reach out toward them, never quite touching them, but menacing them constantly.

"Perhaps you'd better wait for me out there," he cautioned. "This is treacherous. I don't know—"

"I'm coming with you," she cried. "We're going to see the tree together, Kolby, and you're going to get your apples. And Ura and his land will be healed. You'll have your name, Kolby. You'll have a family and a clan."

He put his arm around her shoulders. "Once, I wanted those things for myself, my love. Now I want them for you. Only if I have them can I have you without bringing dishonor to you."

She shook her head. "If the Great Mother Goddess ordains it, you shall have me whether you have a clan or not."

They reached the end of the pathway. In the center of a beautiful greensward stood the huge apple tree. Its boughs were heavily laden with fruit, and its fragrance engulfed them.

"Oh, Kolby," Raven cried. "It's so beautiful, so magical."

"Aye, my lady, it is."

He held up his hand, his fingers trembling. He could hardly believe it when his hand closed around the first apple. The end of his quest was so near. When he returned with the fruit, Ura would be healed. The land would prosper once again. He plucked the first one. And then another and another. His arms were full. He had counted twenty.

When he finished, he gazed up at the tree. "Thank you, Great Mother Goddess," he said softly. "I shall return your magic to the land from whence it came. This I vow."

Raven nea Pryse, once High Priestess of the Cloister of the Grove, knelt at the foot of the tree and touched her hand to the root. "Give me your leave, Great Mother Goddess. I beg to go to be a keeper of the Northland with my love."

From all around them came the tinkling of tiny bells.

She rose and led the way back through the brambles, which neither hissed nor clawed, but rather glowed golden as they passed.

Kolby carefully placed the apples in the center of his pallet and rolled the edges around them. He tied them securely on the back of the saddle and lifted his lady up before him. Together they began their journey back to the forgathering.

Although both were happy that he had found the apples, an air of melancholy hung over them. In the badlands, they inhabited a different world with different laws. They could be together here. They could love. But not when they returned to the Highlands. Both of them thought of Pryse mac Russ, the High King of Ailean. Both of them thought of Raven's vows, from which two more priestesses must release her.

About noon, they stopped to water the pony and to eat. Before they remounted, Kolby opened his pallet roll. Still caught up in his miracle, he wanted to touch the apples to reassure himself that they were real. He pulled one out.

"Nay!"

"What's wrong?" Raven hurried to his side. Her eyes widened. She was looking at dried and withered fruit. Just this morning it had been beautiful, ripe, and succulent.

"These can't be the magical apples," Kolby said.

But for Raven, they were the most magical of all. "But they are," she cried. "You can't disbelieve in them now. We are still in the grip of magic."

He pulled out several more. All of them were
withered and dry. "How am I going to make wine out
of these?"

"You will," she promised, taking them from him
and returning them to the roll.

Outlaws lined both sides of a pathway for them.
Amid cheers and the thunderous clanging of weapons, Kolby and Raven rode toward the mead hall.
Damona and Vaghn stood on the steps in front of the
building with a white-haired old man.

The four Vikings, still dressed outlandishly like the
outlaws, leaped down the steps and ran to take their
chief's bridle and escort him and his lady up the
passage. Durin looked up at him inquiringly, and
Kolby nodded.

Aren grinned over his shoulder. "We brought in
the two thieves."

"Good man," Kolby complimented him.

"I thank you, Aren." Raven added her praise. "You
have always taken care of my needs."

When Kolby and Raven reached the mead hall,
Kolby slid off the horse and turned the reins over to
the youngest Viking. He held up his arms to bring his
lady to the ground. "Aren, have you a gift for my
lady?"

The youth grinned and sped away.

"We were beginning to worry about you," Vaghn
said as he studied the scratches and bruises on
Raven's face and arms. "Another day and your men
would have gone in search of you."

"Another day and I would have expected them to,"
Kolby said. He untied the roll from the back of his
saddle and tucked it under his arm.

"My lady, do you need treatment for your
wounds?" Damona asked.

"Thank you," Raven murmured. "We've doctored
them, and they are healing now."

The old man stepped closer and inspected Raven's arm. He lightly touched one of the scratches. "Thorns caused these," he muttered.

"Aye."

"Most don't survive the brambles."

"The man who abducted me didn't expect me to," Raven admitted. "He dropped me in them and left me to die." To their pleasure she related her story for all to hear, beginning with her kidnapping at the stream. "Lord Kolby of Apelstadt rescued me."

The Vikings led the crowd in cheers.

"What about the Irishman?"

"He will die," Kolby promised. "I have sworn it."

At that moment Aren came running up and presented Kolby with a long cloth-wrapped object. Kolby turned to Raven and bowed formally. "For you, my lady."

Wonderingly, she pulled the cloth aside. Her eyes filled with tears. There lay her brooch, polished and splendid, pinned to the leather of a handsome scabbard that held the sword for which she had bartered so much that she held dear.

"For you," Kolby continued. "With the hope that you never have to draw it except in practice."

She smiled as she pinned the brooch to the shoulder of her cloak and looped the scabbard over her arm. "That is my fondest hope also, my lord."

"I'm glad we didn't have to ride any deeper into the forest than we did," Durin said. "'Twas an eerie sight."

Vaghn cleared his throat and motioned Kolby forward. "I have promised to introduce you to the man who has seen the tree. You have seen the brambles, but your goal is not yet reached." Before Kolby could speak, Vaghn motioned to the old man. "This is Ovar of Wicke. He is my friend and adviser, and the only man who can finally give you what you seek."

Ovar laughed. "I'm his adviser only when I agree with him."

"Come. Let us parley in my tent." Vaghn led the way from the mead hall.

Damona caught up with Raven. "Do you wish to go to my tent? I'll be happy to give you more suitable clothing."

Suddenly Raven remembered how scantily clad she was. "Oh, aye," she said. "And with much pleasure."

When the three men were in Vaghn's tent, Vaghn poured each of them a tankard of ale.

"You wanted to talk to me about the sacred tree, Viking?" Ovar asked.

"I did," Kolby replied. "But now 'tis no longer necessary."

"Why? Have you found the answer you sought? Or have you given up your search?"

"I found my answer," Kolby said simply. "This morning."

Ovar looked deeply into Kolby's amber eyes. At last he smiled. "I saw the tree in the afternoon. The sun was bright. The brightest I had ever seen. 'Twas the only time I ever saw the tree."

"The brambles protect and shield it," Kolby said. "And the light must shine in a certain way before one notices the tree growing out of the midst of the brambles."

"I didn't go into the thicket," Ovar said with a sigh. "I saw the tree from a distance. Did you pluck any of the fruit?"

"Aye, enough to make a healing wine and to replant the orchards on my liege's estate."

"Are these apples golden? Are they big, beautiful, and tasty?" Ovar asked.

"Aye." Kolby hesitated, pondering how much to tell them.

"They are?"

"They were."

Both Ovar and Vaghn smiled.

"They are shriveled up now. I don't know if they are going to be worth—"

"Aye, my lord," Ovar said. "They are worth more than all the riches of the world put together. You have plucked the magical apples of the Great Mother Goddess. You have truly walked among the hallowed."

"Does this mean your sojourn in the badlands has ended?" Vaghn asked.

"Aye, my friend, it has."

Vaghn sighed. "I suppose I must return a great deal of your cloister treasure." Then he brightened. "Mayhap you will return from time to time for a visit. I would play games with you again, and try to win back at least part of the treasure. I must retain my reputation as an outlaw."

Kolby smiled. "Whenever I yearn for adventure, I will return."

Vaghn laughed. "And now will you be journeying to the Northland?"

"Aye. On the way I shall take my lady to her cloister. She wants to meet with her friends and family. Then—if the Great Mother Goddess wills it—we shall journey to my home across the sea."

Vaghn sat back with a satisfied smile. "I had thought there would be a marriage between you and the lady."

Kolby sobered. "The Great Mother Goddess and Odin All-Father would have to work together on that one. How can a high king's daughter marry a Northland Viking?"

Chapter 17

Raven accepted Damona's clothing gratefully. Vaghn's wife clucked like a mother hen over the scratches and bruises on Raven's white skin. Tears sparkled in her eyes at the terrible thorn wound in her thigh. "I fear that may leave a scar."

Raven pulled on black wool trousers and black fur-lined boots like the other outlaw women wore. "A small price to pay for finding the sacred apple tree."

"You actually saw it? You stood beneath its boughs?" Damona's voice was filled with awe.

"Aye." Raven smiled. "And watched while my love plucked the twenty apples for which he had searched two years. His quest is now at an end. He will present them to his liege at Apelstadt."

Damona smiled too and clapped her hands together in delight. "'Tis a miracle only a goddess could perform."

Raven fastened the placket on her red silk tunic with Kolby's brooch. Lastly she buckled on the sword.

"You really don't need to wear that," Damona said. "You are safe here."

"Kolby cared enough to retrieve it for me," Raven replied. "I will wear it until he bids me take it off."

The two women left the tent and walked back

toward the mead hall. Around them was the hustle and bustle of midday. Victual sellers noisily hawked their viands, breads, and fruits. Purveyors of ales described the virtues of their brews in loud voices. Damona stopped to haggle with one. Though Raven was hungry, she walked on, anxious to return to Kolby.

Suddenly a hard arm dropped over her shoulder. She felt the prick of a blade at her ribs. "Scream and it'll be the last breath you ever draw."

She recognized the voice instantly. "Donnal!"

"Surely you didn't think you could get away from me, woman. Triath will pay gold for you." He hustled her into a space between two tents where the merchant had left his cart. Twisting her around, he pushed her back against the solid oak wheel.

She looked into his handsome face. So handsome. So evil.

Still she tried to reason with him. "Don't be foolish. You're risking your life for something you'll get anyway when Triath dies. Let me go. Tell him I died in the brambles on the rocks above Loch Ness. Tell him you barely escaped with your own life."

"Nay!" His teeth gnashed over the word. Tiny flecks of spittle appeared at the corners of his mouth. His eyes glittered. Alba's eyes, but with more than Alba's hint of madness. Clearly he was more dangerous, more unhinged than Alba had ever been. "I'll take you back. He'll set the wedding date."

"Wedding date?" As if caught in a living nightmare, she lost her breath. "What do you mean?"

"Didn't I tell you? He intends to get more sons from you. But he'll never live to bed you." Donnal's hand dropped from her shoulder to her breast. He squeezed it cruelly, then tried to push his knee between her legs. "He'll meet with an accident. So sad. A fall from a horse. A fire in the rushes in his chamber. I'll wed you in his stead. And then—"

She couldn't bear this captivity any longer. Better to die than endure this mauling. If she tried to scream, he would feel her fill her lungs with air.

"Monster!" She drew back her head and spat in his face.

He jerked back, startled.

And she flung herself sideways, rolling off the wheel and somersaulting over her shoulder when her body hit the ground. Her right arm slapped across her body and she came up on one knee with sword drawn.

With a roar he leaped after her, but skidded to a halt with the point an inch from his belly.

She opened her mouth to scream, then a smile twitched the corners of her mouth. As he stared at her, she rose and backed up step by step until she was out into the road that led to the mead hall. She kept her wrist rotating, moving the sword's point in a tight circle, always trained on his belly, getting the feel of the sword.

For a fleeting moment she thought of Wolftooth, the flawed blade Vaghn had sold her. Its added weight had served her well. Her new sword *Craebh Ciuil* felt light and deadly. Her hand and arm were strong.

With a sneer Donnal drew his own sword and followed her. The instant he appeared on the road, Damona screamed and dashed toward the mead hall, calling for Vaghn and Kolby.

"'Twill all be over by the time they arrive," the Irishman growled. "Unless you drop that toy and come with me, I swear my blade will drink your blood."

"It's easy to kill men who don't expect to die," Raven taunted him. "Let's see how you are face to face in broad daylight in front of witnesses."

In his madness he did not spare a thought to the circle of outlaws fast forming around them. Instead he roared again and slashed with his sword. She leaped sideways to avoid the blade and riposted. He had put too much of his weight behind the blow to draw back before her sword tip slashed across his upper arm.

He howled as blood appeared in the rip in his tunic. He clapped his hand over the wound and jumped back.

The outlaws gave a cheer.

"I'll give odds on the woman," one enterprising outlaw yelled.

"Done." A couple of men dug into their pockets for their purses.

"Odds on the man here," another called. "She got in a lucky hit. His reach bests her by a good six inches. She's done in three passes."

"I'll take that."

The ring of spectators widened as Raven and Donnal circled each other, their swords moving, slashing the air, threatening.

Raven's mind was full of Kolby's teachings and the words of her father Pryse mac Russ, a famous swordsman in his day. A direct frontal attack would never do. Her reach was too short. He would kill her before her sword could ever touch him, simply by straightening his arm.

She must get him to commit and then draw back. She must duck low and follow him in. Above all, she must keep circling to the left because he was right-handed.

Keep behind your opponent's arm, Pryse had said. *If he tries to take you on an overhead, dive in and stab up. Dive in and stab up.*

"Throw down your sword and I won't hurt you," Donnal yelled, his face contorted with fury. Besides watching her constantly whipping blade, he saw the hostility in the faces around him. Raven was known to these people as a friend of Vaghn. He himself was a stranger in camp. "Don't believe I'll spare you because you're a woman."

"Look to yourself," Raven called. "You're the one who's bleeding."

He roared again and slashed back and forth at her face. She gave ground before the onslaught. Behind her the circle scattered and closed in behind him.

Kolby, Vaghn, Ovar, and Kolby's Vikings burst through the door of the mead hall. Kolby would have thrown himself down the steps and attacked Donnal with his bare hands had Ovar and Vaghn not caught him.

Vaghn held the Viking's right arm in a hammerlock. "She must answer this challenge herself."

The old man grabbed Kolby by his left shoulder. "She is fighting as she must," he counseled. "Look at her. Clearly she knows what she is about."

At that moment Donnal uttered a terrific oath and lunged straight at Raven.

She dodged and slashed at his hip as he plunged by.

He screamed with rage and whirled. Again she gave ground before a hail of slashing cuts right and left. He seemed to have no thought of striking but merely of driving her back and relieving his frustration.

"Look at her," Durin whispered in Kolby's ear. "She's playing him like a fish. The madder he gets and the more energy he wastes, the better she fights. You've taught her well."

Kolby relaxed slightly. He wished he could take credit for Raven's fighting, but in truth he had trained her little. Only the strengthening exercises that made her keep her arm steady and her point up were his doing. He could see that her opponent was clearly flagging. Blood was running from his arm and down the outside of his thigh.

But the fight was not over. He would be more

cautious now, more calculated. She could not win. Kolby struggled to tear himself away from Vaghn and Ovar, but they held him fast.

"Surrender," Donnal cried. "You'll be a high queen in Eire."

Raven laughed in his face and slashed at his sword. Steel clanged on steel and sparks jumped. "Do you think I'd return to the family who shamed mine? Alba rejected me. I spent nine years in a cloister because of the shame he put upon me. Then he attacked my sister and shamed her too. The O'Illands will never touch me again."

"We can talk." For the first time he gave ground, favoring his right leg.

"Odds on the woman," came the call. "She has him on the run."

A cheer went up and more outlaws rushed to place their bets.

Donnal spared a glance around him. Sweat streamed down his face.

"My mother died because of you," Raven called. "Your men wounded her and she died. Run if you want, but I will find you."

He made as if to leave the circle. She lowered her sword a couple of inches. Then he swung round, sword high above his head. With a roar of rage, he ran at her. Kolby shouted a warning. Damona screamed. The crowd howled.

"Great Mother Goddess," Raven whispered. She stepped aside and dropped to one knee. The *Craebh Ciuil* drove upward in a flash of gold and steel and slid into Donnal's body below his rib cage and up through his lungs and heart.

He took one gasping breath. Blood like a river poured from his wound as Raven lost her grip on the blade. She flung herself back, scrambling away from him across the ground. He took one staggering step, then another. His sword point dropped. He pitched forward and rolled over, clutching with both hands at her sword hilt.

The crowd was suddenly silent. Shakily Raven climbed to her feet and stood over him. She didn't look at him. Instead her eyes stared into the distance, seeing Melanthe's face.

On the steps of the mead hall, Damona pushed herself between the men and raised her arms in triumph over her head. "Raven the Vindicator!" she shouted. "Raven the Vindicator!"

"Raven the Vindicator!" yelled the outlaws. "Raven the Vindicator!"

Kolby sprang down and plowed his way through them to reach Raven's side and boost her to his shoulder as if she were a child.

"Raven the Vindicator!"

Shrouded in a silver-white mist, colored by the fragile light of the setting sun, the cloistered community looked mystical. The whitewashed dwellings shone with pristine radiance; the straw on the roofs gleamed golden. Circular in design, the village spread outward from a single round edifice with four doors. All the other structures were built along four main streets that stretched from those doors like spokes on a wheel.

Standing on the last hilltop before they descended into the valley, Raven paused to contemplate the cloister with the sense of dear familiarity. She reached across the intervening space and laid her hand on Kolby's arm. "Order and civilization. 'Tis wonderful. All is as it should be. Clean and peaceful. Nothing can happen to break the contemplation and quiet thought."

The corners of Kolby's mouth quirked up. "Sounds dull."

She squeezed his hand. "It's the life you are considering now, my lord Viking. When you return to

Apelstadt, you'll be planting and building to create order."

He nodded solemnly, knowing that she spoke the truth.

"Think of it." She pointed to the community below them. "The house of worship is built in an arch shape to represent the womb of the Great Mother Goddess, the Great Gateway to our Mother. It is the farthermost building.

"In the center of the three circles of life are the infirmary, because we are healers, so that all our paths and all our thoughts are directed to that building.

"The four rectangular buildings are the cooking house and dining hall, the residence of the sisters, the home of the novitiates and the guest house, and the warehouse for supplies and stores."

"And the trees," Kolby said softly.

"Yes, the trees." A gigantic orchard marched out across the valley in every direction and up the surrounding hills. "In spring this is the most beautiful place you would ever hope to see. Every tree will be in full bloom, their tiny white buds glistening in the morning dew and reflecting the golden light of early day. The wind will blow and a gentle fragrance will permeate the air."

He drew a deep breath. Clasping her hand in his, rubbing her fingers, he asked, "Ura's steading is poor compared to this. Are you sure you want to go with me?"

"If it's possible for me to do so," she whispered. *Or even if it isn't possible,* she thought. "I shall be with you always."

The cart finally rumbled up the incline and Aren pulled it to a halt at Kolby's side. He looked down at the cloister and the great North Sea stretching away to the horizon. " 'Twill be good to sleep in a building again. And even better to feel the deck beneath my feet. We've been too long on land."

"Aye, lad," Kolby agreed. He touched his heels to his big golden stallion. The beast followed Raven's mount down the slope. "Let's go and find the sea."

Raven wore a blue wool tunic that covered most of Damona's black trousers and boots. Her black hair hung down her back, and Kolby's brooch held her tunic at the neck. As she rode down the street, she could feel color rising in her cheeks. The priestesses and novices who lined the streets stared curiously at her. She doubted if any recognized her as their high priestess who had ridden away covered from her head to her fingertips in dark green wool.

When she reached her residence in the large U-shaped building, she dismounted. Mother Barbara, the high councilwoman, stepped forward to meet her. Every part of the elderly woman's body was enveloped in her robe. Only her face showed, shadowed beneath the cowl.

I can't return to that, Raven thought. She felt the sea breeze lift her hair and bathe her throat in coolness. "Mother," she said. "I have returned."

"Raven, my child, we have been so concerned about you. When only half of your guards returned with the tragic story that you had been attacked by outlaws and that Melanthe"—Mother Barbara closed her eyes and shook her head—"my dear, dear sweet sister had died as a result of wounds she received, we put everything aside and prayed for your safety. I myself have been sick with grief."

Impulsively Raven embraced the elderly woman, though such contact was forbidden. "Aye, good mother. This is the man who saved me. Lord Kolby Urasson of Apelstadt. He is from Northland."

"My lord." Barbara inclined her head. "'Tis a

pleasure to meet you. Thank you for protecting our young mistress."

After they had shared the civilities of introduction, Barbara said, "I immediately dispatched messengers to your father and to Lord Brian and Lady Gwynneth. All await you in the council room." She looked a little uncertainly at the five massive Vikings who stood shoulder to shoulder at Raven's back. "You . . . er . . . men must come too."

"Then let us go inside, Mother Barbara," Raven said. "I am anxious to see them all."

As Raven walked beside the priestess, she could feel her whole body going stiff. Her future would be decided in the next hours. Her whole life would be changed forever, either for better or for worse. She stepped closer to Mother Barbara. "I must speak to you on a private matter."

Barbara stopped abruptly. "Perhaps it would be more seemly if you were allowed to go to your room to bathe and change your clothing first. Perhaps to put on a new robe?"

"Nay. I wish to speak to the High Council and to all the Dryads at the cloister."

Mother Barbara's face crumpled. She clenched her hands. "Raven, I fear we should put aside this matter until—"

"Mother Barbara, I will speak as I am."

Barbara's round face paled with worry. Shaking her head, she motioned to the sister who had followed a few paces behind them. "Ring the bell."

Before they could speak further, the door to the council chamber opened. "Raven! Sister!" Gwynneth nea Pryse, the wife of Brian mac Logan, rushed into Raven's arms. "You're safe. We were all so worried. But we shouldn't have been."

She took her sister's arm and pulled her through the door. "Brian, look who has been with her all the time. Kolby of Apelstadt. We were foolish to worry."

"Kolby!" The two men clasped hands.

"Daughter." Pryse mac Russ came forward to embrace her. His eyes ran over her body clad much as her sister was, although her clothing was shabby compared to the fine materials and exquisite decoration of Gwynneth's garments. "Tell me about Melanthe."

From the bell tower atop the arch-shaped building came the tolling of the bronze bell. Everything was happening too quickly. Raven wanted more time to tell her father all about how it had happened. Later he would know all, she promised herself. For now she said words that would ease his heart. "Her last words were of you. She loved you."

Equal parts of pain and gladness drifted like shadows in his eyes. He closed them and turned away. Raven and Gwynneth on either side of him led him to the high king's chair on the dais, so he could take his place for the deliberations to come. To his right hand sat his daughter, Lady Gwynneth, Queen of the Isle of Cat. Behind her stood her husband, Brian mac Logan. At Brian's insistence, Kolby stood at his side and his Vikings ranged themselves behind the royal grouping.

Soon robed priestesses hurried into the council chamber and took their places at the long straight tables. Mother Barbara assumed the high seat at the head of the first table.

Raven stood at the foot of the first table. When all were seated, she took a small silver bell and rang it.

"Good sisters and friends. I'm overjoyed to be home, to see all of you. Indeed, there were times on this terrible journey when I did not think I would ever see you again. Then I wept and prayed to the Great Mother Goddess to protect Mother Melanthe and me on our pilgrimage."

Those assembled listened quietly as Raven told them of their journey to the shrine and to the trading port, of the subsequent attack by the Irish bandits, and of their rescue by the Vikings. When she came to the theft of the sacred shawl and the cloister jewelry, the women shook their head in sorrow at the report of such evil in the world.

Raven described the journey into the badlands and how Lord Kolby had risked his life to retrieve the sacred objects for them. When she told them about Melanthe's death, her voice grew husky. She ended with the announcement that she had renounced her vows and would not be returning to the cloister.

"Nay," resounded all around the room.

She held up her hands for silence. "Thank you for wanting me to remain, but I cannot. I can never return to a cloistered life. I have killed a man."

Gasps of horror and many shaking of heads greeted this confession. Almost as one the priestesses looked at the sword that hung on Raven's left hip.

"My dear." Mother Barbara rose stiffly. "You are being much too hasty. Your experiences have clearly torn the fabric of your reason. But rest and prayer will restore you. You are a keeper of the land."

Raven knew a moment of despair. Her next words were for her father and sister. "I chose this life for the wrong reasons. You both know what drove me into the cloister."

Pryse stiffened. He raised his hands helplessly. Gwynneth dropped her eyes.

"I was ashamed. I believed that my shame had brought shame on the family. When Alba O'Illand rejected me, I feared you would go to war with him, Father. I wanted you to live. I entered into the cloister, where I have lived for nine long years." She held out her hands. "For nine long years, Father, sister. No one touched me. Not even my mother."

Gwynneth bowed her head. Pryse shook his head. "Surely—"

"No one," Raven insisted. "This is a cloistered, celibate order. We are covered from head to toe. Our faces are shaded from the warmth of the sun. Even our hands are covered." She pointed to Kolby. "He pushed the cowl from my face and brought me out into the sunlight."

The silence was profound. Brian dropped his hand on his wife's shoulder. Gwynneth raised her head. Her cheeks were glistening with tears. She leaned toward her father. "She must be released from her vows."

"Aye," he said. "She must."

Mother Barbara bowed her head. Only her mouth was visible below the cowl. Her lips were moving. At last she looked up. "Where do you wish to go?"

"Wherever Lord Kolby would take me. My home is where the Northlander is."

Scandalized, Barbara twisted round in her chair. She looked at the Viking, huge and fierce and menacing. "You are in love with this warrior?"

"Aye. I want to go with him."

"You can't. You're a keeper of the land, Raven. You cannot leave Scotland except on fear of death. You have been ritually bonded to the land and you belong to the Great Mother Goddess."

"My mother—Mother Melanthe—has already released me from the bond," Raven said. "My father the high king and my sister the high queen have declared that I should be released. Only you and Mother Feich, who is Brian mac Logan's foster mother, protest."

Brian mac Logan spoke for the first time, his voice booming through the room. "I know Mother Feich will approve. She can perform a reversal incantation."

Barbara hesitated. Then she wilted in the chair, covering her mouth with her fingertips. At last she spoke. "We were so concerned, my dear, all three of us. You were a daughter of the Nameless Day. The goddess might have forgotten you or found you unworthy. We sought to protect you. Now we have only brought you pain."

Pryse rose from the high king's chair. "She must be freed to go where she wills. She has served the Cloister of the Grove for nine years. Perform the ritual, dear Barbara, for Melanthe's sake, and set her daughter free."

Mother Barbara rose also. She bowed low to Pryse, who bowed in turn. "For Melanthe's sake," she conceded. "It shall be done."

Kolby gathered his priestess-turned-outlaw in his arms and held her close against him. Her kisses warmed him to the depths of his soul. Were they not in the priestess's apartments in the cloister, he would have pushed her down on the narrow bed and given way to his desire.

When he paused for breath, Raven twined her arms around his neck. "Do you think your liege will accept me, now that I'm no longer attached to Scotland?"

Kolby nodded. "When he learns that my father-in-law is the high king of Ailean, the same as the seafarer Brian mac Logan, he will come to believe that he chose you for me."

"Then we will never be apart."

"Never."

A knock sounded at the door. Reluctantly they drew apart. Kolby adjusted the front of his tunic. Raven smoothed her hair. "Enter."

"Raven!" A young woman peeked around the corner of the door. "Look who I have brought for you." When Raven hesitated, the robed novice entered the room with a huge gold cage in her arms. "I kept her for you while you were gone."

"Black Night!" Raven cried. "Oh, thank you, Agnes."

She took the cage and hung it from a tall pole in front of the window. The young girl withdrew.

"Hello, Black Night." Raven opened the door and put her hand into the cage. The raven hopped onto her wrist, and she pulled her out. Holding out her arm, she made the introductions. "This is Black Night, Kolby."

The Viking stepped closer. "Hello, Black Night."

The bird stared at him with glittering eyes.

Raven picked up a long, delicate chain. "This was hers," she said. "One end encircled her claw, the other I pinned to my robe. But I shall no longer need it."

She caught the bird in both hands and drew it to her face. She brushed her cheek along the gleaming back.

"You remind me a great deal of Midnight Wind," Kolby said.

"Now she will remind you even more," Raven said. She walked to the open window and tossed the bird into the sky.

With a powerful flap of black wings, the raven circled high above them, cawing hoarsely. Then it soared down and landed on the window casement.

"You're free to go," Raven called with just a twinge of pain.

Standing behind her, Kolby put his hands on her shoulders. "Do you think she'll ever come back?"

His lady leaned back against him. "For a visit perhaps. She's been a resident of the cloister too long to forget it entirely. But I shan't be here. I'll be with you."

Before he could drop a kiss on her temple, Kolby heard a familiar cawing. He leaned out the window. Black Night was circlng in the air. She glided with her wings outstretched, dove for the window, then swooped up again. Kolby was about to turn away when he saw another flash of black—a second raven.

Raven joined him at the window. She waved at them both. "Black Night has found a friend."

Both ravens flew into the room, one of them lighting on Raven's arm, the other on Kolby's.

"Midnight Wind has found a friend," Kolby said.

Man and woman joined in soft laughter.

The two ravens flew out the window.

"Where do you think they'll go?" Raven asked, following them with her eyes until they were out of sight.

"That's easy," Kolby replied. "To Odin."

"Odin?"

"Odin All-Father.

"They'll tell him all the doings of earth. Everyone has always believed that Midnight Wind was his messenger."

"But what about Black Night?"

Kolby thought for a moment. "Why, I do believe she's his Valkyrie."

He took his own raven in his arms. She slid her hands up his chest and locked them around his neck. She touched her lips to his in a sweet, warm kiss.

Epilogue

$\sim\!\!\!\sim\!\!\!\sim\!\!\!\sim$

The orchard was small, only twenty trees, planted in four rows of five each. The trees themselves were small yet, but all gave promise of the magnificent specimens they would be when they reached maturity. Their slender limbs sagged with golden fruit from which more seeds would come and more wine. They bore the promise that orchards of the Urasson steading would one day be great again.

Raven Prysesdatter, as the tradition of the Northland named her, sat at her ease in the chair her husband had made for her. From the rise behind the big house that Ura had given to them, she could watch her men tending the trees. Happiness almost past bearing flowed from her breasts as her infant son Lang nursed. She waved her hand as she caught sight of her husband and their first son Pryse, now a sturdy lad of three, coming from the back of the orchard.

Lord Kolby Urasson of Apelstadt waved back with his free hand. In the other he carried a basket of golden apples. Little Pryse skipped gaily at his side. As Raven watched, the big man knelt and put his arm around his son. Their two blond heads bent so close together brought tears of happiness to her eyes. Father and son spoke earnestly. In her heart she could hear the childish treble begging a question and the

373

deep rumble replying fondly. Then they both nodded. The man bestowed a quick hug around the boy's
waist before rising and taking his hand.

Together they walked, father and son, through the
avenue of trees with the bright golden sun behind
them, keepers of the land for future generations.

The End

Avon Romantic Treasures

*Unforgettable, enthralling love stories,
sparkling with passion and adventure
from Romance's bestselling authors*

SUNDANCER'S WOMAN *by Judith E. French*
77706-1/$5.99 US/$7.99 Can

JUST ONE KISS *by Samantha James*
77549-2/$5.99 US/$7.99 Can

HEARTS RUN WILD *by Shelly Thacker*
78119-0/$5.99 US/$7.99 Can

DREAM CATCHER *by Kathleen Harrington*
77835-1/$5.99 US/$7.99 Can

THE MACKINNON'S BRIDE *by Tanya Anne Crosby*
77682-0/$5.99 US/$7.99 Can

PHANTOM IN TIME *by Eugenia Riley*
77158-6/$5.99 US/$7.99 Can

RUNAWAY MAGIC *by Deborah Gordon*
78452-1/$5.99 US/$7.99 Can

YOU AND NO OTHER *by Cathy Maxwell*
78716-4/$5.99 US/$7.99 Can

Avon Romances—
the best in exceptional authors and unforgettable novels!

Discover Contemporary Romances
at Their Sizzling Hot Best
from Avon Books

THE LOVES OF
RUBY DEE   *by Curtiss Ann Matlock*
78106-9/$5.99 US/$7.99 Can

JONATHAN'S WIFE   *by Dee Holmes*
78368-1/$5.99 US/$7.99 Can

DANIEL'S GIFT   *by Barbara Freethy*
78189-1/$5.99 US/$7.99 Can

FAIRYTALE   *by Maggie Shayne*
78300-2/$5.99 US/$7.99 Can

Coming Soon

WISHES COME TRUE   *by Patti Berg*
78338-X/$5.99 US/$7.99 Can